GATEKEEPER

Kay Sexton

Gatekeeper

Copyright © Kay Sexton, 2014

Jacket image copyright © Michael Cummings 2013, reproduced by kind permission of Michael Cummings www.worldwildlifephotography.org

All rights reserved.

No part of this book may be reproduced by any means, nor transmitted, nor translated into a machine language, without the written permission of the publishers.

Kay Sexton asserts her right to be identified as the author of this work in accordance with sections 77 and 78 of the Copyright, Designs and Patents Act 1988.

All characters and incidents portrayed in this publication are fictitious and any resemblance to real events or persons, either living or dead, is purely coincidental.

Condition of Sale
This book is sold subject to the condition that it shall not, by way of trade or otherwise, be lent, re-sold, hired out or otherwise circulated in any form of binding or cover other than that in which it is published and without a similar condition including this condition being imposed on the subsequent publisher.

I-13: 9781503116429

This book is for Tony, who walked the wolves with me.

CHAPTER ONE

Claire could see Liam was tense, his eyes pale against the black bala-clava, his hand clenched around the bolt cutters he was holding. The others avoided his gaze: Ansel patted down his balaclava where it jutted over his beard while Mick tapped his gloved fingers against the wall of the van, but Claire held it, staring him down as the vehicle lurched over the rutted farm road.

It was a relief to get out of the van, to run to the hut, and begin the work that she'd been half fearing, half anticipating for months, releasing the dogs from the misery of their pens. She'd never have believed that it would be more pleasant to break into an illegal puppy farm than sit in a van with a fellow activist, but when that fellow activist was Liam, the menace was almost tangible.

The group had been working for less then five minutes when she knew something was wrong. She checked over her shoulder to be sure she was out of sight of Vidya's camcorder before signing out her message, 'Where is Liam?' but the others pretended they couldn't see her finger-spelling L-I-A-M in her double-thick rubber gloves. She looked into the black space of the night, framed by the hut door. Vince, standing guard outside, should have stopped anybody leaving, but nobody liked to interfere with Liam when he was hyped up.

She assessed the dark rectangle and took a deep breath. Beside her the others worked silently, aware of the video tape logging every sound and movement. They had torches taped to the underside of their left wrists and dog-catcher poles in their right hands so that cones of light danced across the wire. She hesitated, looking into the next cage, where a tiny West Highland terrier rewarded her scrutiny with a tooth-bared snarl. Behind the bitch were several puppies, still too young for their eyes to have opened. They squeaked, opening rosy muzzles, crawling to try and get behind each other as they reacted to the panic and adrenaline in the hut.

Claire hissed through her teeth. The feeling, heavy with doom like a migraine, would not go away. Liam was dangerous, a liability, risky to be near and frightening to turn your back on. She needed to go and see what he was doing.

In the doorway, breathing fresh air, she realised how noisy and fetid it was inside the hut. The combination of the filthy floor and the fear-sweat and aggression of the bitches meant the place stank, and the cacophony of growls, barks and yaps from the puppies had been painful to her ears. She turned off her torch and rubbed at her face with her gloved hands, pressing the balaclava against her skin, trying to soak up the sweat running off her, pooling in her collarbones and sliding down her back, making her squirm. Vince looked across as she stepped into the full-moon brightness of the yard, his eyes two white holes against a black mask. She made the okay sign, watching him as he glanced involuntarily at a hut opposite the puppy factory. Liam would be in there.

She sprinted across the muddy yard and up the hut's concrete steps. The door was open and dark, and before she entered she closed her eyes for a second to allow them to adjust to the reduced light.

Liam was there, his back to her, his fingers spread over some of the small wire cages that stretched along three sides of the hut. He looked stocky and dense in the moonlight, a blackness that swallowed the light, and she knew he was poised for something. Everything about his body, the springiness of his movements, the harsh breathing, said he was preparing for action. She walked down the room, trying not to tiptoe but unable to prevent herself. They were breaking the law; they would go to prison if they were caught, but it was Liam who frightened her, made her silent and cautious, and it was because he frightened her that she couldn't leave it, couldn't let him get on with whatever he was doing.

He was crooning under his breath - when she got close enough to touch him she could hear little clicks and sibilances from under his mask.

'Liam', she spoke quietly but he jumped, turning round, his hands spreading over the tops of the cages as though trying to hide them, his wrist torch illuminating her from hip to breasts like a searchlight. 'What are you doing?'

'Fuck off, Claire. Do your job. I'll do mine,' he spoke without emotion, but there was venom beneath the even tone. His eyes, pale even in daylight, were empty whiteness in the frame of the balaclava.

'This isn't your job. You're supposed to be with us.' She peered into the cages, switching on her own torch, although she already knew what she would see. This hut smelt acrid – it could only contain predators.

The mink, still in their flat summer coats, glared back at her. She watched them curling and turning like fish in a bowl, moving with unbelievable speed and agility.

'This is illegal. This is wrong!' Liam turned and spoke to the mink, not to her, trailing his fingers along the cages again. The mink reared on their hind legs and snapped at his hands as they passed. She could tell he was smiling at the creatures although the balaclava hid his mouth. 'Mink farming is banned in Britain. This is evil, bloody evil!'

'Okay, I'll send Vidya over. She can film it. We need you to help us with the dogs, Lee,' she hated herself for cajoling him, using his nickname, but they did need him – and he was rarely amenable to reasoned argument.

'No. This is wrong. They've got to be freed.'

KAY SEXTON

'Don't be stupid! They aren't native, they'll ...' But he'd stopped listening: he was pulling the bolt cutters from his belt, setting them against the small padlock holding the nearest closed cage.

Claire froze, breathing deeply, trying to work out her options. If the mink were freed they would destroy the local habitat – it was impossible Liam didn't know that. The predators would kill every rodent and small bird for miles around, as well fish; even poultry from farms. But if she shouted for help from the others, the sound might get picked up on the video, ruining months of work. There was a ringing note as the padlock hasp gave way under Liam's cutters, telling her she'd run out of time.

She stepped well back, out of arm's reach, then lifted her right hand and tapped Liam on the shoulder with her dog-catcher. He swung round, aiming a punch, but she was far out of range and already responding, bringing her left leg up in a low roundhouse kick that caught him square in the abdomen. She'd guessed he would choose violence.

Liam fell to the concrete, arms folded across his belly, breath whistling as he tried to get his legs under him. Claire saw a mink streak past her like an unanchored shadow from the open cage.

'Come on,' she murmured. 'We're here for the dogs.'

She turned to leave, keeping her eyes to one side so she could watch Liam's shadow juddering around the walls from the movement of his torch as he pushed himself upright. She saw the shadow reach out for the pole leaning against the cages and raise it over its head, giving her time to throw herself flat as he brought it down across her shoulders. Her action saved her from the force of the blow and she rolled to the right, under the cages on that side, prepared for him to bend down and try and haul her from her hiding place. Instead he kicked at her and she caught his heel, continuing the upward swing of his foot until his calf smashed into the wooden frame supporting the cages. He roared with pain. She crawled backwards and got out from under the cages while he was still leaning

4

GATEKEEPER

on the bank of mink, cursing, trying to hold his stomach and his leg at the same time.

'Come on, Liam,' she said again. She steeled herself to walk past him, daring him to lash out at her again.

'Cunt,' he said, but he followed her down the steps. She stepped aside, afraid he might rush her from behind, but the presence of Vince and the trussed-up guard stopped him, and he limped back to the dog hut. Once she was sure he was inside, Claire went back, avoiding glancing into the mink cages, to recover the dog-pole he'd dropped, feeling hundreds of pairs of eyes, like rabid pearls, watching as she left.

'I'm sorry,' she said in the doorway, and then felt stupid.

Back in the dog hut she handed the pole to Liam and resumed her place. He began to work slowly, with his head down. Vidya had gone to the other end of the hut, where the big dogs were kept. Claire shut her ears to their sounds, the belling howls and throaty barks, she refused to go and look at them in the enclosures that had been pig pens and now had wire roofs to stop the dogs escaping. She couldn't afford to know anything about them, because they couldn't take large dogs on this trip. It would pierce her heart if she met their eyes and still had to leave them behind.

When the last small dog was in a carrier, she and Mick began to carry them out to the van, where Liam and Ansel helped Vince load them. Vidya moved around the farm, vanishing into the mink hut and emerging a few moments later. Her dark eyes were so shadowed by her balaclava that no expression could be made out, but Claire sensed her body was rigid with tension.

The final job was to load the guard, still on his chair. They set him between the two ranks of cages along each side of the van. He faced forward, towards the blacked-out window between front and back, but they still covered his head with a thin pillowcase. Vince and Vidya were in the front seats, balaclavas off, looking like any young middle-class couple collecting second-hand furniture from a

5

family friend. Now Ansel and Liam, Mick and Claire could take off their own balaclavas, maintaining silence but able to see each other's faces in the van's dim interior light as well as reading hands.

'F-u-c-k-u-p?' Mick spelled out.

Liam glared at him and gritted his teeth, the line of his jaw working wildly, then looked away. They travelled in swaying silence, apart from the whining of the dogs, until Vidya knocked on the window, alerting them to replace their hoods.

They stepped out of the van into a narrow alley between a former farm and a chain link fence. Vince gave the thumbs up and they unloaded the cages, laying them out along the wall, clipping plastic water bottles with metal spouts against the front of each cage. Finally they lifted down the guard and set his chair by the wall too, next to the sign saying 'PDSA – Veterinarian Centre and Kennels'.

When they got back into the van they stripped their gloves and threw them into a bag for Ansel to dispose of. Liam pulled up his trouser leg to show a bloody purple bruise to Mick, but his eyes were on Claire, threatening. She shrugged. They drove for ten minutes before the van stopped again. Vidya got out. Her next task was to ring the PDSA's national number and the local newspaper, radio and TV stations, playing the tape-recorded announcement that an Animal Liberation group had raided an illegal puppy farm and describing where to find the dogs and the guard. Later she would post copies of the video to the same places. Vince would take the van and clean it. Claire and Ansel would jog up to her shared student flat on campus, while Mick and Liam went to a friend's house in Brighton to obtain an alibi for the evening.

'Bitch,' Liam said, standing in her way. 'You're in trouble, bitch.'

Claire tried to stare him down, but his pale blue eyes were ugly, painful to look at, and she glanced away. He gave a short, choking laugh.

Ansel shrugged and held out the bag for people to deposit their balaclavas and torches along with the gloves.

GATEKEEPER

'Bitch,' Liam said again, before slapping Mick on the back and moving off with him.

Claire waited for Ansel to put the bag in his backpack, then they began to jog. She felt she'd been running for hours, her muscles cramped with loss of fluid and her throat tight with spent adrenaline. Ansel had warned her it would be like this when the raid was over. They continued in silent exhaustion until they reached her flat. Ansel patted her on the back like a clumsy bear and left. Claire almost crawled up the stairs and into the shower.

Under the hot water she could let go of her fear. She began to shake as she worked through the events of the night in her mind. Liam was mad. The kind of zealot who frightened her most: somebody whose response to suffering was to find somebody to blame and make them suffer in turn. She imagined dozens of mink running through the countryside, swarming branches and swimming rivers, killing every creature smaller than themselves with metronomic efficiency. She was sure he was going to go back and set them free as soon as he could talk somebody into going with him. He'd probably say it was to rescue the bigger dogs but it would be for the mink. He would put the release team and the local ecosystem in danger for his own obsession. She stood with the water running off her shoulders, too tired to soap her body or wash her hair, and tried to imagine how he could be stopped.

Finally she wrapped herself in her robe and went down the hall to her bedroom.

'Claire! It's nearly four in the morning. Have a good night?' It was Mala, peering round her own door, candlelight and some aromatherapy fragrance spilling out around her silhouette: obviously she'd been communing with the Mother or some other Earth Goddess activity.

'Yeah. Yeah. Knackering though.' She smiled and waved as she continued to her own room and didn't remember until she got into bed that she was supposed to have been out on a date. No wonder Mala had been giggling.

7

CHAPTER TWO

At six Claire woke. All her senses were unnaturally alert: her muscles tensed, her ears straining, her eyes wide open and staring at the white ceiling above her bed, cold in the dawn light. She could hear her heart labouring like an engine under strain; the rush of blood through her body made her hands clench.

Over the panic she heard a sound and turned her head to see a white triangle appear and disappear under the bedroom door. It appeared again, making a gentle susurration like a snake. The triangle stuck against the bottom of the door, and vanished. It reappeared, a white tongue, slightly further along the door, grew, became rectangular and stopped.

Somebody had pushed an envelope under the door.

There was no logical way any stranger could have got into the first floor flat, let alone slide an envelope under her bedroom door. She was still keyed up from the previous night and the adrenaline rush that had been waiting below the surface of sleep to propel her into a full-blown fight or flight reaction, grabbed her again. Should she pull open the door and see who was outside? It could be Mala, leaving her a note about buying milk or going away for the weekend. Instead she lay still, watching the envelope, waiting for her body to calm so that she could fight intelligently if she had to, if the door handle turned.

As she waited, she investigated her feelings, trying to establish why she was still so scared. Because Liam wouldn't have accepted what had happened, she realised. Because last night wasn't over - she still had to deal with the consequences. And if Liam could get into the flat, there was no knowing what he might do.

For a long time she didn't move, letting her eyes travel the bare room, taking in the cold morning light, the two small photographs in simple frames on the top of the white bookcase that held her textbooks. One picture showed a fat corgi, the other a brindle greyhound. They were Queenie and Jack, both dogs she'd cared for at an animal shelter. Queenie had been the pet of an old woman who'd died, leaving her dog overweight, arthritic, diabetic and with kidneys damaged by years of eating chocolate and snacks and never taking exercise. Jack had been thrown from a moving vehicle after years of abuse that caused him to urinate uncontrollably whenever a door was slammed or a voice raised. Nobody knew what his original name had been, and Jack was the name of the shelter administrator's nephew, a thoroughly loved baby. They'd hoped it would be a good omen to share it with an unloved dog, but health problems meant neither dog could be re-homed. They'd become shelter mascots, evidence of the inhumanity of people to beasts. Claire kept their pictures to remind her that cruelty could occur through deliberate intent or indulgent ignorance – and that most people weren't fit to care for animals.

Eventually, she rose and collected the envelope, getting back into the narrow bed to open it. The note was unsigned but the handwriting was distinctive. It was Ansel's meticulous script, small and foreign, the flat top to the m and n giving it a gothic air. 'Meet me in the library at nine' it said.

She exhaled, trying to calm her breathing. It certainly wasn't over. It was good news that Liam hadn't found a way to get to her, but how had Ansel managed it? A mystery rather than a full-blown threat, but still it was unsettling to know somebody was wandering in and out at will. She got up and headed for the shower again.

When she found Ansel, he looked as if he'd just got out of bed. His sandy hair stuck up at the back and his clothes were as creased as if he'd been sleeping in them.

'Are you okay?' Claire was still tired, but a second shower and half a packet of digestive biscuits had fuelled her for this encounter. Anyway, she liked Ansel. His remote friendliness was disarming; he was the template for tweedy, pipe-smoking, bird-watching masculinity, with his Norwegian accent elongating vowels like slow thoughts. His post-graduate research allowed him to spend long days standing in lakes and rivers, thigh deep in cold water, netting and cataloguing the fish stock, and he looked as though he'd been born to the task.

'Are *you* okay?' he replied.

She caught sight of herself in the glass-covered panel behind which Student Union notices were pinned. She looked diminished. Her hair was lank, brownish, flattish. Her eyes appeared sunken; pale blurs above shadows like fading bruises. At best they were grey but at worst they became opaque and pale, as though cataracted.

She shrugged.

'Let us walk,' he said. Often, his simple phrases became portentous through the formality of his diction, but this time she guessed it was not accidental.

They left the library and began to tour the campus, walking slowly so Ansel could fill his pipe.

'Liam has been talking,' he said.

Claire shrugged again. 'So what?'

Ansel scratched his forehead with the stem of his pipe, looking miserable. 'Liam is good at undermining. I think his argument will be that you took things onto yourself, instead of going to Vidya, or something like that.'

She stopped herself shrugging again. Fatalism wasn't going to help.

'So what should I do?'

This time Ansel shrugged. 'Nothing, I think. There will probably be a meeting, I don't know if you will be invited. He has already spoken to everybody.'

'Everybody? Even Malcolm and Elaine?'

'No. No, he did not speak to them. Vidya did.'

Claire forced a bitter laugh. Malcolm and Elaine, the group's controllers, were notoriously paranoid. They were former hippy anarchists, anti-nuclear protesters, vegans, cannabis legalisers, commune residents and free-love advocates who had become the *de facto* leaders of the Animal Rights Collective by holding the minuscule budget and even smaller contact list which allowed the group to operate.

'How did you find all this out?'

'When I left you, I emptied my pack to get rid of the bag. There were some cigarettes in there, and I remembered Mick asked me to keep them for him, so I went to the house and Liam was talking on his mobile. As soon as I came in the room he left, so I knew something was wrong. I sat and talked to the other one, Jazz is his name?'

Claire nodded.

'Jazz; the one who gives the alibi. After a while he went to bed, then Mick began to talk about the operation and finally he said Liam was complaining about you to Vidya and asking her to take the issue to Malcolm because you were a security risk. So I asked what had happened and Mick said you had attacked Liam – we'd all seen the injury to Liam's leg, and it showed you were not to be trusted.'

'But he didn't mention the mink?'

Ansel shook his head.

'Bastard! But it's on the video. I saw Vidya go into the hut to check, so how is he going to get around that?'

Ansel shook his head again. 'How are you going to argue against him if they don't let you attend?'

KAY SEXTON

She folded her arms, hugging herself. 'They wouldn't do that. We're a Collective. We all take the same risks and share in the decision-making - that's the whole point.' She hoped she sounded more confident than she felt. 'I've got to get to lectures now, none of us can afford a break in our routines that might attract police attention, right?'

Ansel nodded and smiled, acknowledging the Collective's agreed procedure, but the smile was strained and Claire wondered how he would react when he found out exactly what Liam was planning.

She didn't have long to wait. Vince was hovering outside as she left her second lecture – he gestured her to follow and once they were out of earshot of the other students he folded his arms and said, 'There's been a meeting. You're out.'

'Why?' Claire asked.

Mick shrugged 'You attacked Liam. You ignored the chain of command. The Collective doesn't want you any more.' He could have been reading from a rule book.

'But Liam was about to release dozens of non-native predators ...'

Mick cut her off. 'He says he was just looking at them, trying to work out how to report illegal mink farming. Then you laid into him.

'It's on the video!' She tried to keep her voice low, aware of other students walking past. 'Vidya went in there, she filmed the open cage, everything.'

'We've watched the video, Claire,' Mick broke in. 'We saw the cages; none of them looked open to us.' She saw Mick's face and knew nothing she said would make a difference. Liam had won.

She walked away, angry with them all, but furious that Ansel had not spoken in her defence. She didn't want to face him in her current mood because she didn't want to hear whatever lame excuse he would produce for his cowardice.

12

At the bike racks she stopped dead. Her bicycle had been vandalised. When she walked over to it, she realised it was more than vandalism. The seat and tyres were shredded, and the frame looked as if it had been attacked with a hammer. The whole bike had been the victim of a violent assault - and it stank. Somebody had urinated over it. For a few moments she stood, swaying in shock, then she looked at the chain, which still dangled from the rack – the padlock was cut, as if with a pair of bolt cutters. Liam. His way of showing her it still wasn't over.

For a week she managed to avoid Ansel, and during that time doubt coloured all her thoughts. Why hadn't he supported her? Why hadn't he contacted her since? And above all, how had he got into the flat?

There was substantial news coverage of the release, locally and nationally, and she saw grainy cuts from the video over and over again on the TV news. She sat and watched it, sipping mug after mug of tomato soup which reminded her of her mum, listening to Mala's outrage that puppy farming had been going on right under her nose. There was no mention of the mink.

Claire was surprised at the gap in her life now she was no longer a part of the Collective. Seven days ago she would have said it was just something she did, like Tae Kwon Do or taking photographs; fulfilling but not crucial. Something that stopped her thinking about home. Now she was faced with the realisation that she'd thought of herself as an ARA, an animal rights activist - it was part of her personality. Losing her place in the Collective had knocked a hole in her identity.

Mala cornered her one evening as she sat watching the news, from which all mention of the puppy farm had disappeared. 'You look totally down, Claire. I guess he didn't work out?'

Claire had to think swiftly to remember she'd given Mala the impression she was going out on a hot date to cover for the release

KAY SEXTON

operation. 'Oh yeah, well, bit of a flash in the pan really. Nice enough but ... you know.'

Mala nodded, her voice full of sympathy. 'I know what you need; you need to get in touch with your yin principle. No, don't laugh. Not all New Age stuff is rubbish – come along to my Egyptian Dance class tonight, it's bloody good. You'll get back in touch with your female side, you know, being creative and compassionate and stuff. And it's a bloody good work-out, gets the old abs in shape.'

Claire grinned. Mala acted like a nitwit a lot of the time, but below the dizzy conversation and belief in the mystical powers of femininity was a firm grasp on reality and they'd become something close to friends in the two years they'd been rooming together.

They'd been drawn together by unstated but shared experience. Mala didn't go home either. Her parents and younger sister had travelled to Sussex every week during the first year of university, collecting her from the dorm and dropping her back after dinner. Claire had seen the blankness of Mala's face each time the car pulled up outside. She and her sister looked alike, olive-skinned, long dark hair pulled back in ponytails and wide dark eyes. They were a pair of matched dolls, plush-skinned and wholesome. Their mother was achingly beautiful, hollow-boned as though the wind could sing through her and with hair cut as short as a convict's to show her elegant skull bones. Their father was charming, a little plump, a little rumpled, with an easy smile. But Mala dreaded those visits and Claire, knowing how her own father would strike people – such a nice man, such a kind and gentle soul – made sure that whenever Mala returned she was on hand to make chamomile tea and sit with her in the kitchen, waiting in silence until the tautness left her friend's face and she could begin to talk again.

In their second year they'd got a flat together, a tiny, anonymous, concrete box just off campus. It suited them both, and they lived privately, not interfering with each other and never bringing people home. It seemed to Claire that they were both marking time but while she refused to put down roots, Mala spend all her time creating a personal nest; she spent hours moving the furniture around in her room, putting up postcards and making cushion covers, while Claire kept her space as bare as a cheap airport hotel. Even so, they got on well.

'I'll do it, if you come to Tae Kwon Do with me,' she offered.

Mala giggled. 'Deal,' she said.

It was the one bright moment in the week.

Eventually Claire capitulated, seeking Ansel out on Sunday at his usual lair, a dewpond on a Sussex down-land farm. He was seated by the pond when she arrived and smiled hello, passing over his notes for the day for her to read. Top of the list was sand martin, and she could see the birds skimming above the pond, taking insects from the air. Below that he had recorded burr reed and damselfly.

'Where is your bike?' he asked.

'Why didn't you stand up for me in the meeting?' she countered.

'What point would there be? They'd all decided before you arrived. The Collective won't continue anyway, it's going to fall apart and everybody knows it, except Liam.'

She sat in silence, forcing him to continue.

'Malcolm and Elaine will move on to something else. Vidya will be in charge then, but everyone will know it is really Liam pulling strings. She cannot trust him, so the group will fall apart.'

'If she doesn't trust him, why did she support him in the first place?'

Ansel took his pipe from his pocket and began to fill it, still watching the martins scooping insects from the air. 'Claire, you should ask yourself about motivation. Malcolm and Elaine want to be in a group – it doesn't matter what the group does, as long as they are the core of it. That is their motivation. Vidya wants to be needed. Liam wants power. The others are just along for the ride, or because they want to feel important. So I think Liam told Vidya a story to make her feel wanted. You can work out the kind of thing he said.'

Claire shook her head. 'Not really. I can't imagine what could have made her believe what she saw in that hut was less important than letting Liam have his way.'

'Then you don't understand people very much.' Ansel lit the pipe and propped his chin in his hands. 'Suppose he told her this: he went to look in the hut and you followed and asked him to have sex with you there, he said no so you attacked him and now he is as ashamed as if you had tried to rape him. Or maybe he said you were taking drugs, shooting up perhaps, and you went crazy at him so now he's frightened you will stalk him ... I don't know what he said, Claire, but it will have been a story that made Vidya feel he needed protection. She will be trying to make sure he is safe, by ensuring he isn't questioned.'

Claire began to bite her thumbnail. 'You've got a pretty sick imagination, Ansel.'

'Maybe. Maybe not. But by now she will be seeing the holes in his story, and she'll abandon the group because she will be scared of him and probably disgusted by what she has done. I have seen it happen before.'

'But that still leaves me asking why you didn't speak out.'

'Because a group is only good if it gets things done. People like Liam destroy groups, so the sooner it happens here, the better.'

He puffed grey clouds of aromatic smoke into the air. They dispersed without lifting, held down by the weight of cooling air over the pond. There was silence for a long time. Finally he turned to look at her. 'What do you see out there?'

She focused on the dewpond, a shallow saucer reflecting violet-grey sky. The birds scooped the air like darts, their white underparts flashing across the water, as they fed on the autumn haze of spinning insects fluffing the air above the pond. The grass near the water was trodden down by sheep into little troughs of tea-coloured seepage, each with a halo of midges. 'Nature,' she said.

'I see man. Everywhere I look, I see humanity changing the world.' He hunched forward. 'When I was in the Bering Sea, fishing the crab, I saw this all the time. I could show the others how interconnected the world was, how the gulls fitted into the pattern, how each female crab with her load of eggs was a tiny part of the whole in which we fished. I showed how the bait made a part of this pattern, how what we threw out in slops and waste from the vessel fed the top feeders, who fed the predators who gave out waste that fed the brittle stars that were preyed on by cod, who were caught by us and used as cage bait to catch the crab ....' He smiled sadly. 'But they couldn't understand. They only asked if we should make more scraps to get a better haul next year.'

'There are limits on the fishery, aren't there?' This was familiar territory – Claire had heard the story a hundred times.

'Yes, but that is not the point. When I look at the world, I see a spider's web, fragile and beautiful and constantly being changed and repaired, but wherever there are people, I see that web grow dark. No pattern, no change. Just dark holes where we make the world ours, and destroy the pattern.'

'Whoa ... that's a bit heavy.' She'd never heard him sound so bitter.

'Heavy. Yes. You see, I am not a person who cares just a bit about nature. At one time I thought I might go mad, because when you can see something so clearly and you cannot get other people to see it too, you become crazy in the head. I knew I couldn't persuade anybody, or make big speeches. I'm good old Ansel who is everybody's friend. And what I do is find people and put them together and because they trust me, they will trust each other and so things get done.'

Claire thought while the sand martins dipped and called and a rabbit appeared out of the thorn scrub on the far side of the pond and gazed at them before scuttling off into long grass.

KAY SEXTON

'Would you say you put *me* in the Collective?'

Ansel glanced at her. 'Maybe.'

'That didn't work out so well, did it?' She sounded bitter to her own ears. She thought about softening the complaint but decided against it. She'd felt betrayed enough, without Ansel suggesting he'd moved her around like a pawn on a chessboard.

'You don't think so?' He stretched and the birds accommodated his new height in their flight pattern, lifting higher above his arms as though he was an obstacle. 'You think such a group should continue, with a bastard like Liam twisting everything for his own gain?'

'Yeah, but you didn't put me in touch with them just to pull the group down, did you? That wouldn't make sense. I mean, why would you?'

'No, I wouldn't, but that doesn't mean it shouldn't happen. People like him, you cannot trust. Should such a person be allowed to take time and funds that other groups could use better?'

'So why then?'

'There is nothing better. Not here. Come with me this weekend, there's somebody I want you to meet.'

Claire felt defeated. It didn't seem enough. But Ansel began to pack up, and she left with him.

'How are you getting home?' he asked.

'Bus.'

'Okay. Should I give you a lift to the bus stop on my bike? You could maybe ride on the handlebars?'

'No thanks,' she waved him off, recognising his obvious relief to be rid of her. She drew her coat around her and tried to stride out, but she felt isolated and small. Her long shadow headed down the grass ahead of her and darkened her path. She realised she'd forgotten to ask how he'd managed to get the note under her door.

18

CHAPTER THREE

Ansel took her bird-watching at Hickling Broad in Norfolk. They arrived just after dawn and sat in a hide among the reed beds, watching waterfowl swirling like tea leaves. If you could tell the future from birds, Claire thought, hers was looking gloomy.

A figure appeared, walking the path that had brought them to the hide and Ansel sighed and straightened. 'I want to introduce you to somebody,' he said.

Claire watched the man approaching. He was compact, trim, short, dressed in standard bird-watching attire - thick trousers, waterproof jacket, binoculars - but on him it appeared out of place. He wasn't at home in the clothes he wore.

'Who is he, then?' she asked, but Ansel held up his hand while he lit his pipe, puffing hard to release a scented blue cloud.

By this time the man was alongside them, smiling faintly, not relaxed, totally in command of the situation.

'This is Claire,' Ansel said, by way of introduction. The man held out his hand, and Claire shook it, feeling the firmness of his grip.

'And you are...?' she asked.

He smiled more, causing a fan of wrinkles to spread outwards around his eyes. He was probably in his fifties, but had older skin, the face of somebody who spent time outdoors, a skier's face, chiselled by the elements, and tanned. His eyes were blue and she sensed his colouring and build were Scandinavian, an intuition he

KAY SEXTON

confirmed by glancing at Ansel and dropping into Norwegian. They exchanged two or three sentences before he turned back to Claire.

'If you don't mind, I'll keep my name to myself until later.'

For a moment she was annoyed and then the recognition that this was not a social meeting dawned, and she nodded, trying to hide a surge of expectation. This must be Animal Rights business. Her mind flew to potential projects: artic fox, maybe even polar bears, although she wouldn't mind something smaller, marine mammals maybe, or even fish, given that Ansel was a fisheries specialist. She smiled.

'Fine by me.'

The man turned and walked away, beckoning her to follow. She lifted her backpack. 'Leave that,' he said. 'Ansel will take care of things.'

They'd driven for over an hour, listening to Mahler, and the one question he'd asked was, 'I believe you are not menstruating?'

'I believe so too,' she said, uncomfortable.

'Good. Wolves respond strongly to blood. Even ambassador wolves.'

Claire sat silent, unsure what to do. Wolves?

After a while he spoke again. 'What is the name of that American magician who tricks people into thinking he can survive what would kill others?'

Claire thought for a long time, watching the scenery pass. 'David Blaine?' she said, hating how tentative her voice sounded.

'Yes, good. You can call me Blaine.'

As he spoke, he slowed the car and parked. When they got out she noticed it was a rental vehicle, and shook her head, thinking she would soon be as paranoid as Malcolm and Elaine.

The first thing she saw was an eight -foot chain link fence

And then, on the other side of the fence, a wolf appeared. She stood less than five feet from Claire, her ears faintly forward and

20

her face alert, radiating a curiosity almost ferocious in its intensity. When she'd stared at Claire for a long second she turned her head to Blaine, her ears and expression relaxing, before running off. She moved fast, and in total silence. The shock Claire felt at her appearance had not worn off before she'd vanished as though no wolf had ever been there.

'Unbelievable,' Claire said.

'You see why I said nothing before. To warn you would have been unfair. You have to see wolves for themselves, without pre-judgement. Her name is Kaya.' Blaine began to walk along the fence.

Claire followed, thinking that he'd also wanted to see if she could keep her mouth shut, follow without information, be a good soldier. When they reached the gate, Kaya was there. Blaine whistled, and a figure appeared inside the enclosure, walking towards them.

'On my way,' it called. 'She's faster than I am, you know.'

It was a woman, the kind of headscarf-wearing upper-class matron Claire most despised. The type who thought hunting was 'a bit of fun' and would still be wearing sables if she could get away with it. The woman pushed the wolf away from the gate and unlocked it. She held out her hand to Claire who shook it.

'Come on then. Now, I know what's going on and what you're doing with *him*, so we don't need introductions' she jerked her thumb at Blaine. 'I'm going to explain a few rules and then you and Kaya can get to know each other. When you look at her, either glance and look away, or keep your eyes lowered and your face slightly averted. If you stare at her she'll see it as a provocation. Don't bend over her - crouch down instead. Don't touch her head – she'll think you're trying to dominate her; take out any earrings you're wearing, tuck necklaces inside your top and if you have any dangling items: keys, bracelets, those stupid mobile phone things, give them to me. If she wants to play she can be a bit rough, so I'll keep an eye on you from a distance. Don't run, whatever you do, she's faster than you and has a strong prey instinct. Now go on, she's waiting.'

Claire looked at the wolf standing three or four paces away. 'That's it?'

'Yes, go on. She's a sweetie, really.'

Claire took a step forwards and the wolf bounded sideways, circling on itself to end up facing her again. She glanced at the woman for guidance. The woman laughed. 'She's playing. Just keep moving, she'll soon come up to have a good nose at you.'

Claire took another step, the wolf circled again, her mouth open, pink tongue curling over long teeth, eyes quizzical. It was another kind of test, she realised, but this time the animal was testing her. She looked away, walking into the enclosure, although her instinct was to stay close to the gate. She was alone and unarmed with a wolf between her and safety. She looked behind her. The woman and Blaine stood outside the closed gate; Kaya behind and to one side of her. As soon as she caught Kaya's eye the wolf turned circle again, watching Claire the whole time, as though inviting her to do something. Claire was nonplussed. She raised her eyes to the woman.

'Do what she's doing. Go on!' It was like being lectured by a games mistress, the same hectoring no-nonsense tone.

Feeling stupid, Claire spun on her heel, Kaya turned, she turned, and then the wolf straightened, walked up to her and pressed its chin against her thigh, gazing up with orange eyes, half-challenging, half-appealing, before moving away again.

Claire walked on unable to stop watching the wolf over her shoulder. Kaya ran up behind her, her gait so fluent that Claire gasped. The wolf's head was low, her eyes seemed to glow, it was all part of the myth - and the next part was when the lone traveller felt the hot and fetid breath as the wolf's jaws closed on human flesh.

Kaya stopped abruptly, ears forward, surveying her. Claire slowed, instinct making her legs tense, her hair bristle, throat tighten. She wanted to run. The woman had said don't run, whatever you do. She looked at the long muscles in the wolf's shoulder and knew running would be stupid.

Then Kaya sat down. She rolled onto her side, lifting one long forepaw into the air in a clumsy gesture. Claire watched, frozen. The wolf pawed the air, came upright, gazed at her and rolled onto its side again, paw raised. The body language was unmistakable, Kaya wanted to be friends.

Claire approached. The wolf stayed down, watching her without fear but also, she saw, without the intention to please that a dog might display. Kaya was doing this for her own sake, not Claire's.

One pace away, Claire crouched as the woman had said and the animal rolled right over towards her, remaining on the ground. They were close enough to touch. Claire reached out and the wolf brought her head to sniff Claire's hand. The long muzzle was half-open and she had to force herself not to flinch. Then Kaya was gone again, on her feet and loping ahead, turning about six paces away to look at Claire, who followed, still awed by the power and speed of the dark body but also certain that the wolf knew some formula for this encounter.

They walked for an hour, Kaya sometimes pressing against her leg like a big cat before moving ahead again. The enclosure was large but they covered it twice, pausing sometimes for Kaya to scratch at the soil. At one point she tracked a blackbird, falling into the liquid slinking that had alarmed Claire earlier. Finally Claire sat down and after a few desultory paces back and forth the wolf sat too, within arm's reach, panting slightly, watching her, alert but unafraid.

Claire decided she was also unafraid. Her feelings were complex and she was intensely aware of the wolf's movements and expressions but she'd forgotten to be scared and no matter how much she focused on the wolf's teeth and muscles, she couldn't regain any of the earlier terror. She was certain Kaya would not attack.

KAY SEXTON

The woman came out, carrying a saucepan and Kaya leapt up, running to her and around her.

'Stop it, Kaya. Enough!' She held out the pan to Claire. 'Milk. She's potty for it. Go on, you hold it – let her drink.'

Claire took the pan and Kaya stuck her muzzle in. Her strength was astonishing; Claire needed both hands to hold the pan steady as the wolf guzzled. When all the milk was gone and every drip had been licked from Claire's hands - an activity Kaya took extreme care over - the wolf wandered off.

The woman sat down. 'I'm Eleanor. Let me tell you about Kaya. She's Canadian, six years old, socialised obviously. My husband bought her when he was thinking of turning his grand old pile into some kind of safari park. That idea went kaput and so did the marriage. He kept the house and I kept Kaya. She'd been somebody's pet, but when they couldn't cope with her anymore they locked her in a cage. She was impossible when we first got her. Scared, defensive, destructive – but never aggressive. It took about six months to get her to respond to us. Before that she'd stay as far away as possible and not look at us. Now, as you can see, she's as happy as a lark. Fit for nothing of course. Can't breed her, can't free her. A terrible wasted life.' She sighed. 'If I'd let that bloody idiot have her, she'd have been sold to a circus, or worse. So we're together. Pair of females nobody wants.'

Claire glanced sideways at her. 'I think you're talking bollocks.'

'Ha! What makes you say that?'

'You're fond of her and proud of her. She's stimulated, responsive, alert. And if you're involved with Bl... with him,' she pointed to Blaine outside the gate, 'you've got some kind of role that suits you.'

'He said you were smart, didn't mention bloody rude though.'

'More outspoken than rude, I'd say.'

'Well, you would, wouldn't you? Now look, *he* says you can stay the night. Got a toothbrush and stuff for you in the car, apparently.

GATEKEEPER

Thing is, if you say yes, you're in – understand? You've had your free taster with Kaya. From now on it's in at the deep end or out the door.'

'In,' Claire said. 'I think.'

'Thought so. Right, back to the house for eats and orientation, then off *he* goes and you and I get down to brass tacks.'

Lunch was a vegetable soup eaten in the kitchen of a small bungalow. Claire had expected something more palatial and said so.

'Can't be arsed,' Eleanor said. 'Spend all day outdoors: clean and warm is all I ask for when I'm inside.'

Claire was feeling a kind of vertigo, a dizziness of isolation from her own world. She looked over at Blaine, leaning on the kitchen counter. He had unlimited capacity for standing and silence, she thought. But he interpreted her glance correctly, putting down his spoon and nodding.

'Here is what will happen, Claire. First I will tell you about what we expect from you, then I will leave and Eleanor will give you some understanding of the wolf in captivity. Tomorrow we will go through some practicalities and if everyone is still happy, I will drop you back at the bird sanctuary. If you decide this is not something for you to do, you can stop at any time. If we decide you are not the right person, we will stop also and take you straight back to enjoy the rest of your weekend. But after this, once you agree to go ahead, we hope there will be no stopping.'

She ate, considering his words. 'It's a bit like being recruited as a terrorist,' she said.

'How so?'

'The isolation, all these mysterious first name only introductions, being swept away from my friends and taken somewhere I don't know. The inducement of Kaya. It seems to add up to some kind of indoctrination.'

'Good,' Blaine said. 'You can see clearly how easy it would be to attract the gullible and foolish to work with us. Now look at it

25

KAY SEXTON

from my position. Who can I trust? The obvious answer is I can trust people who have been tested. Who are those people? They are activists. But if a person is known for loyalty to their cause and trustworthiness and effectiveness - they are no good to me. Can you see why?'

She shook her head.

'If I know them, or if they are 'known' to be trustworthy, then the police will probably know them too, in this country and in other countries where there are many agencies keeping track of dissident behaviour. Animal Rights can seem nearly as dangerous as calls for more democracy, because both threaten the status quo. So the people I most want are the people who are most watched. As a result we must find good people who are not yet watched, and hope they will understand our behaviour because to them we seem too secretive. Is that the word? Secretive?'

She nodded again, fascinated by this glimpse into an Animal Rights underground that spanned nations.

'I am not a person who is watched or, if I am watched, it is not for these reasons, nor is Eleanor. Ansel, yes, we know he has been observed, but he is seen as a safe and sensible person, he has been known to argue against foolish actions and so he has a special thing, a rare thing, he can move into the more watched world and still be considered quite safe. But your group – this man who freed the mink ...'

'Liam,' she supplied. Eleanor looked enquiring. 'I'll explain later, if you like,' Claire said and the older woman nodded.

'Liam. He is already watched. You did not know this? He has been in many things, and always with violence. On protests he has been fighting, and he has vandalised some places: factories and research centres that use animal testing. So Liam is useless to anybody serious, because as soon as his name appears in a file or report, there is a little warning that ripples through the world and people begin to look closely at what he is doing.'

26

Claire felt a hot satisfaction. 'I'd say he was useless for more reasons than that,' she muttered.

'Yes, that too. He is instable.'

'Unstable.'

'Yes. We need people who think. They maybe have to think fast, but they must think before reacting. This, Ansel believes, you can do. Anyway, we eat and talk, agreed?'

They continued to eat while Blaine outlined his ideas. His proposal, more of a manifesto, was preposterous. So preposterous that Claire listened to the whole thing in attentive silence, unable to begin framing her questions and objections.

There had not been a live wolf in Britain since the 1600s, nor in Holland, nor in Belgium, for over a century. His aim - The Project - was to raise a pack of European wolves, to live in one of two locations. A pack that would be somewhat protected by its location, by key individuals and by a complex system of selective conditioning, but in all other respects would be released to see if it could find an accommodation with its environment that would allow it to survive and thrive.

'Crazy,' said Claire eventually. 'Impossible. I'm sorry, but it's such a non-starter I can't even begin to believe it's viable.'

'Tell me why. Let me answer your questions,' Blaine urged.

Foremost was the land issue, she said. No community would permit such risks to be taken in its own back yard.

'We are not going to tell them,' Blaine replied. 'Or not all of them. For fifteen years now we have been working in two locations. Our donor has purchased land, legitimately, and we have made it suitable for wolves. We have some people in each place that we can trust — they will protect the wolves to a certain extent and act as advocates for their retention. But we are not going to ask anybody's permission, so it won't be 'we don't want wolves', it will be, 'we've got wolves, now how do we deal with them?"

And that was the second problem, she insisted. Raising a pack.

'Not one pack but two. Two packs, but the strongest only will be released. The detail of how we will raise a viable pack of self-determining wolves is not your problem. In fact you will have nothing do with it. Such information would be counterproductive. But I can say we have specialists and volunteers ready to undertake the raising project.'

And her third objection – if Liam would have been insane to release mink, what would wolves do to an ecosystem?

'Nothing bad,' Blaine said, then held up his hand to forestall her argument. 'They are native Claire. They are meant to be here. You think that a few hundred years is enough for an environment to adapt to life without its big predators: wolves and bears? Not to mention the omnivores like wild pigs. It's not. There are holes in the living world that we have made – when we kill the predators we leave not just a gap, but a mess. Did you know that vultures are dying out in India?'

She shook her head, confused by the change of subject.

'Yes. You know why? Because there used to be so much death for them to feed on: carrion, goats and wild pigs, even deer. But the population of India now scavenges all those dead things, uses every part of them, and all that is left for the vultures is human flesh.'

'Human flesh?' she stared at him.

'In the Jain religion, bodies are put in trees for vultures to pick clean. Because the birds get only one food now, they have developed an illnes; it is killing them. We think it is like Kuru, like Kreutzfeld Jakobs disease – something they get from eating only people. It is the same with wolves in Europe. We do not know what long -term harm we have done to the world by removing them from the food chain, but they belong here, unlike the mink your unstable colleague was so keen to release.'

Claire shook her head. 'I feel like somebody slipped me some acid. This isn't real.'

'So, it is difficult I know. Now we talk about you, Claire. Why you? Can you guess?'

GATEKEEPER

'I haven't the faintest idea. I keep expecting Liam to jump out of a giant cake and yell 'surprise'. Nothing makes much sense.'

'I will tell you: you are resourceful. You're unknown. You've been cut free from animal rights. We need a young personable woman for each place. Young - because young people are more adaptable. Female - because men can end up in dominance battles with other men, while women can back down without losing face, and personable, because looks are persuasive as well as words. Each of you will be the gatekeeper for a pack we are raising and one of you will get to stand between the pack that is eventually released and the community in which we release it. Both of you will be given training, although you will never meet, and when the pack is released, the successful gatekeeper will be completely alone, with only her wits and strength to help her work on the wolves' behalf. We will not be able to help you then.'

He looked at her, waiting for a response.

Claire stared out of the window but the kitchen was on the wrong side of the bungalow; Kaya's enclosure was out of sight.

'Let me get this right,' she said. 'I'm to give up an unspecified amount of my life, to probably *not* work with wolves, with no guarantee that what I'm training for will ever transpire. I'm in competition with another woman, whom I won't know, for one chance to act like a combination PR schmoozer and ordinary member of the public. I'm not allowed to tell anyone what I'm doing, and if it comes to the crunch I'm on my own.'

'Exactly,' Blaine said. 'And in addition, I will insist that you don't study wolves, or visit wolf parks, or do anything else that could alert people to your interest in the species. In fact, you will be helping us if you cut yourself off from all Animal Rights activity.'

She thought about it. It was a lunatic enterprise ... and yet she'd already met one wolf – where there was one there could be many, if this worked. She knew nothing about Blaine, but Ansel vouched for him, and she trusted Ansel. And what did she have to lose? Her

29

choices were stark, finish her degree and find any job that allowed her to stay as far away from home as possible, or return to her father and continue to live with a lie that had warped her entire life until now.

'It may not sound like the chance of a lifetime,' Blaine said, seeming to read her mind. 'But it is. Not your lifetime, and not your chance – but for the pack it will be their chance, their lifetimes. How much does that weigh with you, Claire?'

'Your English seems a lot better,' she said, avoiding an answer.

'I am a little rusty. I've been speaking another language for several months now. It takes the mind a while to catch up.'

It decided her. He spoke so matter-of-factly and yet hid his actions as if concealment was second nature. He was practised at this. She could either trust him or walk away – but she would never get to walk back.

'I'm still in,' she said. Blaine smiled. Eleanor banged shut the door of the dishwasher.

'Then you can politely sod off while I talk to Claire,' she said to Blaine, who picked up his coat, nodded to Claire and left.

'Right. Let me lay down some rules. *He* isn't going to feature in your training. If you make a real effort you might even be able to find out who he is, but I'd advise you not to. You're going to spend a lot of time thinking about this – try not to get paranoid.' Eleanor grabbed a folder from the kitchen drawer and sat down next to her. 'This is the part that's going to be hard for you to understand. Some of the people who are going to be involved in getting you ready for your role won't know that's what you're doing. Do you get that? No funny handshakes or passwords.'

'How can they not know?'

'Easily. Let's say *he* decides you need to know how to operate a hot air balloon – can't imagine he ever would, but take it as an example. Do you think we're going to convert a hot air balloonist to the cause? No. We'll send you a letter telling you that you're the

GATEKEEPER

lucky winner of a course of hot air ballooning lessons and to contact Mr. So and So who's going to teach you. We'll have paid, of course.'

'But then how will I know what is coming from you, and what isn't?'

'That's where paranoia sets in. You're going to have to guess – your friend Ansel might be able to help you a bit, but if you ask me, I'd say you should try and rely on yourself as much as you can. Don't turn him into a sounding board.'

Claire shrugged. She wasn't likely to become reliant on anyone – she knew where that led and the idea chilled her.

'I can give you some guidance in what to expect. You'll be offered work that helps you build a base of competence, maybe something in government, not high level but policy related. Over the next year you'll get to meet some people who can help get you to the right kind of position to be useful. Skills you might need – we assume you can read maps, and you're pretty fit – your martial arts training is a bonus: but we'll add climbing, skiing, a few outdoor activities like that. The one you're going to have most problem with is shooting.'

'Shooting?' Claire shook her head. 'No way.'

'Then, madam, you're out. Shooting: for two reasons. One, it sets you outside the circle of Animal Rights - moves you into the other camp so you'll be trusted by people in a rural location. Two, there are a dozen reasons you might need to shoot and shoot well. Suppose for some reason we need our pack to be fed, who else is going to kill the animal that's going to feed them? What if you have to shoot something else – a rabid cat for example?'

'There's no rabies in Britain.'

'Wrong. There is rabies here, and it could be a threat to our pack. What about a pack of wolf hunters turning up, all high-powered rifles and testosterone? Who else is going to shoot out their tyres so they can't get to the wolves?'

'Rabies? You're having me on.'

31

KAY SEXTON

'Claire, trust me. Any ecosystem is permeable – and just because you don't get told about things like rabies it doesn't mean they aren't here. There are rabid bats right across Europe, trust me. It's a sign of how distant most people are from their environment that they expect to be cushioned from risk. Think about Foot and Mouth and Bird 'flu – all the panicking and rushing around making stupid decisions, not just ordinary people but governments too.'

'But shooting is ...'

'Cruel, fascist, frightening, abusive?'

Claire nodded.

'And if you get sent to Alaska, where you need to survive on what you can hunt, trap or fish - how will you cope then?'

'Get sent?'

'Oh yes, you're going to be doing quite a bit of travelling.'

Claire sat back, trying to digest the range of ideas being thrown at her. 'Why didn't Blaine mention that?'

'We wouldn't want anybody who was more impressed by the idea of travel than by The Project.'

'You're going to take me shooting, aren't you?'

'Smart girl,' Eleanor opened the folder. 'This is an air rifle – takes .22 ammunition, will kill a rabbit, maybe even a fox at relatively close quarters. Learn the parts of the exploded diagram, then we'll clean one and go out and do some target shooting. After that we'll move on to a Browning – expect your shoulder to ache like hell tomorrow – and tonight you'll practice with a night sight.'

'Is that it? I spend the whole time shooting?'

Eleanor smiled. 'No. Tomorrow morning we'll take Kaya for a walk. She has to go out before six so we don't meet members of the public. Are you up for that?'

Claire felt herself grinning, tried not to, sure her face was stupid with excitement, 'You mean walk her on a lead?'

'Oh yes. It's illegal of course, but what the hell, she's better behaved than most dogs. If we do meet people, they tend to think she's a very, very big Alsatian – at least at first glance.'

'Don't they complain?'

'Would you complain about a wolf - if it was in front of you? Or would you walk away and thank God you'd survived?'

Claire snorted. 'I can't believe this.'

'Wait and see. Anyway, you're the one who's going to work with a wild wolf pack, if this comes off – what Kaya and I do is small stuff by comparison. By the way, you're to grow your hair – he thinks you look too boyish with that haircut, something you can put up in a bun would give you gravitas, he says.'

CHAPTER FOUR

Back at university, Claire found her mind dividing into compartments. She could be sitting in a lecture and would find she had been taking notes while her conscious thoughts were with Kaya, straining at her chain in the early morning light as the wolf scuffed at leaves that might conceal a rabbit burrow. Or she would be telling Mala about the weekend – the edited version - and part of her would be back-tracking events, noting that she had changed her opinion of Ansel: now she admired him more, but trusted him less. Much less.

The erosion of their friendship had begun as soon as Blaine dropped her back at the nature reserve. She'd found Ansel where she'd left him – she half-expected to see dew on him, as though he hadn't moved - but he had.

'I took some pictures for you,' he said, holding out her camera. 'Now you can show people photos, as if you'd been here all weekend. You already know how the rooms look, so you can talk about them naturally'

'You went into my backpack? You used my camera?' The invasion of privacy brought her earlier concern to mind. 'And while we're on the subject, how the hell did you get into the flat to leave that note the other morning?'

He gave her a calm stare. 'I thought you should have photographs,' he said.

'Well maybe, but it would have been nice to be asked. And don't duck the issue – how did you get into the flat?'

GATEKEEPER

He reached into his tweed jacket and pulled out a ring of keys, selecting one and unsnapping it from the clasp. 'I made a key.'

'What? How the hell did you do that? And why?'

'When I knew you were being considered for The Project I thought it might come in useful. I took Mala's keys from her bag one day, said I was going out to buy tobacco, got a key cut, and put hers back. It wasn't complicated.' He smiled and in his face she saw the dark side of his mind, a cratered place like the moon, full of fractured excitement. She felt like stepping away from him, but this was Ansel, good Ansel, her reliable friend. She turned the camera in her hands as he continued. 'It's part of my role. Like going to find Mick and Liam after the release operation, to judge what was going on.'

She reached out and took the key. 'Never again. You can text me if we need to meet. I really don't like what you did. Do you understand?'

He nodded, but the smile was still on his face. He'd enjoyed it, she realised. This was his thing – good Ansel liked to creep around and play the spy. It was horrible to think that she'd confided in him. Never again.

Now she felt fractured; part of her had stayed with Kaya. She'd never met a big predator close up before and suddenly she'd understood how people devoted their lives to a single species, becoming obsessed with them.

Kaya had been much bigger than the space she took up in the world. She'd been uncompromising, easily bored and demanding. She'd been funny too – she played differently to a dog, expecting humans to contribute to her amusement and yet not leaving it to them to determine that amusement, she invented games and gave them up within minutes in favour of a new idea. And she was beautiful. Claire had spent much of her time as an ARA arguing that all animals had equal value – that human notions of utility or lovability should not feature in decisions about animal welfare, and yet on her

35

first meeting with a wolf she'd fallen in love; she was smitten, head over heels, adoring the whole species.

Kaya offset Ansel. That was how she saw it in her mind as she spent her days avoiding bumping into him, and fooling Mala that everything was fine, and wasting most of her lectures trying to find emotional balance instead of making notes. She'd gained Kaya, and lost Ansel. It hurt. Ansel had been around since she'd started at Uni, he'd introduced her to Animal Rights activism and he was one of the few people who knew about her mother's death and its aftermath.

She remembered their last conversation at the dewpond – his dark web wasn't a metaphor, he really did care more about the world of 'nature' than people and he took pride in the way he moved people around to repair his web. She'd pretty well ignored her anger at his deception but as a kind of fear began to grow in her, she knew she needed to confront him. She was becoming scared not of Ansel but of the past, at the point where she was reviewing a relationship and seeing scars and sickness in it, where before she'd had a vision of health and contentment. It wasn't the first time she'd had to do this.

She knew where to find him.

She caught the bus to the dewpond again. He sat, as always, with his notebook and pipe, and smiled up at her as though she hadn't been avoiding him since their return more than a month before.

'It's been weeks,' she said.

'Yes, I've missed your company.'

'I don't mean that, I mean I haven't heard anything.'

He looked down at the notepad. 'It takes time, I think.'

'No you don't think Ansel, you bloody know! You've done all this before. You're ... you're a creep!'

'Claire, don't confuse me with Liam, or with what happened before.'

GATEKEEPER

'Before has nothing to do with it!' She wanted to hit him, beat him to the ground and knock out his teeth, destroy the smile she'd thought was benevolent and wise.

'I think it has. I think your mother's death and what happened with your father has a lot to do with it.'

She shook her head. 'Don't you dare, Ansel. Don't you bloody dare! If I'd known what kind of a shit you were, I'd never have told you about that.' Anger pulled her hands into fists.

'Claire, sit down. You're scaring the birds.'

She looked out over the pond, where a flock of sparrows had lifted into the air at her raised voice and was skimming the sky like iron filings pulled by a magnet. She shook her head again, but sat.

'Please listen. You feel betrayed. I understand. When I became part of The Project I had similar feelings. But yours will be worse because of your parents. I know this is the most difficult time. You want to be involved and yet nothing has happened to make you feel part of The Project. I promise, it has started for you. I do know how hard this time is – that's why I haven't looked for you, although I have been worried. You need time to adjust to the idea, and I knew that you would feel I had been … unfair.'

'Not unfair - fucking outright illegal and abusive, breaking into the flat, using things I told you in confidence against me!'

'Okay then. I don't see it that way but you do. Now let me say what I think. If you hadn't had the experience with your mother and father, I think you would not feel so strongly about this. I think you might have seen my actions as unpleasant but necessary.'

'My parents have nothing to do with it.'

'They do, Claire. When your mother died you were devastated. You told me so. Your father's health meant you had to take a second year off university. And then you found out you'd been living a lie. Now you think I also have been making you live a lie.'

She clenched her teeth to stop herself yelling. It was true that there were parallels. Towards the end of her gap year she'd gone on

KAY SEXTON

holiday to Greece, and she'd persuaded her mother to come with her. Not her father, because his health meant he couldn't tolerate the flights, the strange food, too much sun. But her mother had loved it. She'd swum twice a day, eaten everything put in front of her, and sunbathed until her tan matched the oak kitchen units in their Berkshire kitchen. Claire had realised for the first time how much her mother gave up to look after a husband who was 'not strong', and she'd been delighted to watch her open out like a butterfly emerging from its chrysalis, drying her wings in the sun.

A few weeks after their return, while Claire was packing for her first year at university, her mother had driven into a motorway piling. Possibly a stroke, the coroner said, recording a verdict of accidental death.

'It's not about that, Ansel. It's about how you manipulate people: how you manipulated me. No, it's not even about that ... it's about how you enjoy it.'

'Claire, I see you're upset, but the reasons you're taking this so hard need to be understood. You think this is like your family – you feel you're being used.'

She stood again, pacing the rabbit-bitten turf. 'No. I admit that there are similarities, but I'm over that, Ansel. This is different.'

'Are you over it? I don't think anybody can really be 'over' such a thing.'

She was over it. Not just the death, but the other thing – the one she wished she'd never told him about.

'Tell me, when did you last go home to see your father?'

She turned on him. 'None of your bloody business – you're too much of a snoop as it is!'

'Maybe, but your reaction shows you are not over it. How could you be? It was your whole life.'

She wanted to walk away but if she did, she'd be admitting something.

'You're changing the subject. This is about you, not me.'

GATEKEEPER

'And I've said I'm sorry. I think I've only done what was necessary, but I cannot blame you for feeling otherwise.'

Silence. But not the companionable silence they'd had before. Now hers was filled with doubt and his seemed accusatory. The distant sounds of sheep were mocking: faint gurgling laughter like a TV sitcom audience.

'There has been a heron,' he held out the notebook. She took it. He'd drawn the heron tracks he'd seen in the chalky mud at the edge of the pond. She sighed. Only Ansel could think an absent bird's footprint was a sensible peace offering.

'I am over it,' she said.

He nodded, but she could tell he didn't agree.

This time he didn't even offer her a ride on his handlebars. She walked back to the bus stop, trying to remember the last time she'd seen her father. Over a year ago. They'd spoken by phone on her birthday, and he sent her a letter every month or so, full of his doings: allotment, indoor bowling, outings to garden centres. She read them and tore them up.

When her mother was alive Claire had been happy at home, and her father had always been the same: quiet, gentle, taking her round the garden to show her plants that had come into bloom. They'd sit in silence until her mother came out to call them into dinner. Her mother was always the same too. She broke into their tranquillity like a gong, melodious but loud. The way she'd thought of it was her father was a wash of watercolour, a sensitive impression that grew and developed the longer you spent with it, full of gentle subtleties, and her mother was a curve of Indian ink splashed onto that watercolour, a bold arc that might be a Chinese junk sailing on a dawn sea, or a length of bamboo spearing into a pale landscape. They'd complemented each other. And it had all been a lie.

After her mother's accident Claire had put university on hold. Her father needed her. For a while she'd taken on the tasks the older woman had always completed: cooking bland meals her father's IBS

39

could tolerate, filling his inhaler prescriptions, making sure he carried the pills for his migraine. 'Your Dad's got to be careful,' Mum had said. 'Not that he's less of a man than any other, but he has to be careful.'

One day, hanging up his jacket, Claire had felt rustling in his pocket and pulled out a pork pie wrapper. She'd put it back and waited, sure there would be a summons to his room in the night, and she would have to lecture him about eating things that upset him. Then it would be a month of simple food for him. Nothing happened.

A few days later he rang to say he was going home with a workmate to help him fit a new sink. He would eat there. She said nothing, knowing he would pay for it with migraine or terrible stomach pains. He didn't. Weeks further on, alerted by a repeat prescription form from her father's doctor, she checked his inhaler. He hadn't used it in three months; the protective cellophane wrapper was still sealed around it in his pocket. Then he started going to the pub after work. Drinking beer. Eating crisps. She found the packets in his lunch box. He was never ill.

She went to see the doctor, who refused to discuss with her why a man who'd been a semi-invalid all her life should now be able to eat what he liked and do all the things he'd been unable to do before.

She felt she was going insane. Her entire life had been based around her father's condition. 'Dad can't do anything today, love, he's not feeling too good,' her mother would say, and they'd stay home instead of making the trip to the park she'd been promised. They took holidays on the Isle of Wight or in Morecambe, because 'Dad won't do well with foreign food and we don't want him to be ill, do we?'

She'd loved him for it. His peacefulness, his fragility, had brought her hours of happy companionship. He was the one who'd taught her to love landscape, to watch birds for hours, to observe the

GATEKEEPER

small lives of insects in the garden. And it had all been a sham. She still couldn't understand why her mother had colluded in it – that vital woman, full of pleasure, who'd worshipped the Greek sun with her body, who had denied herself so much to cater to this man's limitations, and raised Claire to do the same.

For a couple of months she'd researched his condition in the local library: hypochondria? Munchausen's? Munchausen's syndrome by proxy? Facts didn't help her make sense of her life as it had been, or as it was now. That Tae Kwon Do class her mother had enrolled her in when she was ten, 'because you need to be able to take care of yourself love, and Dad can't teach you how to be safe' – had it been a sign of mental instability in her mother, or a sensible action? She'd never been stopped from climbing trees or riding her bike – perhaps that meant her mother didn't love her, didn't need to wrap her in protection as she had her husband? Or perhaps it meant that the collusion between them had stopped there, and she'd had a normal childhood. She couldn't tell any more.

She rang the University and asked if she could start late after all. They said it would be better for her to wait out the year. So she found a job at the local animal shelter, mucking out dog pens and cat cages and socialising animals that had been beaten, starved, abandoned, abused. She knew how they felt – when loved ones betrayed you it was hard to trust again.

From there it had been a natural step to take up with the Animal Rights groups when she got to Uni. And apart from minimal interactions in the Hall of Residence, she was free to be alone. Within weeks she was volunteering as a dog-walker, then working with Vidya on a campaign to get free-range eggs used in the cafeteria. That campaign had been co-ordinated by Mala. Claire's activism and Mala's eco-feminism gave them a comfortable relationship in which few questions were asked. As soon as she was introduced to Ansel, the progression to illegal activism was easy. Ansel had become a natural confidant. Over the months spent planning the

41

release operation she'd told him about her father and her mother's death and the way her entire history had been churned into ugly shapes by what had happened since.

Now she decided to ignore The Project. It would be better to concentrate on her studies and accept that the day with Kaya had been a huge practical joke played by a bunch of lunatics with a half-baked idea that they could never pull off. Soon they'd be asking her for money to help finance the scheme and then she'd know it was a confidence trick.

She found a second-hand folding bike for a few pounds on the campus intranet. She couldn't ride it far; it lacked the right suspension and gears, but it could be brought into the flat at night. There was no way to protect it out on the campus, but if Liam trashed it she could afford to replace it again. She began to think about a post-graduate course so that she could stay on in Brighton. All she wanted was something to do, to fill up her days so that she didn't have to think about the future – if she'd had any religious belief at all she'd have thought about becoming a nun – anything to avoid going home.

Sussex suited her. There was something about it, the thin soil over the chalk, the scouring winds, the stunted trees, that matched her mood. The gales that swept across the coast were bracing, like a spring clean; they swept away anything weak or unanchored and she would have been happy to have the same thing happen to her; to be lifted and taken up by something stronger, that was all she wanted. She had no certainties to keep her anywhere.

A week or so later, she received a letter telling her she'd won £1,000 in Premium Bonds and a cheque. She didn't own any Premium Bonds. She put the cheque in a drawer and waited. Ansel turned up the following evening.

'How are things,' he asked.

'Much as usual,' she said.

He stared at her and she stared back, blanking him.

GATEKEEPER

'You have come into some money?' he asked.

She smiled. 'Yes, a win on my mother's Premium Bonds. Just in time for Christmas.'

He blinked.

'I've used it to pay off my student loan,' she said, ignoring his frown.

'Well ... ah ... well,' he said, tucking his hands into his pockets.

She sat, leaving him to do all the work.

'I didn't know your mother had Premium Bonds,' he said.

'You don't know everything, Ansel. No matter how much you creep around and ferret things out, you can never know everything.'

He nodded, serious-faced as though her words were a valuable precept he was pleased to learn.

I think the money was for something else,' he said.

'Like?'

He placed a slip of paper on the table. She craned to read it without picking it up. A shooting range offering half-price membership.

'Can't get there,' she said. 'Too far away.'

He pushed the paper over, as if moving it closer would shorten the distance to the club. 'The money would pay for a year's membership and a new bike.'

'I've got a new bike.'

She hitched her thumb towards the foldaway, propped against the wall.

'Ah,' he took up the paper, put it down again. 'But you could buy a better bike?'

'So Liam can trash it for me? Thanks, but no thanks.'

His smile was crooked, and she saw the dark underbelly of his secretive nature, before he nodded again and left.

Claire thought about it though, looking at the flyer without touching it, remembering the satisfaction of Eleanor's rifle against her shoulder. Something simple to fill up her time was what she'd been asking for and now she'd been offered it.

43

KAY SEXTON

There was a bus timetable in the drawer of her desk: two buses would get her there, maybe an hour and a half's journey, including waiting for connections. She could shoot without buying a bike – a compromise, the kind of skill Blaine had wanted her to build.

Next she rang the club and asked if they would give her a student discount on top of the half-price offer, putting the membership within her price-range. She wasn't going to take the money – not yet. Not until she knew what the price would be. She'd made that mistake before.

CHAPTER FIVE

Claire fell in love with target shooting. It was true magic. With a .303, she could change the world half a mile away. She enjoyed the long pause while the universe held its breath, the trigger pressure as gentle and remorseless as a caress, and the final satisfaction of walking down the range to retrieve her target and see the close-clumped holes of her shots. Her eye was good and she became a grouping groupie: dedicated to bringing the five shots ever closer together. It was guilty love, like an affair - going home on the bus she would lift her hands to her face to drink in the chilled metal and cordite scent of the gun. She told nobody what she was doing – especially not Mala, who was busy making rag rugs for the flat. She'd offered one to Claire.

'Nice for the chilly mornings,' she said, spreading what looked like a gigantic sunflower on the kitchen floor.

'I like it cold,' Claire said, knowing that Mala would feel rebuffed, but this wasn't the time to get involved in home improvement, she wanted to be free, unhindered, pure. Sparseness and utility were what she wanted, not luxury and comfort. She watched her diet and kept up her Tae Kwon Do practice to be at peak fitness, and pared away anything else that anchored her to her old world. She didn't talk to other students after lectures, nor go to the bar or any societies. Instead, she worked in her room when everybody else was being sociable or she took long walks over the downs when the weather was bad enough to keep other hikers at home. Mala tried to

KAY SEXTON

get her to go along to the belly-dance group a few times but Claire insisted she had too much to do and eventually the other woman gave up.

The weather got colder, and the hours on the bus were exhausting. She picked up the cheque fifty times or more, but put it back in the drawer. For now at least she held the power – until she cashed the cheque she wouldn't have bought into Blaine's world, or anybody's world – she was escaping all her ties.

Ansel spoke warmly when he saw her, but never came to the flat again, and Liam and Mick sauntered behind her whenever their paths crossed, laughing loud enough for her to hear, but never approaching close enough for her to determine the joke.

Her isolation was absolute, apart from the cold kiss of the gun against her cheek and Mala's bubbling inconsequentialities. The flat had never seemed blander or more anonymous and she had never been more content to exist within it without making it a home. She had a purpose; it kept her busy; she was happy.

Snow blanketed Sussex in February and everybody took the day off. Both universities spilled their students onto the South Downs and Claire and Mala kitted up for a long walk on Devil's Dyke. The bus was crowded with tobogganers and smelt of hot wool. Once on the Downs, Mala bumped into a group of her feminist friends and became involved in building a snow mother. Claire watched for a few minutes, thinking how vital her friend looked in her yellow waterproofs, her dark eyes small and bright like those of a cartoon duck – something about Mala drew comparisons with fairy tale and childhood stories. Claire saw one of her tutors, Peter Kemai, with his two little sons, and joined them in a stumbling snowball battle, hampered by three-year-old Joshua's inability to form snow into a missile and Peter's own tendency to throw his arms wide and smile, celebrating the miracle of snow, and making himself a perfect target.

'When I was a little boy in Kenya, I said to myself, "One day, I will live near a river." It was the big dream of my life'. He smiled

GATEKEEPER

down at his sons and then tipped his head backwards to watch the slow spiralling of new snow from the sky. 'And here I am, not just a river, but a sea on my doorstep, and not just sea, but snow! Claire, I am a blessed man.'

She nodded. Kemai had become a river specialist, researching the ribbons of water that had seemed mythical to him in the driest part of Kenya. She felt unwanted tears rise up and told herself it was the bitter wind, but his statement was one she wanted to share, and his sacramental response to the landscape made her feel selfish and empty. It seemed natural to celebrate weather. All the young bodies around her were sacrificing their heat and energy to the shortest days of the year. It was right to play-fight and laugh and feel the sting of snow against hot skin.

If people could live with one finger on the pulse of nature, this euphoria could be part of everybody, every day. She redoubled her efforts, bending to make piles of snow for Joshua, scowling dramatically when the older boy, James, scored a direct hit on her, leaving him giggling so much he had to put his hands on his knees to keep his balance, landing her own perfect one-two-three on Peter so that for a few minutes the front of his coat bore three white circles in a line, like giant buttons.

And then she felt a stinging blow on the back of her head. She fell, thinking that she must get her shoulder under her and knowing she wouldn't quite make it. Her cheek split as she landed, with a sound like a squeezed grape.

The next thing she knew was commas and flowers of red on the snow. She was kneeling. From far away she could hear Mala, bellowing. Somebody had their arm around her shoulder. Peter. She could see his dark fingertips and blue half-moons on his fingernails. Joshua was crying, but over his sobs she could still hear Mala. Peter lifted her, saying things she couldn't hear, and turned her to the path, supporting her with his shoulder. As they walked, the little boys trailing them and bawling, Claire felt the blood dripping from

KAY SEXTON

her face, but the back of her head hurt more. She felt sick and bent forward, trying to indicate her nausea, but nothing happened except more dizziness. Then Mala was in front of her, bright and vengeful, her voice deep, as though travelling a long dark tunnel to Claire's ears.

'I saw you, you bastard! I know where to find you!'

Claire turned her head, fighting the pain, to follow Mala's outstretched arm like a streak of yellow doom, knowing what she would see at the other end. And there was Liam's back, his shoulders hunched against the voice, Mick huddled with him, lighting a cigarette: both of them acting as if they didn't hear and anyway, it could be none of their business.

Claire looked back at the path again. One foot in front of another to Peter's old car. His hand loomed into view at waist height, holding a shape balanced on his flat palm and Mala's hand reached out to take the thing. A flint as big as a child's fist.

'He put it in a snowball. James dug it from the snow and brought it to me while I was helping you up.' Peter's voice was high with incredulity.

Mala made the stone vanish into her pocket. 'Let's get her to the hospital.'

Claire protested, but they didn't hear her. Her own voice swam up the long tunnel but got lost before her mouth. The dizziness came back and she closed her eyes.

She came round again in the car and was able to walk into Accident and Emergency where they waited hours for an eventual diagnosis of mild concussion and shock. Peter and the boys wanted to stay and drive her home, but Mala, rosier than a boiled ham in her outdoor clothing, sent them away, promising to call soon.

Back at the flat Claire drowsed upright in a chair in the kitchen, her socked feet warmed by the sunflower rug, knowing Mala watched, feeling safe for the moment, but fearing the battle ahead. That fear brought her out of her stupor by morning, but it was

GATEKEEPER

too late. Mala had called the University and begun a complaints procedure.

'I know who he is, Claire, or at least I know what he looks like and I can find out his name easily enough. I saw what he did. I'm guessing that he was the one who vandalised your bike too. This isn't about you any more. I can't pretend I didn't see him deliberately do you harm, and you can't expect me to ignore it. Suppose he'd hit one of the kids instead?'

Claire winced. Speech was painful and nodding impossible. There was a lump the size of half a golf ball on the back of her skull and voices still had to travel a huge distance to reach her ears. Mala was right, but the consequences of formal action against Liam could be disastrous.

'Would you let me try and sort it out myself?' she asked, wondering if The Collective could be persuaded to rein Liam in.

Mala thinned her lips. 'Don't ask me that – you know it's unfair. Don't brush it under the carpet.'

Claire held out her hand in apology and Mala took it, gripping hard.

Between them lay silent years of buried secrets; if Mala wanted to speak out now, Claire knew that stopping her would be cruel. Perhaps it was a first step to resolving whatever the girl was trying to escape. She owed it to Mala to back her up.

'His name's Liam O'Doherty. He's in the Economics Department. The bloke he was with is Mick Pendle, also Economics. And thanks, Mala, you're a real friend.'

They sat in silence for a long time, watching the twilight flatten itself into night, the leaden snow making everything one- dimensional and bringing darkness early.

Claire took a week off lectures, spending the time in her room, exercising with hand weights four or five times a day, pushing her muscles until her head rang with the cymbal crashes of a bruised skull. On the third day Mala came home, her lips thin again. 'He's

KAY SEXTON

gone back to Ireland. Family problems, his supervisor said. Left the evening I made the complaint, before they could notify him – so there's not even any evidence that he ran away to avoid being charged with assault. It'll have to wait until he returns.'

Claire tried not to feel relieved. That weekend she went to the range, but couldn't position the rifle lying prone, because it pressed against the healing cut on her right cheekbone. One of the instructors taught her to shoot from a standing position, estimating the sights rather than settling her vision along the line of the gun – it was difficult, but the idea it could even be possible was enough to keep her going. Her grouping was atrocious and after three or four minutes her arms ached as if she'd been carrying girders, but she persevered, taking long breaks and rubbing the muscles of her upper arms to relax them. By afternoon she could support the gun and estimate the target with reasonable accuracy and she was elated to discover that her grouping began to coalesce again as soon as she mastered the technique well enough to relax her breathing.

The club secretary came out and said somebody had dropped out of a team shooting contest taking place the following weekend at the Bisley range in Surrey. Would she consider filling in? They'd understand if her injury made it too difficult. Claire said yes without thinking, without the momentary pause for evaluation that had been part of her life since she met Blaine. She could tape over the cut to shoot, and it would get her out of the flat for a night, away from her thoughts and Mala's watchful silence.

The morning of the contest carried the last hard frost of the year – the grass rimed with white and the sky lifted with infinite clarity over the range, so that she squinted against its unconquerable brightness. She shot reasonably well on the first day, although she thought she could have done better if she'd known how big the event was – the crowds of olive -and- dun- clad shooters were like a migration – she'd never guessed so many people owned guns, let alone came together to compete so ferociously. It was like being part

50

GATEKEEPER

of a shoal, everybody turning to the sound of the shot, everybody applauding when results were announced; a swirling crowd of rifle-toting individuals, all moving as one. She'd loved it though, and that night at the hotel she stood at the bar replaying the events with the rest of her team and barracking other participants.

It wasn't until she went to bed that she noted the ringing in her ears, despite the defenders she'd worn throughout her events. It was impossible to sleep. The synthetic fragrance of pot-pourri on the bedside table gave her a headache and she put the bowl of acid-coloured petals and wood shavings into the wardrobe. The roaring in her head still kept her awake and she didn't want to take pain-killers in case they dulled her shooting for the next morning. She opened the windows as far as possible and sat on the floor, resting her head against the cold metal sill, inhaling the frigid air.

She realised she'd become a different person – changing tribes was as easy as changing mobile phones. She wasn't an ARA any more, even though her habits were still the same: she still wore camouflage clothing and sensible shoes and spent time in the countryside, drank fair-trade coffee and bought recycled paper - but now she was the enemy.

At two in the morning the weather changed and she woke, crick-necked from slumping against the wall. She felt the temperature waver and then rise – spring was on its way. Not the false spring of forced flowers and asparagus flown in from Africa but the great buzzing wall of hatching insects and migrating birds that would flood the countryside, warming, filling every pocket of space with tiny life – she could feel it. She got back into bed.

The second day's shooting was an anti-climax. Her enjoyment had been tainted by her night thoughts. She scanned faces, trying to find the Liam-types in the crowd but all she could see were happy, healthy people, enjoying the day and cheering on their friends. Perhaps she had been wrong, and the activists were the mad and bad after all. Or perhaps the problem was in her: she was incapable

51

KAY SEXTON

of judging people, her eyes – so keen to see the target and group her shots close to the bull's-eye – were a distorting mirror that had made monsters of her parents and evil into good. She tried again to understand her parents, her relationship to the Collective, why she'd ended up outside and Liam inside, but the only result was that her awareness of the crowd faded and she shot better, improving on her previous score and winning a small plaque for 'best novice'.

One of her team -mates offered her a lift back to Sussex but she made an excuse to travel alone. She'd already purchased her return ticket and the coach trip would give her time to try and sift her understanding before facing Mala again. If she'd been wrong about everything else, maybe she was wrong about her, too. Perhaps what the other girl needed more than anything was to talk about her past, share her experience, not be part of some conspiracy of silence. She was spending the weekend at some weird womanly consciousness-raising event, as she so often did. It was probably a way of saying no to her parents – filling her weekends with courses and festivals was easier than refusing to go home – Claire understood that all too well.

Claire hefted her bag at Poole Valley Coach Station, felt the ache in her shooting arm and opted for a taxi back to the flat.

When she saw the wood across the windows of the flat she was still in the back seat, digging through her purse to find the right money for the tip. She was tired and cold and her mind slipped mechanically into the procedures agreed by the Collective for any kind of security risk. She leaned forward and gave the driver Ansel's address.

When Ansel answered the door, his surprise seemed genuine, but she watched him closely, waiting for the smiling lifeless pleasure that had disturbed her before.

'I don't know what's happened,' she said, shouldering into his flat with her bag. 'The front window's boarded up at home, and Mala's not due back until late tonight, so I thought I'd better come over here first. Is that okay?'

He nodded. 'You did the right thing. I don't know what's going on either, but it's better for us to know first. Maybe just a burglary.'

'Us' meant the Collective. 'Maybe' meant perhaps she'd been the subject of a police raid. She took the phone he held out to her. 'Call the police,' he said. 'This is the number of the local station. Then call your landlord.'

She handed the phone back. 'I'm sure it's Liam. Mala brought a complaint against him and he ran off to Ireland. If he didn't break into the flat himself, he got Mick to do it.'

Emotions moved across Ansel's face, cloud-shadows of shock, calculation, and then the covert smile she'd been expecting. 'Okay,' he said.

She pulled her own mobile from the bottom of her overnight bag where she'd left it all weekend. As soon as she turned it on, text messages and voicemail notifications tumbled onto the screen. The first was from the police, telling her she'd been the victim of a burglary and they were contacting her at the instigation of her landlord. The second was from her landlord telling her that the police had boarded up the windows. Then a text message from the police appeared giving her the number of the local station. Another voicemail from the landlord with the number of a cleaner who would help put the place back together and telling her that the glazier would be around on Monday afternoon. Could she please confirm that one of the tenants would be able to let him in?

She took a conscious breath, sucking air so deep into her lungs she saw blue lights flashing behind her eyelids. If they needed a cleaner it must be bad. Really bad. Her hands shook, banging the phone against her ear. 'Bastard,' she said, under her breath. 'Bastard, bastard, bastard.'

She felt Ansel's hand on her shoulder, pushing down, and her knees gave way as she sat. After a couple of seconds she lifted her head to find him squatting in front of her, his face calm.

'Mala should not see the flat,' His voice was calm, but suppressed energy boiled below the surface.

'Yes, yes of course. I'll ...' she shook her head.

'Call one of her friends. Is she coming back by train?'

She nodded.

'Then get them to meet her from the train and give her a bed for the night. Say that you're clearing up tonight and she can come and take over tomorrow – make it sound like she's doing you a favour by being rested and ready to pitch in.' He stared at the mobile. 'Then we can go and see what Liam has done this time.'

It was worse than she'd imagined. Ansel had packed light bulbs, a flask of coffee, cleaning equipment and an air freshener in his backpack; as soon as she'd pulled the card from the doorjamb that told her the police had been inside the house and who to call, he'd moved ahead of her.

How had he known the bulbs would be smashed?

Her mind began to examine the facts: he could have been the one to break into the flat, although she couldn't understand why he'd want to. He knew the flat well, so he could find his way around in the dark if he'd smashed the lights, but what reason could there be for such vandalism on his part? Her shoes crushed glass underfoot with popping sounds like breakfast cereal. She stood still. Something from the ARA manual, '*Animals see better than humans, so when planning release operations, remember that your need for light is much greater than theirs. The closer you bring the release site to natural conditions the more chance they have of getting safely away - and the more chance you have of evading capture.*' So maybe it hadn't been Ansel, perhaps Liam, or Mick, or the two of them together, had smashed the lights out of habit.

Ahead of her she could hear Ansel muttering under his breath as he tried to grip the metal fixture which was all that remained of the bulb. He prised it free and inserted a new one. She flicked the switch and the tiny hall was lit with sixty watts of uncompromising light.

GATEKEEPER

The flat looked as though a dozen crack addicts had lived in it for a month. Through the doors into each bedroom she could see slashed carpet, bookshelves toppled, paper, clothes and bedding strewn and torn. Ansel moved ahead to the kitchen and she could tell from the cracking of his footsteps that plates, cups and glasses had been smashed to the floor. He opened the bathroom door and grimaced. Claire reached out, touching the hallway walls on either side with her fingertips, like Samson. She wanted to push until the bricks gave way and buried the ugliness in dust and fragments. It would be impossible to clear this away. Nothing that had been part of this attack could ever feel clean or decent again.

'I'm going to make some calls,' Ansel stood in front of her again, his face smooth, only a jumping tic in his right eye showing the extent of his feelings. 'Come outside with me.'

She pushed past him, into her own room, half-squinting to avoid seeing anything except the desk. The drawer had been pulled out and the cheque was gone.

'The cheque, they took the cheque!' She wanted to make it a statement of fact but her voice wobbled.

'Maybe not,' Ansel took her arm, led her to the kitchen. In the sink a pile of damp curled ashes. She lifted a knife from the floor and stirred the grey heap; a smell of urine like a cat-ridden alley stung her nose. Small things had been set on fire: she saw photograph edges, what might have been certificates, her driving licence - unused since she'd arrived here - curled in its plastic sheathing, her picture burnt.

'They burned the most precious things – difficult to replace.' Ansel's voice was as toneless as she'd wanted hers to be a few seconds ago.

Claire gripped the edge of the sink. She'd seen the twisted pictures of Queenie and Jack on the floor in her room, stamped on until their frames had shattered. She had no other photos here, because

55

KAY SEXTON

she didn't carry reminders of her childhood any more. The burnt pictures must be Mala's — irreparable memories destroyed.

She pushed back into her room. The urine was a clue, but if it was Liam who'd trashed the place, there would be something else to tell her he'd violated her home — he'd want her to know for sure. She knelt by the folding bike, feeling the frame, and over her shoulder Ansel played the torch over its bodywork. Each spoke had been snipped in two, the clean cuts identical to those made by bolt cutters.

'Bastard!' She said it like a prayer. At least she knew for sure now.

He led her outside and they stood in the dark while he filled his pipe. He inhaled, filling his lungs with smoke and exhaling with sharp snorts. When he was sated, he reached for his mobile.

Claire put out her hand, aware this was the first time she'd touched him since she took the key from his hand at the bird sanctuary. 'Who are you calling?'

'You know,' his voice was even, but there was energy underneath, like her own desire to smash the flat to the ground. 'This must be stopped now.'

'I'll do it.' She gripped his wrist, making him look at her. 'Tell Blaine to get me another cheque so I can buy a bike. Then I'll stop him, Ansel.'

The next day she received a cheque, by courier, with a slip stating it was to replace 'former un-cashed winnings lost in burglary'.

The bike was beautiful. She spent a week getting used to it, and then met Ansel at the S.U. bar.

'Find out where he drinks,' she said, and Ansel nodded.

'How is Mala?' His concern was genuine, but the slyness of his earlier behaviour had never left her mind and she found it difficult to discuss her flatmate with him.

'She's fine. I thought she'd flip out, but she's been totally focused about it. Getting the insurance and stuff sorted out seems to have kept her calm. Doing better than me, probably.'

56

GATEKEEPER

That night he called her and told her to meet him again at the S.U., where he handed her a complete list of Liam's haunts and habits. He must have been researching it since the night of the break-in, well ahead of her request. She shivered as she felt the cold side of his personality pass over her.

'He's been living at Mick's. Working for a fencing firm.' Ansel's voice curled away from Liam's name as though it disgusted him. 'He can't return to university with the disciplinary hanging over him, and yet he doesn't seem able to stay away either. I don't think he ever left, just told his friends to say he had. Mick seems to spend half his life out of the flat, avoiding Liam, most likely. You should be careful. I think Liam's dangerous, Claire.'

She let the thought warm her. A dangerous Liam was worth fighting, worth destroying – he threatened Mala, he'd released the mink; he was out of control. She didn't need to think any longer, she could just stop him.

The next night was a Friday. She pulled on thin latex gloves, and thicker biohazard ones over the top - they'd worn the same kind when they released the dogs, to avoid leaving fingerprints and as protection against dog bites and scratches. Over them she pulled a padded suede jacket, purchased from a charity shop the previous day, along with a pair of thin denim jeans. It was acceptable, a bit hot for a night in March perhaps, but not unusual enough to attract comment. She tied back her hair, cursing Blaine's insistence that she grow it, using three hair-bands to bind it back from her face. Long hair was a liability in a fight. A pair of cheap trainers, laces double-knotted, completed the outfit. She'd dump them as soon as this was over, along with the jacket and jeans. She wheeled the new bike out, admiring its lightness and the raked contours of the hard saddle. In a way Liam had done her a favour, at least on the bike front; she was sick of the fold-up.

Cycling to the top of town was hard work, but it warmed her muscles. Once she'd left the bike chained to railings on the far side

57

of the graveyard she had an hour or so until kicking-out time, walking to keep her body warm and loose and rehearsing the many scenarios that might follow. She was confident that she could overmaster Liam in a fight - that wasn't the issue. Keeping him subdued was the problem. There was something irrepressible about his malice, like a stamped on insect that still wriggled out from under the boot.

She let Liam get to the top of the hill, heading back to Mick's flat from the pub. He was alone. She walked parallel, tracking him along the side streets, remaining behind him and never crossing a road until she was sure he was already on the opposite pavement. He was oblivious, jingling coins in his pocket, head down. He seemed lonely rather than alone, but she suppressed the thought. She needed to avoid any sense of sympathy. Instead she focused her mind on the wrecked flat and Mala's fear.

As soon as he reached the flint wall that bounded the cemetery she had to act fast. She sprinted to gain speed, clambered up the wall and ran along the grass inside, bent double, both to hide from him and to ensure that if she tripped on a concealed gravestone she would be able to stop her fall before breaking her nose.

High risk, high risk. If she hit gravel he would hear her. If she fell she could do herself more harm than she planned for him. Her bike might get stolen while she was stalking Liam. Even so she felt a spurt of pleasure like warm bubbles frothing her blood into a mild frenzy, like a good night on a dance floor. She'd felt it in the van heading for the puppy-farm, she'd felt it with Kaya. Every pulse hammering a different beat, every sound louder, each breath fuelling muscles that ached to act – this was how a predator felt.

As he turned the corner into the narrow alley where no lights showed, she vaulted the wall behind him. Three running steps and she was on him, as he began to turn at the sound of her feet. Her clubbed hands struck him between the shoulders, driving him forward so he hit the ground. She stamped hard on the back of his

GATEKEEPER

knee, drawing a thin squealing from his emptied lungs, and then kicked him in the ribs, so he curled and turned on his side. She bent down, checking the flicker of his pale eyes as he planned his move, and as he reached out for her ankle, slammed the heel of her foot into his thigh so he shrieked again. Now she bent and half-lifted him, shoving him against the flint wall so that he slid down into a heap, groaning and cursing.

'Should have done this last time,' she said, letting him hear her voice, making sure he knew who it was. She lifted her foot and watched him curl away from it. It wasn't enough – she wanted to stop, but she'd have to come back again if he wasn't terrified, and he wasn't yet.

She let him stagger to his feet and then moved into front stance. He lunged forward and she used punch-pull technique to pummel his face, snapping the punches to about half-power so he didn't bounce his cranium off the wall, and avoiding his nose because she didn't want to drive his septum back into his skull. After eight punches, four with each fist, she stepped back.

It was too easy. Seductively so. She'd never used her Tae Kwon Do offensively before but Liam was no match for her. He hissed through swollen lips, clutching the wall behind him to hold himself upright, and kicked out. She caught his leg with her right arm and pushed up. His spine scraped down the wall as he fell, and as he rolled onto his front she saw blood seeping through his shirt from the sharp stones. She stepped back again, waiting. This time he came to his knees, hanging his head, and grabbed for her ankle. She stamped on his knuckles, reducing the force so as to bruise his hand rather than smash the bones.

This time he stayed down, crumpled at the base of the wall, hand between his knees. She lifted his head by pulling on his hair, ready to kick if he made any attacking move, but he was spent. His eyes were closed.

'Look at me, Liam.'

59

He tried to shake his head, but she tightened her grip on his hair until she'd dragged him to his feet, leaning against the wall. 'Bitch,' he said through blood dripping down his chin.

'Nice,' she said. 'Look at me, or I'll make you sorry.'

He opened his eyes, trying to glare, but the emotion most evident was a fearful hatred.

'Come near me, or anybody I know, ever again, and I'll cripple you.' She let go of his head and he drooped, cursing.

She looked at him, not sure she'd done enough and he kicked out. Almost without thinking she kicked in turn, accelerating his elevated leg. It was the weakest form of roundhouse, but it tipped his body until he lay on his side on the pavement. She put the toe of her trainer against his Adam's apple.

'If I kick you here, Liam, you'll die. It will drive your larynx back down your throat and make it swell so it closes off your breathing passage and you suffocate.' She bounced her toe a couple of times, letting him feel the pressure. His eyes opened, showed nothing but a blank panic.

'Just give me a reason, Liam – now, or any time - and I'll be happy to put everybody out of your misery.' She bent down, confident he was broken. His face was inches from hers and she could hear the breath catching in his lungs as he flinched. 'Try me, Liam. Just try me,' she suggested, before turning and walking away.

She peeled the bloody gloves as she rounded the corner, tucking them into the jacket pocket. She was shaking now – adrenaline and shock at her own ferocity. Her hands barely cooperated as she pulled the bands from her hair, shaking it down. She removed the jacket, folding it over her arm and felt confident she looked like any other young woman walking home from the pub.

She unchained the bike, bungeeing the jacket behind the saddle, and headed for the seafront. The gloves went into a bin there; the jacket she left in a deserted bus shelter. As she neared the flat she checked her face for blood in a hand-mirror from her pannier but found none.

Mala was in bed, so luck was with them both. Claire bundled the jeans and trainers into a bag and walked round to a skip five streets away, tossing it into the middle of a pile of builder's rubble and old furnishings. Back at the flat she ran a bath and sank into it, remembering the time she'd stood under the shower wondering what Liam would do next. Now she knew – he would do nothing.

She slept a dreamless eight hours and didn't even ache the next morning. She should have done it long ago.

The day was warm but heavy. Mala sat in the kitchen, looking at the new mugs and plates, dull in the overcast light. Claire sat down opposite her.

'I've …put a stop to it,' she said.

Mala looked at her incuriously, then smiled with a large insincerity that must have hurt to produce almost as much as it did to observe. 'It's all right, Claire. I'm not worried.'

'Good, that's good. But I've still made sure he, Liam, I mean, he won't bother us again.'

'Us?' Mala's voice broke on the single word. 'What us? I know what you've done. I know why you've been training so hard. You didn't ask me if I wanted you to do it, though. You didn't stop to think about me at all. You went straight ahead and did what you thought best.'

Claire straightened, trying to be calm. 'It's not as simple as that, Mala. I know you thought going to the University authorities was the best way, but the complaints procedure …'

'I don't care what you say!' Mala was strident. 'I'm sick of people trying to tell me they know what's best for me! I thought at least you would know better than to take over my life. I'm not a bloody pet!'

'I'm not trying to take over anything,' Claire turned to the kettle, hiding her face from her flatmate.

KAY SEXTON

'Oh come on! We've both been dancing around this for years, haven't we? I don't know what your parents did and you don't want to know what mine were like. No, don't interrupt, you really don't want to know – it's too ... pathetic. But I had hoped for some respect from you. And then you just go out there and do whatever you did. Beat him up, I suppose?'

There was a long silence which Claire filled with spoons and coffee and pouring boiling water with slow, careful efficiency.

'Did you? Did you beat him up?'

She nodded, inhaling the steam from the mug.

'Jesus, Claire! What's wrong with you?'

'With me? After what he did?' She swept her hand around the kitchen, indicating the new crockery, the cupboards without doors where they'd been kicked in and not yet replaced.

'But that's *him*, Claire. I don't share this place with him. I share with you. If you're as bad as he is ...' Mala stopped, her mouth working, eyes closed.

'Mals, I'm not as bad as him. But sometimes you have to fight fire with fire, that's all. He wouldn't understand anything else.'

Mala shook her head.

'I'm glad this is our last term, Claire. I'm going to look for a job somewhere a long way away from here. I don't even want to think about this place once I've graduated.'

Claire shrugged, 'Don't let him spoil things for you.'

'Not him, Claire. You. It's not about 'fire with fire' - it's about you sinking to his level.'

She thought about answering but in the end it was simpler to take her coffee back to her room and let Mala adjust in her own time.

After a few hours though, she knew it wasn't enough. She went and banged on the other girl's door.

'Look,' she said. 'Whatever you think, I need to know that you are going to be safe. I don't think there's any risk from Liam, ever again, but perhaps he has friends. You know what to do if anybody approaches you?'

Mala nodded. 'Scream, run, pull the toggle on my rape alarm.'

'Good.' Claire had forgotten that the weird groups Mala hung around with were also fairly militant about female safety. 'But I want to show you one thing, something you can use after 'scream' and before 'run', which will help you get away, okay?'

Mala frowned but finally nodded. 'Just to help me if I ever need to get away?'

Claire nodded, bending her knees and clasping her hands in front of her, preparing to teach. 'That's all it is, and I promise you, nobody will run after you if you learn to do this right.'

KAY SEXTON

Rearing Project

In early spring Blaine began to plan for the wolves. Everything else was in place. The bottling plant in East Germany and the cigarette lighter factory in the Czech Republic were both operational. Each factory was a small and sordid outfit on a large expanse of waste ground that had been hacked out of the forest, behind which lay a large area of land, rented at virtually no cost and fenced off by his teams.

So far the factory hands had shown little interest in what happened beyond their noses; their primary concerns were to see how many lighters or bottles of vodka they could filch from the assembly line to sell. He'd designed the factories so that such practices were possible and even prevalent and he'd appointed factory managers who blended larceny, menace and a degree of charm. The factory staff - keen to keep their jobs – unwittingly provided cover for Project workers moving around the site.

Gatekeeper One, a biathlete with a reasonable standing in the Swiss ski-shooting team, was currently employed by a mountain venture company that ran adventure holidays. Gatekeeper Two would soon move to Rome where she would spend a part of each year visiting wolf territories as part of her PhD research. Both women had proved able to remain patient and keep their cool while The Project appeared to forget all about them. For Blaine this was the key criterion – it would be two years before he decided which pack to release, and it had taken two and a half decades to get this far. Impatience was not an option.

Now the Gatekeeper Two was ready to slide into her role, it was time to prepare for the arrival of the cubs. They would be born in April, but before that, relationships would have to be consolidated and bribes negotiated. A wolf pack had to be built from strong foundations and there was no point The Project working with less than superb stock.

GATEKEEPER

Captive wolves were common in Eastern Europe, where right-wing political parties and drug barons alike found owning a wolf to be a potent symbol, but the offspring of neurotic cage-dwelling pets weren't going to give The Project what it needed. Their cubs would have to come from breeding packs that had selected their own alphas. No free-ranging packs were available in Europe, where wild wolf birth rates were below replacement levels, so the cubs must come from zoos and safari parks.

There was just one problem. No such establishment would sell to a private purchaser. Rather than have cubs fall into the hands of unsuitable keepers, they spayed adult females, vasectomised males, or culled the young animals at twenty weeks. To get two potential packs would involve buying some animals from less than reputable parks and stealing others from under the noses of their keepers, not to mention their parents.

He rang a mobile number. 'We'll rescue your cubs,' he said.

In early April the first three cubs, to be known as the H cubs, had been born to the alpha female of a captive wolf pack in a British zoo. She was a young wolf and the litter was strong and healthy. A covert operation removed all three cubs at ten days old. The keeper who'd allowed The Project access to the wolves had been involved in a cub cull the previous autumn, which led to him contacting an Animal Rights group who had passed him to Blaine. The man said he couldn't shoot another litter of new borns, especially as this alpha mother was an animal he'd known since she was a cub herself. It was because the relationship between keeper and mother wolf was so strong that Blaine decided to risk the rescue mission. That, and the fact that she'd cubbed in an above-ground bunker rather than a deep den.

The alpha male had to be tranquillised before they entered the enclosure, always a high- risk process with wolves; some had been known to shock themselves out of anaesthesia with a massive jolt of adrenaline which often gave them a heart attack.

KAY SEXTON

They held off the other wolves with cattle prods, although their interest was intense rather than threatening. One operative was bitten by the female alpha but she chose not to fight for her cubs, possibly because she'd been hand-reared herself. Another rescuer tripped in the dark and tore open his leg on a concrete post. These minor wounds were treated by the veterinarian, who checked the cubs as soon as they were in the vehicle.

The disappearance of the cubs was not released to the newspapers, Blaine had coached the keeper to suggest they had been killed and buried by the beta female, a former alpha.

The H cubs were transferred to a private yacht and crossed the channel.

In The Project enclosure their foster mother waited. She was a collie/Alsatian cross who had been kept in lactation by having a mongrel pup to suckle instead of own litter. She'd accepted the pup as her own immediately – a good omen for the young wolves. The Project had prepared for their introduction by removing the pup at intervals and then restoring it. This time, when it was returned, it would not be alone – the H cubs would accompany it.

At the factory, the wolf cubs were given a swift examination in the control room to ensure they had not suffered during the voyage, and then Blaine headed for the enclosure and reached into the den. The foster mother raised her head, curling her lip in warning, but he persisted, getting a firm grip on the milk-rich body of the puppy. The mother growled and he paused – she'd sensed something, whether in his demeanour or because she'd caught the cubs' scent on him - and was ramping up her threat display. He faced a dilemma; by removing the pup now he risked antagonising the mother and making her less receptive to its reintroduction, but the longer he delayed, the more the cubs would need hand feeding which would break down their natural fear of humans. He lifted the pup. The dog snapped, tearing through his latex glove and opening a gash on the back of his hand. He retreated swiftly, the pup in both hands.

GATEKEEPER

Outside he handed the squirming animal to a volunteer. 'Put her in with the cubs,' he said and moved to the CCTV screen to watch while he cleaned and covered the wound. The wolf cubs, already hungry, restive and confused, kicked and snarled as the puppy was deposited in their small cage, then converged on her, seeking the source of the milk they could smell. One cub located the pup's snout and licked it, finding traces of the food it sought, and within minutes the puppy was being licked and pawed by the whole group.

'I can't take them back in,' Blaine said absently, his eyes still on the screen, 'she'll smell this.' He held up his hand. 'We can't risk her lashing out and getting one of the cubs instead.'

'I can do it,' Ansel said, his eyes also fixed to the interaction of the cubs and the pup.

'No. You do it.' Blaine pointed to the female volunteer, who nodded.

Blaine knew he couldn't risk the cubs becoming familiar with Ansel's scent because he was the link to Gatekeeper 2. He would be needed to carry instructions to her if her pack was the one that was released. If the wolf cubs became comfortable enough with his scent not to fear him, his presence might draw them out of hiding.

The pup, with its full belly, slept, and the cubs drowsed, waking every few minutes to sniff it, before dozing off again.

They had transported the cubs on old bedding from the factory den, so they knew the smell of the foster mother. Blaine hoped that this, along with the cubs' insistent hunger, and their familiarity with the pup, would be enough to persuade the mother to accept them. It was a risk, but so was every stage of The Project, and he was able to watch with a scientist's disinterest as the volunteer carried the cage outside. Once through the gate she lifted the puppy, and the smallest of the cubs, knelt beside the entrance to the den and crawled inside. There was a long silence in the control room. The den was too dark to see much and the volunteer was between

67

KAY SEXTON

the camera and the mother. Ansel sighed loudly and Blaine knew he was frustrated by not being able to view the decisive moments in the gloom of the den.

The girl appeared again, giving a thumbs-up to the camera as she bent to gather more cubs. She would leave the largest until last — knowing that wolf hierarchy meant that the biggest would feed first and most often, so the vital moments when smaller cubs bonded with the mother could determine their chances of survival.

When she'd taken all the cubs inside there was another long pause, then she stepped out briskly, stripping her gloves and grabbing the cage as she left the enclosure.

'Fine,' she said, back in the control room. 'No problems. They all got the idea straight away. The cubs literally pushed the pup off the nipple, but the mother shoved them around until it latched back on again.'

Blaine nodded, allowing himself to smile with relief.

'I don't think it stands much chance though,' the volunteer continued. 'It's not big enough to fight for food, and anyway, it's a bitch.'

'Don't worry. In a couple of days we'll take it away and meantime, we'll watch to make sure it gets enough milk. We can supplement with hand feeding when we take it out every day. It's a good thing it can't take on the wolves physically — that's why we picked a bitch-pup in the first place. A dog can't win a fight with a wolf, even when they are only weeks only — if the pup asserted herself they would injure her, you know that.'

Blaine stopped abruptly, aware that his pleasure at the successful fostering had made him talkative. His preference was never to explain or persuade. People had to be motivated from within themselves and willing to take orders without discussion. He'd met persuasive leaders in the Afghan mountains, men who could enthuse others to fight the Russian army, but when it came down to it, each man fought alone: waist deep in snow, hidden behind a farm

68

GATEKEEPER

building, dodging from bush to bush. If a man lacked the inner belief that he was doing the right thing, he would look for help … and put all his companions at risk.

The puppy bitch was supposed to be euthanised when her purpose ended, but he doubted that people who could raise wolf cubs would follow his orders to kill a canine pup. Some volunteer would smuggle her away to be raised elsewhere. He expected that, the sentimental approach, and would take care not to ask what happened to her. It was foolish to patrol peoples' emotions, it made them question your decisions or lean on you instead of acting for themselves. As long as they organised their mercy mission effectively he would ignore it. The important thing was that the foster-mother was free of encumbrances.

By the end of the same month the M team had purchased four cubs: two males and two females, all litter mates, around sixteen days old. They moved the cubs to the M raising site in the Czech Republic where they were nurtured by a Bohemian Spotted Dog bitch. They were joined by another female cub two days later. The pack was not ideal – another female had been promised but not delivered – and Blaine considered shutting down the entire M Project. The standard DNA tests on the cubs, performed on samples taken during transit, revealed that M1, 2, 3 and 4 were not all siblings. M1, 2 and 3 were related but M4, the second female, was genetically unrelated and must have been produced by a second pair. It gave the pack a chance of breeding without the risk of the genetic oddities that could develop in a single bloodline. The pack could survive on that basis, and he left it alone. It was time for him to leave. The final additions to H pack would be made in his absence.

The volunteer reported that the British cubs, H1, 2 and 3, two males and a female, easily accepted the final pack members. Two German cubs, H4 and 5, were both females which had been hand-raised in an East German animal park. The bitch, H Mother, accepted the new arrivals and nursed them. H1, 2 and 3 were

69

KAY SEXTON

monitored on webcam in the den, but they also took the new arrivals calmly and only roughhoused them by accident.

Human contact was to be kept to a minimum; the cubs were observed on webcams around their enclosures and food was delivered remotely. Young cubs needed minced meat, lubricated and broken down by digestive enzymes, which should have been provided by a pack of adults regurgitating meat for them. The Project used a mincer and special pharmaceutical fluids developed to help stomach cancer victims digest proteins. The slushy mix was poured down a pipe lowered into the den from outside the enclosure.

On the day the cubs received their first 'real' food, the puppy was removed, never to return. The foster mother sensed its absence, but dealing with five wolf cubs was demanding; she had no time to seek out the missing puppy.

As soon as the cubs were part weaned – around two weeks after their arrival - the foster-mothers were removed from the enclosure for several hours each day, forcing the cubs to assume quasi-adult roles. It was something that had never been tried before and Blaine knew the risks were high. Both foster-mothers had a role in teaching the cubs behaviours that would help them in the territory they would be given if released, and the cubs needed a strong maternal figure to support them through their early months. But dogs were not wolves: there was no alpha male to demonstrate pack discipline and no omega to act as nursemaid and clown. Each foster mother was all the packs had, and she had to provide everything the cubs needed for emotional and physical development, she must teach them her own habits and give them a sense of cohesion as a pack. Above all though, she had to be removed before the first hunting instinct appeared in any of the cubs because she would try to suppress it, and if the cubs failed to hunt they would die.

The two project teams, H and M, were unaware of each other. Each team thought they were raising the only pack, and team members were known by their roles rather than their names. Blaine had decided on this system because three people had to work with both teams: himself, the vet and the architect. Information about the existence of the other pack would be easier to conceal if people in both teams were called 'the chef, the groundsman, the geek, the vet.' He was 'the Boss'.

The first Project turnover was about to happen. Each team was about to lose its first member. 'The architect' was the same person for each site. He had planned the enclosure, working around mature trees and running water, laying out the footings that went a metre below the fences and then a metre inwards, with mesh fencing set in concrete. A cubbing female could dig a den with a nine metre tunnel – designing an enclosure that seemed large and approximated the terrain into which the pack might be released was important, but preventing the packs digging out had been the major preoccupation.

Now the sites were in operation, the architect was no longer needed. Blaine sent him home. Later he would come back to observe the wolves before assessing both release sites. Together they would agree which one was optimal. Blaine had not visited either release site for a decade – his presence would not help, and might harm, the community relationships he was building there.

With two unrelated females for the males to choose from, the M pack was viable again and M3 was spayed. Wolves avoided incest but in forced circumstances there was no certainty and he'd decided to remove any risk of genetic hazard by enforcing sterility for sibling females.

At sixteen weeks H3 was also spayed, requiring her to be removed and kept away from the other cubs for 48 hours. For several days the other cubs treated her with intense suspicion but eventually accepted her again. She could have been euthanised once the other females were accepted by the males, but Blaine decided that on balance it would do no harm to get the wolves used to the occasional disappearance of one of the pack for medical treatment. He was also conscious that the team would struggle to accept her death, even for the cause.

When the packs settled again, he told the volunteers to remove the foster-mothers, leaving it open to them whether they re-homed the animals or put them down. His only stipulation was that the cubs should have no sight, scent or sound of their ersatz mothers from the moment of their disappearance. Hierarchy was impossible to break and even though the cubs were now bigger and stronger than their 'mothers' they would always respect them, seek to be with them, and obey them. In the wild, when a mother lost her alpha status it would be one of her daughters that took her place, or one of her sons that was alpha male, so she would be in a position of authority still.

If the cubs believed their foster-mother was still around they would half-kill themselves to escape and find her. The vet went to both sites and gave a lecture on the subject to ensure the packs weren't put at risk.

With the foster-mother removed, the cubs were forced to take on adult roles. H1 and H2 showed signs of territoriality very early, scent-marking around the den, and at five months began to fight in earnest for alpha male status while the oldest female, H5, assumed alpha female status without challenge. Two weeks later, the H team introduced live food to the enclosure. Rabbits – first domesticated ones, and later, humanely trapped wild rabbits - became 70% of the H group's diet. H5 became an expert hunter. H2, the beta male, showed no interest in hunting and preferred to take kill from his H3 sibling. H1 and H5 began to develop adult calls, and group howls began.

At six months H5 made her first bird kill, stalking and bringing down a black tern in reeds near the enclosure pond the architect had designed.

The M pack followed a similar pattern to the H group, although M4 took Alpha female status and the males, M1 and M2 seemed less certain about their hierarchy, continuing their sporadic ritualised fighting without one or the other gaining control.

There were packs. Now they needed territory.

CHAPTER SIX

After what she thought of as 'the problem-solving incident' things began to move and Claire felt sure The Project had just been waiting to see how she dealt with Liam. Within a few weeks, the Assistant Supervisor of the Geography Department called her into the office to tell her she'd been suggested as a temporary tallier for an ongoing bird migration project in Morocco, starting after her final term ended in June. His face was blank and she decided not to ask who had suggested her. She took the application form, the visa form and the thick four-ring index that contained photographs, silhouettes and habitats for more than sixty species of migrant bird and sat in the cafeteria. She spent some time tapping her pen against the stacked documents and staring at the table top before she realised she was expecting Ansel to turn up and explain what was happening. Once again she felt a momentary dislocation – it could be a Project activity or just coincidence, but it was up to her to decide what to do. She gathered up the paperwork and stuffed it into her bike pannier.

At the dewpond she lay back on the turf and watched the sky. There were no clouds, and if she stared long enough she saw invisible amoebas crawled across the blue like gigantic jellyfish sliming the atmosphere.

Her mobile rang. She ignored it. After a few minutes it beeped, saying a text message had been received. She rolled over and read it.

'Job 4 U in Rome. FAO. Call me need 2 apply soon. Ans.'

FAO. She had no idea what it meant. Rome she understood though. And all at once, on one morning, she was supposed to smile and be happy as the pieces fell into place and The Project wrapped itself around her. A job in Rome. She'd never thought further than a job. Her sole ambition had been to line up something when she graduated so she didn't have to go home to her father. Now she had a chance to go to Africa as a volunteer and then take up a job in Rome. Claire had no doubt now that 'they' could organise all this around her. The quietness of The Project, the lack of ostentation, the long periods of inactivity, added up to something more than evidence of competence. It was the antithesis of Malcolm and Eileen and their feverish conspiracy. That alone would have been enough to reassure her, not that it mattered anyway. She'd have washed dishes, painted walls, dug potatoes, anything not to go home.

She thought about Kaya. Although she'd obeyed Blaine's injunction not to research wolves, she had allowed herself two latitudes. The first was a captive wolf pack in the United States that could be observed on webcam. The wolves were rarely around when she could check on them via the university computer room, but she'd seen enough footage to know that they were lazy risers, playful until the middle of the day and then inclined to rest until dusk. So she could imagine Kaya stretched out in her enclosure, snoozing, her dark fur giving off the dust and blood smell that had been so peculiar, yet so right.

The second transgression was a copy of 'Building a Terrorist: how extremism is inculcated' she'd bought in a second-hand bookshop in The Lanes. When she got back to the flat she'd cut the covers and spine away with a knife and reattached the pages inside a copy of 'Essentials of Geography'. It wasn't a perfect fit, but unless you examined it closely it looked no worse than any other student handbook. She'd read each essay a dozen times: looking for clues, for a map of the journey she might be making. She wasn't naive about

KAY SEXTON

it – she knew that terror and activism were a razor's edge apart – the only distinction was in who held the blade.

Kaya has been her touchstone for the past few months, and while she understood that a captive wolf could not be freed, she focused on the idea that if wolves could live in managed freedom in the UK, then there would be no need for any future imprisonment of Kaya's species.

She'd used this as the talisman that drove her to attend lectures, to study hard, to shoot well, to cope with the crap Liam and his cronies. And then she'd used it to fuel her rage against Liam.

Wolves were part of the landscape, they belonged in the food chain, in the environment, in the consciousness of every Briton. The lack of big wild predators was like one of Ansel's gaps in the global spiderweb, a blankness where there should have been awe and beauty, and fear. She could help to put that right. It was only incidental that working towards that future meant she could tire herself enough, mentally and physically, not to get sucked into thinking about her father.

After her mother's death, she'd discovered a new kind of pleasure in strenuous activity: the adrenaline rush she'd got from release operations was as sensual as orgasm. Now she faced the fact that The Project, whether it came off or not, was another replacement for what she thought of as her 'past' - but the wolves weren't therapy. Although it was right they should exist wherever the ecosystem was designed to support them, there was a better reason than her own needs to bring them back. The world needed them. With wolves on the loose, every silly drunken girl who fell out of a pub on a Friday night would know, bone-deep, that the world was a dangerous place. Every yob, prowling for somebody to frighten, for easy pickings, would need to check over his shoulder from time to time, for the primal shape of the predator who prowled more silently and struck more terrifyingly even than himself. Women would be more cautious, men would be less inclined to assume they were the kings of the dark.

GATEKEEPER

She knew what Ansel would say, that she wanted people to be less trusting because she'd been misled and made to feel stupid by her parents, but it wasn't that simple. She wanted the world to contain everything that it should, not just the parts that humanity found useful or attractive. She wanted things to be fair.

So she called Ansel, feeling her T-shirt fall into damp, chilled creases as soon as she moved, like the carved drapery of marble monuments, reminding her body of its fragility. She didn't feel fragile though. She was exultant, full of a power she couldn't name.

When he arrived, they worked through the forms together. Claire felt him looking at her. There was something chilling in his constant glances but the heat she'd stolen from the sky continued to radiate out of her and she chose not to ask what was wrong.

'Your PhD thesis outline,' he said, holding out a folder to her.

She took it, scanning the pages. 'The Role of Eco-Tourism in Transitional Landscape Use in Rural Mountain Communities?'

He nodded. 'You'll do it as a distance-learning student, part-time – it's all organised. Three areas of research: Anatolia, Carpathia, Scottish Highlands.'

She rolled onto her back again, holding the wedge of paper between her and the sun, feeling the T-shirt settle back into its folds, shrouding her spine. 'Right. Good. What's FAO?'

She expected a lecture, but instead he began to strip a grass head of its seeds, picking them off one by one between blunt fingertips. Squinting from under the blue shadow of the papers she could pick out the scars and calluses on his fingers that marked a commercial fisherman. It seemed impossible that such damaged hands could work so finely.

After a long period he spoke, 'Perhaps this is not such a good idea?'

She remained silent, reading the dense pages of text but taking nothing in.

KAY SEXTON

'A doctorate, you know, you have to work for it, not just get through it. Maybe you should think again. To do this would change the course of your life.'

He was unhappy. The realisation seeped into her like the damp.

'And if I decide not to do it, do you get my place?'

'No. You know I don't.' His head was still bent over the grass stem. 'That's not the point. I think this is too extreme Claire, and you're not the right person.'

'Really? Why?'

'You aren't as strong as you seem. This is another stick you've grabbed to save yourself from drowning, that's all. And I think it's wrong to use your vulnerability against you.'

She flexed her fingers, remembering the feel of Liam's hair in them. 'I'm not vulnerable, Ansel. Quite the opposite.'

'Just because you can fight, doesn't mean you're strong, Claire. It's the fact that you fight that worries me.'

She rolled onto her side, away from him. 'Says here I'll have to do field work in each location, including surveys and interviews, and that there may be a way of funding this research in conjunction with transitional land-use projects run by the FAO. Sounds great. Except I don't know what the FAO is.'

He sighed. 'The FAO is the Food and Agriculture Organisation. It was founded in 1945, as part of the United Nations, and it works with all countries to try and improve agriculture, forestry and fisheries, and to end hunger. People who work for it travel the world, teaching about best practice, developing policies and negotiating agreements. Your job is already organised. You will go to the Maghreb first for ... acclimatisation. The interview for the Rome placement will be done from there by telephone. Your appointment will be recommended by the person who is leaving, so it will never be formally advertised.'

'I thought I'd be working with animals, not people.'

Ansel frowned. 'What good would that do? It is people you need to understand. The FAO placement means you can travel, and

78

we can organise training for you without raising suspicions. He has
been very clever about this.'

'He' meant Blaine, of course. Claire let the sun beat into her
spine. She wanted to feel something more than satisfaction but no
matter how hard she searched her emotions the only thing that
emerged was a dry pleasure that this was something that Liam and
his kind couldn't take away from her. No matter how difficult or
unproductive it was, this was her task and they couldn't reach in and
spoil it. All she had to do was finish her degree and move on. She
didn't have to go home.

The Maghreb was exactly as she'd been led to expect. She was
picked up at the airport by Hein, a solemn Dutch WWF official,
who drove her to a concrete bungalow in the desert. The three
rooms contained one bed, one table and one shower. A small portable fridge and three saucepans completed the kitchen equipment,
and Hein unloaded a box of crockery and cutlery from the back of
his Land Rover.

'When you leave, pack it up and bring it with you – the saucepans too. I'm surprised they are still here,' he said.

She was given coffee, flour, rice and sugar, tinned beans and
canisters of tinned margarine.

'No meat?' She was testing the space, such a small place to call
home, and yet she knew when he'd gone she would feel it was empty.

'Don't worry – people will turn up soon to sell you meat, and
cloth and cushions, silver jewellery, and drugs.' He tipped his head
to one side. 'Don't buy the drugs. They will be police officers trying
to trap you. If you need ...'

She waved a hand to cut him off.

'Will you be okay on your own?'

She wondered what would happen if she said no. Would they
take her back to the airport and send her home? She couldn't tell if
Hein was Project or not.

'I'll be fine. Just fine. Anyway, it's only for three days, isn't it? Until somebody comes to check on me, I mean.'

He nodded again, looking around the bare concrete shell as though it was something rare and strange. 'Three days and Tiljad will visit. We work with the Berbers here because they've got a better handle on migratory species than Moroccan Arabs.'

'And he calls by twice a week?'

'Yes. He brings letters and food from town to everybody working out here. Five organisations pay his wages: us, FAO, Save the Maghreb, Planetary Tree and Lynx Trust. So he knows everything and everyone and he's pretty trustworthy.'

'Only 'pretty' trustworthy?'

Hein gave her a long look. 'There are problems. Not just political. You have to understand – if you sleep with a native here, they will lose all respect for you. It seems unfair to women. It is. But that is how it works.'

She nodded. 'So he'll offer to keep me company at night and if I say yes, he'll exploit me – is that it?'

'Yes,' his relief was palpable, he relaxed, his face falling into softer lines. 'I never know what to say to women who come here to do fieldwork. You know, I've been here nearly fifteen years. Things change – here they have changed a lot. Moroccan people and Berbers are both supposed to be Muslim – but the Arabic speakers have carried out Jihad against the Berbers in the past. This is a chaotic time for all of us, Muslim or not. All outsiders must step carefully, but especially women.'

Claire began to put the food on the narrow shelves that were high on the wall to evade ants and termites. She turned her back on Hein so he wouldn't be able to read her expression. This was a test – a Project test. She was being assessed and it felt good to know that she was about to be measured.

'There's another woman out here. Maggie Grieve, she specialises in ungulates. She'll be over to see you soon enough. People drop in all the time, believe it or not.'

GATEKEEPER

She nodded, still with her back to him. She wanted to own this space, make it her home, and she couldn't do that until he left.

He hefted the bag he was holding. 'In the shed behind the kitchen there's a generator that Tiljad takes care of. You can plug in your computer, but there is no internet. Here is your radio, because there is no telephone. I'll show you how to use it. Tiljad will bring you a cell phone if you ask; this thing is only for emergencies.' He slapped the radio casing. 'It's not so friendly.'

She wondered what that meant; desert raves, hash parties or perhaps just people wanting to talk without half Morocco listening in? They practised with the radiophone for ten minutes. He drove away and she stood in the cement cell, feeling the heat reaching for her from the desert. She was beginning her training at last.

CHAPTER SEVEN

Hein had been right about visitors. Tiljad arrived with a mobile phone and a handful of prepaid phone cards as if he'd known she'd want them. He showed her the workings of the generator and how to check the level in the water tank. He spoke Arabic, Berber, French and English, making her feel inadequate and parochial.

'Where is your Jeep?'

'My Jeep?'

'Bird Land Jeep. Where is it?'

'I don't know. Nobody mentioned it to me.' Apart from her tickets and visa, and her folder on bird recognition, she'd been told almost nothing; all Ansel had said was that she needed to break her ties with England, distance herself from her old friends. That wasn't any hardship – the only friend she had was Mala, who had maintained her distance since their argument about Liam.

Day after day she came back from her desert hide; an overturned canvas pot that boiled her alive, to find some stranger sitting on her step, drinking her beer. If they were European they brought their own beer too – blood-warm bottles of froth that they stacked in her fridge to replace the chilled ones they'd drunk. Moroccans came empty-handed but sent gifts later: goat meat, cheese, and for her, because she refused alcohol, cans of soft drink scented with melon and tasting of sugar and plastic. It was a strange peripatetic party that was carried on by Jeep and Land Rover, bodies in motion across the desert, transmitting gossip via bumpy journeys that made beer

82

GATEKEEPER

fizz and heads ache. Travel seemed to be its own purpose, as though people had caught nomadic behaviour from the landscape.

Often they were heading for a film crew, some or other epic being shot in the desert and requiring a night scene. Ouarzazate was a popular location for thrillers and spy movies, and Hein seemed to have a radar for the nights they were out, or maybe he owned some equipment that tracked the huge trailers and cameras as they rolled slowly through the desert. Night shooting meant catering and that meant roast meats, more beer, a crowd of Berber onlookers who were so used to being recruited as extras they came with their own camels, guns, and knives. Often the camels were decanted from lorries – you didn't ride a racing camel to a shoot and expect it to perform well. She got used to standing in the cold, because the desert chilled as soon as the sun left, clutching a greasy tinfoil package of lamb and beans to her chest and eating with her fingers, watching a villain or a hero bouncing around in a 4 x 4 while Berbers curvetted around on camels and yelled threats, waving old rifles that they fired into the air one-handed.

She had too her gun. She had thought transporting a weapon to Morocco would be difficult, but it wasn't. The gun had been offered for sale through the Rifle Association and a copy of their newsletter, with it highlighted, had been posted to her anonymously, along with eight one hundred pound notes. Her club had signed one set of forms, her local police sergeant another, and she'd been shown how to lock her gun in a box, ammunition to be stored safely separate.

The rifle was beautiful. A walnut-stocked Browning Micra with A bolt action, scaled for 'smaller hunters' it said in the literature. She could have carried it every day of her life without tiring, and it slid into her shoulder like a small child needing a cuddle.

She met Maggie Grieve over a spitted lamb. The film crew were on a break, slicing the roast, handing out polystyrene boxes of meat topped with sauce and a dollop of couscous, when a bellowing horde of camels whirled into the film site. Wild ululations filled the air

83

KAY SEXTON

and the film camels began to kick and wheeze, pulling at their tethers. The crew ran for cameras that had been left in position for the next shot, hauling dollies back by hand and screaming insults at the arrivals as dust filled the scene.

Hein was juggling a can of beer and three lamb boxes, dumped in his arms by panicking camera operators. He squinted into the dust, blown gold in the lights. 'Maggie,' he said.

Claire was prepared to dislike her, even before she picked out Maggie's large blondeness, like a heifer among greyhounds. The woman slid from her camel and made for the fire, surrounded by the wiry Berbers.

'Maggie Grieve,' she held out her hand and Claire shook, trying to set aside her immediate prejudice. The other woman's grip was strong, unnecessarily so. Claire felt her knuckles grate under the pressure and allowed her hand to become limp. She locked out her shoulder, then elbow, then wrist, transferring power down her arm until she snapped it through her hand, flexing the first knuckles apart in stepping motion, spreading the width of her hand so that more of Maggie's palm was against hers. Then she transferred the force into her grip, powering the compression until Maggie winced.

'Claire Benson.'

Hein moved forward, trying to hand them both meat boxes, defusing the situation.

'You've upset them again, Maggie.'

She nodded, scooping meat into her mouth. When she spoke her voice was ripe with Middle England, private school inflections overlaid with some unidentifiable twang. 'So what? They hire clapped-out camels and treat them like shit. Shouldn't be allowed to get away with it. Now they've seen how well healthy animals can perform, they might pay decent rates for a change.'

She turned, checking for something in the dark desert. Claire couldn't pick out what she'd focused on. She swung back, 'You're the bird woman, right?'

84

GATEKEEPER

'Only temporarily. I'm a geographer …'

'Yeah, right. The guy you took over from's gone home to try and fix his marriage. You single?'

Claire nodded.

'Me too. Stupid to try and do this kind of work and keep a relationship together. You ringing 'em?'

'Just tallying.' Claire wondered if Maggie usually spoke like this.

'Good. Tell you what, come with me next Thursday, we're doing a roundup – need all the bodies we can get. You too,' she waved her box at Hein.

'I don't think so, Maggie; last time half-killed me. I'm simply a bureaucrat after all, not a …' His words trailed away, Claire listened, fascinated, wanting to know what he could possibly call this woman who seemed incapable of normal behaviour. Instead he smiled and gestured towards the camels.

Maggie turned back to Claire. 'You bottling out as well?'

Claire shook her head.

'Good. Then you'll learn something. You'll have to take a day off bloody bird counting though – we leave an hour after dawn. Tell Tiljad to bring you.' She headed for her camel, handing the box of food to one of the crew. The Berbers followed, tipping back their heads to finish soft drinks and spitting until the clay around the camels was dark and wet.

'Jesus,' Claire breathed, amazed at their arrogance.

Hein closed the lid of his box and dropped it into the fire where it flamed green and stank like a chemical spill. 'Like Lawrence of Arabia,' he said. 'She gets results – the Berbers respect her, but yes, Jesus, she is hard to bear.'

Claire watched the dark sockets of his eyes, moving like weed in the firelight. It must be painful to be out-toughed by a woman, especially in the desert. A lesson to be learnt here. Men were fragile, and in harsh environments it would be a good idea to give them

85

scope to feel good about themselves. She tucked the thought away, smiled at Hein. 'So what can I expect on Thursday?'

'Oh, she knows everything about camels. If you want to understand anything with hooves, she's the expert. Expect to be impressed.' His face flickered. 'And in pain,' he added.

Claire nodded, turning back to observe the film crew. She intended to ensure that pain was not an issue. Maggie wouldn't find her easy to impress either.

Claire found that smells were different in the desert. The action of heat on stone changed their nature and their action: there was no vegetation to capture them, so every odour was a column reaching into the air, heated to stretch rather than spread, and because evaporation was almost instantaneous there were none of the normal smells of humanity. Fires burnt up into the sky carrying nothing but shimmering power. Sweat fled the body and left nothing but its mineral smell because bacteria were annihilated by the arid heat. But water could be smelt, when you were almost on top of it. The scent of it stood in the air like an invisible wall – when a camel hit the smell of water it turned as though it had mashed its nose on brick and walked along the odour until the source was found. She learnt this from Maggie.

Dealing with Maggie was almost impossible; it would have been easier to snog Liam, she decided, than to get on with a woman whose every word was an unintended insult. Their first meeting could have been a template for all subsequent ones.

The only saving grace was that she knew the terminology. Isolation and disorientation preceded bonding and re-education. Maggie might just be a bitch, but her behaviour was that of a recruiter for a terrorist organisation. Claire was starting to understand what Ansel had meant when he'd said she was fragile. If she had something to fight against she was fine, but in circumstances like these she was weaker than water. In the desert she felt alone, afraid, ridiculous.

GATEKEEPER

It said in her terrorist training book that challenging new recruits, forcing them to defend their beliefs against a hostile audience, was a way to change their thinking, to force them into a bunker mentality where everybody who wasn't an 'us' was a 'them' – that was how suicide bombers began their training: arguing for their cause until their beliefs became so entrenched they were instinctive rather than reasoned.

She wanted this. She wanted it so badly she could taste it in the warm mineral tang of the water and the fat of the lamb dripping from the meat to burn orange in the fire. She had escaped. Nothing could force her to go back. Even if The Project ended tomorrow and she had to hunt for a job in England, she was a different person to the one who'd arrived at Brighton University and she couldn't be put back into the shape she'd had then, or the thoughts she'd believed were truths about the world.

It would be better to stay out here forever. Not here in Morocco but outside the comfortable insanity of society. Now she'd been cut free, she had to measure everything against a new standard. In choosing 'this' over 'that', was she making a future that helped wolves live in Britain? The question might be simple but the answer often impossible to find. Was making an enemy of Maggie helping the wolves? Was talking to Hein helping the wolves? Oddly, it made life manageable. She pointed herself at the day and got through it with the questions at the front of her mind. That way she didn't have to think about anything else.

It took two months before somebody decided she was ready. Maggie drove up one day and leaned out of her jeep window. 'So ... what do you know about wolves?' she asked.

87

CHAPTER EIGHT

The next four weeks were what Claire came to think of as survival training. She spent mornings and evenings in the hide, and in between sat in the bungalow with the stack of books and monographs Maggie had brought over in a beer cooler. The material covered everything from the Feral Children of India to the Strategic Management Plan of the Yellowstone National Park. What every publication had in common was wolves: captive, free, breeding, hunted, hunting, adopted by dogs or adopting small children.

It was so hot that the pages refused to bend: they stood like sails and broke at the binding when she turned them. Their edges were the colour of old toenails. They seemed ancient and cryptic, although some had been published less than eighteen months ago.

Sometimes, when she went outside, the light sliced the world in two, half-white, half-blue and she couldn't tell if she was in sun or shade. It made no difference to the heat. At night she could hear the blood thickening in her body, refusing to push itself round, settling in her heart like sand falling to the seabed. Then she would force herself up, to practice in the dark, panting as she kicked and punched until the blood ran freely again. There was nobody to talk to about it, except Maggie – to whom she would admit nothing.

The books sat in her head like toads. She thought that with all the facts she now knew, wolves should run through her dreams like water, but they didn't. She didn't dream at all. She woke, stunned by a headache that vanished when she dragged herself upright, she

GATEKEEPER

counted birds, she read, she practiced Tae Kwon Do, she went to arc-lit film sets and drank melon-flavoured water - and she slept.

Sleep had become a drug. As the sun set, she felt as though the landscape rose up and smacked her face. Perspective and dimension both vanished – the desert became a sheaf of grey paper, fanned in front of her eyes. She couldn't walk outdoors without stumbling and holding her hands out like a drunkard, so – unless Hein or Tiljad were collecting her to go to a shoot – she would get under the thin ochre sheet left by her predecessor and pull one of the wolf books from the cooler. Within minutes she would be asleep, the book open on her chest, and she would wake eight hours later, in the same position, oblong creases on her skin, every page's edge imprinted on her like a concertina of knowledge.

She wanted to dream about wolves. Instead she found herself muttering random words into the gluey heat; 'dominance, territoriality, predation, tolerance, adaptation'. The information stayed at the top of her brain, refusing to become part of her thinking. The photographs remained abstract, images of dog-like creatures that slunk on and off the pages in unnatural postures like pantomime villains. It was silly and tiring and she was sick of it.

And one day she woke up. She'd been drowsing in the hide, trying to feel enthused about the walk back to the bungalow and when she woke she felt different, as though half her blood had been drained and replaced with champagne. Energy twitched in her fingers and her hair felt static instead of limp.

Tiljad - arriving late in the afternoon with canned beans, pappy oversized apples and last week's Sunday papers passed on by Planetary Tree - nodded at her description of her sudden wellbeing.

'It takes a long time. Some people never get used to desert – they sleep, sleep, sleep.' His grin was derisive. 'It takes a long time with you; nearly time to leave isn't it?'

She was sickened by her apathy. The Project might have written her off by now. She'd let Maggie dictate to her. Even her Tae Kwon

Do had been no more than going through the motions. She'd sat in her place like a weak bird on the nest, waiting to be fed a morsel of information.

'Will it come back? The sickness?' she asked him, helping carry the supplies with a vigour she'd lacked for weeks.

'Drink very much, eat more meat, less beans,' he said. 'Do less reading,' his eyes swept over the cooler of books and the bird ID folder with something like contempt.

'Is there filming tonight?' She wanted to go out, she wanted to laugh and dip lamb into fiery sauce and watch an improbable heroine being terrorised by a pack of snarling villains.

'No.'

She faked a smile. 'Okay, this place could do with a clean out. I'll do that instead.'

He rocked his hands on the crate of fruit, weighing up some course of action.

'Come with me,' he said. 'We get the Jeep. You bring it back.'

'You know where it is?'

'I don't know where. I guess. You come, we can try and find it.'

'What about keys?'

He lifted the huge metal canister that was always slung at his waist. 'All keys,' he said.

It was like Ansel all over again, although Tiljad's face hadn't changed.

'Keys to here?' she pointed to the bungalow, locked inadequately at best with an ancient mortise lock in which the dust and sand screeched when the key turned.

He opened the canister, shoving large bunches of keys aside to scoop up one small ring. 'Jeep, house, generator, radio-phone,' he announced, counting them off.

He put them on the table, looking sideways at her. 'I need all keys,' he said. 'But if we say they stay here – on table – then we agree?'

GATEKEEPER

She tried to fathom his meaning. 'You mean you are supposed to have the keys but you'll leave them with me?'

He pursed his lips, not liking the arrangement to be spelled out, but nodded.

'Why?'

He put his hands on the table again, making the rocking movement she realised must be his version of a shrug. 'You can trust,' he said.

The enormity of it shocked her. Trust was what she wouldn't do, maybe even couldn't. Only animals were reliable and then not because they were better or more noble but because their agendas were short term and unambiguous.

He pushed the keys towards her. 'You keep. But ...,' he glanced sideways again, an oblique feminine habit she'd notice on many men here, Arab and Berber. 'If I need, I kick in the door, okay?'

She shook her head. 'It's all right, Taljid. If you need them, I understand. I trust you.'

She said the words without meaning them, and felt embarrassed when he shook her hand. She'd lied. She understood why he needed the keys: she might break her leg at the hide, or wander off into the desert, the generator might break down, or a storm blow up. But she didn't trust him, she just relied on him.

In Building a Terrorist it said, *Trust is contingent on shared values. The terrorist in training will be befriended and betrayed by at least one person during the deconstruction period. This teaches reliance solely on core and common aims, not on friendship or blood ties. The terrorist trusts nobody and relies on others only where reliance cannot be avoided. Human relationships – pared down to mutual need and mutual fervour – are intense but short lived: a fellow believer may be considered a more reliable contact than a parent, spouse or child, but even then, only as far as the aims of the terrorist are concerned.*

She understood that.

Tiljad didn't tell her where they were headed, but as soon as she saw the motor homes and lean-tos scattered off the road, she knew.

91

KAY SEXTON

'Maggie has the Jeep?'

He pulled in behind a flat-roofed compound that looked to be built from asbestos sheeting.

'I don't know,' he swung out of the Land Rover and she followed, feeling exposed. Off to one side, three corralled camels watched them. 'She will be out,' he said. 'Camel drive today.'

The relief Claire felt seemed disproportionately strong compared to the unexpressed hostility between the two women. She thought about that for a second, as Tiljad unloaded mail, beer and tinned goods. She didn't like the idea of Maggie reporting back on her suitability, that was part of the problem, and the other part, she decided, was visceral – the woman rubbed her up the wrong way.

The Jeep was parked behind the compound in the shade of a mud wall. Tiljad handed her the key from his ring and she turned the ignition. He grinned as though she'd achieved some major feat and she smiled back, but inside she was burning. She was going to pay Maggie back for this, one day.

She asked him, when they were back at the bungalow, how people would react if she took the rifle out some evenings and practiced. He wanted to see the gun and when it was in his hands, insisted on going to a wadi to try it out. The gun, she conceded, was of more interest than all her attempts to befriend him had been, and once she'd demonstrated her skill and allowed him some praise for his, there was a new candour to his smile. She drove the Jeep back and felt as if she was finally doing what she was meant to do. The only problem was the nights, when she had nothing to fill her hours.

She sat for a while, looking around the bungalow, but nothing needed cleaning and then pulled out a postcard produced by one of the film crews and wrote a brief message to Mala. She'd give it to Tiljad to post.

She was still practising Tae Kwon Do that evening when Maggie turned up. Claire had punched and kicked until there was no power left in her body, just the weak heat of exhausted muscles.

GATEKEEPER

She'd stopped perspiring after the first thirty minutes and a patina of dried sweat crackled on her skin.

'You found the Jeep then,' Maggie said.

Claire nodded, concentrating on a series on combination punches.

'If you'd asked, I'd have gone one of the boys to drive it over.'

Claire stepped back, aiming her left heel for a point in the air that would approximate the jaw of a six foot man. The kick was weak, but the placement was good.

'No problem,' she said.

Maggie seemed ready to argue, but unwilling to start. Claire stole glances at her between stretches; her mouth was pinched and her legs set wide in a combative pose that Claire couldn't emulate – she could barely stand upright after her intensive training session.

'You seem full of the joys of spring,' Maggie said.

'Making up for lost time.' Claire saw no point to denying her incapacity, the woman would have been observing her closely enough for the change to be evident.

'Desert prostration they call it,' Maggie said with bleak satisfaction. 'Some people never acclimatise. Not something I've ever had.'

'It would have been nice if I'd been warned about it,' Claire began to sip a can of melon drink, rationing herself so she wouldn't get stomach cramps when the sugar hit her gut.

'Weren't you?' Maggie stared at her, demanding that she accept the challenge.

Claire watched her for a second over the rim of the can, weighing her choices.

'No problem,' she said again. Maggie as a covert enemy was bad enough; overt hostility would destroy any chance she had of succeeding as Gatekeeper.

'You sound like an Aussie,' Maggie complained. 'No problem, no worries ... anyway, I've already asked them to keep you here another week. That'll give you a chance to catch up.'

93

KAY SEXTON

Claire turned her blink of surprise into an appreciative closed-eye smile, tipping her head back to drain the last drops of drink. 'God, that's good stuff!' Inside she was raging. What a bitch! To extend the training period without warning or discussion, as though she was a camel needing more time to learn how to cope with a bridle.

'As you're obviously feeling better, I wondered if you wanted to get on with the real point of your ... visit,' Maggie paused before the final word as if picking her terminology. Claire was on guard.

'Purpose?'

'Well, you didn't think you'd been packed off to Africa for a jolly, did you?' Maggie's smile was insufferable, but Claire ignored it, fighting the temptation to rise to the bait by revealing what she'd learned from *Building a Terrorist*.

'I don't think I should discuss my understanding of this 'visit',' she put ironic emphasis on the word, 'with you. I was advised to behave as though every encounter was with a hostile.'

Maggie's mouth slammed shut and she got into her 4 x 4 without speaking.

Claire stood in the courtyard, towelling her hair, wondering if a little tuneless whistling would be gilding the lily of her unconcern.

After a few moments Maggie stabbed the window button and yelled, almost before it had opened, 'Are you coming or not?'

Claire strolled to the vehicle. 'Or not. I don't know where you're going or what you plan to do when you get there. I'm not traipsing across the Maghreb just to keep you happy, Maggie. I have plenty to be getting on with here.'

Maggie glared, her eyebrows drawing down in an expression that made Claire want to step away. It was well-developed, as though Maggie spent part of every day honing her hatred to this stark pitch.

'Forget the bloody books,' she said. 'There's a wolf pack you can observe.'

94

They were desert wolves, smaller and redder than Kaya, and instead of her bouncing high-eared approach, this pack crossed their territory like water, flowing round corners, sliding into crevices, appearing out of tunnels: lurking, slinking, observing.

'Watch out,' Maggie pointed to the electric fence that ran outside the wire mesh fencing. There was another line of electric fencing inside the enclosure and the wolves, despite appearing to move fluidly, never came close to it.

Claire spotted the alpha male, his tail carried higher than the others and his quiet but constant keening, a sound on the edge of human hearing, calling his pack to help defend the territory. He patrolled the perimeter of the enclosure, swirling like red smoke around the corners, vanishing into the concrete bunkers and tunnels to reappear at another point, his eyes always fixed on them. She tried to pick out the alpha female but couldn't. The omega was obvious, a somewhat threadbare wolf with a tail tucked right under his body and a muzzle crossed with small grey scars where other wolves had snapped at him. The rest of the animals were a russet blur.

She crouched, and each wolf dropped its eyes to her head height. She'd read about that, the mirroring posture of a wolf pack, but the speed of it was shocking. Just as when Kaya had trailed her, she felt adrenaline spike her gut. Nobody could outrun a wolf pack. They seemed to think faster than her, respond before she'd even completed a movement – as though they were more intelligent than she was.

'They're a cross between desert wolves from Saudi Arabia and red wolves from America,' Maggie spoke behind her, voice low. 'The idea was to breed a pack for hunting. Didn't work.'

Claire didn't take her eyes from the alpha as she dug in her backpack for her digital camera. 'Whose idea?'

'Some Alawi.'

'One of the Moroccan royal family?' Claire glanced back at her companion.

KAY SEXTON

'Noble rather than royal – quite a remote Alawi, I think. There's something about hunting with wolves in an ancient Persian text and this guy thought he could do it. But he couldn't.'

'Why not?' Claire held the camera at chest height, keeping the pack focused on her eyes, watching how they followed her movements as she pressed the button again and again. The alpha flowed forwards, surging almost to the electric barrier before running parallel to it, his head low, one bright orange eye fixed on her as he loped past.

'They put electric collars on 'em. Like attack dogs wear – to make them let go of their prey - but wolves ...' Maggie's laugh grated. 'They sat around in an orderly fashion and chewed each other's collars off. Did it at night. Next morning, the hunters came out: big heap of electric and leather crap right in front of the door and one pack of wolves laughing their heads off.'

Claire smiled, feeling sympathy with the wolves.

'Then they tried training some of the lower pack members. Same thing every time. Take the wolf out hunting. Wolf escapes, kills every dog sent after it, comes back within three days and sits outside the enclosure waiting to be returned to the pack. Then they thought if they trained the alpha, he'd train the rest. Same thing, slight variation. Alpha escapes handlers, kills dogs, comes back and attacks handlers, refuses to re-enter enclosure and refuses to be scared off.'

Claire straightened, feeling sick. 'Did they kill him?'

''Course they killed him. Shot him about twelve times. What else could they do? If they let the rest out they were scared the wolves would attack the compound, if they left him alive he definitely would attack, and the rest of the pack were going crazy, running into the fence, howling: the whole 'mad wolf' nightmare in front of their eyes.'

'So what happened then?'

96

'This is it ...' Maggie gestured to the enclosure. 'They haven't worked them, or trained them, or anything. The new alpha is the old one's son.'

'Do they still breed?'

'Yup. No problem there, although I keep pointing out to the head keeper that soon they're going to have to split the pack if the alphas keep it up – there's fourteen wolves in there, three of them males old enough to challenge the alpha, and soon one of them will. Then they'll be killing each other. They've lost a couple of juvenile females to injury as it is.'

'That's pretty common though,' Claire said. The words were auto-pilot; her emotions were centred on the wolves in front of her.

'Yup. But it'll be carnage if they get power struggles in the males and nowhere for them to escape to. Got any ideas?'

'I suppose they won't release them?'

'You suppose right. The Alawi who owns them likes to bring his mates out here and show off.'

'Then they need to build satellite enclosures. One east and one west.' Claire thought back to her days watching the captive wolves in America on webcam. 'They can run them off the main enclosure with tunnels, set electric doors for them, get some wolves comfortable with using them through reinforcement behaviours. The easiest way is to get the alphas and the betas to travel through the tunnels to a new enclosure regularly; leaving the omega and older wolves behind, then, when they've got the wolves they want in one place, they can shut the doors. They might have to herd the wolves a bit – that's why it's best to take the alphas in one direction and the weaker members in another, it makes the current central enclosure more like neutral territory. Once they've got the right wolves in the satellite enclosure they can let the dominant ones back into the main space. Then they just never meet again.'

Maggie nodded. 'Not bad. I'll mention it to the head keeper. Where could they find plans, do you reckon?'

KAY SEXTON

Claire reeled off the website address for the captive American wolf pack and Maggie jotted it down.

'Really, they should let them go,' Claire had to say it again, even though she knew it would do no good.

'Agreed. Not going to happen though. No Animal Rights Activists out here to kick up a stink. Best we can do is flatter the owner into improving their conditions by telling him it'll be more interesting for his chums to come and see separated packs.'

Claire spent four hours watching the pack. The alpha calmed enough to stretch out on a concrete block near her position, watching her but no longer pacing or whining. Other pack members trotted along the fence, each turning its head to observe her. Several times the alpha came down and urinated in her direction, scratching with his strong back legs to spread the scent as far as possible, marking his territory. Claire wondered if he'd seen his father shot and how it had affected his view of humans.

The alpha female made herself known, joining her mate on the platform and staring at the women with haughty dislike.

'They're so nosy,' Claire said.

'Bloody predators always are.' It sounded dismissive but Maggie sat alongside the cage for the rest of the evening, watching. After the moon rose, five long-legged round-eared pups emerged from a hidden den and shrieked and tumbled over the older wolves.

When the two women rose to leave, Claire had cramp in both legs from crouching so long. Silent Arabs in khaki watched them return to their vehicle.

'Isn't it odd that they didn't come and talk to us?' she asked.

Maggie sniffed. 'Don't like foreigners, don't like women.'

Claire wanted to ask why they'd been allowed in at all, but the fragile truce she'd established with Maggie was too new to jeopardise with questions.

That night she wrote another card to Mala, and – after a long period when she'd stared at the picture of 'a typical Moroccan souk'

GATEKEEPER

- turned another card over and jotted down a few words to her father. Isolation made the terrorist reckless, except in her case, isolation was what kept her sane. Even so, she had to act like a normal person and that meant keeping in touch with her father, in case he became concerned at her silence. For a moment she laughed – what kind of world was it that made releasing wolves back into their natural home into an act of insanity, but her father into a role model for 'normal' behaviour? Then she heard the cracked sound of her own laughter and pulled herself back to reality. The wolf pack needed her to be strong, she wanted to do this for them, and for herself – there was no shame to recognising that her own weaknesses had value in this kind of work. Every pioneer had to go beyond what other people thought was well-balanced, whether to climb a mountain or discover a new theory of physics – she was using her own problems to help the wolves and if she had to learn to get along with her father again to achieve that, then it was an acceptable price to pay.

The next evening, when everybody else went to a film shoot, she drove back to the wolf enclosure, marked on her map by Maggie with a deeply indented X, and sat, watching them.

After an hour or so, when the alphas had got used to her again, the cubs were allowed up to play. They mock-growled their way around the pack, fighting and jumping straight up in the air like startled cats. They had small round eyes with a bluish cast like sloe berries and they wriggled their hindquarters before pouncing on each other, or on adults. The omega male suffered most; at one point he had a cub hanging from each ear like a malevolent earring, but the adults were good-natured, wrinkling their foreheads as the cubs bit them and at most pinning the wriggling bodies down with soft forepaws and gazing down at the squealing, wriggling, auburn bundles. She heard herself laughing again, but with pleasure at the cubs' antics, and the wolves, after a startled pause, seemed to understand that her laughter was no threat.

From then on, she spent each evening with the wolves.

99

CHAPTER NINE

Going back to England after the desert would have been a shock, but it was one she didn't have to endure. Instead, she went straight from Morocco to Rome, calling her father from Marrakesh airport to announce that she'd been offered a job in Italy and she'd be in touch again once she was settled. He sounded vague but pleased for her, and told her he'd got a dog 'for company'. She thought about asking what had happened to his asthma but bit down the comment.

She'd packed up her stuff before she left for Africa, and stored it in Ansel's place, so she emailed him to ask whether he had any suggestions for getting it to Rome. Then she flew on to Fiumicino airport and found herself gaping in shock at the bare-legged Roman women striding through the terminals. After nearly two months in Morocco they looked naked to her. One thing the Maghreb had done for her though. She no longer feared the sun. She no longer saw her mother, dressed in a garish swimsuit, paddling in a bright sea. She was over it.

Professore Giordano, her new boss, was beautifully dressed, a man with immaculate silver hair and the ability to speak without saying anything that committed him to a course of action. She'd developed no sense of him during her radio-phone interview, and she couldn't pin him down now she'd met him face to face. He seemed comfortable with her, although he didn't seem quite sure what she was meant to be doing, which suggested she had been foisted on him. She couldn't imagine a man less like Blaine – Giordano with

100

GATEKEEPER

his smooth phrases, his manicured hands, his breath mints, and Blaine with his weather-scoured skin and long silences. The lever that had moved her into the Food and Agriculture Organisation must have been applied very cleverly, she decided.

In any case, she had little time to consider it – the one thing Giordano did know was that within three months of moving to Rome she was scheduled for a field visit to Anatolia, examining the relationship between poverty, cash-crops and tourism in the remote mountains. After a week she sent Mala a card showing the Coliseum, and described her new job. She included her new address, a tiny flat on the outskirts of Rome, over an hour's commute from the FAO offices, although she doubted there would be a reply. There hadn't been to the cards she'd sent from the desert. She didn't allow it to bother her much, although sometimes sitting alone at night in the clean, miniature surroundings of her new home she missed Mala's bright enthusiasms. She had enough to deal with, fitting herself into the fury that was an international organisation in the world's most sophisticated city.

Everything about her was wrong for this new role. She looked rough and battered, her clothes - compared to those of the Romans - looked like stuff that a charity shop would throw away, and she spoke no Italian. She felt like an anthropologist observing the strange species that had built this ancient society and peopled it with impeccable votaries, complex rituals, unspoken unbreakable choreographies of administration and diplomacy.

It wasn't long before she realised that there were two kinds of people in the FAO and she was straddling the divide. 'Real' FAO was the preserve of the elegant staffers in their air-conditioned offices: the people who fought for budgets and space with the ruthless, bloodless weapons of committee, allocation and resource. The 'other' FAO consisted of field-workers: chunky, appearing only half-clean, and obsessed by 'their' project, whether animal, vegetable or mineral. These clumsy creatures appeared in the corridors

101

KAY SEXTON

like neutered bears towed by priests. They were led to meetings and debriefings by members of the Directorate General that they belonged to, and they performed their rough tasks, presenting data, revealing disasters or successes, with a kind of innocent earnestness that made the staffers smile. Without the field-workers there was nothing to fight for, but without the staffers the field-workers would be starved of money and support. Together they were like a symbiotic relationship; an orchid blooming with pale beauty on a rough branch.

She dressed like a field-worker but had a staff job. She was a freak, an offence against the nature of FAO and while she realised that an important lesson had to be mastered, she didn't know how to begin the process. In the past few years, something had atrophied in her. She could see what she should become, a confident and polished woman with the shine of Roman experience making her smooth and easy to deal with. She just couldn't work out how to get started. She didn't want to mope the corridors like a field-worker but she found it impossible to imagine herself with the same veneer as her administrative colleagues.

At the end of her second week she went shopping, in her interview suit because it was the only thing she owned that she would dare wear into Rome's boutiques. Even so it was too heavy, too clumpy and badly-cut; she could tell all that now. She looked at the pale linen dresses, the jewelled shoes, the tiny cardigans and ruffled jackets, without trying anything on, and came back empty-handed. She'd lost whatever it was, the impetus to adornment that came from personal relationships.

If her mother had been alive, they could have shopped together. She thought this at night as she lay in bed. Her Roman neighbours seemed to start their evenings at nine, and didn't stop laughing, cooking and throwing things into cupboards until long after midnight. She couldn't sleep, and when she couldn't sleep her mother was at the front of her mind.

GATEKEEPER

Things came too close in Rome. People on the bus crowded against her. The head of her bed was separated from her neighbour by the width of the wall; she heard him, or her, snoring. Her feet swelled up in the soft Italian heat and her whole body seemed puffy and soft, after the desiccating furies of the Maghreb. And she was so big! Next to the fine-boned women of Rome, her body was as slab-sided as a Holstein cow.

She waited until a Sunday afternoon and then, with fatalistic precision, picked up her mobile and called Mala. They talked about Mala's new role as a junior consultant on a biodiversity action plan for a health authority. Claire talked about her job. Mala thanked her for the postcards. There was a pause.

'Come and stay,' Claire said, surprised at her own weakness. 'Whenever you like – a Roman holiday.'

'I don't think that's what you mean, Claire,' Mala's voice bubbled with humour. 'A Roman holiday is where one person suffers for the pleasure of others watching.'

'Well, maybe that is exactly what I mean. I feel like some kind of ape here, all hairy and hulking, and soon I'm going to have to go shopping for clothes or they'll put me in a zoo. I'm not looking forward to it. They're going to laugh at me.'

'Next weekend?'

Claire felt her lips curve into a smile. 'Really? You'd come and stay?'

'I'm earning more than I can spend right now – why not a weekend in Rome?'

Claire had to sit with her Italian dictionary for half an hour to understand the backs of the cans and bottles in the kitchen cabinet. The supplies, including a scant cupboard's worth of dried and tinned food, were supplied by FAO, along with a folder listing the contents of the flat and useful telephone numbers, none of which offered to translate ingredients. Nothing shared a brand name with products

103

KAY SEXTON

she knew in English and her two-day orientation at FAO hadn't included domestic hygiene. She was studying in the language lab one afternoon a week, along with two Somalis, one Swede, three Germans and a large and serious group of Koreans, but they hadn't got past the formality of greetings, weather and directions to places of interest. Now she wanted the place to look good for Mala — and that meant mastering the arts of Roman housework.

The instructions still seemed puzzling when she'd translated them word for word. One tin was floor polish, she understood that much, and applied its contents, via an old t-shirt, to the dusty, plasticine-coloured tiles on the kitchen floor. To her astonishment they turned a glossy, dusky pink, like a starlet's lipstick. Once she'd been to the corner shop and bought shaggy, coppery chrysanthemums for the vase and hung up the beaten silver necklace she'd bought back from the Maghreb as a souvenir, she thought the place looked civilised. But would Mala think so? She'd been the one who'd made their flat look less like a student squat and more like a home — Claire hadn't had the knack or the inclination. Now she wanted Mala to see that she'd valued that domesticity, learned from it even. It wasn't easy, as she lacked most of her possessions. Ansel would be bringing them soon but she hadn't told him about Mala's visit. He might think it made nonsense of the months she'd spent in the desert, supposedly severing contacts with her old life.

It wasn't until the next morning, standing at the sink filling the kettle, that she realised she must have mistranslated something. Her shoes stuck to the floor, and when she prised them loose they made a sound like Velcro ripping. She had to leave or she'd be late to the office and she was meeting Mala from the airport in the afternoon; there was no time to sort out the floor before she left.

All day she dithered about the polish, wondering if there was time to get home in her lunch break, which was typically long, and deal with the problem - but she wasn't yet clear about what had gone wrong; and her colleagues were not the kind of people she

104

GATEKEEPER

could ask. Professore Giordano wouldn't know what floor cleaner was; she wasn't sure he would even grasp the concept of somebody cleaning something – it was the kind of thing that happened when he was out of sight and he seemed unlikely to have troubled himself to understand such processes. His secretary, Signora Malvino, had a high lacquered hairstyle like a flamenco dancer and spoke Italian with such force and venom it was clear that she hated the idea that other languages existed, let alone might be spoken in her office.

Giordano had a Personal Aide who might have been approachable, but the running feud between him and Signora Malvino meant that he showed up when she was out of the office, so his meetings with his boss were limited to lunchtime discussions and booked sessions in one of the many conference rooms where the Signora could not interrupt them. Theresa, the secretary, might have helped, but Claire didn't want to admit her inadequacies to someone who was essentially the office typist.

She'd spent her first week watching the way the organisation worked and getting lost on the buses. Everything seemed chaotic and amusing – it could hardly be taken seriously. Each of the people she met must have some secret inner purpose like her own, otherwise they would go mad in this bureaucratic labyrinth. The thought consoled her when she felt lonely – perhaps Malvino was on a quest to make her superior fall in love with her, or seeking out fraud in the Agriculture budget. Perhaps Giordano lived for the hours he could spend with his mistress or his harpsichord. Theresa's motivation was simple - she was getting married and spent all her working hours poring over bridal magazines in her desk drawer or calling her mother and sisters on the office phone to talk about wedding plans.

Somebody here was Claire's ally, her secret confederate – even if that seemed almost impossible. Clinging to the thought got her past the period of what she refused to acknowledge as homesickness. With Mala's arrival she hoped to become something else; a person who fitted in. Ownership of Rome might kill her growing

105

KAY SEXTON

loneliness. Showing somebody else around the sights could help her feel at home – that was her theory.

Around lunchtime she had an idea. If she approached the floor problem as though it was a wolf problem, what would she have done differently? She would have established as much information as possible without exposing her interest.

When the others had left, she wandered the corridors until she found a cleaner's cupboard, but it was locked. Descending two floors to where stationery was kept, she tried again. Success. There was an entire room of supplies: water cooler cups, yellow warning signs, floor polishers and vacuum cleaners – and a wall-length shelf of cartons and bottles that cleaned, polished or made things smell good. She picked out all the ones that had pictures of tiles on them and carried them back to her desk. A dark-haired man smiled at her in the lift and she smiled back, realising after he'd got out that he probably thought she was a cleaner on a rush job.

By the time she'd deciphered the first box she was starving and she'd gained nothing, it was another polish, not a polish remover. She decided to run out for a sandwich and eat at her desk.

The dark man was there again, outside the building, talking into his mobile phone, she approached him, mentally rehearsing the Italian for sandwich, but as soon as he hung up and she began her prepared speech, he cut her off and answered her in English.

'There are many places – nice places,' he said, beckoning her along the marble frontage.

'Fast is more important than nice,' she said, already aware of Rome's obsession with good food served slowly and eaten with appreciation.

'What can cause such hurry?'

She looked into his eyes, dark, sharp, amused. 'If I told you, you'd laugh.'

'To laugh is good,' he suggested.

106

GATEKEEPER

She realised he was flirting with her. And wasn't she flirting with him? Hadn't she chosen to approach him instead of finding a lunch spot on her own? For a second she felt traitorous: Kaya and her kin, the wolves in the desert compound, The Project, all depended on her – she shouldn't get frivolous. Then she remembered what Blaine had said about schmoozing people into the wolves' camp. She needed to practice that, surely? Anyway, this man was like an advertisement for Roman charm, he was doing nothing more than he did with any woman from twelve to eighty who came into his orbit. Still, she decided to keep quiet about the tile disaster.

'I'm trying to translate something, and I wanted to do it while my colleagues were at lunch,' she said.

He took her arm and she felt a flicker of warmth in her belly as she caught his scent, a rich, clean fragrance like autumn.

By the time they parted Claire had given him her name, her FAO extension number and her first impressions of Rome. In return she'd received his name: Bruno Contadino, his extension number and a large flat bread stuffed with peppers, layered with sharp cheese and dripping with oil – which he'd insisted on paying for.

Back at her desk she checked the packets against an online translator she'd found on the internet and identified one that seemed capable of dissolving the earth's crust, let alone a bit of floor polish. She tucked it in her bag, scooted the rest back to the supply room and was back at work by the time her colleagues returned.

She felt smug. It was a small mission, but she'd pulled it off. Let it be an omen for the challenges to come. And each time she though about Bruno she felt like a green twig being bent to the ground to put out new roots. Something good had happened and she hadn't been suspicious or defensive about it.

She was still thinking about him as she waited in the terminal, which was why, at first, she only stared as Mala approached. Mala, but not. Her long, beautiful hair had gone. Instead of looking like Cleopatra, inscrutable and lush, Mala now looked like a Shaolin

107

monk, her hair so short it stood from her scalp like fur. The bright clothing had become severe charcoal trousers and a smoke-grey shirt. She had always turned heads, but now, instead of smiles, she garnered dropped jaws as she crossed the concourse.

'Claire,' she held out both hands and - after a moment when they both hesitated – reached them wide.

Claire, hugging this new sombre Mala, wondered what tragedy had made her so different, so finely wrought.

But it was Mala who stepped back and scanned her, frowning before saying, 'You've changed.'

The journey back to the flat started in silence, then Mala spotted a battered old cat basking on a roof and began a conversation about feral populations, then town planning, soon they were discussing how to manage invasive species, and if Claire didn't look at Mala they could have been back in Brighton.

She forgot about the kitchen until her hand, searching her bag for keys, found the box.

'Shit! Look, I'll make you a drink and you can relax in the living room, I've got to sort something out in the kitchen.'

Mala raised her eyebrows but didn't comment. Within seconds though, Claire realised she wasn't going to get away with it. She'd have to get changed or ruin her only good work suit. Then she'd need to find something to kneel on, and Mala wouldn't be able to watch her going back and forth between bedroom and kitchen without getting inquisitive.

She smiled, trying to make the confession amusing rather than pathetic. Why did she care so much what Mala thought anyway?

Before she'd finished explaining, Mala was in the kitchen, dabbing at the floor with a finger and grimacing.

'Idiot. This is some kind of glosser, but you're supposed to put a sealant on top. We have York Stone slabs at home – same difference. Lend me some old jeans and flatten out a cardboard box.'

GATEKEEPER

When they were both kneeling on folded cardboard, Mala scrubbing at the goop, Claire following behind to rinse with floor with fresh water, she felt desolate. She was incompetent. She couldn't even polish a floor without making a mistake that someone else had to put right.

She must have sighed, because Mala spoke without turning. 'What?'

'Nothing,' Claire savaged the floor again, rubbing the cloth so hard into the tiles she half-expected them to crack.

'Okay.'

A pause while they both worked, and Claire tried not to sigh again.

'This is good,' Mala said. 'I wanted to talk to you and it's easier when your hands are busy, isn't it? I owe you an apology.'

Claire sat back, watching the shaven neck of her friend moving rhythmically as she scoured the floor.

'No, I think I owe you one, Mals. More than one. For the mess,' she slapped the bucket with the cloth. 'And for Liam.'

Mala sat back too, but kept her eyes on the floor. 'It's looking better, don't you think?'

Claire couldn't see any difference but she agreed, and they returned to work.

'I didn't come here for mutual apologies – I came because I wanted to see you, and explain.' Mala's voice was level. 'We always got on well together, didn't we?'

'Of course,' Claire filled the gap, hoping she sounded warm and positive – what the fuck was this about?

'But we were never close. Maybe people thought we were, but really, we were very good at not talking about things. We … respected each other's need for silence.'

'Uh huh,' Claire wanted to be anywhere but here. She couldn't play show and tell with Mala. Whatever her old friend had in mind,

109

KAY SEXTON

there wasn't going to be a reciprocal revelation from her side, and that would send Mala home more distant than ever.

'And I still do. But something happened that I must tell you about, because without you it would have taken much longer, maybe never.'

Mala had been rubbing away at the same tile for several minutes, her knuckles bone-pale and her back locked into a taut arch. Claire slopped the cloth around to sound busy.

'You don't have to tell me anything, Mals. We're mates – whatever it is, I'll take it on trust.'

'No,' Mala glanced round, grinning. 'I'm going to make you listen, so we might as well get it over with.'

Claire bent her head again. 'Okay, go for it.'

'You know my family is ... very close. But you don't know why. My mother is ... my mother steals. From shops. A shoplifter.'

Claire whistled and then clapped her hand over her mouth. 'Shit! Sorry, Mals, but – fucking hell!'

'For as long as I can remember she's been like it. Long before my sister Lottie was born. She's six years younger than me and I can remember Mum doing it from when I was four. We had to take care of her. When we went shopping – one on each hand, little girls stopping their mummy stuffing her bag with chocolates or face cream.'

Mala stopped scrubbing. She put the brush in the bucket and sat back breathing deeply before turning and facing Claire. Her face was calm, nun-like.

'And as we got older and couldn't hold hands, we had to tell her which shops she wasn't allowed into because she'd been caught there before. But we couldn't say it was she who was banned because she'd smile and ignore us. We had to say, 'Oh Mummy, Mala can't go into that shop' or 'Mum, Lottie is banned from that place' and then she'd walk past with her head in the air as though shaming the shopkeeper.'

'Bloody hell. How often...?'

110

GATEKEEPER

'Every weekend, more or less. It was my father's idea. He used to go to the shops if she was caught, and pay for the stuff and apologise, asking them not to prosecute and saying she wouldn't ever go in there again. Often he would take me with him, or Lottie when she was old enough, and we would say to the shopkeeper, 'Very sorry, it won't happen again,' and hope they'd believe it was one of us who had taken the stuff, and tucked it in the bag, not her. Dad would say to us, 'Take care of your mother' and we knew what that meant'.

Claire heard her own breathing in the silence. She sounded as if she were running. Rage came up her throat like bile, a fury so hot she couldn't contain it, even by jamming her teeth together and clenching her fists.

'Bastard! What a total bastard!'

'He's my father. He loves us - he didn't mean any harm,' Mala spoke with unnatural serenity. 'But I had a plan. I would get away, to university, and once I graduated and got a job I would go and get Lottie. We talked about it on the way to school in the mornings – how she could come and live with me and we'd have lots of fun. Lottie's got problems with food – you can imagine, can't you, how much she wanted to control something? Food was the easiest thing.'

'So what happened?' Claire couldn't imagine a good ending to this story and the fact that Mala had shorn her hair and moved into mourning colours suggested things had become worse, if possible, than before.

'I realised that it wouldn't work. If I took Lottie away she'd feel so guilty about abandoning Mum, she would break down. If I went home I'd feel so torn apart that I would break down. So I took my father aside and told him he had to do something.' She looked down at her hands. 'He denied it. Said there was no problem. Said my mother was just under stress and would be fine as long as Lottie was with her.'

111

KAY SEXTON

She stopped again. Claire waited. The silence became insupportable and her ankles ached from the pressure of staying still on the hard floor.

'What happened?' She asked.

'I hit him,' Mala looked up, eyes glowing. 'The way you taught me after Liam trashed the flat. A two-handed blow to the solar plexus.'

'Jesus!' Claire sucked air, feeling as if the room had become too small. 'You hit your Dad?'

Mala nodded. 'And he fell over, holding his stomach. I told him that was how it had felt each time he asked me or Lottie to take responsibility for Mum when we were little. Like being hit in the gut.'

'What did he do?'

Mala looked away. 'Nothing. But I did. I left him on the kitchen floor and went and told Mum what I'd done. I explained that if she wouldn't make a decision to get help, I would never be able to come back home, because I couldn't promise not to do it again.'

Claire got up, hobbling from the long sitting, and crouched next to Mala, rubbing her friend's stiff back. 'That was brave; it must have been difficult for you.'

Mala shook her head again. 'No, not really. I'd done all the difficult stuff beforehand, when I was little – this was the easy bit.' She shrugged but began to cry. 'Mum was the really brave one. She rang Lottie's school and asked to speak with the Head Teacher. She told him what ... what ...'

Claire shushed her, trying to be comforting although she knew she wasn't good at it - if she'd been the one to hit her father, Mala would have known what to do and say to make her feel better.

'She asked him to organise counselling for Lottie, and then she rang the police and asked them how to proceed. They were very nice. They put her in touch with a support group and she ...she ...'

112

GATEKEEPER

Claire lifted her, half-dragging her into the living room before running to the bedroom and pulling the quilt off the bed to wrap round Mala's shivering body. For a long time there was no sound but Mala's convulsive breathing as she got her tears under control. Claire held onto her, rocking her backwards and forwards as advised in *Building a Terrorist* as a countermeasure to extreme sensory deprivation or emotional trauma.

Out of the window the teal-blue haze of a Roman evening filled with starlings and veils of cirrus cloud began to layer the horizon. The sky became purple and Mala straightened up.

'Sorry,' she said.

Claire laughed. After a second, Mala laughed too, a cracked gurgle that sounded like her first happy moment for weeks.

Dinner should have been a trip to a local trattoria, but they ended up chewing boiled spaghetti and tinned fish from the cupboard.

'Tell me again,' Claire said, trying to be gentle. 'You really think that thumping your Dad made that much difference?'

'No,' Mala grinned and Claire realised she was waiting for the other woman to tuck her hair behind her ears, a gesture that was now impossible. 'But it made everybody realise that I wasn't going to put up with it any more. As long as we were all being civilised about it, nothing changed. But once I broke the rules ...' she flourished her fork.

'And I taught you,' Claire rubbed her forehead, amazed at the reversal in their positions.

'Mmm,' Mala spoke round a mouthful of food.

Claire twiddled her fork in the pasta, knowing that in any normal relationship she would reciprocate with the story of her own parents, but she couldn't be sure that talking about the past wouldn't lead to interrogation about the present and anyway, she had no resolution to offer Mala.

'So everything's good now?' she asked.

113

KAY SEXTON

'No, everything's terrible,' Mala said and then giggled at Claire's expression. 'But it's a good sort of terrible. We're a complete mess – a totally fucked-up family, but it's in the open. Mum's got a self-help group, Lottie's having treatment through the school and Dad's ...' she stopped. Claire waited.

'He's in denial still,' Mala admitted. 'But he's stopped flinching when I get close to him.' She snorted with laughter and Claire joined in.

'I wanted you to come shopping with me,' she said.

'Great – one thing I can do is shop,' Mala raised her head with a proud smile. 'Shopping I can do backwards. Something good comes out of everything, if you look for it. I believe that now.'

CHAPTER TEN

Bruno Contadino was Personal Aide to a Division Director responsible for Genetic Diversity in Staple Food Crops. He was sophisticated and polished, a typical Roman, with his wafer-thin watch and his perfectly tousled hair. But he was also funny – a trait she had never come across in a lover before. And she realised she was thinking of him as a lover, even before he made anything that could be described as a definitive move on her. After the desert she felt she was owed something – a break from thinking about her role in The Project – and Rome, while it might be a stepping stone, was not a Project location so she was not required to be 'on duty' as constantly as she had been in the Maghreb.

A Roman holiday – she thought about the phrase ten times a day: whenever Bruno's elegant figure appeared in the offices of her DG, carrying invented messages or asking for meaningless information. Somehow he pulled off his constant visits without seeming creepy, and that helped predispose her to him. He was charming to everyone and although not good-looking in any conventional sense, he was neat, clean, delectable – as fresh and wholesome as a hazelnut straight from its shell.

Everybody in Rome was scented, from Professore Giardano's cachous which smelt like a maiden aunt's linen cupboard, to Signora Malvino's icy fragrance and Theresa's vanilla perfume. To reach a seat on the bus Claire waded through odours like gateposts to people's personal space: coffee, hairspray, garlic, sweat, sun lotion and pomade. People glinted: tiepins, religious medals, earrings, hairpins like spears, hairbands like pearled nets. Everybody spoke at once, all the time. She was learning to love it, like living in an opera. It was the opposite of the desert, and she was coping with it.

She now had suitable clothes, thanks to Mala's systematic trawl through COIN and La Rinascente followed by a Monday morning dash to the second-hand market at Via Sannio before her flight left. Claire took pleasure in having moved one step from 'turista' to 'indigeno'. She wasn't invisible yet, but like a new cog, she'd begun to spin in unison with the great machine around her.

Food was revelatory. Colleagues began to invite her to trattoria for lunch and took such pleasure in her enthusiasm for the Roman diet that she began to ham it up; rolling her eyes and sighing at each new delight. Signora Malvino even brought her a small salami, made by her parents from the pig they'd slaughtered the previous year. Claire's appreciation was sincere – these people had polished the art of pleasure until it shone like a mirror – nothing had prepared her for her response to it. She twirled in the current of Rome's love affair with itself and was happy to submerge her identity in its demanding self-absorption.

It helped that she found her work fascinating. She'd always thought of tourism as a commercial trap: a purely artificial construct designed to give people a spurious reward at great cost – a whore's orgasm. Now she had to abandon that prejudice and learn a new way of thinking. Her task was to examine how tourism could add value to weak or marginalised agricultural regions. Her first trip to Anatolia completed her transformation. She became a staffer.

'They eat the same thing every day: chick peas, lentils, a little bit of goat meat,' she told Bruno, over a wild mushroom risotto at lunchtime, the day after she returned to Rome. 'And yet they've got an oral heritage of food preparation and special feast dishes dating back to the time of Alexander. Those recipes could easily become a revenue stream. They need capital investment of course, to build

GATEKEEPER

a restaurant, or maybe two, and to send people to Kastamonu for catering training. Once that's done, the boost to the economy could be substantial. Already they have climbers visiting, not just for Mount Ararat but right across the mountain chain. Imagine if the locals could offer the visitors traditional dinners – one on arrival, one before departure. That could lead to reinvestment, seed capital for new ventures, maybe a food cooperative ...' She stopped, watching Bruno pick mushrooms from the serving plate. 'Am I boring you?'

'No, Claire. It is very interesting. But you will need a budget, a field-worker, links into the tourism department of the region – forgive me, but this will not be easy and you are not ... senior.'

She blew her fringe out of her eyes, thinking she must find a hairdresser soon. 'I know, I know. But it's so obvious what needs to be done! There's even a guy, Akhun, he was my translator, who goes up to the climbers most days on a trial bike. He takes cigarettes, imported chocolate, stuff like that. Just think if he had a hot box. He could sell kebabs, maybe even create a provision route ...' She laughed. 'I'm doing it again, aren't I?'

Bruno touched her hand. 'You have found a passion. That's good. When you look at us here in Rome being ... is urbane the word I want?'

She nodded, amazed as ever at his vocabulary, richer and more cogent than her own.

'Urbane. Remember, we have our passions too. We fight for our secretaries and budget lines because we believe in our projects, just as you do in yours.'

The word project brought her back to reality. She was here for The Project, not for Akhun Halic and his motorised delivery service or the broad, smiling women in the villages of Anatolia. This was cover, pretence, camouflage. Still, nobody said she couldn't do as good a job as possible – as long as it didn't interfere with her work for the wolves.

117

KAY SEXTON

'I've been thinking about seniority,' she said, watching his face, liking the way he weighed everything in his mind before speaking. 'If I came up with a PhD project on tourism in mountain communities ...?'

'Hmmm,' He loaded his fork with mushrooms and spilled them onto her plate. 'These mushrooms are from the woods around here. The best mushrooms are wild, like these were, but these have been preserved in oil. In autumn there will be fresh ones and then everybody will be demanding them.'

She ate, waiting for his verdict on the idea.

'Yes, that would be a good research project. It gives focus to your intentions for the Anatolian food programme and there will be meaningful data to measure. That should help with a budget.'

She thought about the outline, on her laptop already. Guilt crept over her like a damp cloud. It was wrong to deceive him, even in a good cause. As time went on it would become more difficult not to tell him her real purpose if their friendship developed. Perhaps it was best to create distance now, so that she wouldn't have to shut him out later.

'Great. I'm glad you think it's a good idea. I'll get Ansel to help me draft a proposal. I'm sure one of the faculty in Brighton will agree to supervise me.'

His face hardened. She sensed the disappointment he wouldn't show.

'So you wouldn't consider doing your research at an Italian university?'

She shook her head. 'It's going to take a lot of travel, and planning. And I've still got a job to do here in Rome. Better if I work with somebody I already know, in a department I'm familiar with – it's one less thing for me to juggle.'

He nodded. 'That's sensible.'

She put out her hand, copying his earlier gesture. 'If you were able to find the time to look at an outline, I'd really appreciate it.'

118

GATEKEEPER

'Of course, I'm very interested in your ideas.'

And in you, was the unspoken message, and she lowered her eyes to her plate. He was far too much of a good thing. Too much, too early - in the wrong place and time. She deliberately spent the rest of the meal talking about Ansel and his work. Bruno was polite but not enthusiastic. As they walked back to the office he slid his arm around her waist and she couldn't help herself doing the same to him. With a table between them she could pretend indifference but flesh to flesh she couldn't lie.

Using Ansel as a barrier made her feel slimy – as if she'd sunk to his level: prying and caching secrets for later use. But at least Ansel himself didn't know. Their relationship, conducted through emails and phone calls, was cordial, although it had never regained its original level of intimacy. He was, she supposed, her handler, her contact with The Project, and she worked at making him think well of her, while reserving all personal information. It was a shock when he sent an email to say he was coming to Rome for the weekend and wanted to stay with her. Also, if she could find a friend, perhaps they could make up a foursome with Bruno for a day at the Monte Mario Nature Reserve?

She rang him immediately but his cagy responses to her questions made her realise that one of them was being listened to. Not her, surely? Signora Malvino didn't speak English and Theresa was as ditzy as a Barbie doll. She put down the receiver and thought about it. Just because Malvino refused to speak English, didn't mean she couldn't understand it. And Theresa might appear facile, but Mala had concealed her bitter secret behind an equally giddy façade for nearly two decades – nobody should be judged by surface appearances

Ansel rang that night on her Maghreb mobile, startling her. She hadn't thought about the handset since she left the desert and it had sat, silent in its charger, for months.

'You must understand,' he said, after the briefest of greetings, 'each side has its supporters.'

119

KAY SEXTON

'Each side?'

'You and the other Gatekeeper.'

She sat back, watching the starlings circle the sky. She knew only four Project members for certain: Blaine, Eleanor, Maggie and Ansel. Of those, she felt she could rely on Ansel, Maggie would oppose her for sure and Eleanor would be incidental to the process. She was confident Blaine would be impartial when the moment came to decide. So she had one certain supporter – nice Ansel who'd turned out to have a nasty side. She hoped he was using both sides on her behalf.

'And?'

'You aren't telling me everything, Claire. That has been noted. You didn't mention Mala's visit. You haven't told me anything about this Bruno Contadino. It worries people'

She stayed silent.

'How can I fight for you, when you aren't honest with me?'

'I thought keeping my own counsel was an important part of the job?'

'But not with me, Claire.'

She capitulated, agreeing he could stay for the weekend.

The visit was more of a success than she'd hoped. Ansel and Bruno got on well and Theresa, drafted in to make up the numbers, managed to stop discussing wedding plans for long enough to tell stories of the FAO, translated by Bruno, that were both funny and informative.

Ansel had arrived by road, in a blocky 4 x 4 that he handled with precise care, infuriating Rome's more improvisational drivers. On the Sunday, when Bruno was sharing a family dinner with his parents, Ansel told Claire she was buying the car from him.

'Why?' She looked out of the flat window at the vehicle, parked half on the pavement because of the narrow street. 'What would I want with a bloody great wagon?'

120

GATEKEEPER

'You're going to drive it to Anatolia next time, and to the Carpathian mountains and – with luck – to the Scottish Highlands.'

She waited for him to continue. Out-waiting Ansel had become a cruel game, one she didn't like herself for enjoying.

'Do you know much about the Renaissance in Italy?'

The question threw her. 'No, nothing. Should I?'

'It might help you to understand The Project.'

She settled back for one of Ansel's lectures, but he walked to the door like a big dog waiting to be let out. He wouldn't talk until they were outside.

'When rich Renaissance men made alliances, they did it from a position of strength. So a Duke would parade his army to persuade another noble to ally with him to attack a third. The Project works the same way. The man who owns the land on which the wolves will one day be released is Italian, a rich, powerful man. Such men have private passions, apart from power and money. His is forests. He has forests around the world: Italy, Holland, Scotland, the Amazon, North America. He buys them and he plants new ones.'

'Sounds eccentric.'

'And you think we are not?' He laughed briefly but honestly and she grinned back, acknowledging the truth of his words.

'So to convince such a man, Blaine had to 'donate' the raising projects himself. He is not poor, Blaine, but such an initiative – two sites, two teams, two sets of cover for the work, the bribes, the salaries ... can you imagine?'

She could. She was shocked by the implications. 'It must be costing hundreds of thousands of Euros, millions maybe.'

'You have learned to think in Euros?'

She shrugged. 'It's what we work in.'

'So, can you see how much is invested in this – in getting everything right? Not just the money, but people's dreams. And some people think you are not as committed to this dream as you should be.'

121

KAY SEXTON

The statement resonated with her own thoughts and she went on the offensive immediately. 'Because of Bruno, and one visit from Mala?'

He nodded.

'I needed Mala. When Blaine told me about this job, he said I would have to be opportunistic – use whatever was offered to help the wolves. I had to fit in here, to look right, and Mala was the one person I knew who could help me buy the right clothes, get the right haircut, all that stuff. So I used her. As for Bruno ...'

'I like him very much,' Ansel said quietly. 'But Claire, some people think you are not exploiting this opportunity as well as you could. There are fanatics in our group, you know. People for whom the wolves come first, only and always – everything for the wolves. They say you're not dedicated.'

She looked around, gauging the distance from the flat, ignoring his words.

'You have somebody who can protect your position here when you are away. He is influential – some people say you should be using him to strengthen yourself in Rome so that you have power to call on later.'

'You mean they think I should sleep with him.'

He nodded. 'You are too much of a loner, Claire. Some say you have been seduced by your tourism ideas and you're giving up on The Project. They claim you lack the ruthlessness to see how to use him to your advantage. The other Gatekeeper, they say, would have Bruno in her pocket by now.'

'Then they don't know him at all. Bruno wouldn't fit in anybody's pocket for long.'

'Even so, he can do things for you that nobody else can.'

'Can he?' She was surprised out of her resistance.

'His father is a tax lawyer. Did you know?'

'I suppose I did. I haven't thought about it, to be honest.'

122

GATEKEEPER

'Since Berlusconi, tax has become a big issue for Italians. Signore Contadino specialises in advising rich people. Not the man we have been talking about, but ...'

She interrupted, 'Wouldn't it be easier to tell me his name?'

'I am not allowed to. This conversation should not be happening. But if you meet him you will know; he is rich, Italian and crazy about trees,' Ansel smiled. 'As crazy as I am about birds!'

'But ... even if I get to meet him, what good will it do?'

He sighed, taking her arm. She wanted to pull away, but let him draw her closer.

'Sometimes you are naïve, Claire. What do you think I have been telling you? Blaine thinks he will have the final say on which of you is chosen as Gatekeeper, but he won't. He's already made one concession over the rearing project by providing so much of the funding himself. When the moment comes, this man will insist on being part of the decision. How could he not? And who can say no to him?'

She nodded. 'But suppose he doesn't like me. That could tip him against me, whoever he is.'

'Think about what I have told you!' She heard impatience in his voice, Ansel who was never impatient.

'Trees?'

'He nodded. 'Learn everything you can about trees. And use Bruno to help you get to this man.'

His advice made her feel uneasy. To use Bruno felt wrong. But if she'd followed her feelings she would already be deeply involved with him. Perhaps she could pull off this balancing act. She nodded and they headed back to the flat.

'Do you ever wonder why we do this?' he said.

'All the time.'

'I mean, what makes us into ... what would you call us? Extremists?'

123

He was circling for another attempt at her feelings about her father. She had to accept him as her contact with The Project, but if he was her handler, then was she an attack dog? The image was disturbing and she suppressed it. But she didn't have to put up with his psychological probing.

'We're activists – that's all. One day people will see that we were at the front of an ethical revolution. Martin Luther King did it for black people – we're doing it for animals. Ethical treatment of sentient beings, whether human or not. Respect for their lives and needs. That's it.'

'That's all?'

'Yeah. What else?'

'I think, sometimes, about what people would call us now – not in the future if what you say comes true – but now. I wonder maybe …'

The T word hovered in his silence. Disguised under other euphemisms like eco-warrior or animal activist, it was always there. Terrorist.

'Nah, if you spend too much time worrying about what 'they' would say, you lose your ability to act. Okay, we're on the cutting edge of activism – call it extremism if you must, or fanaticism, but we're not …'

She couldn't say it either. Even with the book tucked on her shelf in its misleading cover, even with every detail of her Maghreb training crystallised to perfect clarity against the template of its words, even knowing she'd just been told to use Bruno ruthlessly for the cause, she couldn't say the T word. She began again.

'Look, if we were working on a cure for AIDS, they'd say we were crusaders: committed, driven, pioneers. But if one of us put that same energy and effort into trying to make somebody fall in love with us, we'd be called a stalker. It's the purpose, not the means, that determines the label – and our purpose will win through in the end.'

'Do you think so?' He looked dark and remote again.

GATEKEEPER

'We share over 90% of our DNA with primates. One day, dolphins and whales will be recognised as sentient species. Yeah, we'll win. Not in our lifetimes maybe – but one day we'll be seen as the few right-thinkers in a sea of smug, stupid murderous criminals and habitat destroyers. We're activists, not terrorists.' She'd said it at last.

He smiled. 'I think so too.'

After he'd gone, she questioned if it had been wise to feed his mania, but she'd been stung by the claim she might be selling out. She looked round the flat after his departure, and searched the 4 x 4 too, but even if she could find a bug there was no way to remove it without tipping The Project off. Ansel hadn't been willing to talk in the flat. Fine. She'd use that knowledge to give any listeners a rich diet of her own commitment.

It seemed odd that life should become smooth and good in chaotic, dirty Rome and she said as much to Bruno as they lay in his bed, watching pistachio-coloured shadows creep up the white bedspread. He nodded. She knew he wasn't listening – he could switch off his hearing when happy or preoccupied; being totally in the moment was one of Bruno's charms. She admired his colouring, a bronze flesh that showed no effect of sun, unlike her own which burned rose on hot days and paled in the rain. She had become obsessed with his feet, narrow, high-arched and as neat as the hooves of an animal. It was easy to imagine Bruno as a Centurion, looking after a hundred men of the old Roman Empire, marching them along straight roads to conquer and administer for the good of all. His general elegance astounded her, Italian men were both stylish and masculine – something she'd never found in a British man. His scent too made her respond as an animal might: when caught his new leather and burnt sugar fragrance on the air, she would follow it half-consciously until she tracked him down; in another colleague's office shredding somebody's reputation; drinking *doppios* in one of the cafes near the FAO;

125

outside her apartment, flattering the Roman matrons who gave her sidelong glances whenever he wasn't around.

She rolled towards him now, fitting the curve of her back to his stomach. The grey-green shadow reached almost to their waists; it was close to the time they would have to get up and dress for the family dinner. His slid his hand up over the sheet, pressing it to her shape and its drapery turned to graphite in the shadow cast by her hip. She pulled forward slightly, feeling him becoming hard against her spine and he bent his head to her neck, blowing on the strands of hair until they parted and he could kiss her skin. Now his hands slid under the sheet, stroking her.

He was an accomplished lover. She had found out quickly that her own experience was limited in comparison, and he was a hedonist. Pleasure meant nothing to him though, unless it was shared. For a while she'd fought against the depth of feeling he brought to sex – it wasn't the simple anonymous physicality she'd experienced with others, but something more complex – a communication of bodies. It frightened her a little at first, as though he might make her flesh tell the things her voice wouldn't, but now she was used to the intensity of the experience and she'd learned to trust him.

She was tired, and a little achy, they'd been in bed most of the day and the muscles she used for shooting and Tae Kwon Do could only take her so far in the exhaustion brought on by sex, but she still wanted him again. She guided him into her, lifting her leg and turning slightly onto her stomach. His hand rested against her navel, a companionable gesture, a friendship within sex, something she'd never imagined was possible. She cupped her hand over his and felt his mouth smile against her neck. They moved slowly for a while, almost lazily, and then the current took her and she felt the orgasm building. His hand flattened, pressing against her body and sliding down, tangling in her pubic hair. She couldn't stop now, aches and exhaustion were set aside and she began to race her body against his to the climax, moving fast, pushing against his fingers.

GATEKEEPER

Afterwards he held her, murmuring Italian endearments into her hair, his voice beginning to fade into drowsiness. She felt herself starting to drift too. She could stay here forever, sleep here every night if she wanted to, he'd said as much, but she still only visited one night a week. She needed to keep her Saturdays free for shooting and Tae Kwon Do, and she didn't want Bruno to think she was getting too serious about him, even if she was.

'Come on, Contadino,' she muttered. 'Dinner with your parents.'

He growled, but there was a smile in his voice.

Sex was great, but more than that, time spent with Bruno made her feel so alive she felt the air around her must sizzle whenever she was going to meet him. He made her laugh with sly observations that turned the world around them into a vast show put on for their enjoyment. His humour was warm though, as often directed at himself as at others. He talked with affection about his parents – claiming he was a disappointment to his mother because he wasn't married and yet, as he put it 'she never likes the women I bring home and she won't accept that anyone could look after me as well as she does'. It was called the Roman Dilemma he claimed; Italian men were not getting married any more. Even so, he had a flat of his own and only visited his parents at weekends. Claire sensed something of her own need for solitude in his behaviour.

He also spoke of his time at Yale. 'Mother wanted me to go to an American university, because of Italian corruption. If you attend university here, you find yourself being asked to do favours for everybody who was in your year – and they expect to do favours for you. It's impossible to free yourself from those obligations. My sister is an undergraduate at Bryn Mawr now, for the same reason.'

So his years in America had made him a maverick, an unaligned force. It explained people's attitudes to him within FAO where he was liked and respected but often watched carefully. His ability to ridicule slowness and the complex 'corridor politics' earned him an

127

KAY SEXTON

audience but often he found himself alone, fighting against inefficiencies, while cronies of his opponents frustrated his plans.

They had so much in common that Claire felt much of her own life could be left unsaid. He didn't need to know what she was doing, or why, it would be enough for him to understand that she too, was playing a solo game.

Rearing Project

At fourteen months the two packs were ready to learn to hunt large prey. Rearing wild wolf cubs without adults to teach them was unpredictable and largely untried, but rearing cubs with socialised non-hunting adult wolves would have been a bigger risk and The Project had decided to avoid the degree of scrutiny that would result from having to obtain a licence to breed captive wolves. The canine foster-mothers had provided food until weaning, social and maternal care, and taught basic hygiene and grooming skills, but for hunting the wolves were on their own.

Now the ultimate feeding experiment would begin. Large live prey would be introduced and the young wolves would have to master pack hunting to bring their food down.

Blaine gave volunteers a chance to leave. Intellectually they all knew that the deer they'd been raising in a separate enclosure were wolf prey, but emotionally it would be a different matter to watch the cubs develop their killing skills, and the emotional charge would be strong because the wolves would begin by hunting very young deer. One volunteer chose to go and Blaine sent him to a Mongolian vulture-tracking scheme. Far from communication systems and integrated into another group the man was unlikely to spread information about The Project.

A ten-month old red deer was introduced into the H enclosure at noon. Within minutes H5 had begun to track it. The pack showed varying degrees of interest in the deer, individual wolves drifting close and wandering off again over several hours. At dusk, when Blaine had hoped it would happen, H5 called the others to her and approached the deer in a typical low slinking run, feinting a snap of her jaws to the right, to draw the deer's head to that side and then launching herself at the exposed throat. Her weight was not enough to drop the deer and H1 and H4 both attacked, one to the shoulder and the other to the flank to bring the young buck down.

KAY SEXTON

H5 used her body weight to close the deer's windpipe, an instinctive behaviour occasionally used against large, thick-skinned prey. The deer gave a few spasmodic kicks, and died.

The next moments were crucial. H1 stepped forward, bristling and snarling in possession posture. H5 growled but gave way. H1 fed first.

The pack was viable – the alpha female could organise a pack kill and the alpha male had stepped in to dominate her, and by extension the whole pack, at the right moment.

The M pack did not cope so well. Their kill was quick and if anything cleaner than the H pack's, but M1 and M2 staged a mock battle over the carcass and by the time they had finished squabbling both females had fed before them. A clear alpha male had not been established and the hierarchy of M pack had been reversed, with the females offering no deference to the males.

CHAPTER ELEVEN

Claire was inching her way across a rock face when she heard the wolves. First one, then even before the howl ended, a second. A pause, then another long calling howl in which at least two other wolves joined.

'Wolves!' said the American on the ledge above her.

Claire swung her right leg, found a crevice, tested it, then heaved her body up and to the right, using her torso to keep her balance. Her fingers found the ledge and she pulled herself onto it, using the strength of her forearms.

The American was waving his video camera around. 'Where are they, Cip? Can we get a look at them?'

Their guide, Ciprian, shook his head, and although he was looking at the American, Claire knew the gesture was meant for her. She turned, looking in the direction of the group howl. The wolves would be out of sight in the trees. Unless they were forced to break cover there was no hope of seeing them.

Luka came up beside her and gave her a thumbs up. He was Ciprian's brother and climb assistant and, Claire thought, a problem.

She knew what Ciprian's head shake had meant: instead of using the rock to guide her to the ledge, she'd used her strength, her excellent sense of balance and the power of her legs to push herself through the last part of the climb. She'd done it to get to the ledge before the wolves stopped calling in case there was anything to see, and if it had been anybody else on the climb, Ciprian would

131

KAY SEXTON

have ignored it. But Ciprian was Project, she was convinced of it, and he was trying to teach her to climb properly, the way she might need to one day, when she had only her own judgement to guide her. 'Forcing' the rock meant using physical strength or agility to power over the surface instead of reading it and working with it to conserve strength and take few risks. She'd just forced her way onto the ledge and Ciprian was disappointed with her. The fact that Luka thought she'd done a good job just pointed up how badly she'd failed. He was a flashy climber, using unnecessary flourishes and taking risks to show off – relying on his upper body strength to get him out of trouble. She ignored him, taking off her pack and stowing the safety line she'd been wearing, running it through her hands as she coiled it, checking for damage the way Ciprian had taught her.

'Luka, take the lead,' Ciprian said, pointing his brother down the goat track that led back to the vehicles. Claire took off her climbing helmet and put it in the pack, fastened it, checked the buckles, hoisted it. Her load was heavier than any of the others, except Ciprian's, and she was always the last to climb, meaning she spent more time exposed to the rock and the weather, giving her a greater chance of exhaustion, or cramp, or low blood sugar problems. It was a conditioning process, a rough and ready training that pushed her further and tested her more than the other climbers, even though they were more experienced. She waited until Luka and the rest of the group were on their way downhill.

'I didn't read the rock,' she said. 'I'm sorry.'

Ciprian shrugged.

'It was the wolves,' she said.

He grinned, watching the rest of the group move out of sight, then he gestured to Claire to lower her pack. She did, setting down as silently as possible. They waited for several minutes without speaking, until all sound of the departing group ended, then Ciprian crouched and she did the same. He folded his hands around

132

GATEKEEPER

his mouth and made a small yipping sound before launching into an eerily realistic howl.

There was a long pause, then the call was answered by a single howl. Ciprian winked at her and repeated his howl. Other wolves joined in almost immediately, as if trying to drown him out, and the group howl went on for a long time, long enough for Claire to realise that some of the calling wolves were way off to the west, so there were either two packs or one pack in two different locations.

When it was silent again they stood up. 'You have to be down low,' Ciprian said. 'The wolf is clever; he knows if the sound is too high up in the air, then it isn't a wolf calling. I don't know how he knows, but if you call standing up, he will never answer you.'

'Can I learn to do that?' she asked.

'You don't need to,' he said. 'You learn to climb. Soon the snow will be too heavy for safe climbing. You should think only about the rock, not about wolves.'

The rebuke stung, and she followed him down off the climb in silence.

She was back in the Anatolian mountains to audit projects like Ciprian's and to suggest ways to bring local food producers in contact with tourists. It had taken her a day or so to realise that Ciprian was treating her subtly differently to the rest of the group and at first she'd thought it was because her FAO job meant that he had to impress her – a negative report on her experience could cost him his grant funding. When she worked out that this was part of her Project training she was shocked at how much her FAO role had taken over her life. It was only supposed to be a convenient cover, but she had come to believe in it, and give it precedence in her thoughts and actions. Compared to dealing with food security and agriculture, The Project seemed a distant scenario, a mad dream that would never come off.

On the minibus, Ciprian told the climbers that they had a free day to enjoy a local festival taking place in a nearby town. Claire

133

KAY SEXTON

took the brochure he handed out and was sitting in her room at the hostel, ticking various stalls and activities that seemed to fit with her FAO interests when somebody knocked on the door. It was Luka. He looked right and left before saying, 'Come climb tomorrow, yes? I have something to show you.'

She nodded, concealing her excitement.

'I come here, six in the morning,' he pointed to his watch and she nodded again. 'You don't tell nobody.'

She shut the door and tipped out her daypack on the bed – she needed to carry her camera where she could reach it, enough rations for a day, and pitons and a hammer in case they hit a virgin climb. As she sorted through her equipment she grinned. Of course she wasn't going to tell anybody. Who would care, anyway, that she was about to see her first wild wolves?

Her sense of unease began when she saw the snow that had fallen overnight, and it intensified when she realised that Ciprian wasn't coming with them. Instead Luka had brought along his friend, Asik. Claire had already met him, at one of the social evenings in the local bar, and had developed the feeling that Asik was a natural follower who ingratiated himself with anybody who seemed stronger than he was – she didn't exactly think he'd kick a dog for pleasure, but she was sure he wouldn't intervene to stop anybody else doing it. The similarity to Liam's sidekick, Mick, was unnerving. But Luka was no Liam, in fact he was almost too charming, with his chiselled profile and flirtatious manner. All the village girls seemed to know him, and Claire felt sure he could have made a living as a gigolo, if only there were some rich tourist women around, but the Anatolian peaks attracted only hardened climbers, birdwatchers and tough archaeology buffs, not bored middle-aged women, so Luka's talents were under-appreciated.

They drove out of the village in a small Fiat, Asik's car, which explained why he was invited along, but made Claire's unease worse.

134

GATEKEEPER

It would have been better to take her 4 x 4. Driving in snow was difficult – a tiny car, like Asik's without snow chains, could easily get stuck, and then they would be stranded and have to walk out. She had supplies for only a day, and while Asik carried a small pack, Luka had only rope, belts and his gloves. She tried to see something positive in this: perhaps the climb was minor, more of a scramble, and at least Luka wasn't stupid enough to suggest they free climb, but the further the car got from the village, and the deeper the snow lay on the road, the more her senses screamed at her and Luka's always erratic English seemed to desert him the more they headed away from Ciprian and common sense.

'What are we going to see?' Claire asked, but he only rolled his eyes and scowled and Asik looked uncomprehendingly back at her from the driver's seat, so she sat back and watched the white road unfurl, noting that they were the first vehicle to travel it since the night's snowfall. She tipped her wrist to look at her watch – they'd been driving for three minutes: she could at least keep track of how far they were from the village. Sixteen minutes later Asik pulled the car off the road and pointed across a snow-covered field to a mountain slope.

'Over there?' Claire asked, wanting confirmation that this was their destination.

'Up, up!' Luka's finger jabbed at the grey expanse above the treeline.

She measured it with her eyes. The mountainside was steep but didn't seem to have any overhangs or crags that would make the ascent too demanding. She could see dark streaks that suggested fissures, but they weren't going to be exploring any caves, unless the wolves had chosen a cave den in this inhospitable landscape.

Excitement pushed her out of the car and she stood, bracing her hands on its roof as she stretched her calves and hamstrings without taking her eyes from the mountain.

Asik watched her and then began to copy her movements. She glanced at Luka, wondering if Asik should be climbing if he didn't

135

KAY SEXTON

even know how to limber up, but Luka was leaning against the car, rolling a cigarette, so warming his muscles obviously wasn't on his agenda. When she was ready she hoisted her pack and Luka pinched out his cigarette. Asik struggled into his own pack and they set off.

Within ten yards Claire knew the journey was going to be more difficult that she'd thought. The field hadn't contained potatoes or pasture – under the snow were the stumps of conifers that had been cut close to the ground, and feathery lower branches that had been cut from the trees. She bent and brushed the snow away with her arm. The stumps were between three and eight inches in diameter and up to eight inches tall. It would have been hard going even without the concealing snow, but now it was lethal. She kicked at the snow until she found one of the long branches and lifted it free, using it as a broom to clear away the snow so she could see where to place her feet. Asik and Luka had moved way ahead of her but presumably they knew the terrain. She was prepared to take her time, after all, they wanted her to see something, so they could wait until she caught up with them.

The two men were almost across the snowfield when Asik fell. By the time she reached them he was sitting up, and she could see blood staining the snow. He'd stepped on a jagged stump, driving a sliver of wood through the sole of his training shoe and into his instep. Luka had helped him pull free but now he sat on his pack in the snow, staring stupidly at his foot. Claire pulled off her own pack. 'Take off his shoe,' she said, as she reached for the first aid kit. She knew exactly where she'd packed it.

'No.' Luka took the branch she'd dropped and began to trim off the fronds with a penknife. 'He can go back to the car, take his shoe off there. Wait for us.' He handed the whittled branch to Asik who stood, whistling in pain as his foot touched the ground. Luka took the branch back and cut off the base to make a sort of crutch which he tucked under Asik's arm. Claire watched, appalled.

136

GATEKEEPER

'He can't go back like that. He could go into shock or fall again. Suppose it snows and we get stranded away from him? We need to take him to a doctor.' She knelt at Asik's foot and began to unlace the shoe.

'It's okay. We won't be so long. He knows what to do.' Luka lifted her up, pulled Asik's pack over his own shoulder, and made shooing motions at Asik, who grinned weakly and began to trudge back across the snowfield. Claire felt uncertain. She wouldn't get another chance to see whatever Luka was going to show her, and Asik did seem happy to wait for them in the car – perhaps such accidents happened all the time to young men in the mountains, like the broken knuckles and toes that marked martial artists, and were worn as badges of pride. She turned and followed Luka.

By the time she reached the first slope he was already climbing, and she took a moment to orient herself, finding the place where they'd parked the car, and seeing Asik trudging towards it. Then she began the ascent.

When she turned again, to check Asik had made it to the car, she knew the visibility was lowering fast. She looked up. The higher slopes were hidden in what looked like mist but was, she realised, snow. Even as she thought it, the first fine flakes drifted down to her. She began to climb faster, to reach Luka, but he climbed faster too, as if defying or challenging her.

Finally she caught him, on a small plateau, where he was buckling on a climbing harness. He tossed another to her and she pulled off her pack and stepped into it reflexively, tightening the buckles around her body and checking the fit of the webbing, before replacing the pack. 'Shouldn't we go back?' she said, half-wanting to return, half-hoping he would say they had only a short journey to make to find the wolves.

'It's okay,' was all he said, before roping up and beginning the climb.

KAY SEXTON

The face was not steep, but it was littered with scree like gravel, making it difficult to find hand and footholds that didn't slide away as she increased the pressure she put on them. She didn't want to find herself skidding down the slope, only stopped by Luka's body acting as an anchor, so she put all her concentration into reading the surface the way Ciprian had taught her, slowing her pace and using the rock, not her muscles to help her move. The line pulled taut and she glanced up into a dizzying whirl of snowflakes. Vertigo threatened, making it impossible to look away, and threatening to tip her backwards off the slope. The falling snow removed her ability to judge distance and the rock face was already studded with white specks – the surface would become wet as well as cold, increasing the risks of slipping. She felt another tug on the rope – Luka telling her to get a move on.

Claire stopped and thought about what she was doing. There was an injured man in their only vehicle who could be in shock from cold and blood-loss; she was in the middle of a two-person climb in appalling weather, without a map, and in the hands of somebody she already knew was a risk-taker. She'd assumed, without reason, that Ciprian knew about the trip, and she'd relied, without evidence, on Luka's expertise and ability to plan a climb. She leaned her forehead against the cold rock, sighed in frustration, and then tugged twice on the rope, indicating a problem.

Luka pulled the rope taut. She waited, but there was no sign he planned to descend to talk things over. Instead he sat above her, a grey blur on the grey rock, holding the line tight as if he could tug her up the slope by main force. Stalemate.

Claire untied the rope from her harness, letting him see what she was doing, then gave two more tugs before letting it fall free and beginning her descent. She could hear him calling out from above her, but she ignored him, heading down slowly, aware that if she fell now, there was nothing to anchor her.

She had almost crossed the snowfield when Luka passed her, a running blur in the snow, and she was suddenly afraid that he would

GATEKEEPER

to get to the car and drive off. He wasn't Liam, she reminded herself, and fought the temptation to move faster: she'd seen how well that worked for Asik.

Once she reached the car, with its white cap of new snow, she found Luka and Asik both inside, smoking in silence. She knelt outside the car to treat Asik's foot; it had stopped bleeding, which was good, but it looked as if splinters of the wood might still be in the wound and it was likely that any dirt that had been on the sole of the shoe would have been driven into his flesh, so she applied antiseptic spray and a loose bandage. 'He needs hospital treatment,' she said and Luka nodded sourly before climbing out of the car to let her into the back seat.

They dropped her at the hostel without a word being spoken and Claire watched them drive away, hoping Luka was taking his friend to get proper medical care.

Back in her room she collapsed on the bed, staring at the grubby ceiling, running through the extent of her idiocy: she'd failed to tell anybody where she was going, she'd allowed a colleague to suffer injury without ensuring their subsequent safety, she'd had no idea of the extent and nature of the climb and she'd had to abandon her part in it without discussion, putting herself and her climb partner at risk. It didn't matter that Luka had acted like a complete idiot, it didn't matter that she'd trusted him because he was the brother of a Project member, what mattered was that the very first time she'd been given a chance to demonstrate cool-headed caution, she'd behaved like a suicidal moron.

The possible outcomes filled her mind: they could have been seen by some other group, they could have been stranded and needed rescue, Asik could have succumbed to hyperthermia, he could still develop blood poisoning – any of which could lead to her becoming an item of local news, or to the FAO having to repatriate her, or Asik suing her for his injury, and that meant The Project could still find out how stupid she'd been.

139

Eventually, when she'd finished hating herself, she made hot chocolate on her gas cylinder and emptied her pack: cleaning her boots and filling them with newspaper to dry and writing down the supplies she'd used from her first aid kit so she could replace them. There was nothing to be gained by sulking. Even if she'd made a fool of herself and put others at risk, the only sensible response was to get on with things. If The Project kicked her out, it did, but she had to carry on as if nothing had happened.

It was after midnight when Ciprian knocked on her door. She let him in and he sat on the bed, staring at her wordlessly.

'I'm sorry,' she said. 'I thought Luka had come from you, to take me to see ...' she let the sentence hang and he shook his head.

'I'm sorry,' he said in return. 'I am sorry for my brother.'

She wasn't sure if he meant sorry for or sorry about, or both. She made some more hot chocolate and they sat for a while, drinking in silence. It reminded her of the times with Mala after Liam had broken into the flat.

'How's Asik?' She asked finally.

Ciprian shrugged. 'He will be okay.' There was another pause.

'Was Luka taking me to see the wolves?'

Ciprian laughed miserably. 'Wolves? Luka doesn't care about wolves. He was going to ...' the words he needed weren't in his vocabulary and he stopped, starting again with a story Claire had heard before, the tale of a Luftwaffe aircraft, variously said to be full of gold ingots, diamonds or looted religious art, that had crashed somewhere in the high Anatolian peaks.

'He was taking you to a cave,' Ciprian said. 'In the cave, a box.' His hands gestured, a big box. 'Wood.'

'A crate?' Claire guessed.

He nodded. 'In the crate, an ikon, very beautiful. But no way to bring it down in the snow, just three of you, so you would give Luka money and he would get climbers to help him and he would send you the ikon.'

GATEKEEPER

Claire stared. 'A real ikon?'

Ciprian shook his head. 'He has a friend who makes them, and the wooden boxes with the German words on the side. Two ikons he has sold this way, to Americans.'

Claire started to laugh, her relief making the situation seem unbearably funny and Ciprian watched her, his own face lifting slowly as he realised that she was genuinely amused.

'You are not going to tell?' he asked.

Claire stopped laughing abruptly. 'Are you?' she asked.

He shook his head. 'He is my brother, I am sorry for. That he should pick you. But you would not have paid.'

'No. What would I do with a looted ikon?'

'For the Americans I am not sorry. They have so much and we have ...' he gestured at the grubby hostel room, his old coat, the felt hat that had probably belonged to his father before him. 'Sometimes I think Luka, he has the right way, to get their money from their greed. I am the fool to work so hard. And he is ...'

'Your brother,' Claire finished for him. He nodded.

'I was a fool too,' she said slowly. 'I wanted ... something ... as badly as the Americans wanted their bit of stolen art – it would have served me right if you'd told people about this. But I've learned a lesson from it. I won't make those mistakes again, Ciprian, I promise you.'

She looked at uncomprehending face and saw that while she'd been scared he was going to report back on her, his only thought had been that she might cause trouble for his brother. What was it like, she wondered, to put somebody else before yourself like that? To see how stupid and dangerous they were, and still to care enough about them to be prepared to go and apologise on their behalf to keep them out of trouble? She thought about her father and shivered. She didn't think she could ever forgive as Ciprian did.

After he'd gone she lay on the bed again. She'd got away with it. Through sheer luck, her reckless stupidity wasn't going to destroy

141

her chance of becoming Gatekeeper, and as long as she stuck to the rules from now on, she'd be okay. She had to learn this lesson though – she wasn't good at ignoring opportunities; she had a tendency to leap at the chance for action without stopping to consider the consequences, and it had nearly cost her everything. In future she had to be more careful.

She had been so stupid! Why had she assumed it was wolves that Luka had in mind? Because she'd wanted to see wolves, because she'd thought that after all this time and all this training she 'deserved' to see wolves. So what she'd said to Ciprian was true – she was as bad as the Americans, just as greedy, just as focused on her own desires, not on the needs and desires of those around her. She'd acted as if Luka and Asik were puppets she controlled, not people with their own volition, and it had nearly ended in tragedy. From now on, whatever The Project said, she was going to think about everybody's needs, not just hers and the wolves. She saw Ciprian's face again, as he talked about his brother, the mixture of love and shame and a strange kind of pride in his brother's waywardness and imagined the same look on her own face as she talked about her parents. It wasn't possible for her to feel that way, but perhaps it was possible for her to accept what they'd been, without understanding how they'd allowed themselves to become what they had.

Claire's proposal for value-added tourism in the Turkish mountains was rejected. She made an appointment to talk to the Finance Division but came out knowing she'd failed to reverse the decision. She endured several days of black depression, blacker even than she'd felt when her mother died. The Project would surely decide her negotiation skills were inadequate but she couldn't work out a way to improve the situation. The funding outline had been good: the links to FAO's key mission clear, the benefits tangible and measurable. If the idiots didn't see that, they were just stupid and, short of re-educating them, she couldn't see how to proceed.

GATEKEEPER

Bruno asked about progress and she told him she'd been refused funding but didn't elaborate her sense of frustration and failure. She was increasingly willing to take his advice, but didn't enjoy revealing her vulnerabilities – in part because she knew his mother was cataloguing them to use against her at the right time. Already Signora Contadino had pointed out that an English geographer wasn't much of an asset in Rome's competitive social circles and how much more useful if would have been for Bruno if she was a social scientist, or Swiss.

Spending time with the Contadino's was like collating reports, an FAO task she did entirely too much of at present. Sometimes she got to the end with information ordered and tidy, and a sense of accomplishment and sometimes she got frustration and paper-cuts.

Most Sundays, Bruno ate with his parents - other people were invited too, colleagues and clients of Signore Contadino, local teachers and politicians, members of the Senate, journalists. Bruno's mother was an avid liberal and baited her people traps with good food and the chance to hear gossip before it became common Roman knowledge. New political tactics were floated at her dinner table, Europe was dissected, business done, rumour hatched. Claire felt like a donkey in a field of racehorses. She'd thought that listening and learning from the debates had given her a good understanding of how things worked and the slap of rejection for her proposal was worse because of it. Despite attending most Sundays, she hadn't met any tree-crazy businessmen – or, if she had, his particular brand of obsession had not surfaced. She was a failure, a double failure.

She felt diminished again. Her value to herself, to The Project, seemed uncertain. She was a well-paid paper organiser in a huge bureaucracy – what good was that to anyone? Bruno enjoyed her company, in and out of bed, but when his mother disparaged Claire's value, he simply smiled. Perhaps she was just a distraction to him, an exotic and rough-hewn interlude like a camping holiday for a town-dweller.

KAY SEXTON

Her normal response would have been to strike back, and when the pressure of her own doubt became great enough, she did. It happened one Sunday when she was getting ready for another Contadino dinner – she was wearing a simple shift dress Mala had helped her choose, twisting her damned long hair up on top of her head because Signora Contadino had said she thought women over twenty who wore their hair loose looked *jejune*, and scrabbling through the drawer under the bedroom mirror for another hairclip when her fingers found the clicker. She took it out, letting her hair fall as it would, and clicked it. Her Maghreb clicker – the bird counter. The tiny sound took her back to the hide and the dry heat of the North Africa desert. All that time, all that money spent on sending her out there, all that reading, and jumping through hoops for Maggie ...

She wouldn't let it be wasted, or not without a fight. When she'd started Tae Kwon Do, she'd been weak and stiff. Now she could kick down a door and not feel it. She would learn to negotiate, the way she'd learned to fight – by taking the pain and coming back for more. After shoving pins into her hair she drove to the Contadino apartment like a true Roman, one hand on the car horn, the other ready to gesture rudely, steering with her knees if necessary – at first driving here had terrified her, now she took it as part of the day. True, you needed good reflexes and a cold eye for opportunity, but she had both those, and she liked winning.

The dinner that night was good, the company interesting and full of gently malicious gossip that she now understood and enjoyed, and afterwards, as the family relaxed – and she was counted as a kind of ersatz family member, she noted – with grappa and a post mortem of the evening, she decided to act. She thought of what she planned to do as being like the feint - clearing her ground so she could come forward fighting.

'One thing I've noticed since I came to Rome, is how little understanding I have of the process of making deals,' she said. 'When I listen to people here, especially at dinner, they spend as

144

much time talking about how they plan to open a deal as they do about the purpose of it.'

She spoke in English, the language they all spoke fluently. She knew Signora Contadino had not been fluent until Bruno went to Yale – then she'd taken courses to ensure that she understood not just every word, but every nuance of every word that her son's friends and teachers used. Claire reckoned she could have managed the conversation in Italian anyway, but she didn't want to miss any detail of their replies and much of their vocabulary in Italian was shaded with meanings she might not grasp.

Signor Contadino sat back, nursing his glass and staring at the ceiling. She knew it was his way of gathering his thoughts for an exposition and that Bruno and his mother would now run with the conversation until he was ready to sum up four decades of experience in a concise fashion.

'Oh yes, Rome has always been the home of the bargain. *Patto*, we call it,' Bruno's mother said. 'A deal between two or more parties that offers benefits to all – that's how the Roman Empire worked, how the Catholic Church works still and the EU, let alone our domestic politics.'

'And our bureaucracies,' Bruno added.

For a while they talked about the Medici heritage, the negotiations of the Risorgimento, Vatican deal-brokers, and Claire squirreled away information: names, strategies, deals gone good and deals gone bad.

'But I'm bad at it,' she said. 'Take my funding proposal ...'

They did. First she had to explain the proposal, then outline every person and department involved in the decision, then describe the abortive meeting she'd had with the functionary in Finance. At the end she was drained.

'So what did I do wrong?' she asked.

'Where to begin?' Bruno's mother replied with a laugh. 'You spoke to the wrong people, made the wrong arguments, alienated the gatekeepers ...'

KAY SEXTON

Claire's heart jumped at the word gatekeeper.

'But most of all – you don't know the value of making a deal,' Bruno finished for her.

'The value of the deal was clear,' Claire said, stung by his comment. 'More income for a poverty-stricken area, preservation of cultural information of priceless value, and empowerment of women – what more could anybody want?'

'No, that's the outcomes. The value is what is transacted between you and the other parties to the deal. You exchange things – intangibles – and that's what makes the deal possible. Am I right, Father?'

Signor Contadino nodded.

'Your main problem, Claire, is that nobody is sure you will be around for very long. Why make a deal with a person who might leave Rome next year and never return? Why invest in a relationship with a transient figure whose future is unclear and whose motivations have nothing in common with yours?'

'Because it's a good project,' she said.

'But so what? We don't get many bad projects you know, and yet some have to be turned down. Of course there's a realistic assessment that goes on, whether a project can deliver what it claims, but over and above that there's something else – there's what you can deliver, and so far you haven't offered anything,' Bruno said.

'You mean a bribe?'

'No. Of course such things happen, but they aren't necessary if you know what you are doing.' Bruno tapped her fingers. 'To make a bargain you have to do one thing you've never done. You have to really care about the other person's position. You have to take their arguments and objections and make them your crusade. I'll show you. Mother, you be the Finance Officer, I'll be Claire.'

'We can't proceed with this proposal because it doesn't fulfil our key criteria – although it's interesting it's peripheral to our work in adding value to staple foods,' said Signora Contadino, parroting what Claire had told her of the meeting.

146

GATEKEEPER

'I'd like to understand that better,' Bruno said. 'I know that some of the work in fisheries has been considered successful and some not; can you explain why?'

Signora Contadino rolled her eyes 'Are you going to play both parts of this conversation now? I can't answer that.'

'Okay, it's because where capital expenditure was made in plant and factories, it was often for projects that were faddy – that catered to a sudden craze for a food that then fell out of fashion; so the projects that worked were factories that fast-froze prawns, the ones that didn't succeed were places that made prawn mousse.'

'Imagine I said all that,' said the Signora, smiling at her son. 'And you would reply ...'

'That's fascinating. I can see why you have to scrutinise projects with such care. It must be difficult to be confident about which projects have a sustainable future. Perhaps the answer for my project would be to show how the capital expenditure could be reapplied if the current tourists changed their behaviour? What evidence would help you in that regard?'

'You see?' Bruno's mother said. 'Recognise their problem, really care about it, make it your own and then ask for their help.'

'But before that, prepare your ground,' said Signore Contadino from his chair. 'They have to think you are one of them. In any negotiation you have to be on the inside, not the outside.'

'Think about battles,' Bruno said. 'When they sat down to write the treaty that ended a war, it wasn't the Generals, or even the Kings, who agreed the terms. It was diplomats and politicians who hammered out every clause, and those people knew each other, probably from birth. They were cousins and in-laws and trading partners with each other. They understood each other's needs and problems. They cared about the other side's needs, because the other side was their side too. If the treaty wasn't fair, they would suffer, either personally or because their extended family would suffer. Do you see?'

'So I have to make their problems my own and act as if solving their problems is the most important thing?'

'You have to be accepted as part of the negotiation and you have to trade something of yourself – you have to be an inside part of the deal,' Signore Contadino said.

'You have to know when to ask for help,' his wife added.

'And you have to be certain that your deal is best for everyone – when you have that certainty, when you've put yourself in the place of both sides and you're certain there's no better way of meeting all needs, then you go to the table with utter confidence – and that shows.' The Signore finished.

Bruno walked her to her car.

'Did we give you a lot to think about?' he asked.

'Yes, a great deal.'

They spoke Italian between themselves. Claire still spent an afternoon a week in the language lab, but she was on accelerated training now, learning specialised vocabularies for her tourism and agriculture work.

'Then I'll give you something more. Will you come to Florence with us?'

She knew the family had a villa outside Florence. They spent their holidays there. The invitation was a marker - it said that Bruno wanted her to be considered part of the family. A Contadino in the making, perhaps. She couldn't allow that to happen, especially with what they'd just been saying about deal-making and insiders. She couldn't risk any further intimacy with him at this point because how would she be able to explain her sudden disappearance to the Highlands if The Project decided in her favour? He might want to come with her, and that would be a disaster. She spoke almost without thinking. 'Sorry,' she said. 'I'm not ready for that.'

He smiled, but she could see he was hurt by the bluntness of her refusal.

GATEKEEPER

'I don't mean to sound hard,' she tried to explain as much as she could. 'I just don't feel I can cope with that level of intimacy yet.'

'Is it Mother?'

'No,' she laughed. 'Actually, the more time I spend with her the more I like her.'

'The same is true for her of you, but she'll never say so.'

She felt herself blush – Signora Contadino's approval was something worth having, but it made the situation more complicated still. She had to get out of this before Bruno began to map out a deal that she couldn't refuse, and anyway, wouldn't want to. 'Look, we get on so well, let's not mess around with things just yet, okay? Anyway, I'm off to Romania in a couple of weeks – I might get eaten by a bear.' She kissed him gently and unlocked the car.

Driving home she wondered if she'd done the right thing, but she couldn't see any choice. She wasn't much of a negotiator in her own life. When he found out she'd used up all her leave to extend the trip to the Carpathian Mountains, he would believe she'd done it to avoid him repeating the invitation. There was no way to explain that she needed to drive the 4 x 4 in mountainous terrain and travelling overland to Romania allowed her to develop that skill, even if it took all her holiday allocation to get there and back. She couldn't explain anything – she was the Gatekeeper and she'd slammed a door in his face.

She rested her arms against the steering wheel and thought about Kaya, roaming her enclosure, alone and restless. Claire wondered if she was forcing herself into a similar position. But the wolves were out there, somewhere, growing and waiting. She couldn't back down now, or they would end up in cages too. Nobody had pretended it would be easy, and she'd said she understood what she might have to sacrifice, but she'd never imagined there could be anybody like Bruno as part of the equation. After she'd locked the car she went indoors to practice her Tae Kwon Do – without The Project she would never have met Bruno – she owed it to the wolves,

149

KAY SEXTON

to herself and to all the other Project members to see this through to the end, but for the first time she thought about how much easier life would be if the other Gatekeeper got the job, and she was free to stay in Rome.

CHAPTER TWELVE

Ansel had called to tell her she was being relocated. Her Highland job was ready, a cottage had been arranged in the village of Glenfail, and her supervisor at Brighton was waiting to receive her PhD proposal. She didn't even have to make an appointment with Professore Giordano. He called her to his office and said he was delighted she'd already found a way to further her research and as long as she agreed to return to Rome when necessary, he was authorising her two-year secondment to the Forestry Service in Scotland, as a researcher, part-time lecturer and supervisor of grant applications for woodland projects.

'You have an FAO flat; the rent is taken from your salary,' the Professore said. 'Do you wish to keep it?'

She closed her eyes. 'Yes,' she said.

'Signore Ottaviano is leasing you a cottage in Scotland. I believe you know the Signore?'

She frowned. A vague picture came to her of a portly man, rather fussy about his food, at one of the Contadino dinner parties. So that was the Signore. She must have made a stronger impression in him than he had on her. At least she could put a name to one Project face now, although it wasn't much help to know the 'Italian connection' just as she was heading for the Highlands.

Then she had to tell Bruno. She decided it would be best to do it on neutral ground, so she waited until they were walking back from lunch, sidestepping Roman matrons with their shopping bags.

151

KAY SEXTON

'I've got the chance to go to Scotland,' she said.

Bruno glanced at her, alerted to something significant by the tone of her voice.

'It's ... long term.' She'd meant to sound more positive. 'A great chance, with some teaching too, which is going to be a great chance for me, exploring some of the primary research I've done as teaching aids. A two year contract, that's what they're offering me.'

He nodded. There was a long silence, punctuated by car horns, and Claire slowed, to get the discussion over with before they entered FAO again.

'Are you running away, Claire?' His voice was calm. She didn't want to look at him, in case his face was as unemotional as his diction.

'I'm keeping the flat here, but perhaps it would be best if we ... put things on hold until the two years are up.' Was that an answer? Enough of an answer? Too much? She didn't know what she was hoping for: an argument, an agreement? Whichever it was, Bruno was too much of a diplomat to offer it to her, instead he took her hand and kissed it, watching her face, then smiled faintly.

'You know where to find me if you want me,' he said, before walking off towards his office.

Claire felt weak. It was as though she'd held the flat rental out as an inducement to him to hang on. She closed her mind to the idea that she wanted to hang on, too. But when she got home that evening, she found herself cataloguing all the things they had bought together for the flat: a salad bowl, a thick rug – things that added comfort and beauty, possessions with a history of happiness. But that wasn't what she'd come to Rome for. She was here for the wolves. She picked up the phone, but ringing Bruno would achieve nothing. He'd been well-mannered enough to let her go without an argument, she had to be brave enough to leave it at that.

She arrived at High Croft in Glenfail at noon, and within half an hour a mist had settled, so thick she had to put the lights on in all

GATEKEEPER

the rooms to be able to navigate the long walk from the drive to the house. It was easy to tell the place had been built long before petrol vehicles. A natural path came down off the hill to the back door of the croft, and an unnatural track made dog-legs from the tarmac road up to the house, ending with an apologetic puddle in a hard standing that was still thirty yards from the croft door. She walked the path with each box and bag from the car, starting with the three most important, the box with food, the one with her drill and rawl plugs, and the locked metal case that held the Browning. Then she carried in the empty linen box.

The first thing was to tour the rooms, looking for a place to put the rifle box. The obvious place was the kitchen, but when she noticed the condensation stains below the windows she felt uncomfortable. A damp gun was a liability and she didn't want to be cleaning it every couple of days to be sure it was safe. The point of the rifle was that it should be a hidden advantage - if she had it laid out on the kitchen table with oil and rags every five minutes, there wouldn't be a soul in Lochaber who didn't know about it within the week.

In the end she put it in the spare bedroom, fitting the lock-box into the back of the linen case and then measuring for screw-holes. The drill fought against the wall, and she had to move the box twice to find a place where she was drilling through mortar, not stone.

Once the gun was hidden, she felt better. There was no knowing when a neighbour would turn up to examine her, and her possessions, and the Browning was bound to cause comment. She put the .22 box in the kitchen, drilling through the plasterboard wall to secure it above the dresser. Most Highlanders would hunt, she assumed, and a pest rifle was a badge of conformity in this society.

She returned to unloading the car and the combination of tiredness and mist meant that she didn't notice the man standing at the foot of the path until she almost bumped into him.

'You'll be moving in,' he said.

KAY SEXTON

She nodded, shaking droplets of condensed mist from the ends of her hair and trying to pick out details of his appearance. He was small and weather-beaten, wearing a green waterproof jacket that was mist-soaked on the shoulders and made him blend into his surroundings. This close she could smell wood smoke on him, and a faint oily odour like car engines. His eyes were Highland pale, and steady. By his side a small black and white collie stood, suspicious and silent.

'Yes,' she said. 'And you are one of my neighbours, I assume?'

'No, I'm with the Forestry. I came down off the hill.' He jerked his thumb backwards and she saw the white blur of the Forestry van parked at the beginning of the true road.

'We come down this way most days. Easier than going back round.'

She nodded again, adrift in the details but wanting to show at least the modicum of friendliness.

'Is your husband following with the van?'

She smiled although she didn't want to – the double presumption on top of the shitty weather made her feel gritty and exposed. 'No, I'm here on my own and everything I'm bringing is in the car.'

He looked past her at the house. 'You'll be needing logs and oil.'

'I gather the oil's already on order. Logs – if you're Forestry perhaps you can suggest the best place to get them?'

His eyes, travelling back to her seemed to harden whitely, like poaching eggs. 'I'm seconded up from Edinburgh,' he said as though the *non sequitur* contained all the information she needed.

'And I'm seconded from Rome,' she continued to smile.

'I know. I put in for your job. Didn't get it though.'

In the unnecessary last sentence she heard the chilly dislike of an older man defeated by a younger woman.

'I'm sorry to hear it. I hope that won't cause any difficulties between us?'

His eyes slid past her to the house again. 'No. We'll have no dealings, so there will be no difficulties.' He turned back into the

GATEKEEPER

mist and opened the passenger door of his van for the dog to jump in. Before driving off he stared at her again, the dog joining him in a joint cold survey of her, her belongings, her car.

She realised as she carried the camera bag indoors that he hadn't even given his name.

She spent the rest of the day learning her way round her new home. The village of Glenfail was a mile down the road, High Croft the last isolated outpost before the hills began. The croft had originally had two rooms, one up, one down, but they had been divided into an upstairs bedroom and tiny bathroom and downstairs the kitchen and a sitting room into which three people could fit if they weren't large. There was no back door. A garden was surrounded by a dry-stone wall which ran parallel with the track past the house. She walked the track until it disappeared into the grass of the hill. Her neighbour had driven down it, but it seemed to lead behind her house and then to nowhere.

A burn ran alongside the road, dividing the village. It circled the hill at the back of High Croft but then became a set of double falls, the lower about two metres, the upper more than six. Once she got past that point, the hills rose around her, grass becoming mixed woodland, which became pine forests before disappearing into the mist. In clear weather she knew she would have seen the blue smudge of mountains. On a dry day it would be beautiful she thought. If a dry day ever happened here.

Isobel Mearns had banged on High Croft's only door at 7 am the next day. Her pug nose, iron-grey pageboy haircut, Wellingtons and matted black cardigan loomed out of the continuing mist like a nightmare of thwarted womanhood – Claire half-expected to see a chicken with its neck wrung, dangling from her hand.

Isobel had started by sniffing a sniff like an organ note, and had moved into the hall of the house, continuing her lusty inhalations as

155

Claire watched, not sure whether to be amused, or on guard against the local half-wit.

'Bloody men!' Isobel's opening comment didn't add anything positive to the impression she'd generated of ill-kempt menace. Then she turned, holding out an age-worn hand. 'I'm you're nearest neighbour, if you don't count my husband John, which we won't because he's a dour man at best and an ill-tempered bugger at worst. Today is worst, so I thought I'd come up to you rather than let him depress you on your first morning. Now then ...'

She swept off to the kitchen and left Claire to follow.

'Honestly, you would have thought they'd have let me know!' Isobel was pulling food from her pockets. 'I'd have aired the place for you. As it is I've brought you some scones, a pot of my bramble jam, and here's a half-pound of butter: if you want more, and I'm sure you will, order it through Katie Sturridge in the stores – strictly speaking it doesn't exist, but one of our local Aberdeen Angus producers runs a hobby dairy. Katie can get live milk and butter for you whenever you like.'

She stopped. 'Och, I'm sorry. I've been cleaning this place for the past two years, so I tend to walk in. You might think me downright rude.'

Claire couldn't help grinning. She'd never heard anybody say 'och' before. 'No, not rude. It's a bit of a surprise to have a welcome committee ...'

'Och, yes, I know. You met that old devil Noel McIver. He told John about you this morning.'

'This morning? It's barely daybreak!'

'The Forestry go up at six most days. Noel stopped at the house to tell us; that's why I came straight up. I thought if you'd spent all night brooding on Noel's manners you might be packing up to leave us again, and we need some young women about the place.'

'So it's not just me he's abrupt with then?' Claire picked her words, watching the other woman fiddling with the range and filling the stovetop kettle.

GATEKEEPER

'No, not at all. Noel's one of the fine breed of Scot who thinks success is a sin and imagination a curse. Now, sit you down and tell me about Rome while I warm these scones.'

An hour later Claire had been given potted biographies of most of her neighbours, a history of the area, a detailed account of Signore Ottaviano's purchase of the estate and his management style ever since, and a list of eligible men. In return she'd described her PhD thesis, talked about Rome, eaten five scones and jam and shown Isobel the cameo brooch Bruno had sent her as a parting gift.

'Och, lovely,' the other woman had said, turning it into the light with blunt but careful fingers. 'I can't say I'm not disappointed though. We were hoping you'd be an eligible match.'

'We?' Claire felt the warmth of gentle teasing relaxing her caution. Isobel's humour was dry to the point of desiccation and she was enjoying the mild sparring, along with the good food and the warmth the other woman had managed to coax from the oil-fired range that Claire had failed to master the previous evening.

'There's a problem with the Highlands. Men love them - women don't. It takes a lot of character to stay here if you don't love the place, and often the fact that you love your man is an obstacle rather than a help.' Isobel smiled but her eyes were serious. 'If you think you can live in a hard place on love alone, you usually find the love dies. We've had half a dozen couples come here in the past twenty years. Normally he's always wanted to fish or farm or climb or croft and she's encouraged him to think that after he's put in his years in industry or government and the children have left home, he'll have his reward. So here they come. And after a year or so, back they go.'

Claire wrinkled her nose. She didn't like the moral of the story she could feel was impending – women couldn't cope.

'And it's not the women that are the problem, not really.' Isobel continued. 'It's that this is a landscape of thin soil, over hard rock. There's little enough to keep one person going, almost never enough

157

for two. Sometimes he'll fail and sometimes she will, but usually they'll be gone before a year is up.'

'Why is that?' Claire pushed crumbs around the tabletop.

'Because there's no room for followers and leaders here. We're all rugged individualists, as they say, because the Highlands demand it. If you have to lean on somebody, even for a moment, this place will bruise you for it. Get bruised enough and you cannot lean any more. People grow apart. And sooner or later when that happens, they either move apart or leave.' She gathered up the crumbs and swivelled in her seat to open the range and throw them in. 'And I've an overactive imagination, John says.'

Claire smiled. 'And Noel McIver?'

'Poor Noel. We went to school together, you know. He's had a tough time of it. His father was a Highlander, went to work on the rigs when there was oil wealth in plenty, and married an English girl. She lasted about as long as the oil did and when she went back south she took Noel with her. He's spent his whole life trying to get back here, really.'

'Well, he looks like he's here to me.'

'Aye. But not really. He's no land, you see. His dad sold up and Noel can't get a place of his own here – not one that he can afford as a second home. His job's in Edinburgh, not here, so at the moment he's renting a house from the Signore, midway between here and Fort William. He wants to move here permanently which is why this job you've got would have suited him to the ground, but ...' Isobel smiled but Claire felt the warning. Another situation where she'd put the man's nose out of joint without even knowing it.

'Is that why he wouldn't tell me where to buy logs?'

Isobel propped her chin in her hands and drummed her fingers across her lips. 'Yes and no. That's quite a problem around here anyway, but it will have annoyed Noel. I feel sure he gave you the impression he works out in the forest?'

Claire nodded, remembering the van, the jacket, the dog.

GATEKEEPER

'Och, he's tied to a desk in a Portakabin. He'll not have wanted to tell you he's an accountant rather than a tree surgeon.'

Claire fought not to smile, looking over Isobel's head to see the shape of the hill through the kitchen window. She could feel her lips trying to curve though and when she caught the other woman's eye they both broke into laughter.

'So ... logs?' Claire said, after a second.

'Well, that depends on you. From what you've said, you'll already be asking a lot of questions of people, and that will make them nervous. They'll wonder if you're really from the Executive, checking up on us, or the Revenue, chasing taxes. If you buy logs from the McDowells, it would be a sign that you're not entirely ...'

'Honest, above board, in the pockets of the authorities?' Claire suggested, laughing again.

'Well, let's say that where Drew and Alan get their supplies is a mystery.'

'Drew and Alan McDowell it is then. Where do I find them?'

'Don't worry, my dear, they'll find you soon enough – I'm surprised that they've not appeared on your doorstep already, but I'm sure you'll meet them before the week is out.'

Isobel had been right. Before the end of that first full day in High Croft she'd seen the two sandy-haired giants striding up the path out of the whiteness and pulled open the door to find wall-to-wall Hibernian masculinity on her doorstep. They weren't identical twins, she decided after a few seconds, because one was shorter and more auburn-haired while the other was taller, wider and carrot-topped. Both were over six feet tall, had beards, moustaches, long hair and thistle tattoos on their forearms.

'We're your neighbours. Over that way, on The Waird,' a brawny arm pointed through the croft wall to one side of the hill. Claire hadn't realised there were any houses past High Croft, and she decided as soon as they left she would walk up and see what was located beyond the curve of the landscape.

159

KAY SEXTON

'You'll need logs,' he continued, while his brother leaned on the doorframe and stared down at her with bovine friendliness.

'Indeed I will. Isobel Mearns mentioned you, I think. You are the McDowell brothers, aren't you?'

'Aye,' said the one who hadn't spoken so far, the taller one. His voice seemed to come from under her feet, rising out of the stone doorstep and filling the whole house with deep slow tones. Claire was impressed.

'Drew here's a champion caber-tosser. Nae bad with the hammers either,' said his brother. 'Represents us at the Highland Games.'

Claire let her eyebrows lift appreciatively.

'World's strongest man,' said Drew gnostically.

'Aye – maybe. He reckons he's in with a chance at the title, but my own view is that he'd need tae take not inconsiderable amounts of drugs tae match the real strong men and I've nae desire to share a caravan with a man on steroids. Also, our mother would throw him out.'

Drew lowered his head and frowned. Claire looked at his hands - it seemed possible he could circle her neck with the fingers of one hand.

'Come in,' she said, wondering how long it would take Drew to get in if he wanted too, permission or not. He looked like a man who could blow a house down.

'No, we'll nae bother you. Just wanted tae make sure you had all you wanted in the way of wood and the like, and tae say we're happy tae do the odd job around the place. Should you need a new back gate say, or a wall re-pointing, we're your men.'

Claire found herself smiling without intending to. They were rascals, working for cash and probably cutting logs on other people's land, maybe even bagging and selling them back to their original owners, but there was a refreshing lack of guile about their approach. In the air-conditioned corridors of Rome their upfront villainy would already have led to them being killed, stripped and thrown in the Tiber, metaphorically speaking.

GATEKEEPER

'Isobel suggested there might be a problem if I bought firewood from you?'

'Well, I'm sure Mrs Mearns didn't mean tae imply actual difficulty. More a question of logistics.' Alan waved a hand the size of a shovel in the general direction of the landscape. 'Your man frae Sicily doesn't entirely approve of us cutting trees.'

'Entirely approve?' Claire questioned, wondering if 'man from Sicily' was meant to be taken as a euphemism for Mafia involvement or whether Alan assumed the owner was from Sicily because it was the only Italian place he knew.

'Well ...' Alan began to gaze through the exterior wall as though the answer was written somewhere inside the house.

'On pain of death we are forbidden,' rumbled Drew.

'That's a touch strong,' Alan argued. 'Not exactly death, Drew. McIver just said we'd get thrown out if we were caught logging estate land again. Our father was well fashed by it all,' he confided. 'He's not keen on the whole issue of defending our rights tae the land.'

'What does that mean?' Claire leaned on the door frame, feeling the cold of the mist beginning to seep into her body, her front becoming chilled and damp while her back was still warm. The brothers seemed unaware of any problem with the weather, relaxed and pink-skinned with their sleeves rolled up as though they stood in June sunshine despite the icy drips condensing and falling from their hair to make dark spots on their shirts.

'It means that a Highlander may have been landless through many generations, but still holds tae his land. Should he be required tae cull the herd or cut the tree, that's his prerogative as the steward of the highlands, nae ownership papers can change the inalienable relationship of a people tae their birthright.' Alan said.

'So you were caught poaching deer and cutting wood?' she asked.

'The poaching was entirely circumstantial, but they took us up with the wood in the back of the truck. There was nae hiding it.' He

161

KAY SEXTON

seemed unconcerned at the impression he might be making. 'Not least because we'd that very day sourced a new caber for Drew. It was hung over the back of the vehicle by a good four feet.'

'Sourced?' She was trying to keep a straight face.

'Aye, sourced straight off the hillside – bad luck for us that yon McIver had taken note of the same damn tree earlier and saw it was missing on his way home.'

'He recognised a single tree?' Claire fought back a giggle.

Alan leaned forward, blocking out what little light still came through the doorway, 'That man knows every leaf and root, Miss. He's obsessed with the land.'

Drew made a noise like gravel being turned with a shovel. After a second she realised it was laughter. His brother observed him with exaggerated shock before grinning in reply. 'Well, perhaps he's not the only one. We have strong feelings about it too.'

'Well, that could be a problem. You know that I'm renting High Croft at the invitation of Signore Ottaviano?'

Alan glanced at his brother again. 'I can promise you, Miss Benson, that not a log we bring you will be from the forest here.'

They'd already found out her name. It wouldn't have been difficult, but it was a sign how close-knit this community was.

'Call me Claire. And as long as I'm not burning the Signore's wood, I'd be happy to have a load of logs from you.'

'Cash,' suggested Alan.

'Of course. In advance?'

Alan held out his hand. 'No, we're neighbours. You'll be wanting more, so we'll trust you for the payment until the logs are delivered.'

They shook hands. It was like gripping rock. She was glad Drew didn't feel the need to cement the deal too.

CHAPTER THIRTEEN

In her first weeks in the Highlands, it was food that obsessed her. She would wake in the night, dreaming of *proscuitto* ham, sliced as thin as a bat's wing and as succulent as fruit, or *carciofi ripieni di pancetta*; artichokes stuffed with breadcrumbs and bacon. She wrote shopping lists that detailed green and back olives and cold-pressed olive oil, coffee beans, biscotti, honey, figs, fresh-baked flat bread, and ice-cream and then she tore them up and bought pies, oven chips, frozen peas, dried apricots and instant coffee. Her throat parched for *Soave*, mineral crisp and toasty on the palate and *grappa* as intense as an open-lipped kiss, but on her weekly trips to Fort William she stocked up on supermarket red wine and whisky. Every time she banged down her Pyrex plate on the Formica-topped kitchen table she remembered the thick Italian crockery of her Rome apartment, and how she would eat, looking out of her window at the constant love-story unfolding between the city and its inhabitants.

From her kitchen window here she could see the hill, slumped in her eye-line like a failed loaf, pressed down by a sky like a zinc tub. Behind the hill was the glen, with its narrow icy burn and falls, and far behind them, Streap. The view was stippled with birch, rowan and aspen which rose to join the ranks of pine that had been planted with Forestry grants more than thirty years ago. New plantings of native species fuzzed the hill, her hill, and would one day provide habitat and cover for hundreds of species, but for now they were forlornly propped sticks on a landscape like a giant's arse.

To the left of the window was The Waird. On a stony outcrop that had once served the community as a beacon hill were two cottages parallel to her own but hidden by the hill. The McDowell family lived in one, and a couple of women who were wool dyers had taken a lease on the other. The Carline Dysters, Alan called them – Isobel had explained that carline meant old woman or hag. Claire had met them and they were a personable plump couple in their late thirties, so she assumed the description arose from their having rejected Alan's economic or romantic advances.

She tried to characterise the differences between the Highlands and Rome and because food dominated her hours, it was food metaphors that developed. Rome was a boiling of people, all hot and rubbing up against each other, contributing to each other's natures like rice turning over in a risotto. What was Bruno's mildness without his mother's exacting personality as seasoning? What value would buttery Professor Giordano have, without the astringent flavour of his personal secretary? Rome seethed and mixed.

The Highlands, she first thought, were like a bowl of oatmeal - bland and featureless. After a week or two she revised this opinion. Life in the village was like something simmering out of sight, a shape in dark stock, a dimly-glimpsed chunk that presented a new but more mysterious sense of itself with each slow turn below the surface. A bone, a fish poaching its eyes white, a hunk of vegetable rotating in the deep currents of barely stirring darkness? Whatever it was, the thing was at one with itself, hidden but immutable.

She thought of the Loch Ness monster and shivered, even though she knew the beast was a hoax. Still the idea of some huge form in the cold depths of the freshwater lake was disturbing. You had to see the lochs to understand how such things could seem possible – once she'd stood beside the frigid water and stared out over the unmoving surface she felt less inclined to scoff at the people who'd been duped.

GATEKEEPER

She'd met a few of her neighbours by walking around the houses, introducing herself, describing her research and asking them if they would be willing to be interviewed. Most men though, seemed to spend all their time away from their houses and when the fourth or fifth wife in a row suggested she go to the pub to talk to her husband because he was more likely to be receptive there, she felt she should follow the advice. As Isobel Mearns said, 'You'll have to overcome their bloody Highland stupidity. A Highland man has an image of himself to live up to, and it doesn't matter how far he is from the ideal, he'll not thank you for pointing out his failures.'

So she began to visit the pub on Wednesday, live music night, because after the first couple of visits she couldn't bear to hear Alan playing the same tracks over and over on the jukebox: Letter from America, Amazing Grace and Chansons d'Amour. She wasn't sure if she was horrified or impressed by his catholic tastes, but she knew she couldn't listen to Amazing Grace more than once a night without going mad. At least on live music night she got to hear a wider range, even if some of it was dire.

'I've got a price for you, for logs,' Noel McIver said.

Claire, still half-asleep, found herself trying to stare down the wall-eyed dog which was regarding her with the same distant hostility as its owner.

'Nice dog,' she said, hoping the conversational gambit would give her time to work out a response. Most people loved to talk about their animals. She was sure that he'd said he couldn't help her get any wood – now she felt wrong-footed, and being still in her night clothes didn't help.

'Nell,' he said, and the dog moved her eyes to his face, something like affection in her gaze. Then she turned back to Claire and the glacial distaste reappeared.

Claire smiled. 'Hello Nell.'

The dog stared her down.

165

KAY SEXTON

'Well, the thing is, Mr McIver,' she paused to give him a chance to offer his first name. He didn't. 'I got the impression you couldn't help me.'

He stared at her, impassive, him and his dog, she thought, like a pair of plaster bookends. 'And it has been a couple of weeks since we spoke. So I've ordered some from ... somebody else.'

He shook his head with such practiced disgust she got the impression this kind of disappointment happened daily. Looking to his right as though talking to an invisible companion, he said, 'I suppose she told you to buy from the McDowells?'

Claire followed his sightline to the bright windows of the Mearns house glowing against the early morning gloom. 'Well ...'

'Then you listen to me, Miss Benson. If those criminals have cut down a single Forestry tree and I find evidence of it in your log pile, I'll prosecute you and them both. Do you understand?'

She forced a smile. 'I'm sure you won't, Mr McIver. Alan assured me the logs were legally sourced.' Now she thought back on it, she wasn't sure he had, but she wouldn't let McIver see her doubts.

He glared at her and she met his gaze, holding eye contact until he blinked. The dog, Nell, lowered her nose and glanced aside as if Claire was no longer an object of interest.

'We'll see,' he said.

'Indeed. Although I believe you'll need my permission, or my landlord's, to come onto my land, and as of right now, Mr McIver, I'm telling you that I do not give you that permission – I hope that's clear?'

She saw something like satisfaction in his eyes for a second before he turned without replying and walked back to his van. Moments later, as she put the kettle on the range, she heard him drive up the hill and wished she'd thought to deny him access to the short cut too.

'Another day, another enemy,' she told her reflection in the mottled bathroom mirror as she pulled her hair into a ponytail. It

166

wasn't the best start to a relationship but she hadn't had much alternative. McIver wasn't the kind of man anybody could get on with. If she spent too much time trying to win him over she could miss opportunities to build support from other locals. Better to cut her losses now. Even his dog was a lost cause.

CHAPTER FOURTEEN

Alan and Drew blocked the light. One either side, they left her walking in shadow. They looked big enough in Glenfail, on the streets of Fort William they loomed like mutants, but despite their size there was something essentially non-threatening about them, perhaps just the good humour of men who knew they had nothing to prove. She'd found them at lunchtime, waiting for her in the college car park, one either side of the Land Rover.

'We tracked you down through Callum,' Alan said

She nodded. It was typical that Callum should be their friend – her worst student; a charming, feckless, drunkard of twenty-two, whose written work was all but illegible and whose typing contained so many spelling errors she'd returned it unmarked, only to have him claim that she should be lenient as English was his second language behind Gaelic.

'Yon McSlyther's been trying tae cause problems,' he went on. 'He tried tae search the van and we saw him off, but then he said you'd refused him access on your land. Is that right?'

Claire brushed back her hair. How much to say? Were they allies or troublemakers? She thought that if it ever came to a show-down, Alan and Drew would be formidable, but she couldn't be sure. She'd met dozens of martial artists who could never actually face a fight and a few mad bastards like Liam who fought sideways, failing to front up and attack fairly. Then there were people, like herself she realised, who fought from instinct. People for whom the

GATEKEEPER

fist was not the last recourse, but the first response. Even if these two weren't fighters, they would intimidate anybody who came close to the wolves. Good enough – time to pitch for friendship.

'Yes it is,' she stopped outside the pub they were planning to enter, knowing it by reputation as a student dive. 'Look, if there are students in there cutting lectures, it'll be difficult for all of us. Can we go somewhere else?'

Drew turned without speaking and headed down an alley alongside the building and Alan made a courtly gesture for her to follow. They climbed a metal fire escape and Drew leaned on the fire door. Nothing happened. He lifted his foot and kicked it. It opened from inside. The men already in the room seemed to have come from the same genetic subset as the McDowells – big, tartan-clad, tattooed. She stared as Drew reached down to a tray full of plastic glasses of beer and handed her one.

'Athletes,' Alan said, indicating the crowd. She felt her stare getting wider and tried to look unsurprised although her eyebrows were crawling into her hairline. 'The Games,' he added.

'Ah.' She was no wiser, but there had to be some reason for a dozen large men to be stood in an upstairs room, drinking beer.

'Carbohydrate loading,' Alan said, grasping a beer himself. 'Getting tae the end of the season now, but still ...' he drank deeply. 'They take their ale seriously.'

Wide backs and tree-like legs moved aside under the pressure of Drew's outstretched arm and she followed through the press to a table at the back of the room.

'Well, we're grateful,' said Alan as they sat. 'Drew here has something for you.'

She glanced at Drew who was pulling something from his knapsack and saw that he was blushing pink.

'Harris Tweed,' he said. She felt that if she put her hand on the metal table top she would feel it vibrate to his voice.

169

KAY SEXTON

She opened the plastic bag to find a length of heavy cloth, a soft grey flecked with heathery purple and black.

'I can't accept this,' she said. 'It must be worth a fortune.'

'You can, and you will.' Alan put his great freckled hand out and rubbed the cloth between finger and thumb. 'Drew wins them; they're prizes at the games. He'll be upset if you don't.'

'But surely there's somebody else you should give it to, a girl-friend ... or ...' she wondered if she'd made a mistake. Drew was now white, with olive-coloured freckles showing like bird drop-pings on his face and his lips had vanished in a thin pale line under his moustache.

'Well, that's something of a sore point,' Alan said. 'Drew's girl-friend isn't exactly speaking tae him at the moment. She wanted him to enter a weightlifting competition to win a car in Hull, the same weekend as the Callander World Highland Games.'

Drew nodded.

'So he didn't go tae Hull and the man who won the car lifted very little in truth, much less than Drew could lift, and tae top it all he was beaten anyway in the caber toss at Callander, so she's not talking tae us.' Alan patted the cloth. 'It's a thank-you for standing up tae McSlyther. Also, our mother says she'll be happy if she never sees another Harris tweed length as long as she lives, she's a drawer-full at home already.'

'Thank you, it's lovely,' she said. 'I'll make it into something special.'

'Aye and anyway, we wanted tae talk tae you,' Alan's voice held all the embarrassment of a man who hated being thanked and con-cealed it with false menace. 'You've got a secret, have you not?'

She drank, wondering what they knew, or thought they knew. 'I don't think so. What kind of secret?'

'John Mearns said he saw you pairforming some art or other,' Alan said.

She parsed the sentence twice in her head before working out what he meant. 'Performing? You mean Tae Kwon Do?'

GATEKEEPER

'Aye, something of that kind. Would you be a martial artist then?'

She shrugged, back on safe ground, but disappointed that this wasn't a covert contact from The Project. 'I hold a black belt, fourth Dan. Probably fifth Dan now, although I haven't been training seriously since I moved to Rome and then here.'

'Well, that's good,' Alan seemed impressed. 'You should be able tae defend yourself anyway.'

'Do I need to be able to defend myself?' she looked around at the giants.

'If you get on the wrong side of Noel McIver you're probably not going tae have the smoothest path,' he replied.

'But he's not violent, is he?'

'No, he's not, but he could drive anybody else tae violence and that's a fact.'

The fire door was booted from outside and it opened to reveal a Chinese man in a white apron carrying four white paper sacks. He put down the bags, shook hands with the nearest men and vanished again.

'It costs a small fortune tae keep a man fit for the games,' explained Alan as the gigantic men began to pull open the bags and take out tinfoil containers and plastic spoons. 'We have an arrangement with some of the good folk of Fort William: the pie shop, the supermarket, Nam Fung's Chinese restaurant, the ladies who run the sandwich round ... They bring their leftover food for the athletes, who make sure there's no trouble around their premises. It's a brave wee laddie who'll spray his name on a shop wall if he thinks two of these will come visit him. It's a small community here, you see, we take care of our own.'

Own sounded like 'ain'. Claire nodded, she could understand that philosophy completely, it was the one she lived by.

'So if McIver gives you any trouble, Claire, you let us know.'

Drew returned with a carton of spare ribs which he ploughed through, pausing only to drink more ale.

171

They walked her back to the car and as she drove home she wondered what Mrs McDowell was like and whether she would ever see her.

The next day Isobel was to introduce her to the Henwife, a Highland woman who had researched the old folk medicines of the region and now ran a healing practice from her home near Loch Ness – it sort of fitted into the research Claire was supposed to be undertaking. In the car, Claire began to probe the bad blood between her neighbours.

'Is there a reason that Drew and Alan are so down on Noel McIver: apart from the logs, I mean?'

'Have they not told you?' Isobel gave her a glance, a prickly suspicious scrutiny that reminded Claire she was still an outsider. 'Och, it's not my job to rake the coals – although I'm surprised they've kept quiet about it. Maybe they're learning some sense at last. Turn right here.'

Claire followed the directions and wondered how far to push her neighbour. 'Is it the kind of thing they'd tell me? I mean, is it embarrassing?'

'Who can tell? Those two are made of brass and bluster, if you ask me. Well, Alan's bluster, nobody hears much from Drew. But no, maybe they'd be ashamed. Perhaps they feel it reflects on their masculinity.'

'They don't strike me as the kind of men who have problems of that kind.'

Isobel smiled but said nothing.

'And it's not as if I can ask Noel, is it?' Claire continued. 'As he isn't talking to me.'

'Is he not? Och he's an old fool sometimes.' Isobel folded her hands, a sign Claire already recognised as the precursor to gossip. 'Well, perhaps it's better if you hear it from me than from them – they aren't the calmest of boys when it comes to what they think of as their grievances.'

GATEKEEPER

'Do they have a grievance against Noel?'

'I'll let you judge for yourself. It would be about six months ago now, maybe more, because it was before lambing. December or January of last year, then. Noel shot one of their dogs – Tina Turner she was called. They'd got her from a beggar in Glasgow when she was about eight months old: a cross Collie-Alsatian. You can say what you like about the McDowell's but they're all fine judges of animals. She was a beauty – and clever. Big too. They took her everywhere. She was too old and a bit too tall to be trained properly for sheep – you have to start a dog in the field at its mother's side to really get a good working dog, but for all that, she had the makings of a champion. So they mated her to one of Tim Gordon's dogs over the hill and she had three pups, all male. They let the pups go because they wanted a bitch to bring on, and they were waiting for her next season. Tam was to train the pup, he'd won many a show with his old dog Rob, that's the dog who sired Nell, Noel's bitch.'

Claire was lost. 'Hang on, let me get this straight. Noel has a dog from the McDowell's?'

'Och, they got on well enough until Tina Turner was killed.'

'What happened then?'

'That's the problem. The only person who really knows is Noel and the boys don't accept his story.'

'Which is?' Claire held her breath, hoping Isobel wouldn't pause to think and decide not to continue.

'He says he saw the dog worrying sheep. We all knew she'd run off - we'd heard the boys trying to find her up on the hill – but the very next day, Noel told Drew he'd caught the dog running down pregnant ewes and he'd shot her.'

'Surely they can't argue with that?'

'If that was the whole of it, no. But Noel said he'd taken her body to the incinerator in Lerwick and had her burnt. The boys were in a frenzy with him for weeks.'

'Why?'

'Because if a dog has turned against the flock, you can tell. It will have mutton in its stomach if it's a killer, or fleece, from nipping at them, if it hasn't quite graduated to killing. If Tina was chasing sheep there should have been evidence – a vet could have confirmed it for sure.'

'Even so ...'

'Even so, as you say. But the way the McDowell's tell it, Noel hit the dog with his car when he was messing around off the road. You know how he likes to range the hills. And to cover up his trespass, he said he'd caught her at the sheep.'

'And then destroyed her body, so nobody could check his story. I see.' Claire grimaced.

'They didn't leave it there though. Drew went to the incinerator.'

Claire could imagine what it must be like to have an angry Drew McDowell facing you. 'Did he do anything?'

'You mean like tear somebody's head off?' Isobel chuckled but the sound was uncomfortable. 'No but he made enough of a fuss and frightened the man there so badly he was prosecuted for threats and given an injunction against any violent act.'

'And did he keep it?

'Och, yes. When Noel McIver's fine 4 x 4 was trashed, Drew was in the pub in Fort William with the Constable, arguing about the Clearances.'

Claire kept a straight face and focused on the road. 'Alan's a big lad though.'

'Indeed. And nobody doubts it was Alan who did it. But doubt and proof are different things. The insurance paid out, but Noel never replaced the vehicle. He has the Forestry van now – and he's told everybody that if it gets so much as a flat tyre he'll call down the company on the McDowells. A company action could lose Tam his new tenancy.'

'I thought they'd been here all along, the McDowells?'

'They're from the Islands. Came over about four years ago, under some scheme the Executive set up to protect the crofting lifestyle. Their little croft couldn't keep three grown men farming, so they were offered a bigger place here. Alan makes it sound as if he was born in sight of Streap: like a Scot off the telly, he is, talking what they call the McGibson dialect around here, for Mel Gibson, you know, in Braveheart? You hear it a lot on those who want to sport their Scots credentials. But Alan's aye coigreach for all that.'

'Coigreach?'

An outrel like yourself.'

'An outrel?' Claire felt the sting of it even before the translation. 'An outsider then.'

The rest of the journey passed in more general conversation and the Henwife, who was middle-aged and well set up, annoyed Isobel enough to be declared a fraud 'only using the stupid to make herself some money'. On the way home Claire received a brisk lesson in some more Scots words, because, as Isobel said 'she'd never master the Gaelic.' That stung too, her weeks of integration dismissed and her linguistic skills denigrated. She wanted to point out that she'd coped in Anatolia and Carpathia and was able to hold her own in a Roman argument, but she was here to influence, not browbeat, so she took her lesson and tried to look grateful.

That night Claire sat down and made a list of all the people she knew in the village. Born and bred locals included John and Isobel Mearns, Tim Gordon, and the Maxwells who ran the beef farm and supplied the shop with clandestine milk and butter. New arrivals in the last five years were the McDowell's, Noel McIver – although Noel counted as local too - the Carline Dysters, John Heddie the pub landlord who'd moved up from Glasgow when his Highland wife Jenny needed to be close to her ill mother and Avril Johnson who had the travelling hairdressing service and lived with Jason McIntyre, a local. There was also the retired couple from London who spent all their time on the Munros.

People whose origins she didn't know included Katie Sturridge at the Post Office and Stores, Jamie Vincent the pub barman and the grim self-sufficiency family who were raising a turf-roofed barn and home-schooling their daughter: the Survivalists, Alan called them.

She felt the number of new arrivals had to be significant, but which were Project and which accidental she couldn't tell. When her list was complete she wondered what she thought she was doing. Lists. How were lists going to help the wolves? She itched to be doing something, making things happen, but she'd promised herself that she'd learnt a lesson in Anatolia and she was going to stick to it. Her job was to react - not act, to influence - not cause. The fact that doing nothing was driving her crazy was her problem – she could just damn well sit still, or go and do some Tae Kwon Do, or learn to sew and make something out of Drew's present – what she couldn't do was interfere.

Still, it was infuriating not knowing who was Project and who wasn't. She had a feeling Isobel was on her side, the amount of information the woman kept handing out was phenomenal, as if she knew Claire needed the history and biography of every villager, but she wasn't so sure about the McDowells any more – they seemed to be just general mavericks rather than actual Project members; would Blaine really have recruited such high profile, and high octane guys?

It was a mystery she couldn't solve, so she got up and went to practice her kicks, instead.

CHAPTER FIFTEEN

She heard the trail bike several times before she saw it, an enraged wasp buzzing over the horizon beyond the hill. It was a familiar sound; Akhun Halic in Anatolia had ridden one, stitching the mountains with a thin thread of sound as he toured his neighbours, conveying tobacco and booze and gathering up currency and gossip in his self-imposed role as mountain jester. For three mornings in a row she stood irresolute, twisting her key ring around her fingers, trying to decide whether to pursue the rider, whoever he or she was, or get on with her interviews while the summer freed her from teaching. As a new arrival she had every excuse to walk the hills and learn the territory her wolves might one day travel.

On the fourth morning she went to the shop for butter and milk. Katie Sturridge folded her arms under her breasts and wove Claire into the monologue that ran every day from opening time to closing, with a Greek chorus of shoppers providing contrapuntal interjections.

'Aye well, what a noise, eh? I don't know, you'd think people would have a little more respect for their neighbours but I suppose the man's an Italian, he's no idea how to do things properly.'

'An Italian?' Claire thought of Bruno on a trail bike, his elegant loafers slipping around on the pedals, and stifled a grin. It couldn't be him, but the pain she felt in her throat as she accepted that fact came as a surprise and stopped her concentrating on the next few words in the constant flow that was Katie in full spate.

177

KAY SEXTON

'... never thought we'd see the day that the land was sold over our heads and I don't care if he is supposed to be restoring ancient woodland, that's not the way to do it. Anyway, isn't that your job?'

Claire frowned, trying to work out what she'd missed. 'I deal with forestry economics and tourism, not planting. You say he's an Italian? That sounds a bit ... odd.' Bloody unlikely was what she was thinking.

'Oh no, *he's* not Italian, it's the Italian who's sent him here. The landlord: the one who's renting you High Croft – the boy's Australian.'

'Ah.' None the wiser, Claire began to stack her shopping on the counter. She knew the shopkeeper wouldn't rest until she'd shared every speck of information, and done her best to gather more.

'Yes, he was in here the other day. Nice enough lad, polite, but I couldn't understand half the things he said. He's got a tent up on the Streap side, he said, but he won't last long in that, I don't think; he'll be down the hostel on the first cold night. They've got thin blood, those Australians.'

'Mmmm,' Claire dug in her purse for change.

'But still, I said to him I thought it was odd. After all, you're the tree expert around here, teaching down at Fort William and all that, and Noel McIver's been with the Forestry all his life. And he said he was just a technician, his job was only to make sure things were going off all right. Seems a long way to send somebody, from Australia, to see how the trees are growing.'

'I'm sure they didn't send him from Australia – he's probably somebody doing a research project, like me. He could be a student in Edinburgh for all we know.'

'That's not the case,' the shopkeeper paraded her knowledge with ferocious satisfaction. 'And I'll tell you why not – I asked Noel and he said there's no such student down there.'

Claire paid attention to packing groceries into her backpack, not wanting the other woman to see how the knowledge affected

GATEKEEPER

her. 'So what's he supposed to be doing then? He's not blazing trees for felling, is he?'

'No, that's not what he's about. Noel went and had a look round where we'd heard that little buzzy motorbike of his and said that there's nothing amiss at all. I believe that it's something to do with counting the different kind of trees up there.'

'Species density and distribution?'

'There! I told Noel you'd have the answers right in your head. That's exactly what the boy said when I asked him. Nice lad – but a bit wild, is the way I see it. Maybe his family have sent him from Australia to here, like we used to send our black sheep over there!' She laughed at her own joke and Claire escaped under cover of the witticism.

A nice lad but wild, being paid by Signore Ottaviano to check the growth of the newly-planted trees on a cross-country bike - it sounded like one of Blaine's people examining the land. Down in Fort William she bought an extra two bottles of wine: a Soave and a good red from the Tuscan hills, and extra bread and cheese from the delicatessen. She would track him down the next morning.

As she lay in the narrow bed she heard a rabbit scream and then stop. She pressed her arm over her face to weigh down her eyelids so they didn't spring wide at every breeze and rustle.

When she woke, the landscape was swaddled in white cloud. She didn't know if she'd be able to hear the bike in such deceptive conditions. The mountain rescue team would be advising all climbers and hill walkers to stay away from high ground until the weather cleared, and then sitting down with radios to try and find the groups already trapped on the hills by the treacherous fog.

It was a bad idea to be walking alone in the damp blindness, but she did it anyway, trekking the hill until she found the place she thought she'd heard the bike, and then examining the ground for tracks. Where there was mud she could pick out tyre-marks but within a few yards the tussocky grass and heather concealed the

KAY SEXTON

bike's passing. She hitched up her pack and decided to walk to the top of the waterfall – at least she could follow the sound of the water up, and if the weather was still bad she could walk down the other side and get a lift back with the Forestry workers.

He was at the bottom of the falls. She saw the beetle-green bike resting against one of the rocks and stopped, wondering whether it was a good idea to announce her presence, or if she should get a look at him first and decide from that if she wanted him to know she'd been trying to find him.

After a few minutes wait, during which she listened but heard nothing to suggest where he might be, Claire tucked her pack out of sight behind a rock and moved to the bike. The tank was cold. She bent to the exhaust, wary that it might burn her, but it was cold too. The metal would chill fast in the mist but it still suggested he hadn't arrived here recently. She began to work in circles out from the bike, but there was no sign of him until she heard a dull metallic clink. It was the sound of a climber: a carabiner banging against rock. She moved backwards, trying to make the face of the waterfall appear out of the mist, but she could see nothing. She waited about fifteen yards from the bike, well out of the range of mist vision, but he headed straight towards her. She stepped forward to meet him.

'Claire,' he said. 'I wondered when you'd find me. I've got photos for you.'

She looked at him. He was young, but like Blaine he had the exposure-weathered features and old skin of a climber or skier. His hair was shoulder-length, more than enough to persuade Katie Sturridge he was wild, and hung in streaming tails from the waterfall's spray – when it wasn't soaked it would be blond. He was wearing an old check shirt and jeans with a climbing harness and boots. No climbing helmet, no gloves. One of those anarchic adventurers who would rather climb solo and die, than rope to a team in safety. It still didn't mean he was Project though.

180

GATEKEEPER

'How did *you* find me?' She indicated the fog around them, keeping her face deadpan.

'Just a bit of luck – fog thins near running water. Up top there I could see you, but once I got halfway down you'd disappeared – I took a bearing on your direction and kept heading that way.'

She nodded. There was a long moment of silence and then he grinned. 'I'm Shaun. Ciprian sends his regards.'

She let herself smile back, recognising the nearest thing to a password she could have expected to hear. The climber moved forward, crowding her space, and held out his hand. She shook, feeling the striated palms and roughened knuckles of a recent climb.

His eyes darkened as he looked her over. 'Want to come up? I've top-roped all the way – it's a pretty nice face.' The double meaning was clear and his interest in her was nakedly physical. For the first time since she'd arrived in Scotland she felt the hot squirming of desire in her body, tightening her breasts and making her thighs heavy and warm. She watched his mouth, seeing his smile fade into a softer and more fragile shape, not quite a pout but not neutral either, the blood-engorged tissue seeming darker and riper.

He tucked his thumbs into his climb harness, unconsciously drawing attention to his jeans: pale and thin, worn to softness; smeared with moss and damp; clinging to his body and outlining the solid weight and faint curve of his erection. She lifted her eyes to his again and saw that the pale colour had gone from them. His pupils had expanded to give him an ink-dark expression. She moved into his space and watched his eyes widen until the black circles were almost surrounded by bright whiteness: a combination of desire and apprehension that made her feel powerful.

'What will I find, at the top?' She thought she sounded like the worst kind of Hollywood *femme fatale* but dialogue didn't seem important. What mattered was the connection between them: a thin singing line in the white mist, something she could use to haul him in like a landed fish.

181

KAY SEXTON

Still he didn't smile, simply blew out a husky breath, the kind she'd heard herself make when she'd rounded a difficult overhang on a tough climb. 'Whatever you want.'

'That's a bit extreme, isn't it?' She thought she was flirting but she wasn't sure – the intensity of his stare made her responses sound menacing.

'If I can deliver it – it's yours.' His voice broke and faded away almost to nothing on the last words. She had to lean forward to hear him and as she did she caught her first smell of him: cold foliage and hot flesh, a combination of old moss and the warmth of a young man, both underpinned with the dense, almost scentless weight of a hill fog that held down the smells of heather and peat. He smelt desirable, like lemongrass and fresh denim and she inhaled, watching him rear his head back like a startled horse.

'Fucking hell,' he said. 'Jesus fucking Christ on a crutch. He'd never have let me come if he'd known.'

'He' was Blaine, she knew it as certainly as she knew that this man in front of her was almost quivering with sexual need. 'Known what?'

He smiled now, a wide smile, showing perfect white teeth. 'I can't take you up the waterfall, Claire. I'm shaking too much. It's about all I can do to stay on my feet – in fact I might keel over at any moment. I hope you know life-saving?'

She grinned back, infected by his outrageous remarks. 'Known what?' she repeated.

'You should be called Diana: I feel like I've just been stabbed through the heart by the fucking goddess of the hunt!' He placed his hand on his shirt. 'Look, you can see the wound.' He pulled the fabric open and revealed a fine line of tan hair running down a sculpted chest to a narrow abdomen. 'You might have to come a bit closer though; this fog makes things hard to see, don't you think?'

She was still smiling as she put her hand on his flesh, feeling the beat of his heart through her palm and all her fingers, but she

182

GATEKEEPER

stopped smiling as he leaned into her, pushing his weight against her, until his head touched hers and his wet hair was dripping onto her shoulder. She lifted her face and felt his lips, wide and cold, against her mouth.

He was still pushing against her, and she took a step backwards, to find herself off balance. He grabbed her without breaking the kiss, and they half-stumbled, half sat, the grass and bracken beneath them as slick as a wet silk sheet, throwing them off balance again and towards each other. She set her hand against his chin and pushed his head back, catching sight of widely-spaced nipples like copper coins, before the shirt swung across to hide them. As she sprawled over him she felt heat rising from the columns of his thighs and pressed down with her pubic bone, grinding their bodies together. He groaned, and she reached down to unzip his jeans, shoving away the bulky shirt to try and pull the wet denim down over his hips. He arched his back to help her, and as his head tipped back against the ground she saw his eyes were still wide and dark and his jaw set in a rictus; desire married to an urgency she knew she would find ridiculous if she gave herself even a second to consider.

So she didn't. She dragged down her own canvas trousers, thrusting them do her ankles where they became trapped by her boots. As she straddled him she saw his head was still tilted back, so his eyes stared into a distance that didn't include her, but as she lifted his penis, feeling the slick movement of his foreskin as she prepared to slide him inside her, he lifted his head, supporting his body on his arms, to watch as she lowered herself, engulfing him. She moved slowly, amazed at her own wetness and at the responses that her body gave to the paradoxes of fucking a stranger in a cold white nowhere place. It made her hotter, and wetter, and more demanding than she'd ever felt, and she pushed down, shoving his body into the ground, not caring if she tore his skin on the rough vegetation. He didn't care either, grabbing the roots of the plants to anchor himself as he thrust back at her, biting his own lower lip until it was almost blue. She rocked from side to side, trying to find a way to take more of him.

He let his arms fall, sliding his head away until he was supine, and then he lifted his hands, making two fists and she felt his roughened knuckles press against her clitoris, bouncing against her body with every thrust, while his other fist rested below her navel. She curved over it, pressing in and down on his hands and felt the head of his penis pushing against his upper fist, thinning the wall of her body until it felt as if she wasn't really there, or was just a membrane between the two parts of him. Her orgasm, when it came, was unexpected and explosive. She pushed away from the ground, feeling as though she could tip the planet from its orbit, and then felt his bones grinding under her as she shoved him into the earth. When he came it was a small plosive moment, a gasp, his back arching, his eyes wide, dark and for one second blind, as though an eclipse had happened in his vision, and then the wide soft smile again, two purple toothmarks in his bottom lip, his arms rising and enfolding her so that she slipped down to rest on his body, her hands sliding inside the shirt to rest along his ribs, still heaving with exertion, the crown of her head tucked under his jaw, her lips against the pulse in his neck. A new fragrance rose around them: crushed herbs and the ammonia smell of semen.

After a while his hands rose to her head and pulled off the hat. His fingers found the bands and pins in her hair and released it to fall around them, so she lay in a dark cage against his biscuit-coloured skin. He combed through and through her hair, stretching it and curling it around his fingers, pressing it between his lips, while she tried to recover from the moment and work out what could possibly happen next. Was she supposed to give this man orders or was he in charge? She didn't even know what he was here to do. Before she could plan a strategy she felt the worm stirrings of his body, the hot stretch of his penis inside her and she arched her back involuntarily,

GATEKEEPER

feeling the fabric of her trousers restrain her movement as though she was shackled.

This time he took her hands and pushed her to sit upright, then lifted himself so she was sat across his body, and they were pressed stomach to stomach. Holding her close to him, he wriggled backwards until his spine was against a boulder, then he pushed up her jacket and top and she tugged at them until she'd pulled them off her body and thrown them onto the wet ground. His hands cupped her buttocks and hers locked in his wet hair, drying a little now and beginning to curl around his face. They moved together, smiling, finding a slow cautious rhythm as though this was a battle rather than a game, and the first one to surrender to orgasm would be the loser. Even as he lengthened inside her she could feel the wetness of their previous orgasms sliding out of her, onto the soil. It seemed appropriate and she grinned at him. She ran one finger along his bottom lip, feeling the swollen heat of his bitten flesh, but before she could explore further she felt his fingers on her body, a web of fingertips massaging her labia so that she came again.

Eventually she lifted her head from his neck and stared down at him.

He grinned up at her. 'Got a tent at the top there. Still, we seem to have coped pretty well without it.'

CHAPTER SIXTEEN

Claire chose not to think about Bruno, or why she'd launched into sex with Shaun without any planning. Shaun was here and Bruno wasn't and this was what she'd come here to do. Work for the wolves. Shaun's interest in her was empowering, and added to his other interest it made him irresistible because at last she'd discovered the zealotry Ansel had warned her about: Shaun was the wolf fan personified.

And he had photos of her wolves. She wasn't allowed to take them back to the croft, so she spent hours on the turf outside his tent, studying the images of the cubs, learning to recognise them from their markings and to understand distinctive behaviours so she could tell them apart from a distance or in poor light.

He would fan the pictures and pass her one. 'That's H1, he's going to be the alpha, we think. Obviously it has to be H1 or H2, being as they're the only guys, but H1's always been dominant. Look at how he curls his lip; that's a real sneer with attitude, isn't it?'

Shaun knew the cubs so well that Claire sometimes wanted to turn her back on him so she could explore the pictures alone, but she needed to draw his knowledge from him. She was jealous of his closeness to her pack though, and it separated the two lives she had with Shaun. Together, but without the photographs, they played and laughed and fucked, eating huge amounts of transportable food as they turned the Highlands into a vast picnic area. When the photographs came out she felt a glass wall slide between them. He was on one side, with the whole world of the wolves and The Project open to him, and she was pressed against the other side, seeing but not feeling. She didn't resent him, or his depth of knowledge, but the exclusion made her feel isolated and cold – an operative rather than a real partner in this dangerous game.

'See H2 in this picture here – standing on this log? He's the subordinate male, we can't really call him a beta where there's only two males. He's got this blackish blotch on his right ear. Very distinctive – you can pick it out in the dark, even at night under trees. He's the class clown, a real dag. If you can fall off it, tip it over, lose it or trip yourself up with it; he's your wolf to do it. Right after this picture was taken he pitched himself off the log and smacked his nose and then ran around yelping until his brother told him to shut up.' Shaun's smile came from far away, a place and time distant from her - where the tumbling pack of cubs wriggled and learned and fought their way to social coherence. She wanted to see them for herself, wanted it so much she had to unclench her jaw to make polite interjections into his commentary.

'Have you seen the other pack too?'

'Yup.'

'Can you tell me about them?'

'Nope.'

She didn't allow herself to sigh.

'Tell me more about the hunting.'

'They hunt live prey now. We opened up the small enclosure – we've got a tunnel that runs to a hunting enclosure see, and when the electric door goes up, they can go through. That means we can put livestock in the hunting enclosure without them coming into contact with humans.'

Claire remembered her suggestion to Maggie, out in the desert. Blaine's team seemed to know their business, 'And they can take down a deer?'

KAY SEXTON

'Yup. It's pretty scary sometimes. In an enclosed area a deer can't get away, so it kicks out, you know? Weird really. In the wild they give up easier, because they're part of the herd I guess and when they see the others heading off they lose the will to fight, but in an enclosure and all alone they sometimes fight like crazy. H4, she got kicked in the ribs by one deer, sent her flying, and for a couple of days they were worried she'd broken a rib. They even flew the vet in, but it seems she was just bruised. They try not to have any contact with the wolves, see, so medical care is a real problem. The sister's been spayed but apart from that, they're pretty well on their own, too much human contact would make them non-viable in the wild.'

He rolled over, tucking the photos back into his daypack and grabbed her arm, tugging her towards him and mashing their lips together in a brutal kiss. He liked it that way, she was getting to learn his triggers and this was one of them: he enjoyed swift, thought-free sex, something as intense and throwaway as a sneeze. She did too, but this time a part of her brain stayed above the fucking, thinking about what he'd said. The clear implication of his remark was that the packs wouldn't be viable until he went back with his report. Her vision lifted above their bodies, twisting together on a grassy outcrop halfway up a hillside, and became an eagle's eye, surveying the whole of the Highlands. She didn't know where the other pack might be placed, she didn't even know if he'd been there yet or still had to visit the location. She didn't know if he'd fucked, or would fuck, the other potential Gatekeeper. The thought that what they were doing now could influence his decision made her pause for a second, both her body on the ground, slamming his into the turf, and her high-lifting hyper-vision, cold and detailed, above the Scottish hills. It was a test. If she hadn't liked him, found him sexually attractive, started to feel that she might be capable of loving this man, it would have been easier. If he were a task, a part of the plan, she could have gritted her teeth and fucked him, seeing him as an obstacle to be overcome, a stranger to be turned into an ally. But

188

he'd already crept under her defences – she'd come to think of him as a friend and a lover in just a couple of weeks. Not like Bruno, of course, but still somebody she liked, and maybe even somebody she could trust.

Poised above him, she looked down. Down into his face, empty of thought, teeth showing, striving to get her to her move, to restore the momentum that would lead to orgasm and down from the high places, empty air whistling past her as she plummeted from the chill peaks back to the valleys knitted with sheep and cattle. There was no sense to it. It should be easier to please a man she liked than one she didn't, but it didn't seem to work that way. She looked away, pretending he was a nameless stranger, a man who might help the wolves if she made him orgasm more explosively then he ever had before. Below her, Shaun's back arched into pleasure, his fists denting the grass, his pupils huge and black, stark with hysteria or addiction.

She didn't want to love a man if she also had to rely on him. That was what it came down to. She realised the darkness of the truth that night as she sat in the croft and worked through her lecture notes for the following week.

She could love Bruno because she would never have to depend on him – he was a companion, a lover, a friend, but never an ally, the value of their relationship lay in the simple fact that they were equals. Shaun believed some of the same things she did and they might find themselves fighting together, but she'd never allow herself to relax with him because she didn't want even a moment of vulnerability that might allow him to see into her personality and use that as leverage against her if they disagreed about the future of the pack.

On the other hand, the sex was good almost beyond control; whenever there was opportunity they both felt an instant pulse that pushed them towards each other and made them into brutal creatures, tearing at each other. The companionship was great too; he was an intuitive climber and walker, willing to let long periods pass in silence, able to pick out birdsong from the breeze and fossils in the rock face and bring them to her attention. She trusted him on the rock and in her bed, but she didn't want him to know more about her than he already did.

She began to push him, demanding more of him sexually, challenging him to hold back on his own orgasm until she was ready for him to come. His response was to match, and exceed, her demands. The more extreme she became, the more flamboyant his desire to excel.

Claire took on more work from the college – project-marking for the geography department. Reams of files filled her kitchen and every time she left the waterfall she sat late into the night, poring over graphs or surveys, checking statistical data on her calculator. It stopped her thinking about Shaun. Something was badly wrong, not in him, but in her. The drive to dominate was a perversity of her own nature, however natural the willingness to be dominated was to his. She knew she was replaying her parents' marriage, trying to find in herself whatever it was that had made them so mutually dependent and manipulative under the wholesome surface of their marriage.

The idea sickened her more each time she gave in to the urge to make him do what she wanted, but she also knew that she'd found the way to get Shaun on her side. While Blaine could never have expected this to happen when he told her she'd have to do whatever it took, she was going to exploit the situation as far as she could, for the sake of her wolf pack.

She played her role to the full: now she took the photos from his hand as soon as he produced them, and held them out one at a time for his comments, not giving him any choice in the order in which they viewed them.

'That's H5. She's one of the females unrelated to our two boy cubs. You can pick her out because she's the biggest female and she's always at the front – any photo, any activity, you'll see her and H1 in the lead. She's the greyest of the pack: looks most like what people think of as a wolf.' He reached up to point to something in the back of the photograph.

'That's where she hangs out, dug herself a little scrape like a mini-den. It's a fantastic sign that she's developing instinctive pack behaviours. There's no role model for them to follow so we have to hope that a lot of their skills will turn out to be hard-wired.'

Claire studied the wolf. She had light tea-coloured eyes, her expression was self-contained and confident; not so much relaxed as at home. She had something of the air of a popular head girl at a good school; an all-round performer. Probably she also had the lupine equivalent of a nice nature and child-bearing hips.

She had nothing of the charisma of H1 though, nor the knock-about charm of his brother, H2. Those two, with their sandy-grey coats, creamy throats and bellies, and deep amber eyes were stunning. Their sister H3 was also impressive. Smaller and paler than her brothers, more brown coated than they were, she looked a little like a coyote, but her eyes, Nefertiti-slanted and bright orange, were astonishingly beautiful and she seemed to demand the protection of her male siblings with a coquettish air that suggested the heroine of a historical romance.

He carried on, 'Most people think grey when they think wolf – but that's the Timber wolf. European wolves have a wide colour variation. Look at H4, she's one of the other unrelated cubs. She's really dark; grey and brown mixed, with a black rim to her ears and no lightness to her underparts at all.'

'Does it have value? I mean, is it a survival construct for European wolves to be different colours?'

'I wish we knew,' He sat up straight, tearing at the grass and piling the broken stems into a little hayrick. 'Sometimes it drives you mad. You spend half your life creeping up on something, looking sideways, pretending you're not that interested, for the sake

KAY SEXTON

of The Project.' He stared at her, challenging her. 'You know, if I could, I'd walk into that huge empire you work for in Rome – I'd find their wolf guy, and I'd sit down and ask him a thousand questions like: is coat variation an evolutionary mechanism? What's the viability of a pack that has only three genetically unrelated members? Will wolves take wild prey over livestock if all other variables are equal? But I can't do that.' He flatted his pile of grass with his palm. 'Because he only needs to ask me one question in return, doesn't he?'

She nodded. The question was - why do you want to know? She watched him shredding the grass, tearing each blade into tiny fragments. 'So what do we know?' she asked.

'Well, not a lot really.' His sigh was frustrated. 'We just have to hope. We get some good information from the people running the Glen Affric appeal, but it all has to be channelled through one person; a volunteer of theirs who's one of us too, and because she's low-level she can't ask too much.'

Claire unlocked her jaw, consciously relaxing. She broke off a chunk of the energy bar she was holding and passed it to him.

'Did you know wolves can point?' he asked.

She laughed.

'No seriously. Apes can't point, but wolves can. Well, to be fair to apes, it's a bit more complicated than that. Gorillas that have been raised in captivity learn to do a kind of pointing, when they want something,' he crooked his fingers and waved his hand generally in the direction of the energy bar. She broke off a bit and fed it to him.

'But they never point for information, right? So you might see an eagle and point to it, or stick your hand out to indicate that you can see Drew going past with his caber, yeah? But apes never learn to share something interesting like that. Wolves do though.'

He grabbed the photos, riffling through them, pulling out three or four. 'Look, see here?' He pointed to H1. The wolf was standing, his head erect, tail medium high, one paw raised. 'That's a wolf pointing.'

She took the photo. 'He just looks alert to me.'

'Nope. This is alert.' He passed her another photo where all four of H1's feet were on the ground and his ears were forward. 'See the difference?'

She studied the images side by side. 'Okay, I think so.'

'Now look – here's H2 pointing and H1 looking.'

She saw the difference. H2 really was pointing, his foot slightly raised, his muzzle indicating the direction of whatever he was focused on. She followed the line of his gaze, peering into the detail at the back of the photograph.

'A beetle?' she guessed.

'In one! Nothing wrong with your eyes! Look at H1 – no, it's no good, you're going to have to name these wolves, Claire. We can't go on using their indicators.'

She felt a brief rush of joy.

'I thought we weren't supposed to name them?'

'That was only while we waited to see if they'd become packs, until they did they were just research subjects, and you don't name research animals: too much emotional investment. Now they've sorted themselves into proper packs, you might as well name 'em. Blaine says it's your reward for being so disciplined for so long. Anyway the other Gatekeeper's already named hers.'

The joy collapsed like a failed cake.

'What has she called them?'

'Flint, Mica, Agate and Beryl. Flint and Mica are male, the others female.' He glanced at her and away, shuffling the photos again.

'Pick out the pointing behaviour,' he said.

She sorted the images. In seven of them wolves were pointing, and in all but two of those pictures it was the males who pointed. She wouldn't have believed it an hour ago, but male wolves really did point, simply to share an interesting view with each other. H5

KAY SEXTON

was the only female who pointed regularly and each time she was showing the others something food related.

Claire kept her head down over the photos, glad to have this task while she got her emotions in order. Then she broke up the rest of the bar and fed it to Shaun, making him 'work' for his rewards: standing on his head, performing one-armed press ups and other silly tasks that distracted him. She was still upset and wasn't sure she could hide it yet. She'd thought she was ahead, was bound to be leading this race to welcome the wolves, and now it seemed she was in second place after all.

When the food was gone she suggested they make a cairn and set Shaun to gather stones while she packed up their stuff. As soon as he was out of sight she shoved everything into the backpacks and zipped them shut, regardless of order. Then she picked up the photographs again. The other woman had a pack of four, she had five. Her wolves were better. Her wolves had to win. She stared at them: H1, alert and handsome; H2, raffish and grinning; H3 their pretty sister; H4 almost never in the picture; H5 as wholesome as muesli. She had to keep blinking the tears from her eyes. She would not let her wolves down. They would come here, they would be free, whatever it took, even if she had to go and get them herself.

When Shaun returned with his first armful of rocks she was already clearing a space and piling up four big flat stones for the base of the cairn. She smiled at him, hoping she looked brilliant and happy.

'What are we commemorating?' he asked.

'Nothing yet. We'll build the cairn first, then we'll fuck, and that'll be what we commemorate, okay?'

He grinned, it was the kind of thing he loved, working for his pleasure.

She made him wait before he came, insisting on three orgasms of her own, knowing that prolonging things was the way to make him happy – for Shaun there was no value to sex he didn't have to strive over.

GATEKEEPER

As they walked back down she listened to him humming a surfer tune under his breath, a sure sign he was contented.

She was thinking of names.

She grabbed his hand and swung it. 'I've decided what to call them,' she said.

He put down his pack and began to grub in it for the photographs.

'Don't bother – I can do it without the photos. Ready?'

He nodded.

'H1, the potential alpha, he's Flow: f-l-o-w. H2, with that mark on his ear and his behaviour, there's nothing else he could be called but Drip ...'

Shaun laughed. 'Good one. You've nailed him for sure.'

'H5, her name's Meander, you know, a big curve in a mature river? Well she's mature beyond her age and when she hunts you said she makes these curving outruns to strike the animal from the side, so Meander.'

He nodded again.

'H3, the sister to the males, she's called Caldera. A caldera is a big depression at the top of a collapsed volcano, often it fills with water but you never know when it might erupt again – she looks like she might be a bit of a hidden force. And H4, she's called Lake, smooth and calm. What do you think?'

'I think those are good names – particularly Drip.'

She let him chatter on as they continued their descent, answering with as much vitality as she could produce, but one part of her mind was with the wolves. She would not allow herself to be distracted from them now – she had to overtake the other woman and win this battle. And the other woman must feel the same. That's why Blaine wouldn't let them see the other pack, she realised, because it would stop them being so single-minded. As long as she only knew Flow, Drip, Meander, Caldera and Lake, she could fight for them, but if she ever

195

allowed herself to think that her success meant the other pack must fail ...

She pushed the thought away. The other Gatekeeper had picked rocks and stones to name her pack. But in the children's game, water wore away rock.

Shaun left soon after she named the wolves, but she was never in danger of forgetting him. His presence remained on the landscape. There were the boulders he'd levered into the burn to make it noisier, the seven hundred bare-rooted shrubs and trees he'd ordered on Signore Ottaviano's account that were planted in October, slightly earlier than she thought suitable. The little plants, dwarf birch and gean, goat willow and osier, rowan and buckthorn, stood like a twig cemetery below the saplings planted two years previously, which now resembled broom handles.

Claire had only the haziest idea what he'd been up to, and she'd refused to probe the details of his work, knowing that there was a fine line between obtaining information and seeming inquisitive. She didn't want Shaun to think she was needy, or to report anything negative about her to The Project. She was surprised to find she was relieved when he left. Surprised but happy – whatever it was that had driven her parents to distort her childhood in such a weird fashion, it wasn't part of her. In her, yes, but she could let it go.

Only when he was gone did she realise that a large part of her tension over the wolves had been the fear that she would find she was addicted to the power she'd wielded over Shaun and couldn't live without it. She liked him, she could even have loved him, but only if he'd been willing to let go of the need to be dominated, which she doubted he could do. Now he was gone, she could allow herself to feel sickened by the behaviour that had excited her at the time. Like a drunkard's child trying alcohol, she'd found that while the propensity was there, it didn't need to rule her life.

GATEKEEPER

Rearing Project

Blaine made his decision when three large prey hunts for each pack produced results similar to the first. The M pack was not viable. It was a shame, because the architect had already visited the Dutch site and approved it for wolves, before moving on to check out the Highland location. Ottaviano had obviously done all he'd promised. Blaine thought about recalling the architect to give him the news, but decided against it; let the work proceed as planned.

Deep down, Blaine had hoped both packs would make it, that the second pack could follow the first into freedom, but he'd also known the likelihood of failure. An unbalanced wolf pack had no future. Lone wolves in captivity were clinically insane, and even captive packs could turn crazy; killing their own lower-ranking members until the pack imploded.

Soon the M pack would become neurotic. Without social harmony its individuals would either retreat into apathy or become frenzied, attacking each other. Already Beryl had begun to exhibit odd neuroses, scent-marking like a male and caching food that she defended from the males but shared with Agate – she was acting as alpha male substitute. But he would do what little he could. He flew the veterinarian to the M team site.

'Can we move Agate to the H pack?' he asked.

The gamble was high. Neither raising team had known about the other; the risk of revealing that three wolves had been euthanised could tip the H team against him. Still, he couldn't kill an animal that didn't need to die. He'd seen too much needless death, both human and animal.

After several days observation they decided that Agate might fit into the H pack hierarchy and the task of killing the M pack began.

He rang Ansel. 'If it turned out that the foster-mother of the H pack could be located, and some of her bedding could be acquired, I wouldn't ask any questions about how it was done,' he said.

197

KAY SEXTON

'What should I do with the bedding, if I can get some?'

'Seal it in a plastic bag and wait until I contact you again.' Blaine was pleased that Ansel, at least, rarely asked questions or needed explanations.

Blaine slipped doses of sedative into the dead kill thrown into the enclosure. The M team volunteers observed their pack becoming lethargic and uncoordinated over several days. Blaine's veterinarian took stool samples and claimed the wolves had bovine tuberculosis. The only answer was humane killing. Blaine called Ansel to fly in and help with the closure of the site, bringing any of the H pack's foster-mother's bedding that he'd managed to locate.

On the final day they fed the wolves sedatives, this time openly; Blaine inserting them into the meat for the volunteers to see. Once the pack was sleeping, the volunteers entered the enclosure and said their goodbyes, for the first and last time able to touch the wolves they'd raised, patting the young animals and talking to them. It was a high risk manoeuvre, especially for Agate, whose continued sedation could cause permanent harm, but the volunteers had to be convinced they were the only Project, and it was over. Blaine stood guard with a rifle as the volunteers said their farewells. To refuse them the chance to say goodbye would have been cruel, but he would have accepted that responsibility – what he couldn't risk was any concealment or hurry that might have eroded their belief that The Project would end with the death of the M pack.

One man wept over Flint - Blaine had to go and lead him back out. Then the M team volunteers left for the airport accompanied by Ansel, who would ensure they all caught their flights.

When they had been gone for half an hour, the vet entered the enclosure and injected the wolves: Flint, Mica and Beryl were given lethal doses of tranquiliser and Agate just enough to keep her stupe-fied for several hours. It was a hard thing to judge – too much could suppress her breathing reflex and kill her, too little and she might regain consciousness in transit, risking harm to herself and others and certainly causing her huge mental trauma. They lifted her onto a stretcher and moved her to a travelling cage.

An hour later Blaine lifted each remaining wolf onto a canvas square and made doubly sure by dispatching each animal with a head shot. He asked the vet to help him lift each body onto a trailer and drove to a trench they had dug that morning in the middle of the enclosure.

He in-filled over the corpses with a small bulldozer hired in Declin, then waited for the Ansel to return from the airport. When he came back they laid a thin scrim of concrete over a large surface area — within hours it would look like the foundations of a house that had never been built, which, Blaine thought, was apt.

The vet monitored Agate throughout the clean up process and then they drove her, in her travel cage, wrapped in a blanket on which the H pack's foster-mother's had slept, to the German border, while Ansel returned the trailer and cement mixer to the town. On his return he would check the site for any remaining evidence of their presence before joining them. The factory would continue to run and Blaine would continue to visit. He alone would know that there was no purpose to the place any more.

Agate was slow to come round. Her eyes remained opaque and unfocused for hours after she regained consciousness in the temporary enclosure built for her alongside the H pack's territory. Her gums were pale and she had difficulty standing. When she did, she was disoriented and feeble, staggering sideways and often lying back down with her ears flat and her tail between her legs.

At dusk the H pack began a chorus howl and she lifted her ears, but neither rose nor replied.

The next morning she was still in the open, and Blaine began to fear she would not recover. Either the drugs, or the trauma, or both, had destroyed her will to survive. A lone wolf was a fragile creature — it was pack support that gave structure to wolf behaviour and a juvenile was utterly part of the group matrix. Without her pack members around her, Agate could go into shock from which she would never bother to recover.

Silent H pack volunteers monitored her on webcams. Blaine had described the failure of the M pack to them as soon as Agate was in her enclosure and after a few questions they had retreated into terse practicalities. The vet suggested setting up an intravenous feed, but Blaine rejected the idea. If Agate would not fight to survive now, she would never cope with introduction to a new pack. It would be better to let her die sooner, rather than later.

At around ten in the morning Drip approached the wire fence that separated Agate's small enclosure from the bigger territory covered by the pack. He stayed about thirty feet from the wire, aware of Agate's presence and unsure how to proceed. Blaine watched. Possession was a wolf's key characteristic; it determined every action and thought in a wolf's mind. Drip was possessing information not available to the rest of his pack and his natural curiosity and desire to 'own' the new knowledge drove him forward until, by eleven, he was a foot from the fence: stiff legged and uncertain, but unable to resist the temptation of novelty.

'Open the chute,' Blaine said. There had been a food chute at that point in the fence, which was why they'd placed Agate there, but he'd expected to wait several days before introducing Agate to the H pack, allowing them to get used to each other with the barrier between them and observing their interactions so he could choose the best moment to effect the transfer. Agate's poor condition meant they had to set caution aside.

The sound of the chute door sent Drip flying away, although his flight distance was less than fifteen feet before he stopped and turned to observe the situation – effectively he'd halved his fear of the new situation in an hour. In a matter of seconds he approached the open chute. The sound of the door was a positive one for the wolves; they associated it with food, and no matter how quietly the

GATEKEEPER

team operated the chutes, the wolves could hear each one from any point in their enclosure.

Now Drip knew he had only a matter of minutes before the rest of the pack arrived. He scented his surroundings, using his tongue as well as his nostrils to trap and examine airborne scent. Blaine knew it must be a tangle of confusing odours: Agate, people, drugs, foster-mother, all shoving for supremacy in an olfactory processing system a thousand times more sensitive than a human one.

To everybody's surprise, Drip waited barely a moment before stepping through the door. They'd removed the chute from the other side, and for a second he nosed around the bare earth where it had rested, before trotting over to Agate, where he stood in a semi-submissive posture, one foot up, tail low and ears back.

'Go on, go on!' one of the volunteers was muttering under her breath, although what she thought the wolf should go on to do was a mystery.

Flow appeared, loping towards the door and stopped thirty feet from it. Blaine noted the fight/flight distance was the same for both males, implying a rough equality of confidence. He would expect a female to stop further away, and indeed, the next wolves to appear, Meander and Lake, stopped several yards behind the male alpha. Flow growled.

From inside the small enclosure Drip replied with a juvenile yip, an apologetic sound, but one that also implied safety. Agate flicked her ears, half-raised her head, and came fully upright into a wobbly snarl, facing the young male.

'Yes!' said the volunteer and several others smiled or relaxed, but Blaine held up a cautionary hand.

Flow was stalking towards the door, his legs stiff, neck hair erect and his throat vibrating with the constant growl that was a serious threat display. The alpha male was upset and defensive, and such posturing could lead to serious injury for Drip or Agate if they failed to respect Flow's orders. He might harm Agate anyway – regardless of her response – because her weakness, unfamiliarity, and the strong odours of humanity and drugs could add up to enough of a threat to warrant the most unusual and extreme action; attacking another wolf.

There was silence in the observation room, people flicking their eyes between the two screens, which reported action on each side of the fence. Blaine felt he could hear Flow's low threat, although they were too far away for that to be the case, only yips and howls were transmitted through the tree-mounted microphones.

Drip sat down, lolling out his long pink tongue and scratched his shoulder with a back paw. Flow stopped, disconcerted by his brother's actions. Agate too seemed confused and swayed from side to side, whether from weakness or as a threat display was impossible to tell. Drip rolled onto his back and began to squirm, and Blaine could tell he was making the *hnar hnar* sounds he always made when he rolled. After a couple of seconds he stood again, trotted over to Agate and leaned against her. She staggered and he yipped in surprise as he fell.

Flow sprang through the opening, in full fighting pose and then stopped, unable to decide what to do next. Drip, dragging himself upright and looking a little ashamed, gave a short surprised bark and bounced up to his brother, shoulder-rubbing him affectionately.

Flow growled sideways at Drip, glared at Agate and stalked back through the gap. Agate sat down again, but this time upright and considerably more alert, and after a couple of glances at his retreating brother, Drip sat beside her. Flow rounded up the females and took them away, obviously feeling that his dignity needed to be restored by a display of power, especially if he couldn't control Drip.

There were a series of exhalations in the observation room. 'That went better than expected,' said Blaine, masking his relief with calmness.

Drip wandered off after an hour or so, but returned in mid-afternoon, by which time Agate had drunk from the pan of water and made herself a temporary den in the far corner of the enclosure. He approached her ingratiatingly, tail low and mouth open in greeting, and lay down beside her. At dusk he went back to the main enclosure but as the pack was not fed that day, he only nosed around for a while and then went back to sit by the doorway. The other wolves had all come over to look at Agate through the wire, but none had gone through the gap. Flow paced the main enclosure for an hour or so, being picked up by the infra-red cameras as he prowled the perimeter, presumably checking for any other new things on the outskirts of his territory.

At ten in the evening, when only a skeleton crew remained watching, and flasks of soup and coffee were being passed around the observation room, Agate stood and howled. It was the high yearning call of a lone wolf. She called twice and was answered with silence. After some minutes she called again, trying to reach a pack which no longer existed. Again she was answered with silence.

At midnight, long after the wolves would normally have settled unless they were hunting, Flow appeared on the roof of the main den. He howled; a deep-throated territorial call. Drip, by the gate, lifted his head and answered with the higher ululating tones of a chorus howl and the females joined in, lifting their voices in concert with the two males. The call lasted for three and a half minutes. Agate did not join it.

For a while there was silence. Then Flow howled again. This time, when the pack females threw themselves into the howl, Agate too raised her head and gave voice.

She was accepted by the pack, and over the next couple of weeks seemed relatively settled in the enclosure, but almost immediately Blaine had to deal with another problem. Over the years he had learned to ignore the formal route with such problems – money solved most things, misdirection usually dealt with the others. But this difficulty had become intractable.

The issue was political and he had too much experience of politics to be hopeful. Born in 1943, to a Russian mother and a Norwegian Communist father, he had developed an early appreciation of the ruthlessness of small men in positions of limited power. He had spent the first decade of his life learning to cope as a 'foreign communist' in Russia's viperous capital. Then his father, once 'beloved of Stalin' had become an outcast on the steppes, his family living on the edge of starvation. It taught him to seek solutions where possible, escape routes where not. Blaine's had been back to Norway, and the military where survival instincts were valued, and his knowledge of Russia was a currency that had brought him success.

Soon after Agate's arrival, the Mayor of Rhumberg, the nearest town, had died in a car crash. His deputy, pending an election, had revoked the factory's licence. A bribe would solve the immediate problem, except that the man who was going to be elected, and who was not the deputy, had made clear that anybody who financed the interim mayor would pay for it when he took over. His grip had already extended to grasp many small businesses in the town. The wolf pack's days in Eastern Europe were numbered.

Blaine had hoped to keep them in Germany for another year while the Gatekeeper bedded down into her location, but he knew that the day after the election the cars would roll and black-suited men would step onto his land. They would be followed by trucks which would take away his plant, his stock and his papers. They might burn the buildings – it had happened elsewhere – and they would find and shoot the wolves.

For a single day he considered the logistics of moving them back to the abandoned site of the M Pack but it wasn't practical for two reasons. Relocation would have damaged the training the H Pack's foster-mother had given them. A training based on their enclosure landscape, which had been planned to seem as much like the release site as possible. Also, if Agate returned to her old home she would probably compete for alpha female status, damaging the pack dynamic beyond repair.

Instead he told the raising project team members to ready the transporter. Then he went to the Mayor-to-be and traded a substantial donation to election funds for a licence to export small arms and guaranteed round-the-clock protection for his factory until election day. With this small illusion he planned to distract any observers. A heavily-guarded security truck filled with crates would leave for the border. After dark the wolves would leave too in their battered lorry. With any luck, local eyes would follow the truck. Blaine would stay and host an election party in town. Once the wolves left, his job was done. Whatever success they achieved would be beyond his control. He wasn't optimistic – his experience had shown him that most of the time, freedom was too difficult, whether for people or animals.

Even so, they had a chance, something that The Project had given them. He'd spent his whole life being watched and doubted, trying to fit into situations where he was viewed as a threat or a risk. The Project was the only thing he'd been able to do without constant oversight, and he'd had to wait until he retired to take an active part in it. Without it as a secret strand of his life, he'd have felt he had no independence at all – to be able to live without borders and constraints was impossible for him, but perhaps, if everything went well, it would be possible for the pack.

CHAPTER SEVENTEEN

Claire had never thought of herself as having trouble accepting good things, but the Highlands made her reassess her nature. She wrote to Ansel, explaining her daily routine: chopping wood, checking the oil tank, talking to Highlanders about the changes they'd seen in land use, comparing their stories to those she'd gathered in the Carpathian and Anatolian regions, teaching, writing chunks of thesis ... it sounded banal and she knew she'd failed to get any sense of her contentment into the words.

She couldn't express how the demands of crofter life made her happier than she'd ever been. Each day contained a series of tasks and a narrow range of choices. Gardening must be done in daylight, letters driven down to the post box by three. Rainy days meant washing had to be hung on the drying rack above the fire, sunny days had to be used to tour the area taking photographs and interviewing chance-met Highlanders and incomers. Snow had to be cleared and neighbours helped if stock went missing.

When walkers got lost on the hills, all the local residents took part in the search. As first she was asked to go to the hall and supply teas, coffees and coordination support to the radio network, but soon she was invited to join a search team, kitting up with Noel McIver and John Mearns to walk the lower slopes while other teams tracked the higher ranges. Four times in three months they were called out. The long hours spent in fog and rain, trudging the hills, seeking for any sign of lost holidaymakers or strayed scout troops, were not

GATEKEEPER

exactly happy, but she found them fulfilling. At the end of a day, sitting in the school hall, accepting coffee and whisky from the support team, she felt more useful than she had ever done.

The restricted range of life made pleasures unconditional. A bath that was hot enough to soak in was an unalloyed pleasure. The first Greater Butterfly Orchids flowering in the croft corners seemed more extravagant than a bouquet of tropical blooms. Fixing her sights on a rabbit and making a clean kill was satisfying, as was skinning and gutting the corpse, taking the head and guts up into the tree line to leave for scavengers.

She would imagine how it might be one day. The pack would be resting up, until the sound of a rifle shot brought them to their feet. To her it sounded like a large book being slammed shut. Flow would cast from side to side, investigating the air with his sensitive nose, while the alpha female, Meander, faced the rendezvous den where the cubs waited. Flow would pace a few steps each way, sampling information carried on the breeze, then he would settle again. Meander would wait a while longer, her maternal instincts less amenable than his to airborne evidence and soon she would turn and nip a lower-ranked wolf; shoulder-shoving them in the direction of the cubs. That wolf would trot back to the cubs' hiding place, giving the short ululating yips that indicated the approach of a friendly adult. The cubs would peer out: cautious, blunt-nosed, long-legged, already aware of the many risks to their survival.

Reassured, they would pour from the den, subjecting the adult to a prolonged bout of play-fighting, honing their skills and establishing their ranks in the junior hierarchy that would one day supplant Flow and Meander as pack alphas. When the light began to fail, the pups would withdraw to their hiding place again and the adult would move a safe distance away before calling.

Down in the village, the howl of a lonely wolf would weave into the soap operas on TV and the music from radios, causing farmers to call their dogs and make one more round of barns and fields. After a

KAY SEXTON

while the pack would answer, calling the lone one back to them, and together they would follow the trace particles of rabbit blood, still rich in the cooling air, to the scraps she had left for them.

The remorseless regularity of the days meant she had plenty of time to think, but there was so much pleasure in the small details of her existence that she was happy to concentrate on the minutiae of her tasks, rather than becoming introspective. It was as if she'd finally learnt to live in the moment, although she knew that impatience burned just below the surface – as long as she was able to keep busy, she could use her newly-learnt discipline of reacting rather than acting, and discovering what was really important to others. It was important that she became a full part of village life, so the mountain rescue work was a crucial step in her integration, it was equally important that she understood why young people left the Highlands and how their parents and grandparents felt about the drain of population to the cities of the South.

Unless she could demonstrate that these things mattered to her too, she would not be able to act as Gatekeeper when her wolves arrived. She'd thought she would miss Shaun, but it was Bruno she focused on when she allowed herself to feel lonely: his humour, something Shaun had lacked; his refusal to play games, whether office politics or his mother's matrimonial ones; his determination to know, understand and appreciate her without requiring her to change to fit in with him. She'd taken it all for granted in Rome, but now, looking at how she'd twisted herself to be what Shaun wanted, just to get what she wanted, in turn, from him, she saw how rare a partnership of equals might be. She'd had the chance to explore something she'd once thought impossible – a healthy adult relationship – and she'd turned it down for the wolves.

Even that didn't worry her so much any more. Distance had given her perspective and she had the feeling that Bruno understood that she was doing something that was necessary, even if she hadn't talked to him about it. She had confidence in him, if not

GATEKEEPER

herself; he knew how important he was to her, so he would know that whatever kept them apart was also important. It was something she'd once possessed herself; a sense of self-worth that came from being loved and nurtured, she'd lost it after her mother died. Then she'd met Kaya and seen something else – the potential for a change that wouldn't just improve one animal's life, but that of a whole species, maybe even a whole eco-system. She'd seen how the world would look if it had wolves running free, in sight of humanity, and the vision had been strong enough to carry her through her training. But in Rome she'd discovered that not every family had ugly secrets and many people cared about health, wellbeing and security of people and species they'd never met. She could feel the ability to trust returning, and with it, the knowledge that Bruno was giving her a chance to sort herself out.

So she didn't think about the pack, except when she was out shooting - but then, she knew, her behaviour would be considered unusual. Her neighbours either fed steaming offal straight to their dogs or took whole rabbits home and cleaned them in the kitchen, only she left the 'inedible' remnants of her kill high on the hill, where a predator might find them without risk of being seen by anybody.

Nobody had commented on her actions, which didn't mean they had gone unnoticed. Highland life required tolerance of eccentricity. In the four months she'd been here she'd learned which of her neighbours borrowed tools without returning them, and which teenagers would be driving home drunk on weekend evenings. Mary Glossop, who worked part-time in the Post Office, was fabled to call on men whose wives were away and not to leave until the next morning. Alan McDowell dealt marijuana, and both brothers took orders for cider and beer from underage drinkers, carrying booze back from Fort William. Katie Sturridge short-changed you if she was in a bad mood or didn't approve of your purchases.

Some of them had to be 'her' people, explicitly part of The Project or implicitly in favour of wolf reintroduction, but she no longer tried to guess which were allies and which might be enemies. Instead she kept her head down, limiting herself to the horizon of each day. There was nowhere else for the pack to go – her site was the best, she was sure of it. It was only a matter of time. She refused to consider that The Project might not choose her. She would not accept that her wolves might not be free.

In November, driving back from her Forestry teaching, with a portable oil radiator that Isobel had asked her to collect from the repair shop, she found the McDowell's re-hanging a gate on the Torlochie road. They flagged her down.

'Drew, Alan,' she said noncommittally.

'Claire, how're y'doin'?' Alan leaned in at the window while his brother propped himself on her front wing, rolling a suspicious-looking cigarette.

'I'm fine. Yourselves?' she waved a hand to indicate both of them.

'Not so bad. Bitty work here for the old man, he fashes over gates, him.'

She nodded. Word had it that Tam McDowell fashed about having two grown sons hanging about his croft living on benefits and polluting his caravan with their riff-raff visitors, and tried to make life as unpleasant as possible for them to persuade them to find jobs and leave home. 'It's a bit different to putting up radio masts,' she suggested

'I wouldn't know about that. Drew worked on the masts.'

Drew raised a meaty hand in acknowledgement and lit his cigarette, taking a deep drag and staring out over the gate as though some absorbing prospect filled his vision.

'So,' Alan continued. 'I expect you're wondering why we stopped you?'

'To pass the time of day?' They were notorious for preferring talk to action.

'Well yes, the pleasure of your company of course. But the old man's been hearing things.' He paused, raising his eyebrows, and his brother chuckled.

Claire turned off the engine and Alan opened the door for her to step out. She glanced from one to the other. 'What kind of things?'

'Well, I hardly like to say,' Alan leaned on the gate and Drew settled back against the car. 'I don't like to think he's subject to delusions or whatever, but he swears he heard a wolf.'

Claire gripped the top bar of the gate. 'Really?'

'Well no, I mean, there's no chance, is there? I reckoned it was Courtney Love, she's got a howl on her that could break glass. But since she was sat with him when he reckoned he heard it ...'

Courtney Love was a cross Alsatian-lurcher, at least as villainous as her owners.

'What did she do when she heard this wolf?' Claire asked.

'Now there's a smart question. According to the old man, she put her ears and tail down.' Alan said.

'Is that what she'd usually do if she heard a strange dog?'

Drew and Alan exchanged glances. It was Alan who spoke.

'Nae, that's not exactly typical behaviour from Courtney. Normally she'd be over for a fight, quick-time.'

Claire nodded. 'I'm sure it's very interesting, but ...'

'And we wondered if you'd heard anything?' Alan cut across her.

'Me? No.' I should have been told, she thought. If the wolves are here, I should have been told.

'Because, by and large, the old man's got no imagination at all. Memory yes, he's not forgotten a thing we've done wrong since the day we could walk, but he's never been one tae make up stories.'

They both stared at her with the lingering dispassion of country dwellers prepared to gaze for hours at nothing much.

'It must have been a dog,' she said.

KAY SEXTON

'Aye. We said as much. There's a fair few new dogs around — have you noticed?' Alan said.

She shook her head.

'Well then, we've a new pup, Axl Rose, goin' tae be a sheepdog, he is, we'd hae preferred a bitch but he's good enough stock. The Sturridge woman has a collie – nine months old – frae somewhere near Fort William, and those other incomers, the Survivalists, you know? Well, they've got two of those Ridgeback dogs: nice beasts by all accounts.' Alan paused reflectively, or perhaps he'd run out of words for once. She noted 'other incomers' without rancour.

'Rhodesian Ridgebacks. They'd be for hunting lions, d'y'reckon?' he continued after a moment spent watching Drew take a deep inhalation of dubiously aromatic smoke.

'For guarding stock from predators: lions, hyena, jackals, maybe, but not for hunting them.' She was leaning on the gate now, affecting a casualness she didn't feel, but prepared to let this peculiar conversation run its course. It was her job, finally. It was what she was here to do – the Gatekeeper. She'd wait until later to think about why she hadn't been told the wolves were here.

'Aye. You've been tae Africa then?'

'North Africa, not South. The desert. More risk from scorpions than lions.'

'Aye? They say it's always the little buggers that do most harm.' Alan seemed to be mining a seam of conversation and turning up platitudes with every spadeful. Drew was watching his brother closely.

'So, it will have been one of those new dogs, you reckon?' Alan had circled back to the main subject.

'Sounds more likely than a wolf,' she countered.

'Aye. But you never can tell. Would you be thinking of getting a dog yourself now?'

She tried to divine the meaning of this. Was Alan part of The Project? Did his question have the force of a command, like Eleanor's

212

invitation to learn to shoot? Or was he just making conversation? Perhaps Courtney Love had puppies they wanted to home.

'Why would I want a dog?'

'Why indeed? Just seems tae be a craze for dogs round here at the moment. Mind you, they do say you've a fair eye with that rifle of yours. Rarely do you come back without something for the pot, we hear.'

'I have shooting rights on the land,' she said, as though he'd claimed she didn't.

'Aye, and we're well pleased to have you using them. We didn't expect you'd be ...' he ran out of words.

'So in tune wi' Highland life,' offered his brother. Alan raised his eyebrows in surprise and then smiled.

'Aye. Exactly. You rose in our estimation no end when we saw you could bring down a rabbit and draw it too.' Alan finished the sentence with the self-satisfied air of a conjuror who'd pulled off a difficult trick.

Claire thought fast. 'We' seemed to mean more than the McDowell brothers, Alan gave the impression of speaking for the community as a whole, or perhaps just a section of it – maybe Project members. 'There's no point being squeamish about land management,' she said. 'When I did research in the Turkish Mountains they had an annual drive for feral goats. We shot thirty-four in two days – if we didn't cull them they'd strip the mountain of trees in a few years.'

'Like the bloody deer,' Alan interjected, banging one hand on the gate.

'Long-leggit vermin.' Drew nodded agreement.

She nodded, not sure what point they were making.

'I'd rather you shot a deer than a wolf, any day,' Alan said.

'I don't have a licence for deer.'

'Aye. Well you don't have a licence for wolf either, I reckon,' Alan laughed.

KAY SEXTON

'I wouldn't shoot a wolf,' she said. 'There would be no reason to.'

'No? If you saw one wandering down the valley you'd not shoot it?'

'No. Healthy wolves don't attack humans.'

'Is that so? But then, you don't keep stock: you might feel different if you did.'

'I hope I wouldn't. I hope nobody would. Wolves rarely attack domestic animals. They don't like coming close to houses and a good guard dog will normally scare even a pack away.'

'Is that so?' Alan seemed enthralled. 'Now, how would you know that?'

She took a deep breath. 'The research I'm doing covers three highland regions: the Carpathian and Anatolian mountains and the highlands here. They have varying degrees of farming and tourism, which is what makes them good comparison areas. And both the others have small wolf populations.'

'So you've had dealings with wolves then?' Alan was gazing at her as though she'd sprouted wings and a halo.

'No. Never. But the communities I research have evolved strategies for living alongside a variety of large predators: wolves, lynx, leopards, even bears. They're farmers too, so if wolves weren't a threat to them, I don't see why they'd be a threat here.'

Alan nodded, taking the cigarette from Drew and drawing deep on it.

'Well, be sure and let us know if you hear anything, Claire.' he said, moving back to the gatepost and rocking it with both hands.

'Aye,' said Drew taking back the cigarette and putting it out on the sole of his boot. 'We'll do the same for you.'

She drove away slowly and concentrated on the road, not allowing herself to consider what she'd heard until she was inside her own door, with the range stoked and the kettle filled. Then she sat at the table, staring out of the kitchen window.

GATEKEEPER

The pack was here. It must be. And nobody had told her. What had Blaine said at the beginning? Something about a perfect reintroduction would mean the Gatekeeper would never be needed. She hadn't thought he meant it though.

When the kettle began to sing she stood and made tea, then used the rest of the water to wash out some underclothes which she hung on the dryer. She heard the Forestry van come down off the hill and past her door. Five-thirty then. When she stepped outside there was still a band of light above the hill, but it was shrinking fast. She went back to the house and took the Browning from its locked cabinet, placing four cartridges in her waist pouch along with a whistle, torch, knife, mobile and waterproof. Apart from cleaning, she had never taken the big rifle from its case before. She chose not to consider why she was carrying it now.

With the gun over her arm she picked her way up to the tree line. About thirty metres under the cover of the branches she stopped, settling at the base of a conifer. She set the gun in her lap and closed her eyes.

For three hours she listened. She heard rabbits and voles and something that made her heart rush, until she opened her eyes and saw it was a farm cat dragging a young rabbit's corpse through the leaf litter. No cat would be hunting while wolves were around.

She gave up and went back to the cottage, locking the Browning away, replacing the cartridges in the back of the bedroom cabinet. Now she could work out why she'd taken the gun with her.

It wasn't for the wolves – she felt no fear at all of them, only fear for them. It wasn't for her neighbours – she'd been trained to keep the gate, not kill those who might enter. Her job was to measure, to examine, to persuade, delay and influence those who came close to the wolves, not to stop them. Other people might be given the task of prevention, but it wasn't hers. It wasn't for herself – she felt safer on the hills than she ever had in Rome and any attacker she met would be doubly hampered: she would know the land and she

215

would know her own abilities, they would not know either to the extent that she did. So the Browning was a proclamation. She had taken it to test herself, to know that she could sit on the hill with the gun to hand and trust herself never to need it.

And with that out of the way, she allowed herself to feel the fury that she'd suppressed since the McDowells told her their news. The wolves were here, somewhere, and nobody had even bothered to give her time to prepare. It was just over two years since she'd been kicked out of the Collective: she'd given up her future, she'd given up her social life, she'd travelled halfway round the world and learned and trained and worked for this, and The Project had dropped the wolves on her doorstep without a single word of warning. Her muscles tensed with anger and frustration and she felt like banging her head on something just to relieve the tension. Couldn't Shaun have found a way to let her know? Wasn't Ansel supposed to be her handler? Was this all that the past two years of her life was worth? Not even a hint, from the people she'd come to think of as being dedicated to the same cause as she was?

A stray thought made her count back on her fingers: yes, it was twenty-five months since she'd first met Blaine, and he'd said that the wolves The Project hoped to release would be born in the spring *after* she agreed to train as Gatekeeper. That meant something was wrong, badly wrong. The 'pack' wasn't even two years old yet, nowhere near ready for survival in the wild, the wolves wouldn't even have their full adult coats and teeth. Either the McDowells were wrong, or something had happened that had forced Blaine to free the wolves nearly a year before they were mature. And in that case, warning her might have been impossible.

She got up and took the Browning back out of the case, cleaned it, and laid it under her bed. She unlocked the ammunition box and put twelve cartridges inside her wardrobe, tucked into a pair of old hiking boots. The premature release might mean there was nobody out there to help the wolves, or her, in which case she wanted the

GATEKEEPER

gun where she could reach it, and the ammunition where she could load it. She spent the next hour practising rolling out of bed, grabbing the gun, pulling the wardrobe door open and loading the ammo. It took less than two minutes, even in the dark. If she heard a window break, or a door being kicked in, she was ready to give somebody the shock of their lives.

That night she woke five or six times, ready to hit the floor and snatch up the rifle, thinking she'd heard a howl, or a thump on the door, but each time she'd dreamed the sound.

At 5 am, with light breaking on the hills, she went to her computer. She wasn't sure where Ansel was: last time they spoke he'd been trying to get a research posting on a Fisheries Inspection Vessel in the Bering Sea, so she emailed all his accounts simultaneously. The message was simple. 'Hi, how are you? Last time we spoke you wanted to go fishing for King Crabs. Any luck? One of my neighbours reckons he heard a wolf howl behind the village. Isn't that weird?'

She signed off and grabbed a pile of multiple-choice questionnaires waiting to be marked. By seven she'd finished all her paperwork and was back in the kitchen, folding yesterday's washing. At eight she was chopping wood. By ten she'd run out of her regular tasks. She could have sat down and worked on her thesis, but she didn't want to.

She cleaned the rifles. She cleaned the windows. She went outside and cleaned the car windows; no point doing more because mud would be up to the door handles by the time she drove down to the main road, and then she cut back the herbs in the garden, trimming the mint and thyme to the ground. The energy came from her returning fury, and each time she replayed the conversation with Alan and Drew her face burned with shame – if they were Project members they must have been laughing at her, and if they weren't it was demeaning to hear about the wolves from somebody outside The Project.

KAY SEXTON

Finally she walked up to the second tree line, carrying her camera. The conifer litter didn't hold footprints and the ground underneath was dryer than bones; an elephant wouldn't make an impression on it. She spent an hour checking all the places she'd seen Shaun working, but there was nothing obvious: no scat, no new diggings, to point to the presence of wolves.

She was left with two choices: find Alan and Drew and ask for more information, or sit tight and wait to see what happened and her pride wouldn't let her approach the McDowells for help. After all, the only thing hurt was her pride, and the only thing out of control was her impatience for confirmation that the wolves had arrived. It would be pathetic beyond belief to crack now – and Alan and Drew's interrogation might just have been a final, cruel test of her ability to keep quiet no matter what the provocation. She walked back in the dark, confident that the only predator in the woods that night was herself.

CHAPTER EIGHTEEN

Two days later Ansel arrived. He had grown a beard which made him look like his own older brother. He was thinner too, his cheeks incurving, making his smile more solemn, yet gentler. He shook hands with her before leaning forward to place one formal kiss on her cheek.

On the drive back to the village he was silent until they reached the Torlundy turning, when he looked out of the car window until the houses had slipped away behind them.

'Have you seen them?'

She assessed his tone – eager, but nervous.

'No,' she fought to make her own voice sound neutral.

'So … are you sure they are here?'

She shook her head. 'Don't *you* know?'

He pressed his fingers against his face, feeling the edges of the beard as though blind. 'No. I know they … went. I don't know where.'

'Then they're here.' She changed down through the gears for the croft road.

'People want them to be here. Hope turns their imaginings to evidence. The other Gatekeeper says there have been reports of wolves in Holland too,' he said.

She concentrated on the path, not speaking until the 4 x 4 was parked on the hard standing.

219

KAY SEXTON

They're here,' she said again. Her certainty was gone though. 'Can't you ask Blaine?'

'I asked,' his fingers dabbled the beard again. 'He said I had no reason to know.'

'They're here,' she said, looking at the hill. 'My people wouldn't imagine things.'

'Your people?' He sounded surprised.

She got out of the car, opening the rear to load him up with his backpack before picking up her own shopping and the extra things her neighbours had asked her to bring from town.

'These people,' she poked her chin towards the village, 'don't make things up. You don't know them, Ansel - I do. I know the wolves are here.' She slammed the door shut with her hip. 'Wait and see.'

But once Ansel was settled in the croft she left him, saying she wanted to get a jar of jam from Isobel for breakfast. On the way down she pulled out her mobile and called up Alan's number. She couldn't decide how to open the conversation though, 'Heard any wolves lately?' seemed too blunt and anything else would lead to more confusion and Chinese whispers, so she put the phone away.

Isobel gave her a hard-eyed look and insisted she came into the kitchen.

'Is that your man from Rome?' she asked.

Claire relaxed. 'No. Anyway, I thought I told you my 'man' is just a friend now.'

'Friends visit.' Isobel fussed with half a dozen jars of preserves.

'Yes, they do. And Ansel is another friend. But not that kind. I've known him since university.'

'That's nice. I'm glad he's not your friend – I've never liked a man with a beard myself. But you must miss ... what was his name again?'

'Bruno,' she said, unconsciously lifting her hand to touch her hair.

220

GATEKEEPER

Isobel smiled.

'Have you heard anything unusual?' Claire asked, trying for a casual tone.

'Och, you mean Tam McDowell and his wolf? The man's gone mad, although when you look at the dance those boys lead him, I'm not surprised he's turning fey. They've been cutting wood again, you know?'

'Drew said they were under pain of death not to.'

'Drew said?' Isobel glanced at her. 'Well, if Drew said anything to you, you're honoured. Alan said he'd taken a liking to you.'

Claire shrugged. 'I'm not sure what you mean.'

'Drew, talking. He doesn't deign to open his mouth to most folk. Between him never speaking and Alan never shutting up, it's no wonder poor Tam's gone loopy.'

Claire took crab apple jelly back with her, along with a box of Isobel's griddle cakes for the next morning. Ansel was staring out of the kitchen window, at the hill.

'We can go up tonight if you want,' she lifted the key to the gun box from the kitchen drawer and took the .22 from its home.

'I ... tonight perhaps ...' he didn't turn to face her and she didn't help him. Whatever he had to say, she would force him to express it.

'Tonight I need to borrow your car,' he said finally. 'I shall go and see some people.'

She laid out the cleaning rod and oil and sat down to work on the .22.

'Claire?'

She ignored him.

'I'm sorry. You know it has to be this way. If you know who is Project and who isn't, you'll tend to appeal to Project members for help. Your job is to influence as many people as possible – to win them over to us, to the wolves. You can't be prejudiced for, or against, anyone.'

221

KAY SEXTON

She looked past him to the hill. 'You didn't come here for me at all, did you?'

'I did, but also ...'

'He sent you. Blaine. To talk to the others. I'm a convenient doss for you while you contact whoever actually knows about the wolves.'

'I don't even know if the wolves are here, Claire.'

'No, but you know who might be expecting them, and I don't. I feel like ...'

She didn't even know what she felt. There wasn't a single word that expressed her emotions. Somewhere out there were her wolves and she'd do her best for them, but also there were people who knew what she was here to do, and they must be watching her, judging ... 'I feel like a lab rat,' she said.

Ansel winced and she pushed the point home.

'Yes, that's it, a lab rat, being observed by some remote monster in a white coat. Can you imagine what it feels like to know that people are judging you, every minute of the day, and you don't even know who those people are?'

'I will find out if the wolves are here. I promise. And I will tell you, even if ...'

His voice faded out again and she realised he wasn't supposed to tell her even that much.

'Jesus! I'm not going to find out the truth from you either?'

'Yes, yes you are.' He came and took the gun from her, holding her hands and making her look at him. 'This is too much Claire, I agree. Nobody can be expected to work in the dark. I will find out, and I will tell you if they are here. By tomorrow morning I will know, and you will be the first person I tell.'

She nodded, trying to free her hands, but he held on.

'Listen. This is the hardest part now. For you. For some of us ...' he faded out again, looking down at her hands. 'For some the hardest part is over. Perhaps you have to understand that.'

222

GATEKEEPER

'I can't understand nonsense, Ansel. It's been two years of my life, so far – for nothing yet. How many people could do that, do you think? If you want me to trust you, tell me what you mean by 'the hardest part is over'.'

He shook his head and turned away. 'I can't tell you. I can't tell anyone. Can I have the car?'

She put the keys on the table, next to the gun.

He hadn't said she should stay home, so after a supper eaten alone, she picked up the .22, checked the Browning under the bed, and headed for the tree line. The air snapped, temperature dropping fast as the weak sun left the hill. The grass was becoming beige and sere, readying itself for snow. Once the weather broke, or 'closed in' as the Highlanders said, it would be obvious if there were wolves nearby. There would be tracks. She thought about settling at the second tree line again, but walked up higher, until she was just over the brow of the second hill, and the lights of the village had vanished. Ahead of her was the darkness of the wild hills. She put the gun over her knees, sitting on a waterproof to keep herself warm and dry, and fell into a kind of waking dream. She thought of it as clicker time, like being in the Maghreb, counting the birds in and out. She let her breathing settle until it became so slow she felt suspended in each moment.

A wolf was watching her. She realised it without moving, without even really thinking, she was so deep in her living dream. A wolf. It was the warmth she saw first, a small faint cloud of vapour hanging in the air, a combination of breath and heat given off by the working muscles of a superbly fit predator. Then, looking without looking, she saw the head, half turned away, aware of her but not looking at her. Not an aggressive posture, more enquiring. She strained to pick out more details, but against the broken ground of the hill and the trunks of the trees the dark form was almost imperceptible. She let her breathing slow even more, relaxing the

223

muscles of her body, even her eyelids, her lips, her scalp. The wolf knew she was there, but she didn't fit a pattern – she didn't move like prey or like a threat. She didn't move at all. She wasn't acting like an aggressor, nor like a meal. She wasn't identifiable and until she was, the wolf couldn't decide how to react.

And then, with liquid speed, it moved. Its head swung, triangulating three impressions: her appearance, her smell, and the environment around her, and it took one step forwards. As it moved from the shadow between the trees she saw its head clearly, eyes focused on her, one foot pausing before touching the ground.

She'd never seen this wolf before. Not in life, not in a photograph. It was a stranger. Claire forced her breathing to remain slow, but she knew adrenaline was pumping round her body, her fingers became slick with sweat and her mouth was dry. The animal lifted its muzzle, sampling the air. It picked up something of her confusion and fright and turned, vanishing silently into the space between the trees.

She broke the gun, unloaded it, and put the cartridges back in her pocket. The rules said never run, even with an unloaded gun, but she had to run now. She had to find Ansel. Something had gone wrong.

Back at the croft though, she thought again. The most she could achieve would be to walk down to the village in the hope he was there. It would look odd, and that might alert people to something being wrong, which was exactly what she mustn't do. If he'd gone further, say to the McDowell croft, she wouldn't find him anyway. And when she did confront him, she would have to convince him that the wolf she'd seen wasn't one of her pack, so she needed to be calm, rational.

She went through the animal's appearance again. Not Flow, no alpha posture. No blotch on the ear, so it wasn't Drip. Not Meander, both too small, which was subjective, and too dark, which was equally subjective but easier to quantify. The wolf she'd seen had

GATEKEEPER

been more sandy than grey and Meander was grey, her coat a solid colour. Not Caldera, because her eyes were distinctive, both bright and highly-slanted, they made her unmistakable. Lake had a dark rim, charcoal if not actually black, to her ears and the wolf she'd seen didn't have that. Was it possible the wrong pack had been released?

When she heard the 4 x 4 coming up the track she forced herself to stay in her seat. Eleven-thirty; he'd been to the pub then. She let him come into the croft before she spoke.

'I saw a wolf, Ansel.'

He nodded. He looked tired and hot, as though he'd been drinking too much.

'I know.'

'No, listen. You have to understand this; I'm not imagining things, or being neurotic. It wasn't one of my wolves.'

She expected him to argue, but he sat down hard at the table, as though pushed into his seat by a bully. 'I know,' he said again.

'You know? How do you know?' She stood in front of him, bending so she could see his face. He looked up at her and smiled; a ghastly pale grin of misery.

'Her name is Agate. She's the only survivor of the other pack.'

Claire sat. The light was too bright. Her eyes hurt. Even though she'd been home for nearly two hours, she could feel her face tightening in the heat of the house, as though she'd stood in front of a fire. She looked at her hands. They were steady.

'Survivor?'

His head dropped slowly, and then equally slowly he lifted it again. 'I can't explain.'

She remembered his help when Liam destroyed the flat and stood up again, to take hold of his shoulders. 'Then that's okay. I ... I'll take it on trust.'

It hadn't been deliberate; using the word trust had been a test of herself rather than him, a way of seeing if she really could balance her ingrained suspicion of people's motives with honest acceptance

225

KAY SEXTON

that those she knew best could be relied on. Even so, it was as if she'd used the worst psychological trick in the book to break Ansel's resistance, his face crumpled and he leaned forward to rest his head in his hands.

'You would not trust me if you knew what I have done.'

He straightened slowly, pointing her back to her seat, and she watched with pity as he held her gaze, telling her about the destruction of the other pack. He didn't look away while he described burying the bodies and transporting Agate, nor when he told about the wolf's acceptance, first by Drip, then by the rest of the pack She endured his changes of expression as he talked about how one of the volunteers had cried when he said goodbye to the animals and how Agate continued to roam the home enclosure, still calling for her family despite being accepted by a new pack.

Only then did he look away.

She couldn't think of anything to say. The enormity of what had been done extended outside anything words could express. She remembered how she'd complained earlier that she couldn't describe how she felt about being judged as a Gatekeeper. Compared to the pain Ansel was carrying, her problems were minuscule. She stood up and walked to him, standing over him again, holding out her hands. He shook his head. She could see tears trapped in the sandy lashes of his closed eyes. She leaned forward, pulling his head to her waist, holding him tight as he cried. His sobs were ugly. His hands, locked around her body, made it hard for her to breathe – he was strong, his wiry arms could pull car-sized pots of crab onto the deck of a heaving trawler. She'd forgotten that strength. She patted his back over and over until the sounds changed to gulping breaths as he fought for control.

'Okay,' she said. 'Okay, I understand. It's okay, Ansel.'

He rubbed his face, his beard sounding like the stridulating grasshoppers at the dew pond. 'It's not okay. It can never be okay.'

226

She stared over his shoulder at the dark window. Out there somewhere, were the wolves. 'Look. I'm not judging you, or anyone. But I've seen wolves in captivity – for what my opinion is worth, it's better for them to die early and clean, than live in a cage.'

'You weren't there.'

She couldn't argue with him on that. 'No, but you can tell me about it over and over until it seems like I was.'

'What good will that do?' His voice was distant.

'I don't know, maybe none. But I'm your friend, Ansel. That's what matters right now. I know I've been harsh before, over the keys. But I've learned a bit since then. Nobody's perfect, especially not me, and if you let this get to you, it'll take over your life. You'll never stop wondering if you did the right thing, and whether you could have done anything else, anything earlier, to prevent the situation. You need to let go of it. It happened, you played your part, that's it. It's over.'

He shook his head.

'Don't tell me it can never be over, Ansel. Right now it's at the front of your mind, but it will take its place behind other things, if you carry on living. But if you hang on to it, keep it always in your thoughts, it'll never develop its proper perspective. I know about this stuff, remember?'

He smiled 'And when did you last see your father?' The tone was gentle but the sarcasm came through clearly.

'Okay, I haven't 'seen' him. But we do write.'

Ansel blinked.

'See? You didn't know that, did you? I started writing to him when I was back in the desert, and now I get a letter every couple of weeks, up at the college. I didn't give him this address for … security reasons. He's got an allotment.' For a second Claire fought with her sense of reality, why was she discussing her father's new hobby with Ansel when there were wolves out there?

227

KAY SEXTON

'Anyway, the point is, if you hadn't helped me keep a sense of perspective back then, I might never have been able to have this much contact with him. I still don't get the whole illness thing; I don't understand how he and Mum lived like that, but he is my Dad and it's ... good to be back in touch with him.'

'He told me not to say anything to anyone.' Ansel twisted his beard as though trying to pull it off his face.

'Blaine, you mean?'

Ansel nodded.

'But he can't have meant me – you're my handler.'

'Yes he can. He never talks. He thinks it's unnecessary.'

Claire shook her head.

'He does! You know he never even talks about—' Ansel stopped abruptly.

Claire waited, knowing that Ansel had already been pushed past one breaking point. Anything she said or did now to influence him would be an abuse of their friendship; he was too vulnerable and confused to be sure of his judgement. She stayed silent and he sighed.

'His father was a Communist,' Ansel had made a decision of some kind. 'His mother was Russian. He was born in Russia, during the war. We didn't know anything about him, or his family until 1965. Then the police turned up at my parents' house – they said he claimed to be my father's uncle' son. They'd found him eighteen kilometres inside Norway. He had walked across the border at Kirkenes, he said. Nobody believed him. You couldn't cross the border there; if the Russians didn't get you on their side, the Norwegians did on ours. But there he was,– a grown man, an officer in the Russian Army, and an asylum seeker, claiming to be related to us.'

'So he's your ... great uncle?'

Ansel grimaced. 'I wasn't even born when he was found. Or as the police said 'caught'. Once my father admitted that the family

228

hadn't heard from the communist uncle since 1942, and had no idea if this man was his son or not, they took him away and nobody saw him again for a long time. I was a teenager before I even knew he existed, my parents never mentioned it.'

'But then ...?'

'He came back. He'd been working with the Norwegian military, then other militaries, sharing what he knew of the Russian system. My parents were pacifists, you know? The war had been a bad thing to them. To have this man, this soldier, in the family ... well, for a long time they couldn't get along.'

'So what happened?'

'Well, my parents were very dedicated to the planet, that's why they called me Ansel: after Ansel Adams, the photographer?'

Claire nodded.

'And he listened to them, even agreed with them. From time to time he would go off on a trip and when he came back he would talk about what wildlife he had seen, never about what he had done, and from that we knew he had been to some very strange places: Afghanistan, Mongolia, even South America. He was very good at listening, and the more he listened, the more I ended up thinking like him.'

He rubbed his face again, and smiled sadly, 'Slowly, I came to think that he was right and my parents were wrong. His way, changing things, that was the answer. Just to care wasn't enough; to name your child after a nature lover, that wasn't enough, but to do what he did, going to places where things were wrong and putting them right ...'

There was a long pause.

'But now, I don't know.'

'So the money ...?' Claire asked gently.

'Well, probably he is a mercenary, don't you think? A man who could walk from Siberia to Norway and could cross the border untouched, who sold his knowledge to other armies, what else can you call him?'

KAY SEXTON

'Must be a pretty senior one then,' Claire suggested.

'Oh yes. Well, why not? To survive Stalin and become an officer, he had to be clever, and then he had secrets that were worth a fortune in the Cold War and nothing to spend his money on.'

'I'm a bit surprised your parents let you get to know him.'

'Well, I think there was a lot of guilt, you know? When the police brought my father to see him and my father said he had no knowledge of his uncle having a son in Russia, that was pretty bad for my father to have to do, but worse for him, for Blaine, because the police treated him badly, I think. I know it took him a long time to convince the Norwegian authorities that he really wasn't a spy. And once he told us he had to stay three years in Russia after his father, my father's uncle, died, because they were watching him. He never said what happened to his mother, I think perhaps he doesn't know.'

'So why wolves?'

Ansel laughed and rubbed his face again. 'You think it's something to do with Russia?'

Claire shrugged. 'I don't know, I'm asking you.'

'I don't know either. When I was younger, I hero-worshipped him. He'd done so much more than my parents would ever do. He was brave, he was – I don't know the word in English – he never talked about it, you know?'

'Modest?' Claire suggested.

'Yes, that's a good word for it. And he spent a lot of time with me, telling me about animals, about the empty places where people never went and animals ruled. He was the first person to take me fishing, out in the Barents Sea, and so when he began to talk to me about putting things right, I knew I would help him.'

Claire patted his hand. 'And you have, and that's good. Now you can decide for yourself if you want to carry on – he can't make you, Ansel. Perhaps he's pushed you past the point your own beliefs would have made you stop, or maybe you can come to terms with what happened to the other pack, but whichever way it works out, the decision is yours, not his.'

Ansel nodded but she could see he was unconvinced.

'Anyway, I'm glad you told me. It makes a lot of things clearer.'

He smiled weakly at that and she left him to sleep, knowing she would stay awake most of the night, listening for wolves.

CHAPTER NINETEEN

It seemed impossible that she could be recalled to Rome just a week after her first sight of the stranger wolf, but the FAO job was her cover and when Professore Giordano went into hospital to have a hernia operated on, she had to go back to her desk and help deal with the departmental work. She was guaranteed she could return to the Highlands for Christmas as the Hogmany celebrations and their eco-tourist potential were an integral part of her research, but for now she was stuck, marooned, trapped.

She hadn't told Bruno she was coming back, but as soon as she had unpacked her small bag, she rang him at his flat.

'Wonderful, my mother will be so furious!' was his first comment and she laughed until she had to sit down. She'd forgotten how much pleasure Bruno could find in any situation: even the frustration of his mother's marital ambitions. 'I'll pick you up for lunch tomorrow,' he continued, as though it was a given that they would take up the threads of their relationship.

'Well …' The image of Shaun's soft mouth appeared in her mind. She wondered if Bruno would guess how her autumn had been spent. Then she realised that he too might have secrets to keep. She'd been away for five months and he was a charming man with an active social life. If she had found time and opportunity for an affair, it was likely that he had too. Well, that was fine. They were free agents - they'd agreed on that. But she found she was holding onto the seat of the chair and her knuckles were white with tension.

'And eat with us on Sunday. My sister Guilia will be home from college, she'd love to meet you.'

She agreed, and then he said something inaudible and cut the connection. The voice he was responding to had sounded female. She felt jealous, even though she knew the reaction was unfair. When they'd agreed that they would not try to maintain a relationship through her two-year secondment, she hadn't felt like this, and now was no time to try and renege on the agreement.

Even so, she lay in the bath that evening with a face-pack smeared across her face, hands and chest, and she planned to make an appointment for a decent haircut the next morning. It was all very well taking her Roman glamour to the Highlands, but there was nothing that life on the croft had given her that would help her feel confident when she faced Bruno's family again. Nothing she could share with him anyway.

At midnight her phone rang. Ansel said, 'I am leaving this evening. I will give the keys to Isobel. I saw two.'

She lay back on the bed, closing her eyes. 'Who?'

'Agate and Drip,' his voice was strained – he didn't even want to discuss the pack in this coded way. The tension transmitted to her. Perhaps her phone was bugged. Blaine had said that activists could have their phones tapped under terrorist legislation, and while she didn't think she had a profile as an activist, it was wiser to be careful.

'That's nice,' she fought for a casual tone. 'Tell you what, why don't you send me some details.'

She could check her anonymous email account at a cyber café before she got to the office. With any luck Ansel would have stopped somewhere on the way home to send her as much information on the sighting as he could. If not, she'd have to wait until he got into the university computer room. As she drifted off to sleep she saw wolves pouring like smoke between the trees behind High Croft. She couldn't wait to get back to them.

233

The next morning she changed her flight so she could leave Rome on Friday, straight from work. She'd miss the Contadino's family dinner but she'd have the weekend to look for the wolves before flying back to Rome on Monday morning. It was going to be tough and it would drain her savings, but she could keep it up for the next few weeks and she'd get as much time to look for the wolves as she could.

By early January, when her boss was able to return to his desk part-time, the wolves' routines had become known to her. She discovered that each wolf had a personal route, a patrol maybe, that they took around their home territory, except for Flow, who was relentless and unpredictable.

Meander prowled the upper tree line, flushing rabbits in the early morning or digging in the snow, for what purpose Claire couldn't tell. Lake and Caldera travelled together, a long afternoon stroll, loping one behind the other like two puffs of smoke on the landscape. Agate sat for long hours alone, looking out from one of several vantage points she'd made her own. Drip though, came right down to the water, his pad marks showing in snow and mud, and his yellow urine staining the same rocks and tree trunks on his visits. He often lay on the big stone in the stream, head down on his paws, snoozing like a fireside pet, flicking his ears from time to time and yawning hugely in the chill sunlight. He rolled too, in the pine litter under the trees and she would find his wallows afterwards; scattered bark and loam, while he trotted back to the pack with pine needles studding his coat.

She used the binoculars to observe them, seeing them so close she felt she could reach out to them.

One afternoon she was coming back down the hill when she heard a sound completely new to her. She slowed, choosing her path, and was rewarded with the sight of Drip, on his back, legs kicking as he wriggled from side to side. The *hnar hnar* was his ecstatic

GATEKEEPER

moaning as he pressed some vile substance deep into his fur. When he had finished and strolled off, a large brown stain marking his shoulders, she found the place to contain the very decayed remains of a crow. He must have stunk to heaven.

She'd read an article in the Maghreb that claimed wolves rolled to disguise their scent while hunting, and another that debunked the first, saying no wolf could plan that far ahead. They rolled, it said, to possess the thing they'd found; possession being a wolf's greatest passion. She hadn't understood it then, no creature could be less encumbered by possessions than a wolf, but now she did.

Drip, heading back to his family, had a rich ripe scent, a thing he'd found and now owned. Taking it home gave him a gift to bestow; he could reward his pack's curiosity with this redolent, surprising possession. He carried his ears and tail high as he vanished into the trees. He would be King of the Wolves for the afternoon.

She realised the value of Shaun's work when the wolves began to howl. From the High Croft side of the hill the howl was audible, although somewhat masked by the rushing of the burn, but from the Streap side, without the water and the heavy secondary woodland that acted as a baffle, it was astonishingly loud. There were only six wolves but they sounded like fifty. Their eerie harmonies rose like smoke through the trees at dawn and dusk. She was sure the whole village must have heard them within a week of their arrival.

Nobody spoke about it. She kept waiting for somebody to mention – in the shop or the pub – 'I could have sworn I heard some wolves today', but not a word was said. She couldn't understand it.

After another week she emailed Ansel, asking him to call, and then had to scramble down to the shop to buy a top-up card for her Maghrebi mobile phone.

'Can you talk?' she asked, as soon as the phone rang. She found her paranoia still returned whenever she had to deal with him, although she couldn't decide if he caused it, or reminded her of the

KAY SEXTON

circumstances that had created it or whether it was just the knowledge that he and Blaine were related that made her so uneasy.

'I can.'

'Okay, so explain this – every day the wolves howl: often in the morning, always at night and sometimes in between too – so why isn't anybody talking about it?'

There was a long silence.

'I don't know. Are you sure other people hear them?'

'How can I be sure, if they don't mention it? Use your brain, Ansel!'

'Sorry, that was stupid of me. So, you hear them?'

'All the time.'

'Is it possible your house is just that much closer, so you hear them better? Other people might think it's dogs.'

'Every day?'

'But Claire, you *know* the wolves are there: they don't.'

'Some of them do,' she interrupted him.

'Yes, some do – but they won't be the first to mention it, for obvious reasons.'

'People out on the hills must hear them.'

'Hmmm. Could they be afraid of making fools of themselves? After all, you are not far from Loch Ness, and that was a famous hoax. Perhaps also your behaviour is blinding you to the facts. You spend a lot of time outside, on land that most other people don't visit. Perhaps they hear only occasionally, and assume it is neighbouring dogs?'

'Noel McIver drives over the hill twice a day – and he's always got his nose in other people's business.'

'And he hasn't said anything?'

'He doesn't talk to me.'

'Oh? So you don't know if he's talked to anyone about hearing wolves?'

236

GATEKEEPER

'Fair point. I don't think he actually talks to anybody – he's a bit of a loner.'

'He sounds it. Is he capable of hearing wolves and keeping the information to himself?'

She thought about McIver. He was an isolated figure in the close-knit community, more than capable of keeping his own counsel, especially if he thought silence might give him some power.

'Yeah ... I genuinely believe the only thing he talks to is his dog.'

'There you are then. The wolves will be spotted soon enough and then you'll regret ever wishing people would notice them. Enjoy this time, while you have them to yourself. It will all change before long.'

She said nothing.

'Claire?'

'Mmm ... okay. I hear you.'

'I know you want to get on with your job.'

'It's not that ...'

'What then?'

'Sometimes I think I'm imagining them.'

He laughed. 'You're too practical for that. You know the wolves are there. It's just nerves.'

They talked about other things for a while and she felt comforted when she put the phone down.

One morning Drip was sitting by the burn. She focused the binoculars, already sure something was wrong. His posture was hunched, ears flat, tail curled around his haunches in a tight protective arc that spelled misery.

His muzzle bore a large gash, obscene and pink against his grey fur. His eyes were closed and he looked like an animal waiting for death. As she watched he lay down, curling into a tight ball.

KAY SEXTON

There was nothing she could do; the wolves had to be wild, and wild wolves died young – illness, injury and accidents would mean most of the pack did not see their seventh year. Had they been born wild, at least half of them would have died before maturity.

Even so, and even though she was supposed to be conducting a survey in the isolated community of Dulnaid that day, she ran back down to the 4 x 4, drove to High Croft and picked up her mobile before heading for her appointments.

As soon her phone registered a signal she pulled over and called Ansel, describing Drip's condition. He said he would contact her when he'd checked with The Project.

She carried on with the survey, recording the opinions of the crofter's wives still at home and then heading into the hills on foot to track down their husbands and sons. She could walk broken ground for hours now – her legs were tireless, even by Highland standards. She gathered some interesting anecdotes about Pre-Raphaelite tourism, when English 'artists' set up home in the Highlands for the summer. Many had hired crofters as models and the income they gained showed up in local records as flocks purchased and new chimneys and roofs for old crofts. It should have been fascinating, but her attention was on her phone.

She got back to Glenfail around four and drove straight to a point where she could see the burn. Drip was still there. She couldn't decide whether to go and wait where she could receive Ansel's call or stay and observe the wolf. She compromised. She would take the vehicle back, check her email and then walk up to watch over the wolf from a distance.

There was no email from Ansel.

Back at her vantage point she made herself comfortable. She'd picked up cereal bars and water and, if necessary, would stay out all night. She'd brought the Browning too, in case she needed to fire it over their heads to break up a wolf fight. That would be inappropriate, she knew. It would interfere in the dynamic of the pack, but as nobody could prove she'd done it, she didn't care. Nothing could protect the omega forever, but she knew weakened wolves were sometimes attacked by other pack members out of self-preservation – in areas where wolves faced other predators like bear, or in India, tiger; a wounded pack member could draw attention to the pack as a whole. It was like a mercy killing, in a way.

She hoped that Drip's choice of location meant he wanted to live. He was reasonably well-concealed by the large rocks and near water – a perfect place for convalescence. She couldn't see if he had other injuries and she knew if his legs were also bitten he would struggle to recover. After a while she realised she was talking to him in her head, urging him to be strong. Poor Drip never did things by halves.

After an hour he got up and drank. Although he only walked a few paces, it was enough to show he wasn't limping and she relaxed, feeling now that he was sulking, rather than laying up to protect a seriously damaged body.

At dusk, when the wolves would normally howl, Flow stepped out of the woods and stood, looking at his brother. Claire scanned the alpha with the glasses. He was more subdued than she had ever seen him. His tail was mid-high, his ears low and he looked uncertain. Drip lifted his head, glanced at Flow, and lowered it again. Claire checked the rifle was in reach. Drip didn't seem fearful though.

After a few seconds in which Flow radiated indecisiveness, something she'd never expected to see in the alpha, he walked down slowly and sat by his brother. Drip immediately rolled on his back, tail curled up under his belly – full submission. It told Claire that Flow had been the one who inflicted the bite. Flow lowered his head, his ears still flat, and sniffed his brother. Then he pawed at him gently. Drip sat up and Flow lay down, allowing his brother to be the taller of the two – a submissive posture that the alpha had never allowed in her view before.

KAY SEXTON

It was a reconciliation and Flow was doing all the work. Drip picked his way over to the water and drank again. When he returned, Flow stood and trotted back up to the tree-line, but Drip returned to his original spot and curled up again. Once more, Flow was uncertain. He went into the trees and then reappeared, returning to Drip and pawing him, but Drip ignored the request to move. Finally Flow sat back on his haunches and howled.

The females replied. Drip twitched his ears but didn't move. Flow's howl was full of emotion. A wolf always sounded mysterious and sad to Claire, but Flow, this time, was expressing something she had never heard from him before and hesitated to name. Whatever it was, he certainly wasn't a threat to his brother.

He howled again and Drip lifted his head and howled too. Claire had never seen a wolf howl from a curled position, although she'd read they would contribute to a chorus howl even while swimming, mating or defecating. The howl *was* the pack – to miss out on it was to become a nothing.

Flow stopped calling and bent over, licking his brother's torn face. Drip growled, she could see his lips curling and his throat vibrating even though the sound didn't travel to her, but allowed the grooming to continue. After a few minutes the two males began to play, sitting on their haunches and batting at each other with their forepaws. Then they romped into a game of chase around the rocks. At one point, Flow's paw caught Drip's slashed muzzle and the omega's yelp was audible. He sat down and curled his long tongue up to try and reach the wound. Flow stopped too and approached tentatively, wagging his hindquarters like a pup. Drip let him lick the wound again, and they sat down, shoulder to shoulder for a while, before loping off together into the trees.

Claire picked up the rifle and walked home. She'd been privileged to see the alpha in a rare moment of vulnerability. She thought how difficult it must be for him: always on duty, always in charge. The affection between the brothers was strong, but she had a new respect for Flow. He had found and gathered up his omega – he was willing to show some gentleness – this wolf was everything they'd hoped for. If anybody could guarantee the pack's future, it was Flow.

Ansel rang at ten, on the house phone, and she picked up the mobile, jogging to the one spot where she could get a signal, to call him back.

'We think maybe they fought: either Drip and Flow or Drip and Meander,' Ansel's voice was weary. 'There's nothing to be done, I'm afraid. It's amazing it hasn't happened before. Drip's not a natural omega – they told me he's actually a bit bigger than his brother, which usually means alpha status – and anywhere else he'd have left by now to be a solitary. It's the unnatural pack dynamic – no older wolves to keep the peace. The foster-mother did her best but she wasn't strong enough to discipline them once they were two months old. There's no senior authority figure to keep them within safe bounds. At least they're doing better than ... than the others did.'

'I think it's okay,' she said. 'I think Flow had to put in Drip in his place but they've patched it up now.'

'Good.'

She could tell he was waiting for her to elaborate but she didn't. What she had seen was private. Even she had felt like an interloper. The brothers deserved to have their moment of tenderness kept secret.

The next time she saw Drip there was a dark scab across his nose. After a few days even that was gone, although a shiny white scar remained. He seemed un-cowed by the experience, and Flow reverted to his formal, authoritative persona. But she now knew how strong the bond was between them, and she was confident that if Drip got into trouble again, his brother would do all he could for the omega.

CHAPTER TWENTY

She recognised him even through the rain, though she'd only met him once. She knew him, even from the back. She saw him as soon as she pushed over the crest of the Carmundie ridge, fighting the cramp in her quadriceps that came from balancing on slippery ground for hours. She'd walked three ridges since 6am, heading away from the hill behind the croft, checking fences and croft walls, exploring the boundaries of any cottage and farm on her route, trying to establish how much would need to be done to keep the livestock on each place safe. Now it was mid-afternoon and despite stopping at a pub near Ben Ghil she was exhausted and hungry. The pack, being smarter than her, would be resting up in a pine wood, warm in pine-needle beds where the rain never penetrated. She envied them.

And there he was, in a sky-blue waterproof, staring into the grey torrent over Torlochie. She descended loudly, hoping to alert him to her presence, hoping he would move off. Let him have come to look at his wolves, to celebrate their freedom. Let it be that. She knew it wasn't though. Blaine wouldn't be here for any good reason.

He didn't turn as she came up behind him. When she looked into his face under the blue hood she saw a man waiting to deliver bad news and thought about walking on, wondering if he would pursue her or let her go. Whatever this was about, she didn't want any part in it. Sudden weakness made her lean against the old stone wall.

GATEKEEPER

'Claire.' He smiled. His face was so drawn her first thought was that he was dying, suffering some fatal disease that had brought him to the wolves for the last time.

'I guess you're not bringing me a medal,' she said.

He shook his head. 'I'm sorry. The only thing I bring is a burden. But you can say no. Nobody ever expected this to happen. It is not part of your job.'

She sagged, wrestling the straps of her pack, sodden and cold, down her arms. Once she was sitting she pulled out the flask of hot water she'd got at the pub and made instant soup, giving him half in the lid while she drank the rest from the flask. The sharing of food was some kind of gesture, she realised – doing this was a way of preparing for what was coming. He seemed to know it too, raising the plastic cup to her with severe grace, making something sacramental out of what could have seemed ironic.

'So tell me,' she said finally, looking at the water that was oozing from his jeans now that he was sitting – how long must he have been standing there for so much rain to soak his clothing?

'Somebody has to kill the omega,' he said.

She blew out air. 'You're mad. That's ... stupid. Why?'

'He's been scavenging. But it's worse than that. It's a long story, Claire. Must I tell all of it?'

She heard the appeal but ignored it. 'Yes. Whatever the fuck you think gives you the right to say things like that is long gone, Blaine. These are my wolves now. My wolves! I'm the Gatekeeper. You told me that once they were here, it was up to me. So before you even think about getting close to the omega you'd better explain what you're talking about, or I'll stop you.'

She felt the tiredness of her body but knew that she was still a match for this man. She could kill him if she had to. She could get away from him if necessary. She could lead him in circles on the cold hills until he collapsed. He looked so old. The other time she'd seen him, Blaine looked like a strong man in his fifties, now he looked a

243

KAY SEXTON

decade older, and frail. She watched his hands, which Ciprian had taught her showed strain better than faces. Blaine's were crabbed and he flexed his fingers around the cup as though testing his ability to sense its shape.

He told her that he had made a mistake. A miscalculation. He had trusted his team to understand the reasons the wolves must have no human contact. 'And so, we had no cameras outside the enclosure. If we had ...'

It was obvious that he meant her to ask, to take some of the burden of confession from him. Instead she stared down the hill, trying to pick out High Croft, but the driving rain hid everything. Finally he finished the sentence. 'Our veterinarian was hand-feeding Drip, through the wire. Because he wasn't getting enough food to keep him healthy in the enclosure, she said.'

'How did you find out?'

'She told us, when he began to come down off the hill. She said a veterinarian should care first for an animal's welfare, only second for wider issues.'

She leaned back against the wall, wanting the support of something behind her. 'He'll soon get over it.'

'We don't think so. He's been going to the The Waird most nights now, turning over the bins. But it's much worse than that.'

She shook her head. 'Much worse? Don't see how it can be.'

'Claire, nobody has ever done this before. This is the first pack to be raised without adults, without human interference, the first to teach itself to hunt ... when you do things for the first time, many of the results are unpredictable. We have a much bigger problem than we thought. A wonderful problem.'

She knew immediately. She hadn't seen Meander for several days and she'd wondered why. The alpha female thought she was pregnant. She must have dug a den and gone there to wait for the imaginary cubs to arrive.

'She's too young, if you mean Meander. It's a false pregnancy.' She saw his glance, knew he was reassessing her.

'You knew she was making a den?'

'I guessed.' She hadn't, but there was no reason to say so.

'Well, I agree. She's too young. Flow's too young. There have never been cubs from a two-year male before: but two-year old females have produced cubs in captivity. The thing is; there has never been a recorded twenty-four month male alpha. We think now that perhaps *any* alpha is fertile - even at a year old; it's just that the circumstances that could produce an alpha male so young have never happened before, or not where we've been aware of it.'

'So you think Flow and Meander mated? I'm sorry, but I saw no sign of that.' She watched the fingers convulse on the cup.

'No,' he said. 'Not Flow.'

'Drip? You think Drip ...?' she laughed, and then stopped. Drip was as big as his brother, maybe bigger. He spent a lot of time with the females when Flow was patrolling the territory, and yes, he was a charmer, he was always grooming, rolling, playing with the girls. Would she really have noticed if he spent more time with Meander than with any of the others? Or had she just put it down to his omega role, the social oiler of all the wheels?

'You see the point?' Blaine put down the cup and tucked his hands into his armpits against the cold.

'I still think it's a phantom pregnancy.' She watched his face - he didn't bother to hide the pain.

'Sadly not. We managed to get some urine from Meander; we've been setting traps - cellophane saucers in the bracken - and the sample was positive. It could be either of the males, but as you say, there's no evidence that Flow mated with her, while there's quite a lot to suggest Drip may have grabbed his chance while his brother was absent. But it doesn't matter which of them is the father – the point is that the cubs will be left with the omega as soon as they're weaned.'

KAY SEXTON

'And he'll teach them to scavenge.' She saw it as clearly as a video, Drip with his sweet, scarred face, leading a bundle of stilt-legged wolf cubs down to The Waird and finding themselves confronted by an irate Tam McDowell who would be expecting nothing worse than Courtney Love or Axl Rose rooting through the overturned bin. Or worse, the holiday cottages in Glenfail being let to a family who left food out on the picnic table and came back to find an archetypal nightmare; a slavering wolf pawing at the back door.

'Oh Christ,' she said, without blasphemy.

'I can do it, if you cannot.' His voice was low, so low the weather took the words and she had to strain to hear them. 'It is my responsibility.'

'But I know them better; I know the places to find him alone.'

Blaine nodded. 'Even so, this is something I cannot ask you to do.'

She felt the tears stinging her eyes. 'I volunteer. I can do it more safely than anybody else. If it has to be done, I will shoot him.'

She let herself cry then for - Drip and for herself - and it wasn't for some time, until the tears were exhausted, that she realised Blaine was holding her and his faded blue eyes were raw too.

'And when I've done that,' she said. 'I'm going to find the bitch who made this necessary. What's her name?

Blaine leaned back, his hands slack. 'You know who it was, Claire. You know her.'

She stared at him, understanding coming so slowly she felt it as a tide in her blood, chilling her. 'Maggie is your vet?'

He nodded.

It couldn't stop there, of course. He had to explain things to her. Shaun was here, somewhere, he'd be the one to help her bury Drip. That it must be done soon, before Meander brought the cubs up from the den and left them to the omega to care for while she hunted. That the den was probably on the other side of the hill, so

246

GATEKEEPER

it would be best if she tracked him on this side, to avoid alerting the rest of the pack. That this might unsettle the rest of the pack, but it was better to risk that, than to allow Drip to bring the cubs into proximity with humans - because the pack was then doomed. That they thought Agate would probably replace Drip as omega and her fear of people would reinforce the cubs' wild instincts and keep them well away from danger points.

She listened without caring: not even registering properly that Shaun was around. All she wanted to know was where to find Maggie. Not now, not while this still had to be done, but later, she promised herself, she would take care of Maggie.

When he'd said all he had to say, she found herself patting him on the hand as if he was an aged grandfather. She didn't trust her voice, so she managed a smile and then stood, watching him climb to his feet and lift his small pack.

'I leave tomorrow,' he said.

She didn't know she was going to move, the action came from something unthinking inside her, and then her hand was under his jaw, pressing the column of his throat, constricting his breathing. She looked into his face. He gazed back at her, eyes pale and marked with pain, but unafraid.

'Does she know what I did to Liam?'

Blaine swallowed convulsively and she loosened her grip a little. 'She knows.'

'Good. Then I don't have to send her a warning.'

His eyes were cold, but approving. He wouldn't support her, but he wouldn't stop her either.

She lowered her hand and lifted her own pack, wanting solitude now, to prepare for the task, but he scrabbled in his pocket.

'Here,' he held out a mobile. 'You use this, to call Shaun, when it's done. His number is programmed in. Then he'll take the phone away afterwards. This way there's no record.'

She took the phone.

247

KAY SEXTON

He vanished into the weather before she was ready – she'd meant to ask him where Maggie was, and whether the woman had played any role in the failure of the other pack. But he was gone, his footsteps dead on the grass, his figure swallowed by the caul of rain.

She gave him ten minutes to get down the hill and then walked slowly, measuring each footstep against the future. The next time she came up here, the next time she passed this wall, the next time she saw that pine tree … Drip would be dead.

For the whole evening she performed on auto-pilot, cleaning the gun, checking the ammunition, and honing her knife before tucking it into her waist pack. She ate, then examined her clothes and boots to make sure there were no loose buttons or worn laces. She laid out the things she would wear the following day on the sofa and went to bed. There was no howl that night. She lay awake until it was nearly dawn. No birds lifted their voices – there was no sun. For the hours she had stayed still, her mind had raced, trying to find another solution. Perhaps they could capture Drip and move him. Perhaps he could be retrained using aversion therapy to avoid the bins and the lure of easy food. Perhaps, perhaps, perhaps.

For every crazy thought there was an answer. Capturing a wild wolf was almost impossible. If the rest of the pack heard they could come to his rescue, putting themselves and Drip's captors at risk. The cubs might be moved to another, less safe den, or even abandoned. Even if they caught him, he might come back, unless they took him out of the country completely and that would leave him like Kaya, but without even human companionship. He would be physically healthy but insane: a lone wild wolf, stripped of his social and emotional framework, never survived long without a pack, but a caged wolf could live years - in misery.

Aversion therapy never worked. Wolves were too clever and anyway, he would revert sooner or later, when he was injured or if he lived long enough to develop arthritis or his teeth wore down too much to cope with large prey. A wolf was an opportunist and

248

GATEKEEPER

Drip could never be trusted not to go back to a habit he'd learned was rewarding. Even the fact that he approached human habitation meant the whole pack was at risk.

The dawn was still grey but the rain was not as dense. She ate again, her eyes on the hill. She wanted to think about the cubs, but her mind kept skidding off the subject.

In an hour Noel McIver would be heading up the hill. She imagined him in his little green van and Drip crossing the path in front of him, his coat slick with water, his eyes the colour of tawny port, his head turning, fixing on the vehicle as his body continued to move through the landscape like a mirage. What would Nell make of the wolf – would she bark or cower? It couldn't be allowed to happen.

Before she could give herself time to think she'd picked up the Browning and hit the TV play button, turning it to a chat show and lowering the volume before checking the curtains were fully drawn so that nobody could see if she was in the room or not. She closed the door quietly behind her and took the back path to the hill so that her footsteps wouldn't show before the rain could cover them.

As soon as she was in the tree line she began to run. There was only one chance to do it properly today – if she could make it to the falls before Drip crossed the burn at the stepping stones he would be silhouetted against the skyline and the waterfall would drown the shot. He would never know she was there.

At the top of the falls she could hear her own breathing like a broken machine and the rain, although thinning, still hid the land – she couldn't tell if he'd passed over the water or not. She loaded the rifle and was standing with her hands braced on her knees and the gun hanging from its sling, still trying to catch her breath, when he appeared.

There was no time to crouch. No time to aim. She lifted the rifle, half-emptied her lungs and brought the sights up from his chest to the point between his eyes. Drip paused on the bank as he always did, right foot raised, wrinkling his forehead at the water. She saw the corrugations appear in his brow, making sandy-grey lines across his head. Then he vanished.

It wasn't until she smelt the oil and hot metal odour that she realised she'd fired. Then she had to raise the gun again, and find his body as he lay on the bank. His left foot was touching the water, making a silver furl in the stream. She fired again, placing the second shot in his throat.

Then she climbed down to the bottom of the fall and was sick into the water.

When she got across the burn, having slipped twice and soaked herself to the knees, she approached the wolf from behind, coughing loudly as all the books said she should, to ensure that any other predator had a chance to move away. Not Drip. She knew he was dead. She'd known from the moment she'd lifted the rifle.

Now he looked big and dangerous in a way he never had before. It took a moment to realise that she'd never been this close to him; it was proximity that made him so huge. She broke the gun although she knew it wasn't loaded and put it down. Then she knelt by the wolf, lifting his big hot head onto her knees. She smelt him, ammonia, blood, and underlying that, the woolly smell of warmed muscles under a wet coat. She pressed down his eyelids with her fingers without looking into his eyes. One hand slipped and she felt his tongue, long and harsh like a cat's, and then her fingers were deep in his pelt and she was crying into his shoulder.

After a long time she felt his body cooling. She straightened her back, knowing her clothes were bloody and her face must be a mess. It was no good acting like this. Drip was dead. She'd killed him. Now she had to protect the rest of the pack. They wouldn't come looking for him for a long time: they were used to him going off on his own and the sound of shooting wouldn't disturb them, she'd made sure of that. But still, her job was to look after them, and she had to be tougher than this.

For the last time she bent over him, resting her head against his, then she put him gently on the ground, lifting his left paw from the water and curling it up against his body as though he slept. She stepped into the water, feeling it burn with cold, and sank down, washing his blood from her clothing. She pushed her head under, keeping her eyes open until the need to breathe tugged at her. When she came out of the river she was shaking with cold. Drip appeared calm, young, harmless – she realised that however strong he looked, he'd still been a baby. Such a short life. His pricked-up ear showed the blotch for which she'd named him. She gathered up the gun and jogged back to the croft.

She was supposed to be teaching, but she rang and told them she was not well. She forgot to add whatever excuse she should have made, but the college receptionist must have heard something in her voice that suggested she was truly sick. It was hard to believe most people were still wandering around their homes, eating breakfast. She felt as if a whole day had passed, but it was only early morning.

For a moment she stood, unsure what to do, and then she remembered the mobile phone. She could call Shaun. He would sort things out. She stripped her clothing and hung it up. She got halfway upstairs before turning and running back down. She pulled the trousers and shirt from their hangers, the socks and underwear from the rack, and opened the range door. The kitchen stank of burning wool by the time she'd pushed it all in, but she shoved the clothes deep and closed the door. Then she pulled the scissors from the kitchen drawer and cut her waterproof jacket into jagged pieces which she shoved into the bin. She looked at her boots. She couldn't burn or destroy them. She went upstairs and pulled on her oldest clothes and Wellingtons then went out to the compost heap and dug a hole next to it, where she buried the boots.

There was only the gun left. She looked at it, wondering if she could burn the stock, but in the end she left it on the table.

She picked up the mobile, looking at the number that would summon Shaun. Was she ready to face him? She put the phone down again, noting with cold interest that while she'd hesitated to pick it up, she'd put it down again without a second thought. Instead she went to the bathroom mirror and plaited her hair, pulling it tight back from her face and hissing with pain as her fingers ripped through the wet tangles. Having her hair so severely tied back made her look dour and old.

She changed her Wellingtons for her old mountain boots and dragged the backpack from the cupboard. In it she placed the length of Harris tweed Drew had given her, needle and thread from the sewing box she'd never opened before, twine, and the kitchen scissors. Then she took the scissors out again. She held them against her plait for a moment – but put them back. She shoved a roll of black plastic bin bags on top, and pulled the knife from her waist pack, tucking it into the big pack. She pulled her old Barbour jacket out of the cupboard and put the mobile in the pocket. This time she let the door slam behind her as she left.

At the waterfall she realised she couldn't lift the wolf, even if she'd wanted to. Instead she rolled him slightly towards the water, placing one edge of the tweed close against his spine, and then rolled him back again, turning him onto the densely-woven fabric.

She arranged him, folding his legs and tucking his tail around him, pressing his head down gently until his muzzle rested between his forepaws.

Without looking, she placed the fingers of her left hand high in his abdomen, feeling for the lowest ribs and then, separating her thumb and forefinger, hefted the knife in her right hand and stabbed between them into the abdominal cavity, releasing the stomach gases so that the body would decay more quickly.

GATEKEEPER

As she knelt, threading the needle, she listened to herself talking to a dead wolf. 'This cloth will keep you warm, Drip,' she heard herself say. 'Warm and safe. You were doing your best, I know. We all were. It just didn't work out. Not for you. But I'll take care of the others, and the cubs. Don't worry about a thing.' As she sewed she had to blink a few times, but there were no tears.

When she'd finished, she lifted the phone and called Shaun.

'Come now,' she said. 'Bring a spade. And the photographs.'

'Where?' His voice was strained.

'The falls.'

He hung up without speaking again.

CHAPTER TWENTY-ONE

Claire sat for a while, looking at the mounded shape in the grey shroud. Then she tugged the plastic bags from the roll, laying several out and rolling the wolf onto them before dragging the whole thing away slightly to reveal bloodstains on the grass. She took another bag and held open it in the stream, feeling the sting of the water. Eight times she gathered water and used it to wash the blood down into the stream. She held the knife in the water until it was clean and put it away.

She sat, her right hand resting on Drip's curved spine through the fabric, until she heard Shaun's bike. Then she ran down to the path.

When he saw her he stopped the bike and took off his helmet. She stood a few paces from him, making herself examine his face. She was so busy noting the details of him: his grey-brown eyes under straight coppery lashes, the softness of his mouth, the gentle hollows of his neck, that it took a few seconds to realise he wouldn't meet her eyes.

'You're not going to do it, are you?' he asked.

'Do what?' She knew what he meant, but it seemed necessary to hear him say it.

He shrugged, unwilling to put a name to the action.

'You mean to shoot Drip? Am I really going to shoot him?' Her voice was out of control, her breathing uneven.

He ducked his head. 'Yeah.'

254

'What alternatives are there, Shaun? Who else is going to do it? Or perhaps you think I should ignore it and hope that nobody else notices a fucking full-grown male wolf in their back garden, maybe with half-a-dozen cubs in tow? Is that what you think I should do?'

Now he looked at her, glancing up and away.

'Fucking hell, don't make it any harder than it is.' She felt as if she'd been hit, as if a fist had met her gut without warning.

He got off the bike and handed her the photographs. She sorted through them, finding one of the whole pack together and then passed the others back.

'I thought you'd want one of him,' Shaun muttered. 'To help you identify him.'

She laughed, trying to hold down her hysteria. 'I know them all just fine, Shaun, thank you.'

'I thought it was odd. I guessed you'd be watching them pretty closely. So what's the picture for?'

She ignored the question, tucking the picture into her waist pack. When she looked up again he was trying to smile.

'So ...' he ran out of words immediately.

'How long have you been here?' she asked.

He shrugged again.

'Weeks? Months?' She pushed up against him, shouldering into his space. He wouldn't answer unless she made him.

'A couple of weeks. Just checking stuff.'

'And they told you not to tell me you were here, right?' She wondered why she felt so angry; it wasn't as if she even wanted his company.

'He thought it would be better if we weren't seen together. I didn't use the bike at all, I've been sleeping ...' his voice faded again.

'I know exactly where you've been. In the caravan at The Waird – that's the one place you could have seen him scavenging, because if you'd been out on the hills at all, I'd have seen you.'

He blinked at the fury in her voice.

'And were you alone?' She wasn't jealous, there had even been a kind of relief when he'd gone the first time, when she'd realised how poisonous the relationship was becoming. So what was driving this anger? She looked away, trying to understand her own paranoia. She'd learned to live with doubt, so what was the problem that was pushing her anger this time? His lack of reaction gave her a clue.

'Was Maggie with you? Fucking hell! Was she actually here?'

'When we got the first report that Meander might be pregnant, she came over to do the test – you can't use a kit from a chemist shop, you know!'

His own temper flared, making his jaw bunch and his cheekbones stand proud in a red flush, and she watched, detached. She'd never seen him angry before and even now, she was sure his behaviour hid something else. He wasn't going to tell her anything while he was in this mood, she could see his resistance building with every second that she stood in front of him.

She took a deep breath, lifting her eyes over his shoulder to look at the heather. It was cold and wet, but that wouldn't bother him. Keeping her eyes on the faint new growth of the landscape, she pushed her hand across her forehead and then reached out to him as if overcome. He took one step towards her, and then she had her hand around the back of his neck and she felt his warm pulse through fingers that were still frigid from the stream. He sighed, a ragged sound that combined defiance and need. He wanted her to make demands on him. She set her own jaw, keeping her head down so he couldn't see her face, and pulled him forwards, pressing her fingers under his collar. The last time she'd touched anyone it had been Blaine, and Drip had still been alive. She closed her eyes and told herself to get on with it, for the wolves.

Her lips were cold too, when she pressed them against his neck, and she felt him shudder as she parted them to let the heat of her breath contrast with her icy kiss. His hands rose to settle on her waist. His gentleness had always surprised her but now it was more like a man frightened of being hurt than that of a man who was afraid to damage a fragile moment. She felt him holding back, fighting the surrender that she knew he craved. She lifted her thumb, pushing it under his chin so that his head was tipped backwards, then she set her teeth gently either side of his Adam's Apple and held them there until he swallowed convulsively as Blaine had done the previous day. Now his hands were shaking, not with fear any more, desire was pushing at him, but his nature made him hold back, wanting to submit, to be taken.

She shoved her fingers up into his hair, tugging his head down so that she could cram her lips against his. She didn't want to be aroused, but she was. His smell, denim and citrus, underlay the wood smoke that she knew now was from the old mica-fronted stove in the caravan. His soft mouth, the inner cushions of his lips like velvet, the tension in his body that she felt like a bass note drumming – they all combined to make her wet and hot in just one part of her body, between her legs, and as she pulled at his clothing and her own, the way she had the first time, she thought about herself as some kind of ice maiden, chill except for her very core. And then she thought of Drip, his body cold on the ground behind her and desire left her. She counterfeited the passion that Shaun wanted, groaning and thrusting at him, biting his lips, forcing him into her body, and yet her thoughts were with the pack.

Underground somewhere, and Claire thought she knew where, Meander would be listening to the sounds of her cubs. Not many, maybe three or four, because she was a young wolf and litters were small for first time mothers. And the father was young too, of course. She pushed the thought away, straddling Shaun, stabbing her straight fingers into his chest to make him lie back and remain passive. Don't think about Drip.

She would be a good mother. That was sure. Something about Meander suggested she would only come into her real power when

KAY SEXTON

she had cubs. She was the kind of solemn, strong, loving creature that became a nurse if it was human, or made a wonderful bellwether in a flock of sheep: a natural leader of the weak and vulnerable. She wouldn't nip at her cubs, except to teach them important lessons. She would groom them and sing to them, the strange breathy yipping howl that all wolves used in moments of tenderness, whether mother to cub or sibling to sibling. Don't think about siblings, she insisted to herself. Don't think about a brother who won't return to the pack.

The cubs then. Strong little bodies, as dark as wolverines, round ears set high on short muzzles. As they grew those ears would sharpen and move back and the long lupine jaws would stretch from the baby faces that were more like kittens than dogs. They would wriggle and yelp, those small blind forms, sounding like foxes at first, until their voices belled down as their eyes opened and the distinctive tones of the wolf emerged.

At first the eyes would be milky blue, then a strange gooseberry green that lasted for the first couple of days above ground and until they settled into one of the narrow range of amber hues that distinguished wolves from their canine cousins. Finally Meander would bring them above ground, blinking, to be inspected by the rest of the pack. Would they be at any risk from their extended family? Agate might find it hard to cope with cubs, especially if Drip wasn't there to ease the pack into a relaxed frame of mind. Don't think about him, she reminded herself.

Shaun raised his hand to her breast. 'Now?' She ignored him. 'Now?' It was the signal they'd developed, his request to be allowed to orgasm. She took one hand from his chest, where it was bracing her movements, and pressed it over his mouth, denying him the right to ask, or to come. He groaned against her fingers, arching his back to try and reduce the depth of his penetration, to make it easier for him to fight his climax. She ignored him.

On the other hand, acting as second mother to the cubs might be all Agate needed to settle her into the hierarchy at last. Perhaps she would become the kind of devoted foster-mum that Claire had seen in the desert pack, shepherding the unruly cubs around with unlimited patience. Drip would have been good at that too. She fought the image of good-natured Drip being bullied by miniature wolves: clowning with them, *hnar hnaring* his wolf-laugh and then getting up and trotting away, grinning back at them as their short legs twinkled through the grass to keep up.

Shaun squirmed under her, lifting his upper body from the ground, tipping her backwards. She looked at him – his eyes were big and black above her hand. He was shaking his head, telling her he couldn't hold on any longer. She smiled – and shoved her hand harder against his chin, pushing him back down.

For the first time since she'd got up that morning she let her mind return to the moment when she'd fired the rifle. The wolf, frowning at the cold water as he did every time he came across it, wouldn't have known what happened. Even if the first shot hadn't killed him outright, and she was sure it had, the second had followed within a heartbeat, a single breath, and that would have given him not even a moment to understand his death had found him.

She hadn't killed Drip. She had only pulled the trigger. His death had happened long before, when Maggie took it into her head to tame him and make him into a creature who thought humans were an interesting source of food rather than a remote activity on the fringes of wolf life. Maggie had murdered the wolf.

Claire lifted her hand, looked into Shaun's eyes and said, 'Okay.'

As he convulsed beneath her she faked her own climax, feeling the heat of her body spreading, her fingers, her toes, every part of her warming in her new understanding. Drip was simply an animal – he didn't know what had happened or who was to blame. But she did. She knew what she was going to do about it too.

When he had recovered, she checked her watch. There was still at least an hour to wait before she could be sure the top end of the village would be empty. The post van came past before noon and it

KAY SEXTON

had to be back on the Torlochie road heading away from them before they could move Drip. She squatted down, watching the rain settle on the grass they'd disturbed, covering up their dark green writhings with silver again.

'Well, what are we going to do?' Shaun said eventually.

'Wait.'

He stood, nearly tipping over in his haste. 'No way, no fucking way! Sorry Claire, but this is none of my business. I'm not going to hold your hand while you wait to murder that poor wolf.'

'His name is Drip,' she said. Then, more to keep him busy than out of real interest, she asked, 'So what alternative is there?'

He shook his head, avoiding her eyes again. 'I don't know, but I didn't sign up for this.'

'If we let him teach the cubs to head for humans whenever they're hungry, this pack won't last six months. You know that.'

He turned away from her, refusing to answer.

'So you think you can abdicate when it gets tough, Shaun? You can play at being God, but when the time comes for dirty work you can walk away and say it wasn't what you signed up for?'

'I could never kill an animal that had done no harm.'

She heard his voice choke with passion, but the energy in it was as false as their lovemaking earlier. He was fuelled by denial.

'Then you're a weak and stupid fool.'

'So you think you have the right to play God, right? To shoot that poor beast? For what – because he hasn't fallen in with your plans?'

She wiped the rain from the grass with her hand and glanced at her watch to see how long it would take for the moisture to settle again.

'Somebody else played God, Shaun. Not me.'

She waited until Isobel would have left to help out at the playgroup, John long departed to the fields, the English couple in their little

260

GATEKEEPER

car off to whatever they did when it rained. Shaun had gone to sit on his bike, his hair had matted to the colour of wood chippings by the downpour. He blinked the water from his eyes without moving. Then she walked him up the hill, and showed him the body.

'Christ, fucking Jesus Christ!' His hands were shaking. It took a long time for her to realise he was scared of what she might do next.

She gave short commands. Lift. Carry. He swore under his breath and did what he was told.

Drip's shrouded body, wrapped in plastic bags, was easily carried by two of them, once they'd knotted twine around him and whipped the loop into handles. Shaun, facing her across the corpse, worked faster than she did; his climber's fingers on auto-pilot. They hefted the bundle between them, trudging over the slick grass until they reached her back wall. Lifting him over the stones was difficult. Shaun waited with the body at his feet until she'd walked down to the road to check all the cars were gone, and then, together, they brought Drip the last few yards, into the middle of the garden.

'You can't have him here, Claire.'

She ignored him, cutting the twine and pulling the bags aside, before turning back to the house to bring the spade from the porch.

'Claire, you can't do this! It's fucking crazy.'

She began to dig, trying to keep the earth neatly piled. 'You get down to the McDowell's. Tell Alan you want the cultivator.'

He backed off before replying. 'I think you've lost it, I really do. This is mad.'

'And if she's still there, Shaun, you tell her that she'd better be gone by the time I've finished this.'

He headed away then, vaulting the wall and scrambling back up to where he'd left the bike. So Maggie was still at The Waird, and he'd gone to warn her. Claire didn't care, she'd only wanted to get rid of him. She'd been so stupid not to see the truth – Maggie was his handler like Ansel was hers. Maggie had even talked about being in Australia, but Claire hadn't put that together with Shaun's

KAY SEXTON

accent. They were traitors and fools, both of them. All of them. Her included.

She stopped digging and bent down to touch the shroud. Then she turned to face the hill. She'd promised Drip he would be safe; nobody would know where he was.

She climbed over the wall again, picking a spot that she guessed would line up with the waterfall, invisible on the other side of the hill. She lifted the turf and dug a hole at the foot of the wall. Lifting his body was harder than she'd thought - in the end she had to lay the bags out again and drag him to the wall, before heaving him over unceremoniously to thud on the other side. She laid the photograph of the pack that she'd taken from Shaun on top of his body and then covered him swiftly, not sure how long she had before Shaun returned.

The turf fitted back reasonably well, but it was still clear she'd been digging. She pulled on her gloves. The worst part was lifting the big boulder from the field corner and rolling it to place above him, crouching above it and pushing it from facet to facet on the wet grass until it was approximately over the grave. She didn't think she would be able to lift it, but she did, just one time, to position it directly over the evidence of the disturbed earth. Then she had to scramble the field corners for fallen wall stones to pile around it. By the time she'd finished she'd made a low cairn that could just possibly be mistaken for a buttress.

She ran back to the hole in the garden, more tired than she'd felt in her life, muscles shaking with exhaustion and nervous energy. She threw the bin bags and twine into the hole, and refilled it. By the time she heard Shaun's bike again, she was spent, sitting on the ground with her hands on the spade resting across her knees.

He paused as he came up the path, assessing her mood. She put the spade to one side and pushed herself upright.

'Did you get it?'

'Have some sense, Claire, I couldn't bring it on the bike. Alan wasn't there but Drew's bringing it over on the truck.'

262

GATEKEEPER

She nodded. 'Now get down to the Survivalists and pick up some seed potatoes.'

He stared, then nodded. 'Okay, that's pretty clever.'

'Go, Shaun. Get on with it.'

'Shouldn't you take a shower or something?'

'Shouldn't you do as I tell you - before something bad happens?' She let him see how willing she was to hurt him for real and he backed off again, smiling nervously.

She listened to the bike receding. She listened to the rain falling. She heard the McDowell's truck labouring up the hill.

Drew appeared, cultivator over his shoulder like a maniac's umbrella. She watched him put it down in the corner of the garden and then he came and lifted her up, wrapping his great hands around her forearms. She looked into his broad face, small blue eyes, freckles smeared with rain. He shook her, and she realised he'd been talking to her without her hearing.

'Get indoors, get yourself cleaned up,' he said.

She shook her head, breaking free of his grasp and moving towards the cultivator. He caught her before she'd gone three steps and held her still. Finally she nodded, but she stayed outside, watching him turning the heavy ground with the machine as easily as a child might drag a fork through sand.

She saw the taxi pull up outside and sparked into a kind of feral panic: tiredness submerged beneath the need to manage this new situation. Nobody came to High Croft in a taxi. Before she could move though, Drew was there. 'It's Alan. I called him,' he said, and relief made her knees shake with fatigue again.

'Right then lassie, let's get you indoors,' Alan slapped his brother on the back in passing and grabbed her up as though she was a bag of shopping. She saw Drip in her memory: a limp bundle wrapped in black plastic, and began to shiver.

'I'm staying here,' she said.

263

KAY SEXTON

'No, you're not. And I'll tell you why. It's time tae be canny now. Drew's one for hard work – it's as good as training for him tae work your garden. You head indoors and make yourself look nice in case anybody comes calling.'

She shook her head. 'I need to be here when Shaun gets back.'

'He'll be a while, believe me.'

'He's only gone for seed potatoes.'

'Aye, he told me. But once he was on his way I rang those nut-cases and told them he was an expert on self-sufficient living – he'll not get away for hours.'

She blinked the rain from her eyes, staring at the dark, turned earth.

'And that gives you time tae get your act together. When he comes back he'll find you and me in the kitchen having a cèilidh; it's about time you learnt some dancing.'

'Then he'll be sure I've gone mad.'

'Then he'll only be sure he can't be sure of anything. And your job's not over, Claire. Do you want tae give him a chance to say you're not up to it?' His face was concerned.

'What do you mean?'

'Well, she's packed and gone. As soon as you called him, she was off out the door ...'

'Good riddance,' Drew growled as he turned the corner behind them, the cultivator churning and whirring.

'Aye, we didn't exactly relish her ways. But she'll be trying tae poison the pot for you. You've got tae give her nothing tae work with.'

'She's out of it,' Claire put her hands to her hair, feeling her scalp burning from the tightness of the braiding. 'Isn't she?'

Alan shook his head. 'I doubt anybody would trust her easily again. But if they need a vet, who else is there?'

She agreed to shower and change her clothes. While she was dressing she heard the cultivator stop and looked out of the window

GATEKEEPER

to see the garden drilled into neat black lines, rain pooling already in the straight furrows.

Alan made coffee and poured whisky into it. 'Drew knows where there are some paving slabs doing nothing. We could lay some steppie-stones for you, so you'd not get muddy when you went for your vegetables. What do you say?'

She drank, feeling the spirit scorch its way down.

'Good idea.' Anything that kept them this side of the wall was good – Drip would rest undisturbed, not even The Project would be able to find him. They'd let him down in life, she would keep him safe in death.

Shaun appeared in the doorway, a sack in his hand. She gave him a level stare - he'd get no more help from her now he'd run to Maggie. The light disappeared behind him as Drew loomed up.

'Don't stand gawping,' Alan said. 'It took you so long we thought you'd had tae dig the spuds frae the ground.'

She shivered when he said dig and all three glanced over at her. Drew took the bag from Shaun's hand and passed it to Alan.

'They could do with a few more days,' he said, poking in the sack. 'Drew'll come over and help you cut them to seeds.'

Shaun turned to leave. Drew stood in his way. Claire lifted her mug and drank deeply, watching over the top. She wouldn't stop Drew even if he twisted Shaun's head off and kicked it around the garden. Shaun had chosen his side, and she'd found hers.

Shaun side-stepped Drew's bulk and as he reached the door, Alan, his head still bent to the sack, said, with perfect clarity, 'Something's rotten in here. I can smell it.'

Drew rumbled and once again it took Claire a few seconds to realise he was laughing. She found she was laughing too and as the hysteria took her, Alan moved behind her and held her shoulders gently until the giggles mutated into tears.

CHAPTER TWENTY-TWO

For two days the rain continued. She stayed in High Croft, watching from the kitchen window as the clouds glued themselves to the hill and emptied their cold tears. She began to believe, against all rationality, that the rain was helping her, washing all traces of Drip's death from the landscape. Drew appeared in a yellow mackintosh, and sat silent in the kitchen, cutting potatoes into neat chunks, each with two sprouts. She took pleasure in his company, remembering the time Liam had isolated her, but she still felt incapable of facing the rest of the village.

As he began to pull on his outdoor gear again he said, 'We're taking the fight to them now.'

She nodded, not caring what he meant.

'Dinnae be surprised at anything you hear.'

What she heard, the next morning, was so surprising that she opened the door, walking around the side of the croft with her coffee mug in her hand to gaze at the hill in the light drizzle that was winding down the valley.

It was Scotland the Brave, played on the pipes - and played very well. She looked at her watch. Six-thirty in the morning - breakfast time by any crofter's standards. And wolf-calling time too. The hidden piper continued until seven and she stood under the eaves and enjoyed Will Ye No Come Back Again, The Flower of Scotland and, astonishingly, Lochaber No More segueing into Letter from America. She knew who it was then and went back into the kitchen to flash the light as a signal.

GATEKEEPER

He appeared ten minutes later, pipes under his arm, his hair plaited so it fell over his shoulder like ropes. For the first time since she'd seen him on her doorstep with his brother, Claire looked at Alan McDowell and saw the true size of him: Drew made him look small, but he was no small man.

'Hidden talents?' she said, as she took his donkey jacket and handed him coffee.

'No. Just the old man wouldn't let me practice before - said it would annoy the neighbours.'

'So what changed?'

'Well, the neighbours right now are your friend and that vet woman ...'

'But they've gone, haven't they?'

'Aye, but the old man doesn't know that yet. I'm taking my chance while I can.'

She spurted laughter and saw Alan watching to see if this time she could control it. She took a deep breath and smiled. 'So he wasn't keen on Maggie?'

'That he wasn't. Nor, I'm sorry tae say, on your boyfriend. So when I asked for the return of the pipes, Father was happy I should get my wind back.'

'He wasn't my boyfriend.' She turned to the range and flipped the griddle cakes over. 'It was ... expedient to win him over.'

Alan sat. 'Well now, if only I'd known, I could have let you win me over instead and saved us all a lot of grief, let alone got some pleasure for maisel'.'

She looked back at him, and saw he was grinning. He must have seen them out there on the hills somewhere. She felt herself start to blush and then shrugged off her embarrassment. It had been part of the job. She wasn't proud of it, but whatever cooperation she'd had from Shaun had been won through sex. She'd do it again tomorrow, for the pack.

'I'll be up again at dusk,' he said as he stood to go, two griddle cakes sandwiched together with butter in his hand and another

267

KAY SEXTON

making his cheek bulge. 'Let's see what clever soul can hear wolves in this valley over the pipes.'

It was the first overt admission of The Project's work.

'And you need tae get yourself back out there with your questions and so on. Folk soon notice things, Claire and you can't claim to be ill for much longer. You're doing them no good while you're in here.'

'Them' was the wolves. She acknowledged his point without promising anything, but as soon as she'd seen him off over the hill to The Waird, she called the college and said she would be back next week for sure. She spent several minutes looking for her boots before remembering she'd buried them, and then laced on her old ones. She could buy replacements in Fort William in the week; for now she needed to go and find out how the wolves were coping.

It took her two days to find them. That wasn't unusual, but she kept thinking the worst, remembering what Ansel had told her about the other pack and Blaine's silence. If Blaine decided this pack wasn't viable either, he wouldn't bother to come and tell her. The wolves would simply vanish.

On the second afternoon she saw Agate, high above her, casting along a bank of bracken. The wolf turned back on herself twice, apparently following a scent she kept losing, then sat down for a while, curling into the tight shape wolves used in bad weather. After twenty minutes she got up again and wandered off. Claire knew her path back to the den, and decided that instead of following the wolf, she would cut ahead to see if she could pick up her trail on the return journey. She stayed further back than usual, sure the wolves must be disturbed by Drip's disappearance, and settled herself on a bank with the binoculars supported on her knees.

She had to wait for nearly two hours, feeling her flesh chill until she was beginning to shake with cold, but Agate reappeared, loping down her regular track to the main den. In her mouth she carried a rabbit, its body swinging wildly with her fast pace. Claire sighed. The new omega carrying prey home meant only one thing – Meander had given birth to cubs and was being fed by the pack. They would continue to feed her until she brought the cubs above ground. It was one small good thing after all the recent horrors.

She sat for another hour and saw Caldera and Lake swing away from the den area on a sweep of their own. At least one wolf was staying near the den entrance at all times, which was unusual. Often the alpha female would cub in a den unknown to her pack. This pack though, were making up their own rules about certain things. Claire guessed that losing Drip had unsettled them and their behaviour reflected the desire to protect Meander, and the cubs, at any cost. From now on until the cubs came up, she decided, she wouldn't come anywhere near the den. If she saw the wolves at all, she would observe them on their hunting trips.

It would be about a month before the cubs were ready to appear to the rest of the pack. For that time she would make sure that she, at least, brought no harm to them.

Some days later she saw Noel McIver's van was outside High Croft. Exhausted by an unusually difficult teaching session, was in no mood for him. She slammed her car door and strode up the path, glancing at the potato bed as she passed, noting how vigorous the plants were. She couldn't see Drip's cairn because it was lower than the wall, but she'd made sure to build another one, bisecting the remaining length of wall, so that it appeared the two buttresses had some structural purpose.

He was standing in the porch, hands in pockets, Nell at his feet.

'I want you to tell Alan McDowell not to practice bagpipes in the morning,' he said.

She glared at him. 'Tell him yourself!'

'I don't talk to him. Or his brother.'

'One, it's nothing to do with me; two I didn't think you were talking to me either and three, I quite like it.'

KAY SEXTON

He looked past her as though she was an obstruction. 'You can ban him from your land.'

'Why should I?'

His eyes finally met hers. 'I record birdsong. His pipe music drowns it out.'

So that was what he did in the early mornings. She felt a pang of sympathy – it was so Ansel-like, the image of a lone man in an empty landscape, all his attention on a tiny creature he could have crushed between his fingers.

'Look,' he walked back to his van. She followed unwillingly. She didn't want to mediate between McIver and the McDowells.

In the foot-well of the passenger side was a collection of recording equipment: fuzzy-headed microphones, leads, black boxes with knobs and dials. Nell leapt through the open window and settled herself in the passenger seat, looking smug.

He leaned in, pressed a switch. Claire realised he must have prepared for this – set up the equipment to show her. It was an unexpected view of his solitary life and she didn't welcome it.

Birdsong played, clear and plangent. 'Redstart,' he said. She nodded. Another call. 'Siskin,' he said. Another. 'Red Grouse. A harsh, almost barking sound she'd never heard before. 'Golden Eagle,' he said, watching her.

'Really?'

'I volunteered for the reintroduction project in '82.'

She remembered the return of nesting eagle pairs. Ansel had talked about it in meetings of the Collective – a sign of what was possible.

'Look – I'll talk to Alan. But I'm not banning him from the land. That would be outrageous.' Too late, she remembered she'd barred McIver from her property. He smiled thinly and walked round the van to drive off without saying thank you.

She mentioned it to Alan in the pub on Wednesday. He growled. 'I don't trust yon McSlyther.'

270

GATEKEEPER

'No, nor do I, but let's be honest, Alan, people must be aware of them by now.' By them she meant the wolves. 'It's his hobby. I feel bad about depriving him of it.'

Alan shook his head, but she noticed that he played later in the mornings from then on.

Meander brought the cubs out of the den in early May. Claire didn't see them at first, but she heard their yips, like bat calls, one warm afternoon as she sat in the trees, marking a bunch of essays she'd brought up in her backpack. She smiled but didn't move. Sooner or later she would come across them, until then it was better if they, and their mother, were able to relax undisturbed. She badly wanted to see them, hoping there would be some evidence that Drip was their sire, although she knew it was impossible to tell. Even if every pup had a dark blotch on its ear, it would mean nothing – Drip and Flow had been brothers, there was no simple way of separating their genetic markers in the cubs.

The first photograph appeared in the Highland News in May too. It was the lead story. The grainy image was a beige blur, legs obscured by bracken, streaking across a rainy hillside. The picture had been taken by a hill walker. Claire identified the wolf immediately as Agate.

She took the newspaper down to The Waird, finding Alan self-consciously sorting eggs.

'Normally Mother does it, but she's away tae Fort William, talking tae the Scottish National Party.'

She sat beside him, brushing the graded eggs with a dry cloth to remove chicken shit and feathers before placing them in boxes. The newspaper lay on the ground in front of them.

'Which one's that then?' Alan jerked his chin towards the picture.

Claire bit her lip. She hadn't named the wolves to anyone except Shaun and Ansel until now. It felt dangerous even to acknowledge them.

271

KAY SEXTON

'Agate,' she said finally.

'Aye. The one who was brought in. I guessed as much.'

They worked in silence for a while.

'Drew's up on the old logging road. Yon McSlyther will be fashed.'

'Why?'

'Building a wall, right across it. We've been moving the stones close enough for months. Shouldn't take more than a day to block it tae cars. McSlyther's the only person who goes there regularly.'

'Noel can use the path past High Croft; I've no problem with him going through.'

'Fair enough, though I'm not as confident as you. He killed our dog, you know.'

'Yes, but ... she was worrying sheep, wasn't she?'

Alan narrowed his eyes and then shrugged. 'Probably. He's not really a man tae make up stories.'

'Then the circumstances are different. The pack are taking deer, not domestic animals and they don't come down to this side ... any more.'

Alan reached over and squeezed her shoulder. 'It was the right thing you did. Difficult, but right.'

She lowered her head over the eggs, hiding the prickle of tears.

'Mother will bring in the S.N.P. for you. The line she's taking is 'Wolves were here before Sassenachs, and they're more welcome than foreigners telling us how tae manage our land.' It's a braw argument that the last wolf in Scotland was killed by the English.'

'I'm English.'

'Aye, but you're a pretty lass and you know about wolves. It's the opposition we need to think about.'

'I think we need to do two things. Keep the uncertainty going for as long as possible – claim it's a dog or a hoax photograph. And then, use the argument your mother's making: why should some bunch of outsiders come and tell us what to do? We're a community

GATEKEEPER

and it should be the community that makes any decisions. That will give me time to establish who's on our side and who's against us.'

'You can bet that McIver will be against – he'll take the opposite side tae us McDowell's on principle. If we're for the wolves, he'll be against.'

'Maybe so, but that's not the battle I want to fight. If you reframe it so that it's us against a bunch of bureaucrats and reporters: trampling the land, disturbing the game birds, vandalising our landscape, then even people who might not be comfortable with the idea of the wolves will prefer to side with us against the 'outrels'.'

Alan sat back, looking at her admiringly.

'Now that's very canny. That takes the ground out from under them.'

'I hope so. Then there's a second line of defence which is, we can all profit from this.'

'And how would that work then?'

'Well, the press will be first on the scene. They'll take over the pub which will mean a fine profit for the Heddies. Then they'll want interviews – for which people should get paid. If we can stop them bringing vehicles in, they'll need guides to take them across the hills – there should be a fair income from that. And as soon as the story really breaks, the tourists and wolf fans will start turning up. And tourists need beds and food and they buy souvenirs.'

Alan thought for a moment.

'Let me guess how everybody benefits. Katie will do roaring trade in the stores and the Heddies in the pub. Mother might sell eggs, I suppose, although I can't see too many tourists taking home live poultry tae raise. The Carline Dysters should be able tae shift all their yarn if they're canny. What about folk like the Mearns though, and the Survivalists?'

'Isobel could sell tea and coffee and cakes. And the self-sufficiency people really want to publicise their beliefs, don't they? So this would give them a wide audience for their crack-pot ideas.'

273

KAY SEXTON

'And McIver?'

Claire shook her head. No matter how many times she'd run through the scenarios she couldn't find a way for Noel McIver to gain from the presence of the wolves.

'Oh well. If somebody has tae lose out, it couldn't be a more deserving person. So what happens next, do you think?'

'Depends if the nationals pick up the story and how soon they get confirmation of the pack. The local press will be on their way already, I reckon.'

'So we're off tae the pub, are we? To see what they're about?'

There was already a newspaper reporter and a radio team at the pub, interviewing John Heddie and Jamie Maxwell, the beef farmer. Claire took her ale to a corner to watch, but Alan was straight into the fray, describing his brother as 'the great caber-tosser Drew McDowell', offering to play the pipes and denying he'd seen any wolves while equally robustly claiming it wouldn't worry him at all if he found one on his croft.

'The point is, if you farm the Highlands in harmony with nature, you've nothing tae fear. Before the Clearances, folk aye kept a shepherd in the fields and brought the cattle in at night. I'm more fashed about GM crops than about wolves and that's a fact. And anyway, if there are wolves about, it's for Glenfail to decide what tae do, not some bunch of officials. The Highlands have had too much interference already.'

'The landowner, this Italian man, what do you think he'll make of this story?' the radio reporter asked.

'Well, he's a busy man by all accounts. I doubt he'll fash himself over a photo that looks like a biggish dog having a wee trot through the heather.'

Everybody smiled.

'But I'll say this. He's a guid landlord – a man who appreciates the way of life we have here. I don't doubt he'll back us, whatever.'

Isobel Mearns, interviewed in her car as she pulled up outside her house, told the reporter she'd never heard such rubbish and they should be ashamed of themselves, chasing a figment of somebody's imagination.

Mrs McDowell, in Gaelic, said exactly what Alan had claimed she would.

Neither of the reporters had actually gone over the hill, preferring to be filmed against the backdrop of the lower burn as they recorded their stories. Claire caught one photographer trying to pass High Croft at dusk. He was persuaded to turn back, more by the Browning in her hands than by her insistence that he was trespassing.

Next morning she flagged McIver down as he headed for work.

'I'm having a gate put across the path,' she said. 'It will be padlocked, but I'll give you a set of keys.'

He stared at her impassively.

She forced a smile.

'It may just be a nine-day wonder, but I don't see why we should have a bunch of gawpers driving around the place. If they want to walk in on foot, I can't really stop them but I can block their cars.'

'If they come in on foot, good luck to them.' He smiled secretively at Nell and then looked back to Claire. 'Keys would be useful. Thank you.'

The words were grudging but at least he'd said them, she thought. She waved him on and realised neither of them had mentioned the wolves.

She rang Alan, remembering she had to walk down to the road and face west to get a signal, and asked him to buy a gate, posts, cement and a padlock.

'Should I charge it tae the estate?' he asked.

'No,' she replied, feeling her way through the possible outcomes. 'I'll pay you. I want it to look as if I'm protecting my home from trespassers. Nothing to do with any supposed wolves.'

KAY SEXTON

She continued on to the Mearns, to tell them about the gate. Isobel was brisk.

'That's up to you, of course. We never go up there; our land is all the other side of the burn. And I hope it all stops quickly. I've never heard such rubbish in my life.'

'So you don't think there is a wolf then?'

'Wolf? I credited you with more sense, Claire. But if there were – I'd go and shoot it myself.'

She walked back, deep in thought. The assumption that Isobel would be on her side – the wolves' side – was obviously wrong. Who else might she be wrong about?

She was supposed to be interviewing a family in Camaghael that day, but she rang as soon as was civilised and cancelled. They were avid for information – was it another Loch Ness hoax or did she really think there could be wolves running free in the Highlands? She gave the speech she'd rehearsed so many times. She didn't know, and anyway, wolves were not a threat to people or livestock. She'd seen farming communities elsewhere in peaceful coexistence with big predators. Nobody needed to worry yet, or probably, ever.

They didn't seem worried though, more excited, as thought something had happened that would put this remote area of rural nothingness on the map. As she hung up she wondered how many more times she would say those reassuring words about wolves being a natural part of the environment, and never attacking a human being.

Five times that day she repeated the speech; once to the Carline Dysters who had driven over in their old Morris Minor, twice in person to reporters and twice on the phone, the final time to the Daily Star.

She expected that interview to appear the next day, so after she'd given Noel his set of keys, she drove down to the stores for the morning paper delivery.

GATEKEEPER

She hadn't bargained on the photograph. It showed Caldera and Lake, sitting together as if posing for a portrait. They looked relaxed and happy and the image was excellent quality, no mistaking them for dogs or a hoax shot. The only thing she didn't understand was that the bracken around them was brown, not spring green – the picture was an old one. It must have been taken with a telephoto because the wolves were far too contented for the photographer to have been close.

She looked at Katie, who shrugged.

'Could be anywhere, that picture,' the shopkeeper said. 'Nothing to suggest it's here.'

But Claire knew the crisis point had arrived.

CHAPTER TWENTY-THREE

She badly wanted to go and check on the pack, especially the cubs, but she couldn't leave High Croft unattended; the gate kept out vehicles but anybody could climb the garden wall and walk up the hill.

They should have thought of this, she decided. One person couldn't be gatekeeper, literally now, *and* argue for the wolves – it would have meant being in two places at one time.

The first reporters arrived at noon. She heard the television trucks like tanks on the road. She checked herself in the mirror to be sure she was presentable, and then, feeling sick and shaky, opened the door to see a convoy heading towards her. She pressed her hand against the doorframe to steady herself before walking out to greet them. To do the job she was here to do.

By three in the afternoon she was exhausted. Drew had turned up to lean against the gate, looking ominous and speaking only Gaelic, to the frustration of the reporters. Claire lied, saying she didn't have the keys to the gate, and even if she had, they would have to get permission from the Signore to be on his land. That was when the reporters found out their mobiles didn't work. She neglected to tell them where they could pick up a signal.

At four a lone policemen appeared and stood around with Drew. Several film crews set off across the field on foot but were chased back, one cameraman with a twisted ankle from a rabbit hole.

GATEKEEPER

Around five they all began to fade away. Claire watched them pass the Mearns' house and sagged. Drew patted her shoulder.

'They'll be back tomorrow.'

He began to examine the ground between the Mearns' house and High Croft, placing stones in two or three spots. She was too tired to ask why.

Alan drove up a little later, bringing several roughly lopped tree trunks and sacks of cement. The brothers dug holes and cemented the wood into them.

'It's nae pretty, but if they come back tomorrow with off-road vehicles, they'll not get through,' Alan said.

By eight she was in bed. She knew she should have gone to the pub, to gauge local reaction, but she was too tired. Her throat was raw and she felt as if she would never be able to stop smiling. Her face muscles had frozen.

She heard the wolves calling as she fell asleep.

Noel McIver's car horn woke her at daybreak. She dragged out to the car, pushing her feet into untied boots, pulling her Barbour over her nightwear. She'd been sleeping in a T-shirt and sweat pants since the first report, aware that the wolves were more active at night and any crisis would probably occur after dark.

He wound down the car window and pointed to the wooden posts.

'To stop people taking off-road vehicles through here,' she said, thinking he could at least have got out of the car and knocked on the door. He was a hard man to like.

The next arrival was more welcome. Mala, in a hire car, with a small suitcase.

'I saw you on the news,' she yelled, before she'd even got out of the car. 'I thought if I rang, you might say don't come ...'

'Never,' Claire assured her. 'You can't believe how welcome you are.'

Mala quirked an eyebrow, but said nothing.

279

Claire carried the case inside and began to show her around, but Mala jerked her thumb at the door. 'Let's go for a stroll.'

Outside, she hugged Claire briefly and stepped back. 'I didn't know if it was okay to talk indoors. This is it, isn't it? This is what you've been working on since Uni?'

Claire nodded, then grinned. 'Yes, this is it. The Project.'

'Wow! I know you can't tell me anything, but as soon as I saw you on the news I knew you must be in this up to your neck. It's brilliant!'

It was only then that Claire realised nobody so far had said anything good about the wolves. Mala's enthusiasm was the first positive response she'd heard.

'Yeah, it's ... amazing. The wolves I mean. It's impossible to describe, but when you see them it's like a missing piece of the landscape got put back in place, something you didn't know was wrong until it was put right. And they've got cubs.'

Mala clapped, her eyes huge with excitement. Claire felt her own tiredness fading. It *was* brilliant, they *had* done it. Whatever came next, this moment was worth celebrating.

'As soon as I can get somebody to watch this place I'll take you up there. Maybe this evening. I can usually find one or another of them – they follow regular routes.'

'I brought you some news,' Mala sobered suddenly. 'As soon as I saw you yesterday I thought about Liam seeing you on TV as well.'

Claire imagined him in the corridor of an overnight train, heading for Scotland, watching the dark landscape rushing by – planning his attack.

'Shit! I'm so stupid, I never thought about Liam.'

'It's okay. Actually, it was pretty weird, to be honest. I dug out my old college address book and started ringing people up. I had a perfect excuse, you know. Had they seen you on TV and wasn't it amazing and who else of the old crowd were they still in touch with ...' Mala mimed a talking hand. 'Yak, yak, yak. So about the third call, somebody gave me Vidya Kavalam's number. You remember Vidya?'

Claire would never forget Vidya's averted face, hollowed by the effort of denial.

'Well, I rang her and damned if she wasn't doing exactly the same ring-around but for a different reason. Yesterday she'd had a visit from the police - they asked a lot of questions and showed her some photographs, demanding to know if she'd ever seen things like that before. She knew what they were, apparently, crimps and fuses for explosives. So she said no, of course, and asked why and they said they'd arrested a former associate of hers who might have been planning an attack on a research lab.'

'Liam?'

'None other. They wouldn't say, of course, but as soon as she started to call people she learned his flat had been raided the previous day. Is that perfect timing or what?'

Claire shook her head. 'No, not timing. Ansel.'

'Ansel?' Mala mimed smoking a pipe.

'None other,' Claire mimicked Mala's earlier words out of a sense of relief. Ansel had done what he'd promised. He had continued to watch out for her. He must have either planted the stuff, or known Liam had it and tipped off the police. Nice Ansel with his dark side – how like him to think so far ahead on her behalf.

'Does that mean Liam's been set up?'

Claire shrugged. A year ago she'd have been horrified too – now she just felt relieved that somebody was covering her back. Liam turning up in the middle of the wolf negotiations would have been a nightmare.

'He's a danger to everybody around him, Mala. Can you imagine him here, stirring up violence?'

'Yes, but – if he was framed, that's unfair.'

'Think of it as deferred justice. You, above all, have some idea how much he got away with in Brighton – now he's paying for it.'

KAY SEXTON

Mala looked uncertain.

'Okay, let me put it this way. Liam succeeds because he allies his behaviour to a good cause, most of the time anyway. People allow him to do awful things for the sake of that cause, whatever it is. But I couldn't let him bring his violence here and claim he'd done it for the wolves, so all Ansel's done is neutralise a threat to my task. He'll probably get off with a caution, but even if he doesn't – would you rather I had to beat him up again?'

'No. No, you're right. It's just a bit of a shock. I mean, Ansel? Such a nice guy?'

Claire nodded, although she'd long ago forgotten how shocked she'd been to discover Ansel's hidden side. His relationship to Blaine had clarified so much about his behaviour that she'd found difficult before; it wasn't surprising that he played the spy, with his mysterious relative as a role model.

Mala shook her head. 'So how big is this thing then? This project? If Ansel can plant stuff on Liam to keep him out of your hair …?'

'Big. Really big. Two decades of work to get to this point. I can't afford to mess up here, Mals. That's why I'm glad Liam is out of the equation.'

'Twenty years?'

'Probably more. I don't know much about that side of things – deliberately. My job is just … to be here. Right person, right place, right time to protect the pack. And to try and guarantee their future.'

Mala fanned her hand in front of her face. 'Phew! Heavy stuff! When I heard about it, I thought maybe it was a bit daft, but presumably there's a whole bunch of stuff going on behind the scenes?'

'Presumably,' Claire was distracted by the sight of the poles. Why hadn't Noel McIver stopped last night? He must have seen them as he came down off the hill. She walked over, heading around the side of the house on the track, before turning and coming back down. Yes, he would have seen them, if he'd driven out past her cottage.

'Claire?'

'Sorry, just an odd thought.'

She came back to Mala's side. 'I'm glad you're here. Really glad.'

'Yeah, me too. As long as I don't have to beat anyone up.' Mala's smile was crooked. 'So what happens next?'

'Good question. I'm supposed to just react to what happens.'

'Supposed to?'

Well ...' Claire felt re-energised. 'It's a bit passive. All I've done so far is hand out spiel to the media and stop them getting past me in cars.' What else should a Gatekeeper be doing, she wondered? 'I can't help thinking I should be doing more.'

'Like what?'

'Like winning friends and influencing people.'

That evening, with Drew sitting on the doorstep like a tartan Buddha, she took Mala to see the wolves.

They made a large circle around the edge of Agate's territory. Claire wanted to ensure that if any wolf was made skittish by their approach, it would be inclined to head away from High Croft rather than towards it. She was anxious to see the cubs, not just for Mala's sake but to establish whether Meander had been disturbed enough to move them to a new den. It didn't seem possible the wolves could have escaped the excitement, but as they walked, and the sounds of dusk began to filter through to her, Claire felt again how small the village was, compared to the wolves' terrain, and how little attention they paid to it. With Drip gone, none of them had ever crossed the stream below the falls, let alone approached the track. She let herself hope that distance had protected them.

When they reached the vantage point she saw the cubs were out, playing with their mother. She handed the binoculars to Mala and sat back to scan the immediate neighbourhood. Mala was silent for a long time, watching the pack, then she tugged Claire's arm and

KAY SEXTON

held out the glasses. Claire squinted at the new arrival; she could always distinguish the wolves, even at this distance.

'Flow,' she murmured. 'He's the alpha male.

'That's the cubs' daddy then, am I right?'

Claire nodded. Not even to Mala would she explain why she hoped not. It made no real difference – only alphas mated and had cubs and the whole pack invested in their upbringing, so Drip would never have been a father in normal circumstances – but she wanted to believe he had a physical continuation, a line that would survive him. All future cubs would be Flow's. Let these three be his brother's. And not just that. She also wanted to think Drip had mated with Meander: that he'd had every experience open to him in his short life.

'They're so beautiful,' Mala said. 'So relaxed. Who could ever object to them if they'd seen them like this?'

They stayed until the light became too dim to distinguish the wolves. As they walked back, Claire thought about what Mala had said. She wanted to do something – to stop being reactive – and Mala was right. Seeing the cubs being cosseted by the pack was a powerful counter-argument to the 'vicious wolf' myth that some of her neighbours clearly believed.

She decided to pick out the most sympathetic and influential journalist and give him, or her, an exclusive when the time was right: a chance to film the cubs. Quite how to do it, she didn't yet know. It would require careful planning to preserve her status as a chance element in the release project.

'I wonder why people say 'ravening wolves' she said. 'Nothing else ravens. You don't get ravening lions.'

'I've been thinking about costs,' Mala countered. 'I still can't get my head around the money that's been spent.'

If only you knew, Claire thought. If you knew about two packs and two sites and two Gatekeepers, you'd be amazed.

'And it's not just the money,' Mala continued. 'Think about the timescale.'

'I don't really know about the history, I could make some guesses, but I won't, even with you. But if you think about it, what's the whole cost? One Impressionist painting? Two biggish diamonds? Three month's running costs for a film studio? There are plenty of people out there with that kind of money.'

'Maybe. Yeah, you're right; the rich are a different species. But the timescale is still boggling.'

Claire stood still. Why hadn't she ever thought of that? She'd been looking for Project members in her own age group, but the core of Blaine's support would be people of his generation. So Drew and Alan weren't just Project, they were second-generation. One or both of their parents could have been with Blaine from the beginning. And Ansel was definitely a child of The Project – no wonder they were all so committed to the cause, they'd been inculcated with it from childhood. She'd probably been the last in; her paranoia had been justified, not because it was based on fear of discovery but because all those around her were bound together through years of silent support for the wolves. She'd been an outsider – unfamiliar with their long, secret history – they'd shut her out because they were locked into cosy relationships established for decades. There had been no room for her.

'Fuck! Ansel told me I was naïve – why the hell didn't I think of that!'

Mala looked quizzical. 'What?'

'Oh, it's not important, or it's not important now, but if I'd realised a couple of years ago ...'

She wouldn't have done anything differently, she conceded. The same blindness to personal motivation had caused her to misjudge the Collective and led to her expulsion. It was part of her – an innate failing.

KAY SEXTON

Mala glanced at her and took the lead, leaving her to follow as slowly as she wished. Claire saw how Mala backed off – recognising her vulnerability and giving her time to manage the new insight with dignity. Mala had always been supportive: of her parents, her sister, her friends. 'Mals?' Claire felt her legs begin to shake. 'What do they call that moment when you can see everything clearly?'

Without turning Mala replied, 'Revelation?'

'Nope, another word,' Claire stumbled and sat down.

'Eureka, insight, epiphany?'

'Mals?'

Mala turned. 'Are you okay? Did you trip?'

'I don't know. I don't know if I'm okay.'

She waited for Mala to sit down next to her.

'Look, I'm not sure how far I can go with this, but if I don't say it now, I probably never will. I just worked something out. You remember what happened with Liam, back in Brighton?'

Mala nodded. Claire could barely make out her face in the dusk. A late bee zigzagged past, racing home against the dark.

'I was thinking that I've done the same kind of thing with this project: been oblivious to all kinds of undercurrents that might have helped me, and I thought 'Oh, that's me, the way I'm made' but it's not. I didn't used to be …'

'Obtuse?' Mala suggested.

Claire snorted. 'Is that a polite way of saying dense?'

Mala said nothing.

'Okay, obtuse then. It's something to do with … after my mother died.'

Mala tilted her face to the evening sky - its pale oval seemed un-shadowed by features. She held up her hand and Claire paused.

A sweet jangling bird song filled the silence

'Blackbird,' Claire said when it was over. 'The pre-dawn chorus starts at 3am and some birds sing until eleven at night in summer.'

'After your mother died …' Mala prompted.

GATEKEEPER

'Yeah. I'm not going to get into the history, it's not important ...'

Mala made an inexpressibly graceful gesture, signifying acceptance. Claire reached over and took her hand, fearing that she might lose the nerve to speak after all.

'Anyway, I did tell Ansel. He knows all about it. The thing is ... I'm not obtuse. I just prefer not to see. I don't want to know ... didn't want to know, any of that stuff about people, really because what I found out about my parents was so wrong, that I couldn't face anybody else's secrets. But even so, by accident I got to see some of Ansel's ... 'weirdness' I think is the best word for it. Since them I've been closing myself off to anything except what people what to show; the front everybody puts up.'

'So?' Mala's voice was cool but the accompanying squeeze of her hand was comforting.

'So ...' Claire sighed. 'Yeah, so what? I've had this moment of truth, but it doesn't change anything.'

'Truth doesn't change things. People do. But perhaps you don't need to change?'

'I don't know.'

'There is another way to look at it, Claire. When we met, at university, I trusted you immediately. You were willing to accept me. You didn't pry into my family or my sex life, or my beliefs. We just got on with life. It helped me to believe other people could have relationships without strings - and if they could, I could too, one day. That did me a lot of good.'

Claire exhaled.

'Thank you. For that, and for listening, Mals.'

'One more thing. You're very good at causes, Claire – you never stop fighting for what you believe in. I wonder what your life would be like if you believed in yourself.'

'I don't know what to say to that,' Claire felt exposed and uncomfortable.

287

KAY SEXTON

'When I first started standing up to my parents, I used to get the giggles. Not outside, but inside a part of me would be laughing because it couldn't believe I was doing it. I would watch myself like something on a TV show and expect the presenter to pop up any minute and say 'Fooled you!' I mentioned it to my therapist and she said it wasn't anything to do with my past. She said everybody feels as if they're playing a role at times. It's part of being human. The thing that makes it dangerous is when we use the role to hide from ourselves. It stops us feeling naked - but it also stops us growing.'

Claire was glad it was dark. So much insight from a woman she'd once thought was a sweet but dizzy creature.

The blackbird sang again. When it finished Mala stood, still holding Claire's hand, and they walked down to High Croft in silence.

CHAPTER TWENTY-FOUR

The wolf story refused to die. A football love-triangle pushed it from the front pages, but pundits kept popping up, for and against, and a rash of unconfirmed sightings across the UK from Glasgow housing estates to Wiltshire farms, filled inside columns with faked or erroneous pictures. At least it took the pressure off Glenfail.

'That's a dog,' Alan stabbed the Wiltshire article with his finger, and three or four pub regulars nodded agreement. 'Are these people, blind, daft or what?'

'Greedy,' Claire suggested. 'They get paid for these stories, remember.'

Alan looked embarrassed. It was common knowledge he was charging reporters £500 for a tour of the wolves' supposed territory, although in fact the terrain he was guiding them over was well off any wolf's regular route.

'If you get caught, I won't help you,' Claire had warned him after the Signore had declared that anybody caught on his property would be charged with trespass and, if appropriate, criminal damage.

Alan had grinned. 'It's better for them tae get a wee tour from me, than head up there alone. I'm doing them a favour, all that fresh air and countryside. They come back with a braw appetite.'

Mala had been gone for three days and Claire was still thinking about their conversation. She'd never planned beyond this point, never thought what she would do when The Project ended.

KAY SEXTON

Of course she still had her job, and her PhD research, and perhaps Bruno, but imagining a life without the pack to give it focus was difficult. What purpose would she have? She wasn't sure she would even be the same person if she had no cause to work for. What Mala had said resonated through the short evening hours she spent out watching the wolves – what would her life be like if she believed in herself, rather than in some cause like The Project?

Bruno had called, once the story reached the Italian press, and they'd talked about the wolves. He'd shared some minor office gossip and made the conversation a success by not asking anything awkward, like when she was coming back. Only when he'd hung up did she think she might have raised the subject herself. It was five months since she'd seen him – perhaps he'd given up on her. She could imagine him at Sunday dinner with his parents, his mother quizzing him about their relationship.

'She's busy being a wolf-mother,' he would say.

'I knew she wasn't right for you,' Signora Contadino would reply.

'Actually, I think she might have been perfect for me. A wife who spent *half* her time on a distant mountain-top would give you plenty of opportunity to make up for her inadequacies in the way of cooking and cosseting me. But not *all* her time – I'm afraid I've lost Claire to a pack of wild marauders.'

And he would smile and turn the conversation to politics and she would become a footnote in their family history: Bruno's wolf-woman.

She grabbed her backpack and headed for the hill. She would go and watch the cubs.

They were some seven weeks old now – nearly weaned; their eyes already dark and their skinny bodies just starting to catch up with their oversized feet. Personalities had been established. Eddy, as she'd named the male, was demanding and pugnacious. Although he treated the alpha male with respect, he already bullied

290

GATEKEEPER

Agate and kept his sisters in their place, often by climbing onto a hillock and jumping on their heads. Torrent was a quiet creature, usually curling up against the guardian wolf for reassurance. And Puddle. When Claire looked at Puddle she felt her eyes fill. She tried to control the reaction, but each new sighting brought her to smiling tears. Puddle was Drip reincarnate. If there was something to fall off or into, she fell; if there was a game to be played, she played it – hiding behind trees and leaping out, wriggling under fallen branches and getting stuck, digging frantically after some bug until her nose and paws were black and her excited yips earned her a warning growl from the duty wolf. And she rolled with a voluptuous *aah aah* – a soprano version of the dead male's pleasure. Even if she lacked the dark ear blotch, she had replaced him – and Flow seemed closer to her than either of the other cubs, as if he too appreciated her nature.

On this day they were drowsy, soaking up dappled sun in a glade near the upper tree line. Eddy bounced self-importantly around the clearing for a while before settling to sleep and the two female cubs napped together, twitching their feet and ears as they dreamed. Agate lay a short distance away. Claire watched through the binoculars for more than an hour. She'd scanned the clearing for any evidence of a kill, something to suggest the cubs were now being fed solid meat rather than that regurgitated by their pack seniors, but she could spot nothing.

When she lowered the glasses Flow was watching her.

He was closer than he had ever been before. Closer than she'd come to any live wild wolf. His eyes were bright but hostile. She lowered her own gaze, knowing that to stare into his face would be taken as a challenge, but it was almost impossible not to lock eyes with him; his intense focus demanded it.

She watched his chest instead, the rhythmic rise and fall of his breath, and realised he was growling. It was so quiet as to be almost sub-vocalisation but it was a warning all the same.

KAY SEXTON

She wanted to look over at the cubs, to see if they were even visible to the naked eye. Did he know what she'd been observing? Stupid question – of course he did. Even if he couldn't see them, he could smell them, and probably hear them, even at this distance.

His stance became stiff-legged, his muzzle slightly raised, a sneer rather than a full-blown snarl, but she felt her body hollow out with fright.

She'd thought that, up close, his eyes would be glowing, fiery, like banked peat, but they were cold. She'd felt a brief fear with Kaya, soon lost in the female's playfulness, but Flow was unnerving. Her mouth and throat filled with hot cotton, her hands began to shake and she was terrified equally to look at him or look away. The instinctive horror of a wolf attack made sense at last. She knew a healthy wolf never attacked a grown human. She knew it. She no longer believed it.

She watched his head droop, like a raindrop sliding down a stem. Now he was looking up at her with his shoulders tensed. He could spring at her if he chose.

There was nothing in his posture but intention, no emotion, no clues to his thoughts. A perfect machine designed to defend its territory to the death.

She began to shake, her teeth juddered together. The binoculars rattled against her boot. He stepped forward.

She was caught in his gaze. She had to look away but she couldn't. A tiny sound came from her throat, like a squeak. He blinked.

She remembered Kaya guzzling milk. She could see Flow doing the same, but with her blood. How could she have thought wolves were safe?

He took another step and she yelped again, her right foot, nearest him, withdrawing spastically from his proximity.

He stopped.

GATEKEEPER

Shaun had said wolves had stimulus intelligence – you didn't know what they knew until the time came for them to use it. Could Flow know she'd killed his brother?

Her rational mind said not – and then reconsidered. What if Flow had gone looking for Drip in the two days she'd hidden in High Croft? He could have smelt out the sequence of events – maybe he'd even seen her that day, with the rifle in her hands.

She didn't know what any of them were capable of, but she'd thought she knew enough not to underestimate them. Faced with Flow's icy calm, she knew she'd misjudged, again. Perhaps he'd always followed, from a distance, watching over his clownish sibling, just as he guarded the cubs now.

Drip had never given a sign that he was being hand-fed in the enclosure, even with eight cameras covering his every movement. Why hadn't she ever reflected on the intelligence it had required for him to elude observation? A new thought came, with the force of a seizure, jerking her legs into her body, making Flow twitch. Stimulus intelligence - had Drip smelt Maggie at The Waird? Was it her presence that had triggered an old memory and led him to seek her out? Would his scavenging instinct have remained dormant forever, without her scent to jolt him back into an established habit?

If her suspicion was true, Maggie had signed Drip's death warrant with her arrival in the Highlands.

The McDowell boys would know when Drip had appeared at their home – she had to find out how culpable Maggie was. But first she had to deal with Flow.

Stimulus intelligence. Behaviour that was only triggered by circumstance. Flow was hostile but not aggressive – how could she persuade him she was harmless? What stimulus would cause him to recognise her as non-threatening?

She licked her dry lips and, looking slightly to one side of Flow's concentrated glare, began to hum under her breath.

'*Amazing Grace, how sweet the sound ...*'

KAY SEXTON

Flow cocked his head.

'*That saved a wretch, like me ...*'

He lifted his head, looking down his nose with what seemed to be scorn. Then he flicked his ears, turned sideways and was gone, running silently uphill.

'*Amazing Grace, how sweet the sound...*'

She got to her feet, shaking, unable to remember the rest of the words. It took several attempts to get the binoculars into the backpack, her fingers fumbling at the straps. She sang the whole time, starting the lyrics again as soon as she reached the end of the lines she could remember. Walking down through the trees, she kept her pace steady: not running even when she reached open ground - it was pointless to run, she knew that now.

Back at High Croft she grabbed her mobile - what could she say to Alan to get the information she needed? How much did she need to code the conversation? She ran out to the signal point and punched his number.

'Alan? Hi. Look, do you remember when you had your problem – the, uh, leak? Can you remember what day the drip started?'

His answer was immediate. 'Third of February.'

'And when did your unpopular guests arrive?'

'Twenty-second of February.'

'Okay, thanks.'

'Hold on Claire ...' she heard him speaking Gaelic and then he came back on the line. 'More news for you: there's going to be a community meeting – the M.E.P suggested it. A chance for us all to get together and talk about 'emerging events' is the way he put it.'

She waited to see if there was more he wanted to say. There was.

'The S.N.P. will be coming in force, mother says. You're not to worry.'

'I won't. Worry won't help. Thanks Alan. Look ... the longer we give people to get used to the wolves, the better it's going to go

294

GATEKEEPER

for us, so there's no rush to get this together, right? Any delaying tactics you can use will be a help.'

'Right. I'll tell mother, but she won't be best pleased; she's not good at hanging back.'

'I understand, really I do. I'm not good at being patient myself, but I've had to learn. Believe me – every day we gain is like a vote in our favour.'

She walked back slowly. So Maggie couldn't be blamed directly for Drip's change in behaviour. She realised how much she'd wanted the woman to be at fault, to make stronger the case against her. And behind that realisation was an uglier one – that Claire herself was moving from one cause to another. Already she was thinking of when the wolves were settled, when this was over. And when that happened she intended to go looking for Maggie.

She felt sick. Physically sick at her herself but sick in her head too, a buzzing like concussion. A dull aching. She'd become something vile. Like Liam. Somebody who wanted to hunt down a victim, to make them suffer. The fact that her hatred for Maggie was warranted didn't make it any better. She had become what she despised.

The date of the community meeting was changed twice: the first time to accommodate the very M.E.P. who'd arranged it and who had to fly back from Brussels to attend, the second to fit in with a wolf expert that Noel McIver – in his role as spokesman of the anti-wolf members of the community - had invited to attend.

Claire became increasingly febrile with each delay. The long hours of daylight made it hard to sleep and yet by afternoon she would be drowsy and slow like a sun-drugged wasp. And about as friendly, she had to admit.

Even though she'd wanted to delay decisive action on the wolves, to gain time to win people over, delays not of her own making fed her irritability. She snapped at Alan and pointed out to Katie that she'd been short-changed in the shop. It was like first-night nerves but the feeling dragged on and on with each postponement until she wanted to smash plates. She began to visit the wolves earlier, staying longer, observing them for hours until her arms ached from holding the binoculars.

As the weather improved, the pack spent more time sleeping in the sun and the cubs ranged further. Eddy often harassed his timid sister Torrent into following him on some spree but Puddle headed off alone, ambling away from the adults to investigate some new smell, returning to curl up by Flow, who tolerated her playful ambushes although he disciplined Eddy for trying the same thing.

Agate slipped back into her omega role as the pups needed less supervision. Often she spent much of the day alone, sitting and staring over the landscape. It was impossible not to think she missed her original pack and her voice was always the first to be raised in the calling howl that Claire felt sure the wolf still hoped would be answered by her old companions. It seemed to annoy Meander, who always followed up Agate's calling howl with a dominance display that made the omega tuck her tail under and crouch in submission.

Pack dynamics were much on Claire's mind as the cubs grew. The estate could support one pack easily if it had the cooperation of the tenants, but two only if the second pack was small. The most likely outcome – the desirable outcome – was that Agate would continue to fission from her group and as soon as Eddy was old enough to challenge Flow, he would splinter off with her to form a new couple. If they were tolerated by the main pack, they could create a secondary unit within eighteen months.

After that things would get more complicated. European packs tended to be small – three to five wolves. Flow, maintaining dominance over four females and three cubs, was at the outer boundary of what could be expected of a young male. If Meander had a larger litter in the following year, and Eddy and Agate's splinter pack also produced young, the territory would be stretched, not in terms of food, but by the need to keep a satisfactory distance between two competing males.

During the day, when she had spare time, she would examine her map of the Highlands, wondering how far the wolves might travel and how they would be received. So far the adults had not strayed much. Their early conditioning, abundant food and – she suspected – Drip's disappearance, inhibited ranging behaviour.

The cubs though, had no such limitations. Already Puddle was exhibiting the confident curiosity that had been Drip's main characteristic. It would be the new generation that moved into territory beyond Claire's reach or knowledge. She feared for them.

The photograph of the two wolves that had been in the newspapers worried her too. It had to have been taken by a Project member and released deliberately. Why? Why that picture, why those wolves? She kept a photocopy of it on the kitchen wall and stared at it while she ate.

Caldera was the most photogenic wolf so it made sense to choose her as the first image most people would see. And she was always with Lake, so a picture of both of them was logical. Flow would have been too much like the wolf of myth: handsome, stern and deadly. Meander was a nice-looking creature, but had none of Caldera's grace. Showing two wolves made it clear it was a pack, not an escaped pet, so that made sense too. The quiet repose and obvious affection between them must have been part of the decision. But ... it still nagged at her. No matter how often she thought it through, Claire was sure she was missing something.

Ansel had vanished on another of his fishing-industry secondments, this time to the Indian Ocean. She emailed him regularly, but received no replies. With Mala she had more frequent contact; they still sent postcards most weeks, but often she would walk up to a placed where she could get a mobile signal and call Mala in the evening to talk – not about wolves but about issues. They discussed feminism, ecological footprints, global warming: ideas

KAY SEXTON

they'd explored at college. Claire knew that if she wanted to, she could reopen the subject of her past, or Mala's, and that knowledge, for now, was enough. She'd learnt to think before acting, and now she was learning to think her way through her own emotions – for years she'd turned her back on her fears and doubts and now she was finding her way again, slowly. She'd even rung her father to tell him not to worry, only to have him say that he'd been buying all the newspapers that had her picture in. She was the talk of the pub, he said. To her surprise she felt happy that he was proud of her.

In June she received a huge ornate invitation to the christening of Massimo Moretti. It was decorated with gilt and smothered in fat babies she immediately identified as the schmaltzy cherubs called *putti*. It was addressed to Claire Benson and Bruno Contadino. She rang him immediately.

'Theresa's baby boy? He's as big and bouncing as any Italian parents would wish. In fact he looks like Mussolini in a bib.'

She sank down onto the windowsill, looking out at the sunlit hill.

'When did you see him?'

'He's been to the office.'

'No way!'

'Oh yes,' Bruno's voice was full of laughter. 'Theresa and Paolo have wasted no time in getting young Massimo on the ladder to success. He's visited his future place of employment and networked with his patrons-to-be. In fact he networked all over Professore Giordano's shirt, but such things are not likely to be held against him. In fact I suspect D.G. VIII have already assigned him a desk in their pleasure at seeing the professor mopping baby vomit from his tie.'

The pang of homesickness she felt was visceral. She wanted to have been there to meet the baby and share in Theresa's triumph.

'Can you come to the christening?' he asked.

'I don't think so. I want to. I hate the idea of missing it. But ...'

GATEKEEPER

'It's difficult for you to leave there at present. I understand.'

She tried to read his tone of voice and decided it was sympathetic but not warm.

'Could you ... could you come here? For a weekend perhaps?' She hadn't known she was going to invite him and her fingers locked around the handset as she waited for his reply. 'I'd like to show you the wolves.' Why had she said that? Why not just admit she wanted to see him.

'I think not. I wouldn't get on with wolves. I'm too much of a bear in the morning, and wolves and bears don't exist happily together.'

She laughed, but his rejection hurt and she knew the pain would increase as soon as she was free to concentrate on it.

'No Claire, you have a job to do there. It's better to keep things separate, don't you think?'

'Yes, you're right of course.' She knew she sounded dull and distant - it was how she felt.

'But shall I go to the christening and take a gift from both of us?'

'As a couple?'

'As a couple.'

It was a clue. No, more than that, it was Bruno saying, as delicately as possible, that she still came first with him.

'Yes, that would be great! I'll tell you what, I'll go shopping tomorrow and courier something Scottish to you as my part of the gift. A little silver dagger, a *sgian dubh* they're called; Scotsmen wear them in their socks.

'Entirely appropriate - young Massimo can use it to stab FAO staffers in the back – we're always doing it to each other.'

There was a pause before he asked, 'When are you coming back, Claire?'

She thought for a moment. 'Soon. I'm coming home soon. And permanently.'

299

KAY SEXTON

'Home?' Now his voice was bright with humour.

'Yes, home! They call me an outrel here – it means outsider. Rome is where I belong,' she hoped he understood that she was asking to be let back into his life.

'You aren't going to stay anywhere permanently, Claire. You're not that kind of woman. But if Rome is your base, the place you return to ...'

She waited.

He laughed. 'Let's talk about it when you get here.'

She sat for a while, thinking of all the possible implications of his words. The undoubted fact was that he was giving her a second chance, without conditions, but she this time she would have to be sure she made things work.

CHAPTER TWENTY-FIVE

Isobel gave her the name of a silversmith in Fort William who stocked ceremonial *sgian dubh* and offered to come shopping with her, a concession that surprised and warmed Claire.

'Actually, I'm going to stay overnight. Get a facial, have my hair trimmed, the works,' she said. It was part of the plan. From now on she would divide her mind as she had at university: part for the wolves, and part for Rome and Bruno. Shopping for the christening fitted into the Rome half and she would make the most of it. She was a Gatekeeper, not a nursemaid, the wolves could manage without her for a day and a night.

'I suppose you want to look for best for the community meeting?' Isobel asked.

'No. Well, yes, of course I want to be presentable, but I'm hoping to see a friend soon and I'd like to be looking nice.'

'Your friend from Rome?' Isobel looked surprised.

'The very one.'

'Is he coming here then?'

Claire shook her head. 'No. My research is about done, and I need to think about heading home.'

Isobel gave her the long assessing look Claire remembered from their trip to the Henwife.

'I'm surprised. Most folk think you're staying in Glenfail for good now.'

'That was never part of my plan. I came here to conduct research. The wolves altered a lot of things, but I never planned to stay for good. My career is in Rome.'

'And your young man too.'

'Yes.'

Isobel smiled. 'I'm glad for you. I wish you every happiness.'

'That's a bit premature.'

'Och, I can see your face, Claire, I don't need to hear the bells to know what's coming. You've decided to make a go of it with him – I hope you're going to get married and raise lots of children.'

Claire blinked. Marriage hadn't even entered her head.

'Will you have to become a Catholic?'

'We haven't even …'

'Och, well, there's time enough. If you do though, I'll ask John's brother to come and look after this place so we can come to the wedding. I've never been to a Catholic ceremony – but I don't suppose one will do me any harm.'

After a second Claire grinned. 'You're pulling my leg.'

'I'm glad to see you more like your old self, that's for sure. Whatever else those wolves have done, they've worn you to the bone.'

Isobel's words were friendly but her concern came as a shock. Claire looked in the mirror when she got back to High Croft. She was thinner, but she thought she looked fine. The combination of hill-walking and Tae Kwon Do had given her a solid musculature and her skin was tanned from the hours spent outdoors. Her eyes did look tired though - tired, or perhaps evasive.

She remembered Flow's gaze, as penetrative as an X-ray and Drip's warm, often puzzled, eyes as he took in every new thing the world showed him. Her eyes looked as if they were only used to measure threats – she had the harried look of a prey creature, fearing what might appear next. She shook off the introspection and went to pack a bag.

GATEKEEPER

Later – as she sat under a Scots Pine, watching Agate trying to supervise the cubs who were play-killing a large piece of bark – the analogy of predator and prey came back to her.

Ansel had said her ability to respond to circumstances was her great strength. But all he knew of her was the last few years: nothing, really, of her childhood. It took a degree of self-confidence to be resilient, to change and adapt, the wolves proved that. Puddle, despite being the clumsiest of the cubs, was indomitable in her belief that she could do anything she wanted, whereas the bigger and more physically assured Torrent seemed to have already decided that the world was a place best experienced from the shelter of another wolf's shadow.

Drip had shown the same ebullient adventurousness as Puddle. Despite being the omega he had travelled more than the other wolves and – she was sure now – had impregnated his brother's mate. In the end his confidence had led him to his death, but without Maggie's disastrous behaviour he could have been an alpha, he could have taken Agate and formed his own pack. He'd been the most complete personality she'd ever met - human or animal – willing to clown, to be serious, to help others, to take risks and in the end – to die.

Not once, not ever, had he hung back. First to leave the den - according to Shaun, first to Agate's side when she was introduced, first to cross the burn. And first to get injured, first to pay Flow's price for inadequate submission, first to suffer the consequences of human interference.

She couldn't ask herself what Drip would have done in her place; the concept was meaningless – but she could decide whether she wanted to be like him or like Torrent. She could go forwards, trusting to herself, or hold back and wait for things to come to her.

No contest, she decided. Go forwards. Live her life, take some risks of her own for a change, meet Bruno more than halfway. Let Maggie worry about when she might appear – Claire wouldn't seek

KAY SEXTON

revenge. In fact, leaving Maggie to expect her at any time might be the best revenge of all.

Puddle fell in the burn again. It was probably the fourth time in the past couple of weeks she'd stood on the edge, watching the flashing water, and overbalanced. Both other cubs had learned to lie down when playing with the water, but not Puddle. Claire was pretty sure she was doing it on purpose.

She put down the binoculars, knowing that what would happen next was best viewed from a distance. Too close a focus would lose some of the details.

Agate sprang to the water, giving the high-pitched yips that warned of a problem. Puddle swam out towards the middle while her siblings bark-howled, running along the bank. Distant answering yips came from the other adults, already converging on the source of the noise. Agate grabbed for Puddle's scruff with her teeth, but the cub twisted away.

Eddy found a place where he could stand belly-deep in the water, watching his sister and began to issue yip-howls, taking on the role of auditory beacon so Agate was free to pursue Puddle.

All wolves could swim, it was innate, and Drip had been a keen fisherman. The cub was in no real danger - she was just bored on a hot day and felt like causing mayhem. Agate though, hated the cubs to enter the water and rarely went to the far bank. She became agitated when the adults crossed the upper burn and could only bring herself to follow when the pack had already left her far behind. Claire wondered if Drip's visits to The Waird had triggered this fear. Maybe his return, still damp and smelling of human things, reminded her of her pack's disappearance.

It was always a toss-up if Flow or Meander would be the first to arrive when a cub alarm was raised. This time it was Meander, flying down the hill, past her other cubs and into the water, without breaking step. She swam past Puddle and turned broadside to the current. The cub was now safe, and trapped. She couldn't get

GATEKEEPER

past her mother, and Agate was closing in for another grab. Puddle would be hauled from the water, rolled onto her back and scolded. For the rest of the evening, every move she made would result in an adult closing its jaws gently around her muzzle while growling – telling her she was in disgrace.

But Puddle had worked out a strategy. She ducked under the water. A stream of bubbles appeared on the surface, and both adults plunged their heads too, seeking her out.

Immediately she reappeared, flung herself onto Agate's back and from there scrambled to the bank.

The two females stood in the water, staring at her. Flow materialised on the far bank. Meander climbed out and headed for the cub, tail high in dominance mode. Puddle dodged and, as Agate put her forepaws on the bank, sprang forwards, pushing the omega back into the water.

Meander stopped and shook herself, watching her daughter sidelong. Agate put a paw on the bank and Puddle shoulder-barged her, knocking her back into the burn. The cub yapped with excitement and pranced, tail high, until her mother growled a warning. Agate regained the bank downstream from Puddle and began to shake herself. Puddle pranced again, using the straight-legged high leap all wolves employed to catch rodents. Agate shook her off, but she didn't growl.

Claire looked over at Flow, who was observing the cub. After a moment he loped into the water, not needing to swim, and climbed the near bank. Puddle threw herself flat on the turf, wagging her tail ingratiatingly. He stood over her, dominating her until she rolled on her back. Agate left, heading into the woods, her tail low.

Claire knew she'd observed a change in the pack hierarchy. Puddle's behaviour didn't just express her desire to be treated as an adult, not watched over as a juvenile. She'd successfully thwarted Agate – essentially she was demanding a higher place in the pack than the omega. It would be a couple more months before the issue

305

was resolved, and hierarchies changed constantly, but Puddle had asserted herself against an adult for the first time – she was claiming her rights. Perhaps one day she would challenge her mother for alpha female status, Claire wouldn't be around to see it, but the feisty display was a good indicator of the pack's future viability. Already the free-born cubs were surpassing the enclosure-raised adults.

It felt like a message to her. The cubs had moved past their parents already – but she'd stayed where she'd been, emotionally, when her mother died. It was time for her to move on too.

The night before the public meeting she was invited to The Waird for dinner. She wasn't surprised to find herself eating chicken.

Tam McDowell was 'on the hill' and his dog, Kneb, lay in the yard, disconsolate. Claire noted that Kneb, like most local sheepdogs, had acquired a broad studded collar. Axl Rose, the pup in training, hated his, and sat under the table trying to scratch it off. Drew bent and smeared the dog's front paws with barbecue sauce to distract him.

'He'll get used to it,' Alan said. 'It's a problem though. Nobody here collars a dog – too likely tae get hooked on a branch or a fence. Teaching folk different will be like pushing water uphill.'

'Why do you need to?'

Alan frowned. 'A collared dog's hard tae mix up with a wolf – that's the main reason: if there's any dogs seen running on the hills near farms, we don't want them mixed in with the pack in people's minds and causing panic. And we don't want tae give McSlyther any excuses to shoot any more of our dogs, so ...'

'He wouldn't, would he?'

'He did before. The point is, we're just trying tae set a good example.'

Claire was more worried about the wolves going after lambs in the fields next spring, and said so.

Drew spoke in Gaelic and strode off. Alan held up his hand. 'Wait now. With any luck he'll explain for himself.'

She waited, watching three broody hens in the croft-yard. Kneb ignored them, but Axl Rose couldn't decide whether to finish cleaning his paws, have another go at the collar, or stalk the roosting birds. He zigzagged between the three desires, creeping a few steps towards a hen, before stopping to lick a foot or scratch at his neck. Mrs McDowell, turning spatchcocked chicken on the barbecue, watched him too. As he decided on the nearest hen she picked up a wooden stake and, as the dog approached the hen, threw it so it landed behind him. He yelped and ran. Alan gathered the wood and put it back on the wall. There were half a dozen such weapons there.

'Mother trains them to be wary of hens. A McDowell dog believes every hen comes with a guardian angel – isn't that so mother?'

Mrs McDowell smiled broadly.

Drew reappeared with a plastic spray bottle.

'Go on then, tell Claire how it works,' Alan urged, but Drew put the container down on a table and ambled off to play with Axl Rose. Alan shook his head. Claire saw that his face was strained and his eyes weary.

'Tell him, mother,' he said.

Mrs McDowell spoke in Gaelic and Alan scowled.

'I'm taking Claire to see the chicks,' he said.

Inside one of the low barns, Claire looked at pens filled with cheeping birds and Alan scrubbed his fingers through his hair, grumbling.

'She's nae help at all!'

'Your mother? It must be difficult for her, not speaking English ...'

'You think? She's doing it deliberately.'

'Doing what?'

He came and stood beside her, looking down on the scurrying birds.

'I want Drew to speak more English. It's nae good if I have tae do all the talking. But he doesn't have the confidence. It halves

KAY SEXTON

our effectiveness for him tae stick tae Gaelic, he can't deal with the English press, nor half the Scots, if it comes tae that.'

She noted how strong his accent had become, as though he was straddling some linguistic barrier himself – speaking English but with Gaelic intonations.

'Is he shy?'

'Well ... he's very young, I suppose.'

'Is he?' She'd never thought about their ages, they were called the McDowell boys as though 'boy' was their occupation and with both being more than six feet tall, it was like guessing the age of a tree. Now she looked at Alan again and saw he was not a boy at all. 'How old are you both?'

'I'm twenty-seven. Drew's twenty.'

'Really?' She would have guessed only a year or two separated them. 'Twenty? I thought he was older than that.'

'Folk do. Always have. When he was twelve, people took him for sixteen. And when he was sixteen, and took the job on the radio masts, everybody treated him like a grown man. I suppose it's difficult for him – but what's the point two of us being out there if Drew won't talk tae anybody?'

'I suppose that at that age a lot of people are self-conscious ...'

'Nae. It's the bloody mother's fault!'

Claire crouched and looked at the chicks, knowing Alan needed to vent his anger and would find it easier if she wasn't looking at him. Frustrations were being magnified by the tension of waiting for the meeting, and concerns about the future of the pack. It was better for Alan to get it out of his system now than bring his bad temper to the public event.

'She's a bloody fraud!' Alan began to bang around with feed cans and the chicks all ran, cheeping, to their food bowls, expecting a meal. 'She speaks English fine, you know. Better than Drew, anyway. It's her fault he's nae confidence except in the Gaelic.'

GATEKEEPER

Claire remained silent, waiting to see if Alan wanted to explain or was ready for reassurance.

'We spoke both at home, until I was six or so, and at school we learned in English with Gaelic as a second language. Then we got a new teacher in the islands, for the little ones, and he only taught in Gaelic – my mother and the rest of her separationist friends had got him appointed. So Drew learned the English but he never really spoke it; it wasn't used at school and mother ignored us if we used it in the house.'

'Well ...' Was this important, Claire thought? Did it matter now, with what they had hanging over them?

But Alan wouldn't be deflected. 'I didn't know how different, how difficult it would be for him. When he left school, there wasn't enough work for three of us and mother on one croft, so he went for the masts. But they didn't speak Gaelic there – half of them were frae England – and they didn't appreciate how young Drew was. He was only a boy but he looked big and strong, so they didn't allow for him. He didn't understand half what they told him but he was too shy tae ask, so they began tae treat him like an idiot. Like a big stupit animal. Then he hit one of them.'

Claire glanced at his face. So there was a point to this after all.

'Hit one of them,' she repeated.

Aye. Well, you have to remember they were none of them wee men. It wasnae like he hit somebody much smaller than himself.'

'What happened?'

'Well, it seems the man managed tae hit him back. Then Drew picked him up and threw him into the radio mast. It broke his head.'

'Broke his head?'

'His skull.'

'Drew fractured a man's skull? Jesus!'

309

Nae, the mast did it, when the man hit against it. Drew only threw him. It wasnae deliberate. Even the man said so, when he got out of hospital. He wouldnae press charges.'

'And you're worried he might do it again?'

'Well …'

'Yes or no?'

'No. He'd never. What I'm worried about is when the real lunatics start turning up. Yon wolf-hunters and shamans and all the rest of the mad bastarts. I doubt Drew would defend himself again, even against a mob, but you know how folk are.'

She did, but she'd forgotten how to look at her neighbours as if they were strangers. How had they seemed to her in her first few days here? Isobel like a witch in a man's cardigan, with packages of food in her pockets. Noel McIver's cold scrutiny. Alan and Drew like giants: intimidating, dubious, dangerous – it was true that when they'd first met, she'd even been glad not to shake Drew's hand.

'Well, I can see at least *you* understand.' He'd been watching her face and she recomposed her expression as fast as she could.

'But if Drew's no threat to anyone …'

'I didn't say that, Claire. He's a threat tae himself. If he comes on like Frankenstein's monster, then sooner or later somebody will decide to take him on. If only he'd bloody speak a little more!'

'I've never thought of him as particularly silent, although Isobel did seem surprised he had talked to me.'

'He took to you frae the start – there's not many he'll pass the time of day with the way he does with you.'

Claire paused, slightly stunned to think that Drew's few cryptic utterances in her direction were considered chatty by his brother. 'What about his girlfriend?'

'Louise? Well … she's a good lass, when they're talking to each other at least. She's a temper on her like a blistered heel.'

'A bit like your mother then?' She couldn't resist saying.

GATEKEEPER

He grinned. 'It'll be a massacre when those two have tae share a roof – her and the mother. Wouldn't you like tae be around when they have their first disagreement? There will be feathers flying to Glasgow, I reckon.'

'Louise speaks Gaelic then?'

'Indeed. How else could she put up with Drew?'

So why can't she pair up with him? Especially if she's got such a temper. I would imagine she'd give any head-case a mouthful of home truths if you think she's capable of taking on your mother.'

'But she's a girl.'

'And so am I.'

'Well ... but that's not how we tend tae do things around here.'

'Then it's a good thing I'm here to point out the obvious to you. If she cares about Drew...'

'Aye, she's very protective.'

'Then get her involved.'

'Her parents won't be best pleased.'

'You asked me for my advice. I've given it,' she stood, dusting off her knees. 'If you don't like it – fine! Just stop making excuses for your own sexism'

'I'm nae prejudiced! I admit I was a little surprised tae work out you were ... the one.'

'You expected somebody bigger, perhaps?'

He grinned in reply but refused to rise to the bait.

'Alan, the wolves have a jaw pressure of 1500 pounds per square inch. Your average Alsatian has the bite pressure of 750 pounds per square inch. A wolf can bite through an arm, even Drew's arm, like you'd bite through toffee. They don't need someone to protect them – I'm here to fight their battles for them; and battles are won when the terms are signed, not when the soldiers are on the field.'

Where had that come from, she wondered? She sounded like Signore Contadino.

KAY SEXTON

Alan was gaping at her. 'I'm nae sure I understood a word of that.'

'Don't worry about it. I'll do my job, you do yours. And let Drew and Louise have a chance to help too.'

'Isobel will be wud.'

'Wud?'

'Furious.'

Claire sighed. Tiredness seemed to make the sound of the chicks discordant and their short lives futile.

'What's Isobel got to do with it?'

'She's Louise's aunt.' He grinned again at her expression. 'Aye, so if Louise comes tae help frae Fort William she'll have tae stay with the Mearns who think this whole wolf business is insane. Is that what you call a foot in the enemy camp?'

'Is everybody here related to everybody else?'

'You know they are. Apart from you, the Dysters, the Survivalists – and us. Although if Drew has his way, and Louise says yes, we'll be knitted in too.

She thought about the battles she'd described so confidently to Alan. They would be civil wars, relative against relative. She kept forgetting that this community was a centuries old one, linked by blood and marriage. It was obvious that family ties mattered in the mountains of Turkey or Rumania, but it was easy to lose sight of in modern Britain.

'So everybody else …?'

'Well, they're all tied in, somehow.'

'Katie Sturridge?'

'Frae Loch Shiel. Married a Glasgow man, divorced, came back here.'

'John Heddie?'

'Like McSlyther. His folks were frae hereabouts but they went tae the rigs, then Dubai. John came tae Glenfail when he was made redundant down South, but he'd always spent all his holidays here.

312

When his father and mother were overseas he'd stay with his granny at The Waird – the Dysters have her place now. Aye, he's local enough.'

She shook her head. 'It's amazing. Where I grew up, people arrived and left all the time. If you stayed five years you were a local.'

She faltered. She'd just told Alan about her childhood – something she had never voluntarily mentioned, except to Ansel, since her mother's death.

'Is that so?' He'd noticed nothing – and why should he? Other people talked about their childhoods all the time. She changed the subject anyway.

'What was in the sprayer?'

'Well, it's a disinfectant, very diluted. That veterinarian busybody woman told us they used it in with the wee cubs, as a deterrent. Whenever something bad was done to the wolves – spaying and the like – they made sure the cubs picked up the smell of it, and when they were bigger wolves and the electric fence was switched on, the raising team sprayed the ground near the fence with it. Aversion therapy, you see. Now we spray it across the hill and at Mallie Top and other places close tae houses. Only … Drip ever crossed it. So we can use it tae keep the wolves away from the sheep pens at lambing time. Drew or I'll go up every day and spray all the walls. The opposite was done when they moved the stranger wolf in. They transported her in a blanket that smelled of this pack's foster-mother, apparently. So when … Drip came across her, she smelled of people and anaesthetic and all, but of their old mother too, which helped them accept her.'

'Clever,' Claire said. 'Very clever.' She noticed that he too had a problem naming the missing wolf. Drip's death had affected everyone, it seemed.

After they'd eaten, Drew produced a photograph album.

'I'm not sure Claire will want tae—' Alan began, but Claire cut him off.

KAY SEXTON

'No, let's see,' she said.

She'd assumed they would be pictures of his triumphs at various Highland Games, but they were wolf pictures. As she turned the pages she saw images of Drip under the protective cellophane pages: Drip hunting, Drip rolling, Drip sitting on his haunches howling. Her hands moved slowly, touching the pictures gently. Some pictures of Flow, alert and powerful, and Agate, as alone as ever. But most of the pictures were of Drip. The photographs were Polaroid, and not particularly good. They had none of the crisp detail of the one shot that had been leaked.

'You didn't take that picture that's been in all the papers?'

Drew shook his head.

'Didn't you?' Alan asked.

She shook her head. 'That picture bugs me,' she said.

'Aye, me too, now. Who took it? We thought you must have!'

She shook her head again. 'It was somebody in The Project, I'm sure. It's such a good picture and nobody's come forward to claim responsibility. But why that picture, that's the question?'

Mrs McDowell laid the newspaper in front of them. It had become crisp in the weeks since it was published but the colours were still sharp and the two wolves seemed to glow with health and contentment.

'I know where it is,' Alan said.

Claire glanced up at him. 'So do I, but I don't know what the place is called, or even if it has a name.'

'Mallie Top,' he said. His huge finger came down to hover over the image. 'That way's the burn, and that way's the trees.' He indicated directions.

'So let's unpick it a bit,' Claire said. 'It's a hard place to find, right? Unless you know the terrain well, you'd never stumble across it. So maybe they chose the picture in case people went scrambling around the hills, trying to locate the 'wolf spot'?'

314

GATEKEEPER

Alan nodded but Drew shook his head.

'No?' she asked, but Drew refused to speak further.

'Well, there's more isolated places – where Agate goes, up on that rocky step, for example. You can't get up there without a hell of a climb,' Alan said.

His mother replied in Gaelic and he tightened his lips.

'Hell is nae a swear word, it's an adjective,' he told her.

Claire stifled a smile.

Mrs McDowell went on for a while and Alan nodded.

'Mother says it's not so far away anyway. Hard to find, maybe, but only about a mile frae Tim Gordon's top field. The sheep field.'

Claire was galvanized. She almost never approached the wolves from the village. Since the beginning she had made wide circles around the territory, approaching from different places on the Streap side so as not to create a regular trail. She knew wolves followed any kind of track and didn't want them using hers to come back down to High Croft. Her caution had blinded her to the true layout of the wolves' territory. She asked for a map. Once it was laid out, she could see that there was indeed a sheep fold marked very close to the wolves.

'So ... what we've got is a picture of two wolves within a mile of some sheep. Has Tim Gordon reported any losses?'

'Nae, not a one. He's a sour old bast ... man,' Alan bit back the epithet with a glance at his mother. 'If he'd lost a single sheep we'd have heard.'

'Okay, so maybe that's it! We have evidence of wolves and sheep coexisting. But ...'

'What?' Alan asked.

'Why such an old photograph?'

'Is it old?'

And then she saw it. A tiny brown furl behind Lake. A seedling rowan, not more than five inches tall. And she knew the purpose of the picture.

315

KAY SEXTON

'Drew, can you go up there tomorrow? I want a dozen pictures – each one including this,' she pointed to the rowan. 'Bring them to me at High Croft before the meeting, okay?'

He nodded.

'So what's the mystery?' Alan asked.

'I'll explain tomorrow at the meeting – if I tell you now, you'll just look smug and that will tip people off that we've colluded.'

'Smug? Me?'

She grinned.

He walked her back down to High Croft.

'I think Noel McIver stayed out on the hill all night,' she said.

'Aye. We know. He had his damn expert with him.'

'Expert?'

'He's got a wolf specialist from some University that he's taking around the place before the meeting.'

Claire nodded. 'Ah. That explains it.'

'Bloody old fool, he is, McSlyther.'

'Don't worry about him, concentrate on our side. Are you sure you know what to do?'

'Aye, get into the Gaelic and get you on the platform. Dinnae fash, we'll do it. Is the Mafia man coming?'

'Signore Ottaviano? I doubt it. He'll send somebody to report back to him though.'

'Don't they tell you anything then?' he asked.

'Nothing,' she said cheerfully. 'Not a damn thing. I'm just a researcher who happened to be here when the wolves arrived. I've got no resources, no back-up, nothing.'

'You've got us,' he said.

'Yes, but that wasn't supposed to happen: the early release caught everybody out. Although, while we're on the subject, how long has your mother been part of The Project?'

'Well, as long as I can recall. Before I was born, I think. It was all about empowerment, the Highlands being self-determining,

316

returning the land to its natural state and its rightful owners, that kind of thing. The wolves sort of came along afterwards.'

She nodded although she was pretty sure the wolves had been the entire purpose all along. Mrs McDowell had been seduced into taking the wolves as an emblem of her wider beliefs, just as Claire had.

'You know him then, Blaine?' she asked.

'Blaine is it? Nae, mother's met him but we've not. We work through a Nationalist contact in Edinburgh. I didn't even know his name.'

'Blaine's not his real name,' she said.

'Well, that's nae surprise. He's Russian, isn't he? They're a very strange bunch – buying football clubs and the like. Makes wolves seem almost everyday by comparison.'

'Russian? Maybe.' She'd assumed he was now Norwegian but it wasn't her place to reveal information about Blaine, or anyone else involved.

'So you've met him?' Alan asked.

'He was here in February.'

'Was he now?' Alan shook his head. 'I wish I'd known.'

'Why?'

'I don't know really. To get a look at the person who made all this happen?'

'*We* made it happen, Alan. Don't forget that. We're not puppets. We chose to make it work.'

CHAPTER TWENTY-SIX

The community meeting was to be held in the old school. Claire had only been there for Mountain Rescue call-outs, otherwise it was kept locked up. There were not enough children in Glenfail to justify a teacher's salary. She'd ensured the McDowells had volunteered to set up the chairs and tables in the hall, and she'd given them clear instructions on how to do it – battles were won when you chose your ground carefully and she knew what she wanted to achieve.

Drew had arrived at High Croft at noon, with a double handful of Polaroids, showing the outcrop, bare of wolves but surrounded by fresh green bracken in the middle of which the small rowan tree, now a foot tall, had sprouted tiny sprigs bearing symmetrically-placed oval leaves. She'd studied the images, making sure of her facts. The tree was ammunition, of a kind. What had Ansel said all those months ago, when she was still in Rome? Something about how powerful men traded by showing they possessed things other powerful men wanted. Blaine wanted wolves, but Ottaviano wanted trees. The land belonged to the Signore, and if The Project wanted his backing, she had to give him a reason for keeping the wolves on his property.

She wasn't ready for this, but she could never be truly ready – too much was riding on the meeting. But then, at each stage of The Project there had been moments when everything could have failed – if she dwelt on the responsibility she bore it would become too much to cope with, so she put it aside and thought about the

318

flat in Rome instead. She was going to need a bigger bed if things worked out with Bruno.

She dressed carefully, choosing clothes to fit in with the strategy she'd defined with Mala's help. She would need to improvise, of course, but knowing what she wanted to have happen was the best way to control events; improvisation alone was like a boat without a rudder – you could row as much as you liked, but you couldn't steer for your landing point.

A plain navy suit, a white shirt, the thistle brooch she'd bought the same day she chose Massimo's christening present. She put up her hair, admitting that Blaine had been right to tell her to grow it. With short hair she could have looked officious, but the chignon softened her appearance, making her seem more feminine and vulnerable. It made people think she was gentler than she was, and that gave her an advantage.

She arrived late, deliberately. She wanted the local people to have taken possession of the room ahead of her, to feel they owned the space. She would be sitting in the audience, at least to start with, and she knew that allowing the community to settle in, choosing who they sat with, was important to their sense of proprietorship. And that was what she was going to play with - their sense of owning their surroundings.

She'd also ensured they had a chance to get the gossip out in the open; Isobel would be telling everyone that Claire was going back to Rome soon, which gave them something to talk about, made her name and doings into immediate local currency. Noel McIver's expert would have to contend with that, when he began to speak.

As she'd requested, the chairs were laid out in a V shape, facing partly towards the table at which the community leaders would sit and partly towards each other. She wanted debate to travel as much across the room as up it.

The two wooden tables pushed together at the top of the room had a large notice pinned to them, reaching almost to the floor – it

KAY SEXTON

read 'Please Do Not Move the Chairs' in English and, she assumed, Gaelic. Behind that makeshift panel were four chairs for the local M.E.P.; Noel's expert; the meeting Chairman: a Justice of the Peace from Fort William, and the Chief Constable of the Northern Constabulary.

She put her bag under her chair and went to talk to her neighbours, encouraging them to see her as one of them. Later, when – with any luck - she moved to sit with the panel, the audience would remember, subconsciously, that Claire had been their representative, she'd stepped up from the middle of the room to speak for them. It would give her a psychological advantage.

She examined the four men. The M.E.P. was a known quantity, safe and unimaginative; the Justice of the Peace was known to be a reasonable, if harsh, upholder of the law; the Chief Constable was not popular – he lacked the valuable condition of being a Highlander; but it was the expert she would have to contend with. He was plump and bearded, and looked pleased with himself. He wore jeans that had been ironed and a pair of polished brown loafers. With any luck his appearance had already alienated his audience. He had a folder of papers in front of him but he was staring out of the arched windows at nothing in particular.

The meeting began with a statement from the J.P. that he had been invited to come and chair a debate about the apparent existence of wolves in the area. Nothing discussed would have the force of law, he said, but it was important to consider how this matter might affect the community in terms of policing and resources, which was why his colleagues from European Parliament and the Constabulary were present.

'Well, what about yon boffin, what's he guid for? And where's the translator for the native speakers?' called a voice from the floor. Claire glanced over. It was Callum, her worst student. Drew must have set him up as a stalking horse. She smiled.

Mrs McDowell stood up, and spoke up, in Gaelic. The S.N.P. representative offered himself as a translator for 'that part of this

320

community that speaks its native tongue'. Somewhat abashed, the M.E.P. and J.P. agreed. The expert looked startled. The S.N.P. man moved to the front and stood beside the table. From then on, everything would have to be translated into Gaelic, giving people time to digest each comment. It would slow the process down, exactly as Claire had intended.

'Now you can tell us about yon gomeral at the end,' Callum shouted. The S.N.P. man repeated gomeral when he translated into Gaelic but didn't mention it was Scots for idiot.

Don't overdo it, Claire thought. Don't get too cocky.

The J.P. folded his hands. 'I'm sure that when the panel introduce themselves, we'll all understand why they're here.'

Callum subsided.

The M.E.P. and Chief Constable outlined their reasons for attending, then McIver's expert spoke.

'I'm Dr Simon Fillard, from East Anglia University. I suppose you'd call me an expert on wolves – insofar as anybody in the UK can be called an expert.' He smiled at his own joke. 'I've been invited here to examine the evidence for this so-called wolf pack.'

'Then are there wolves, or aren't there?' It was Isobel's voice.

The man touched his papers before speaking. 'There is clear evidence of one or more large predators. Whether they are wolves is another question. I've seen at least one feeding site, some scat – that's what we call fecal matter ...'

'So do we!' came a loud voice from the back of the hall, a gamekeeper from Streap, Claire noted.

The expert looked unhappy, not used to being interrupted. 'Yes of course. Well, what I haven't seen is any of the predators themselves, or a kill site. As a result, I can't make any sure determination as to species.'

'Well what good is that?' Callum muttered loudly. There was a pause while the S.N.P. man ran through his translation.

KAY SEXTON

Tam McDowell stood. 'What's the difference between a feeding site and a kill site?'

'Ah,' the expert steepled his fingers. 'A good question. I find it impossible to believe, without concrete evidence such as a sighting or a fresh kill site, that there could be a viable wolf pack in this region. It seems more likely this is a hoax. There was a case in Bavaria several years ago of a man who allowed his wolf-dog hybrids to predate the sheep of a neighbour with whom he'd argued.'

There was a pause for the Gaelic. Tam stood again.

'You didn't answer the question.'

'Didn't I?' The man looked surprised. 'Well, a kill site is where predators actually kill prey, but a feeding site is simply where they've eaten – the evidence of chewed bones, fecal matter ...'

'Scat,' said the gamekeeper loudly.

'Quite. That evidence tells me a large predator or predators have been involved, but not how the prey died. I suspect what you may have here is somebody shooting prey for a wolf-hybrid or dogs to feed on.'

'So you can't tell us anything we didn't already know?' said the M.E.P.

'Not without further investigation, no.' The expert sat back.

Claire kept her face neutral. Now, she thought. Do it now!

Alan stood as if he'd read her mind. He spoke in Gaelic, then English. 'Well, I'm not so sure that's very helpful. It seems tae me that our own expert knows a guid bit more than you do.'

Dr Fillard looked shocked. 'What expert? I was told I was to have exclusive access to the site.'

'Aye, were you now? Exclusive apart from all of us puir folk who have tae live here and deal with things, you mean? Who told you that, anyway?'

The expert looked at Noel McIver, who stared back impassively.

Alan pointed to Claire, 'Well, Claire Benson counts as local, she seems tae know more about wolves than you do and she hasn't asked for any kind of exclusive.' Heads turned in her direction.

GATEKEEPER

She stood and looked at the audience, not the panel, as she spoke carefully in Gaelic. Laughter went round the room. The S.N.P. man looked unsure if he was supposed to translate Gaelic into English. Claire turned to the panel.

'I just said that before anybody called me a gomeral I wanted to apologise for not speaking enough Gaelic to save our translator his trouble. I am learning, but it's a difficult language and my research and teaching work together take up most of my time, the rest I spend on mountain rescue.'

She knew the audience would be on her side now she'd established her credentials as a community member. She took a step forward.

'Alan's very kind. But I'm not a wolf expert. You all know me; you know I'm only a tree counter. I do know a bit about wolf-community interactions though. I've spent time in the Turkish and Rumanian mountains, just as I have here, looking at how agricultural communities can benefit from new land uses. In both those places, wolves live in farming regions. If I can be of any help ...'

She turned back to the audience while the S.N.P. man translated. She was asking them, not the panel.

A ripple of applause began.

'Gie her a chair!' Callum yelled. 'Gie her a place with the head yins. She's on our side!'

The J.P. nodded. Alan dragged forward another table and a chair and Claire walked up to the front. Bending, she whispered in the M.E.P.'s ear. He smiled and stood, taking the new chair so she was seated between him and the J.P. She smiled at the audience and spoke again.

'Before you wonder, I asked Mr Haig to take my place because I've been reviewing grant applications for the Forestry today, in the office, so I'm wearing my best suit. I feel a bit more comfortable with my legs behind the poster.' As she'd hoped, every member of the audience craned to look at her legs. 'After all, you're used to

323

KAY SEXTON

seeing me in my hill clothes and boots, I feel a bit shy of you in a skirt!'

They laughed again. She knew she'd done it. They'd be on her side now, whatever she said.

'And probably I only have questions, not answers, to offer, but I'll do my best,' she finished. Nobody else had offered the community anything. Bruno's father had told her to be on the inside before making a deal, and now she was.

The M.E.P. leaned over and spoke quietly. 'Remind me never to run against you for a seat, Miss Benson.'

She grinned at him and murmured back, 'It would never happen, but thanks for the compliment.'

'Now let's continue,' said the J.P.

'Actually,' Claire raised her hand like a pupil in a classroom. 'Could I go back to Mrs Mearns's question?'

He nodded. Claire held eye contact with Isobel as she spoke. 'Yes, there are wolves. Either five or eight of them, depending on how you look at it.'

The room filled with voices. She watched to see who nodded; who'd known or suspected but not come forward - those people were allies in the making.

'Ridiculous!' the expert said. 'Either five or eight? Can't you count?'

'Well, she can see what's right under her nose, which is more than you can,' said Alan.

Claire bowed her head, waiting for the noise to subside. Then she looked up, engaging one audience member after another with her eyes. 'Yes, I can count. But before I explain, who else has seen the wolves?'

Drew put his hand up immediately. Alan followed. Several more hands were lifted.

'Tim?' she asked. Slowly, Tim Gordon raised his hand.

'John?' He glanced at his wife first, but after a moment, John Mearns put his hand up too.

324

'Thank you. And who's heard them?"

This time many hands were raised.

'Doesn't look like we needed an expert to be sure about that, does it?' she grinned.

Noel sat impassive, arms folded. Claire had to admire his stoicism.

'As to the question of five or eight, it all depends on whether all the cubs live to maturity,' she continued.

'Cubs?' The expert snapped his head round to stare at her.

'Yes. Two females and a male. The adults are four females and ... one male.' She faltered for a second, but nobody seemed to notice. 'If you could pass up my bag? It's under my seat, next to John and Jenny Heddie.' She used their names deliberately, emphasising that she was part of the community, knowing and known to all.

Her black satchel came up, passed from hand to hand. She moved to the projector and turned it on. Then she turned it off again and faced the hall as if she'd forgotten to say something, highlighting her role as one of them, rather than an expert. 'As you know, I'm living at High Croft. Perhaps I was the first to notice the wolves because I live that much closer to the hills. I want to emphasise though, that they aren't close to the village. It took me a while to find them. But when I did ...'

She'd laid the photo-transparency on the projector while she was talking. Now she switched it on again and the image of the cubs sprang onto the screen.

She'd taken the photo weeks ago, when they first emerged from the den. It showed them as furry bundles, pop-eyed and tiny; two curled together in a patch of sunlight and one sitting upright, looking astonished.

Sighs and murmurs filled the room. She slipped another image onto the projector. 'This is their mother ...' Meander lay with two cubs at her feet, and the third, Puddle, climbing onto her back.

KAY SEXTON

'And the father ...' Flow stared out from the trees, a rare shot where he looked relaxed, rather than stern, fierce or outright menacing.

'And the others are already well known to us all,' briskly she flipped transparencies of the original grainy newspaper shot of Agate onto the screen, then the portrait of Caldera and Lake. She continued to speak.

'The questions I'd like answered are: what happens now; how do we cope with the media and tourist attention that's already begun; how can we use this to the community's advantage?'

She didn't move back to the table and as the questioning began immediately, it seemed natural for her to stay at the projector with the two wolves gleaming behind her. She was in control of the process.

'Claire, two questions. Where did the wolves come from is the first. But the second matters more to us - you say you've spent time where wolves hang around farms. Is our livestock at risk?' It was John Mearns, Isobel nodding rapidly at his side.

Claire smiled at John, and shrugged. 'The answer to the first question is that I have no idea. If you mean where, geographically, did they come from, I'd say Eastern Europe, that's the only place I can think of that has wolves that could have been brought to Scotland and released into the wild, but if you mean how did they get here, well, I'm as much in the dark as you are.' She fought not to cross her fingers as she told the lie. It was only half a lie anyway, she didn't know exactly how the wolves had got here, she could honestly claim total ignorance of Blaine's methods. Then she looked across at the panel, inviting them to share in her speculations. 'As for your second question, I think Dr Fillard is best placed to answer that.'

'It's impossible to say, at present ...' he began.

Callum jeered. 'For an expert you don't have much to tell us, do you?'

'Hang on,' Claire raised her hand. 'This is important. We're all involved in agriculture somehow. I research it, many of you have

326

GATEKEEPER

livestock, or use wool, or wood, or meat to earn your living. Even John Heddie wouldn't have much trade at the pub if farm profits were hit. We need to get a clear picture of the situation.'

Around the room, people nodded.

'Dr Fillard, please continue with what you were saying,' she invited, ignoring the M.E.P. who was grinning at her mastery of the audience.

'As I was saying, at present the only feeding sites I've seen are deer carcasses. Wolves leave almost nothing of a kill – what they don't eat, they cache, that is, bury for later consumption. I'd say, from the current evidence, and what you've told us that this pack must be predating deer. But that could change – it rather depends on who released them and why. If you'd like my ideas on that …?'

Claire nodded. 'Of course. Have you ever seen anything like this before?'

He stroked his chin. 'No, nothing on this scale. You get the odd accidental release of predators like mink from fur farms, or did when mink were farmable here …'

For a moment she was back in the van, staring into Liam's cold eyes as she tried to work out what he was planning, feeling the adrenaline rush through her body as she prepared for whatever mayhem he hoped to unleash. She glanced over her shoulder at the wolves on the projector screen to reassure herself. It was amazing how far they'd all come since then.

The mood of the audience was conciliatory now, as Fillard talked about how the occasional puma or lynx escaped from a zoo and caused panic. 'But,' he concluded, 'this is something unprecedented. No recognised organisation has claimed responsibility for this, so I think we must assume that it's the work of a splinter group of animal activists. Whoever they are, they've done something quite exceptional. Unheard of. This event will shape the future of animal release programmes worldwide – and the future of quite a few deer too!'

KAY SEXTON

This time his joke earned a ripple of laughter.

'Thank you. That's very helpful – I suspect nobody minds a few deer ending up as wolf dinner,' Claire added.

'Aye, if they eat the deer, I'm all in favour!' Tim Gordon said loudly. 'Bluidy things get more of my winter forage than the stock does, and they leap the walls. Last year they ate my cabbages!'

There was a general laugh.

'So, we need to monitor the wolves and their food source,' Claire said. 'Has anybody had any stock go missing?'

Silence.

'Tim? Mrs McDowell?'

Still silence.

'So far, so good. But I think perhaps we should decide right now, how to keep track of the wolf kills. Some of us are out most days on the hills and could note any deer carcasses we find. Tim, Drew, Alan, John, Noel, Tam … you're all in a position to do that, I think? And we need a coordinator for it all – perhaps Mrs McDowell would take that on, as she's fluent in both languages?'

Noel smiled sourly, but nodded when the others did.

Claire took a deep breath. 'And if anybody else finds anything – a dead sheep, a deer skull, please inform Mrs McDowell. It's vitally important to safeguard our livelihoods. As I say, I have yet to meet a farmer who's lost stock to wolves, but if it happens we need to be ready to act. Agreed?'

John Heddie stood up. 'That's all very well, but as far as I'm concerned, those wolves should be a protected species. In the past month my income has trebled from the tourists alone. If I thought it would help, I'd put out a trough and feed them lamb chops in the car park.'

There was more laughter.

'That would be the worst idea you've ever had, John,' Claire said when it subsided. 'I think the wolves could be good for the

GATEKEEPER

village too, but any attempt to feed them, or even kill them, could be disastrous for them, and for us.'

'How come?' His posture was belligerent.

'Again, I think Dr Fillard has the answers,' she stepped back, allowing him the floor.

'Yes, in this case I can be rather more definite,' he enjoyed the laugh he got this time. 'Wolves are predators – by nature they are designed to hunt. At present, as far as we can tell, these wolves are doing a good job of feeding themselves. If they teach their cubs to hunt deer, then deer will be their main prey. But predators are always opportunists, much more so than prey species. If anybody starts to feed them, they will swiftly adjust to being fed. From that they will learn to expect feeding and cease to hunt. And if the feeding stops, for any reason, they will have become conditioned to the taste of the food and they'll go looking for it. If you feed lamb chops, expect lots of dead lambs!' He smiled round the room and Claire saw he was shy, and out of his depth, and keen to make a good impression. The villagers gave him the courtesy of short applause and he ducked his head with pleasure.

'Thank you, that's really useful to us,' she said. The J.P. opened his mouth and she held out her hand to stop him. 'Just one more thing. I mentioned killing wolves being a bad idea. Now I can see several of my Forestry and Tourism students in the hall and we recently had a study session on large predators and tourism. Before I sit down, I'd like to invite them to share what they learned with you. May I?' She appealed to the audience, who nodded.

'Callum, you weren't taking many notes that day – not that you ever do! So I hope you've got a retentive memory. Can you explain the different behaviours identified in hunters and eco-tourists?'

Callum stood. 'Aye, no problem. Hunters are generally fully equipped when they arrive at a destination – they don't buy stuff, in other words. They tend to have off-road vehicles and sometimes snow-mobiles, spotter aircraft, marsh-skimmers, depending on the

329

KAY SEXTON

terrain. They often ignore hunting regulations and exceed permits
– there was a guy in Russia shot four wolves from a helicopter, out
of season, with explosive bullets. He might have shot more but he
miss-aimed and blew one of the helicopter runners to bits. The rescue services had to come dig him out the snow. Served him right, if
you ask me.'

'And eco-tourists?' she prompted.

'Oh aye. They're the green sandal or green Welly brigade,
right? They tend to have smaller vehicles, don't shoot, like locally-
produced food, often stay on campsites or in hostels, and have ethical concerns about exploiting people and places. By all accounts
they're not big spenders, but at least they like to support the place
they're visiting.'

'Thank you, I'm impressed. I'll expect to see all that in your
overdue essay.' Callum sat down, grinning.

'Bethany? Can you remember the Michigan Cabin case study?'

Bethany stood. Claire had only two women in her student
group and Bethany was the quieter of the two, it was a surprise to
see her here – perhaps she was another Project plant, in any case, it
was worth showing the villagers that there were plenty of people
around who could support them if they decided to live alongside the
wolves. Bethany wrapped her arms around her body and blushed.
She was shaking her head.

'Oh, hang on, I might have the transparency in my bag,' Claire
said. She did, of course, she'd brought everything she'd thought
she might need. She slapped it on the projector and stood back. It
showed a large cabin with a wolf-skin nailed to the door.

'Oh right, that one. This guy ...' Bethany began. 'He owned
this tourist cabin, and people used to come and shoot and ski and
climb. Well, one day, he shot this wolf, and claimed it had been
menacing his guests. He put the skin up on the cabin. Then the
wildlife services found out it was a collared wolf he'd shot and prosecuted him. Because it's illegal to shoot a reintroduced wolf. To pay

330

GATEKEEPER

the fine he got given, he ... um, took a hunter to shoot an eagle or something ...'

'Bald eagle,' Callum called out. 'Protected species.'

'Oh yes, Bald eagle. Anyway, when the spring thaw came, the Forestry officials found some cubs that had starved to death because he'd killed their mother and they hadn't been weaned, and he was prosecuted again anyway, for helping to shoot the bird, and sent to prison.'

'What might have happened if the cubs had been older?' Claire asked.

'Um ... well, if you kill a wolf, the whole pack will often come and search out the body, is that right?'

'Exactly. So even if the pack hadn't come to find the missing wolf, he could have had six or seven young wolf cubs in his vicinity with that skin attracting them – which could have led to serious problems because they wouldn't have been taught to hunt by their mother, so they could have turned to scavenging instead; making them a threat to livestock.' Claire turned to the J.P. 'Which is why we need to monitor the pack and be sure, before we act, that we'll make things better and not worse.'

She slipped the picture of Caldera and Lake back onto the projector before she sat down.

'More questions?' the J.P asked.

The discussion ranged for an hour. Claire passed as many questions as she could to Dr Fillard, deferring to his knowledge and reminding the audience that she was one of them, looking for answers, not providing them.

Finally Isobel stood up. 'So what are we going to do?' she demanded.

'I'm going to bring in a guest ale and start serving lunches,' John Heddie quipped.

Claire waited.

'Do we need to do anything at present?' the M.E.P. asked. 'It seems to me that the community is not at risk. In fact, there are

331

KAY SEXTON

benefits to some of you from these wolves. Can anybody make a case for interfering at this point?'

There were mutters but nobody stood up.

Claire spoke. 'There is one thing I am an expert on, and I'd like to share it with you, if I may?'

'Go on, you've made more sense so far than the whole clanjamphrie,' Tim Gordon called out.

She walked to the projector again. 'The thing I know about is communities. I don't know much about wolves or reintroduction schemes – in fact Noel McIver is our expert there.'

Noel blinked.

'First, I'd like to talk about the Golden Eagle reintroduction project in 1982,' she said. 'When it was announced that the Eagles were breeding in a number of sites, there was huge media attention. Well, we know all about that here, don't we?' She smiled at the reporters in the back row. 'And despite local protests, the nest sites were publicly identified.'

Noel nodded, then stopped when he realised what he was doing.

'It was a disaster. Can you explain, Noel?'

She'd put him on the spot and he had to answer. He didn't stand, but his voice carried clearly. 'People turned up from all over. Most of them weren't even bird-watchers. That was bad enough, noise and rubbish and people trampling everywhere disturbing the birds. But egg collectors came too. The nests were raided and about five clutches taken. We caught one of the bastards red-handed. Not the others though.'

Claire nodded. '*We* need to make the decisions. *We* are the people affected. These are Glenfail's wolves – if we can make this work, we can all gain from them, but only if we retain control of the decision–making process.'

She pointed to the picture. 'One last thing. A small thing, but – to me – the most important of all. Look here ...' she reached up, tapping the screen. 'It's a seedling rowan. This photo with the

GATEKEEPER

wolves was probably taken about six months ago. I went up there yesterday, to take a look for myself.' She pulled Drew's Polaroids from her bag, putting one on the table for the panel and passing the others down to the audience so they could see the bright green leaves and extra height of the little tree. 'You can see how much it's grown. It's probably nothing much to you, but it's a sign to me. Once these Highlands were largely forest – before the Clearances, and the deer. Then the woods were all cut down and turned into grouse moors for absentee landlords to shoot across and the deer chewed down the landscape until nothing would grow but bracken and heather and gorse. Normally, a seedling tree like this would have been eaten during the winter as the deer grazed on every bit of greenery they could find. It's very significant that this tree is flourishing in a place where the wolves obviously spend quite a bit of time.'

She looked out into the audience, finding the man in the Italian suit, the Signore's representative.

'The deer are still around, and always will be, because as Tim said, they can jump any fence. But as long as there are wolves in Glenfail, many more seedling trees will grow and mature, because the deer daren't stick around long enough to graze them to extinction. We have a chance to help the this landscape come back to life through the growth of these baby trees. We can actually recreate one of the great forests that once covered this land. In environmental terms, that's like finding Tutankhamen or the discovery of the coelacanth. For me, that's a good enough reason to try living with the wolves.'

She went back to her seat in the audience under cover of the applause led by Alan and Drew.

333

CHAPTER TWENTY-SEVEN

Ansel was on the doorstep when she got back to High Croft. She'd guessed he would be.

'I need tea. I need a gallon of tea. I've talked myself dry,' she said, collapsing into a kitchen chair.

'Did it go well?'

'Don't you know?'

'I was here. I can't be in two places at once.'

'Ask Blaine, I'm sure he knows everything by now.'

'I'm asking you, Claire. As your friend.'

She watched him fussing with the tea things.

'You're not supposed to be here, are you?'

He smiled but said nothing.

'Where do they think you are?'

'I told them I was going to watch birds on Windemere. But I also let them think that maybe I was saying that, so that I could take part in a release operation at a testing lab in Liverpool that will happen tonight.'

'Clever. So you lied about lying.'

'I thought you might want a friend to talk to.'

'I don't care if I never talk again in my life.' She swung her legs onto the table, laddering her last pair of Italian tights. 'Damn!'

He remained silent while he poured the tea.

'Okay, it went well,' she conceded. 'Better than I could have hoped. I think that the village will give it a shot, and that Ottaviano will want the pack to remain, because the wolves are going to help him get what he wants – a genuine Highland forest. And because of that, I'm leaving next month, as soon as term ends.'

He raised his eyebrows.

'My work's done. I'm going back to Rome.'

'Your work is hardly done, Claire. We expect you to stay for at least another six months, maybe a year.'

'I don't care what you expect. We knew from the beginning that what we were doing was a gamble and it's paid off so far. But the longer I stay, the more the people here will come to think of me as the person to turn to. That's not going to work in the long term - they've got to make their own decisions. That's why the community around the wolves had to be a mixture of Project and non-Project, right? Because if it was all Project, we'd have failed. We wanted to free the wolves into normal society, not some protected zone – because if the Signore's land was surrounded by a ring of wolf enthusiasts, it would just be a bigger than usual wildlife park. For this to succeed, the community has to work out how to cope with the wolves. If I stay here, then I'll stop being just a Gatekeeper and become some kind of resident wolf-warden instead. That's not the deal. Glenfail has been introduced to its wolves now, and it's up to the village and the wolves to see how well they can get along.'

He shook his head. 'He won't like it.'

'Blaine can get stuffed. We have to trust Glenfail now; the good, the bad and the downright peculiar people who make up this community. I'm going. Next month.'

She swung her legs down. 'I'm taking a shower, then going to bed – I'll take my tea up with me. Tomorrow I'll take you up to see the wolves.'

He smiled oddly. 'You've changed.'

She patted him on the shoulder as she passed. 'No. This is me as I always was. I just … got a bit one-track minded for a while. Crusades do that to you, I suspect.'

She stopped in the doorway, remembering something, two things. 'Thank you for dealing with Liam,' she said.

He ducked his head.

'Not for me, I could have coped with him, I think. If I'd had to. But for the pack – it was the right thing to stop him having any opportunity to mess things up for them. And talking about right things; you once tried to ask me if we were terrorists, remember?'

He nodded.

'If you know when to stop, Ansel, then you're not a terrorist. That's why it's right for me to leave now. I've shown the village how it could live with the wolves, but the bargain is between Glenfail and the pack, not Glenfail and me. They've got to be allowed to work it out themselves. I thought about bringing in a journalist – even got Mals to pick one out, for an exclusive on the cubs. But that's no good; that's just moving people around – manipulating them. If the deal I've suggested is good enough, they'll make it work. If it's not good enough, they've got to work out something else for themselves.

'Don't think that just opening the door means something is free. It isn't, it just means you've opened a door. Being free requires a lot more than that. I don't know why Blaine got into this, although I could make some guesses – it makes perfect sense for a man with a military background who's been treated as a spy to develop an obsession with absolute freedom of action, and he'd be perfectly placed to plan a quasi-military operation like raising a wolf pack, but that's speculation. The point is, we've all got our reasons for taking up causes, but sometimes you have to step aside. That's the really difficult bit, Ansel – knowing when to let go. That's what stops you being a terrorist.'

CHAPTER TWENTY-EIGHT

She'd told everyone she was leaving at noon, so at four in the morning she carried her boxes out to the car, using moonlight to guide her. By five she was packed. She would be gone before the village began its day.

She stood looking at the hill. She could walk up one last time and try to find the wolves. They'd howled in the night and she'd interrupted her packing to go outside and listen. They still sounded like fifty to her.

She didn't hesitate. She put the note to Isobel, explaining her early departure, on the kitchen table and locked the door, before walking down the garden to the back wall. There she stopped. She wasn't coming back, whatever happened. The wolves deserved freedom, however partial, and freedom meant the pack and the community of Glenfail working things out themselves. A gate maybe, but no Gatekeeper. She rested her hand on Drip's cairn. This was her last goodbye. She didn't need to see them again.

She heard Noel's van and turned back to the house. One last task.

He was unlocking the gate. She handed him the keys to High Croft to give to Isobel.

'You're away then,' he said.

'I'm not good at goodbyes.'

He nodded.

337

KAY SEXTON

'I've suggested they offer you my teaching hours,' she said. 'I think you'd do a good job.'

He nodded again. She hadn't expected thanks and she didn't get them. Nell stared at her without interest, as usual.

As she turned away he said, 'I never shot their dog, you know.'

She turned back, surprised. He nodded towards her car.

'Drive safely,' was all he said.

She didn't find the CD until she reached into her glove compartment for the ferry tickets. It hadn't been there the night before. It was blank, no label on the case, nothing to say who had put it there, but she knew could only have been Noel. She'd left the car unlocked – nobody locked a car in Glenfail, or a door either.

She waited until she was just outside Rome to play it. She'd stayed overnight with her father, whose unquestioning acceptance of her arrival had been just another part of the oddness of their relationship. The old greyhound he'd taken on from the rescue centre was called Tess and while they walked the dog he'd told her about his plans for the garden. She had been surprised at her affection for him. She would never understand anything about him, or her childhood, but it didn't matter so much any more.

As the Seven Hills appeared she pulled over and slotted the CD into the player. Birdsong poured from the speakers – a Scottish dawn at full volume. She closed her eyes, hearing the sounds of the hills. The calls faded and she heard the bagpipes begin. Then she knew. She hit the pause button and got out of the car. She needed oxygen.

'You clever bastard!' she said to Rome's distant haze and she wasn't sure if she meant Blaine, or Noel, or both. 'You clever, clever bastard!'

She reached into the car and hit play. 'Letter from America' poured out, from the speakers, from Drew's pipes. Now she knew what Noel had meant. He was one of The Project. All his actions had been part of his job ... to orchestrate the opposition. He'd been meant to fail and he had failed - it had all been part of the plan.

So why had he mentioned the McDowell's dog?

The wolves fitted perfectly into Drew's music, so perfectly that at first she didn't notice them, but as their chorus swelled out of the car, belling into the air, she finally got it. He'd taken the McDowell's dog for the cubs - Tina Turner, prize sheepdog - had been their foster-mother. The wolves had been raised by a mother who actually knew the land around Glenfail, and who'd been trained to live alongside sheep. She would have smelt of the heather and the hills that became their home, and she'd have taught them the habits she'd learned herself: sheep and chickens came with guardian angels and weren't food. Clever, so very clever, to prepare the cubs for the land they would inhabit. No wonder Noel hadn't been able to produce the sheepdog's body; she'd have been suckling the wolf cubs by the time Alan and Drew noticed she was missing.

Finally she knew who'd taken the photograph of the wolves with the rowan sapling. Noel had been out on the hills as often as she had; he was the one who'd sent the anonymous picture to the newspapers.

As the wolves' call faded she had to lean against the car, she was crying for real now. The recording was faint, but she knew what she was hearing. A happy wolf, rolling, the *hnar hnar* sounds as distinctive as the drip-shaped blotch on his ear.

When the tears stopped, she got back in the car and drove down into Rome.

ACKNOWLEDGEMENTS

I would like to thank Professor Sir Ghillean Prance, Dr J Trevor Williams and Dr Melaku Worede for a dinner-table conversation in Rome that led, many years later, to this work of fiction. In addition, I am grateful to Peter Jay for teaching me intellectual rigour and Lord Puttnam for his kindness and patience when the dream was still a dream. Many talented, hardworking writers at Zoetrope Virtual Studio have offered time, energy and invaluable critique, not just to this novel, but to many works of mine. Cove Park gave me a residency when I most needed it, in surroundings that helped bring the fictional Glenfail to life. Michael Cummings generously allowed the use the wolf photograph on the cover and Michelle Finlay was a fantastic editor.

This book would not have been possible without the keepers and owners who shared information about the wolves in their care, and the animal rights activists who took me into their confidence and told me about their operations - to all these people I owe a debt I can best repay by preserving their anonymity.

Two people have been especially significant in my writing life; Brie's confidence in me has helped through many a rocky patch - without her this book would never have seen the light of day. Bunny Goodjohn pushed and pulled me into writing for a living, and then into living to write - better companion no writer could ever hope for.

Also by Kay Sexton

<u>Fiction</u>
Anubis & The Volcano

<u>Non-Fiction</u>
Minding My Peas And Cucumbers
The Allotment Diaries

Printed in Great Britain
by Amazon.co.uk, Ltd.,
Marston Gate.